A LOVE AFFAIRE IN THE MOST EXTRAORDINARY PLACES

LOST IN HOTELS

M. MARTIN

Lulu Publishing Services rev. date: 10/29/2013

CHAPTER 1

CATHERINE

I WAKE UP ten minutes before the alarm in order to turn it off so it doesn't wake Matt and especially not Billy. There is perfection to the morning stillness before the sun rises, before breakfast television programs fill the apartment, or coffee scents the air. These few moments in my life are just for me. I linger in thoughts and memories of people from years ago and the roads that led me to today.

I was the girl who was supposed to be the success story, the child the parents spent a little more for on college, on class vacations to Europe, and braces when there wasn't even money to pay the rent. I was supposed to be the first female president—at least in elementary school—a doctor, an attorney, and then an English major to become a journalist. I was supposed to get that high-profile newspaper job that never came. Instead, I settled for a publishing job that allowed me to climb my way up to a good-paying job, and then to a magazine position where I am today. It sounds better when I talk it up than when I'm actually doing it day after day for the past seven years.

Then I approached that age where everyone around me was married. One by one, I traveled alone to the destination weddings of my younger sister, to my best friend in childhood, and even to my young assistant. It seemed every other colleague except me were married—even those

1

other women in the office who were said too tough, too fussy, or just too dominant to ever find a man.

Matt is a perfect specimen of a husband in this prone state. Manly and vulnerable, he lies unprotected and motionlessness on his back, a single arm raised above his head, and his lips open ever so slightly with symmetrical inhales-to-exhales. My internal complaints about him not being driven, intellectually or otherwise, yield to my awareness that it's been weeks since we've had sex. I dare not touch his unkempt hair that I constantly criticize, but it looks so perfect right now with its fine texture that falls to the side of his strong face. He has his father's nose and his mother's cheeks.

In sheets that are a good week past their need of cleaning, I opt not to do an inventory of the packing that I must do, or worry if there's enough food in the refrigerator to last them a week. Instead, I remember the first time I saw his body, that sinfully toned specimen that reminded me of a mix of John-John and a burly Midwest football player with a painfully sarcastic grin and an inescapable charisma that made everything else about him seem unimportant. In a whirlwind romance, he made me feel like a woman and stripped away my fear of never being loved or having a family.

In a fuss-free city hall wedding and no honeymoon, he promised to make it up to me as we moved into my apartment, and he continued to search for work in an economy that underlined his lack of a college education. None of it mattered to me. I liked the availability of a man who would wake with me in the morning and be there when I arrived home from work. I didn't worry about his wandering eye or finagling with coworkers, his word is unyielding and forever truly means until the end of time. Matt was the sure thing that came at the end of a series of relationships that never got past the second month.

He sleeps with one leg in and one leg out of the covers, and that school-boy erection that lets itself be known every morning like clockwork, even if I choose to ignore it or insist I'm too busy or too tired or too stressed right now. This is not one of those times. My hand slowly makes its way down his chest and caresses the lower part of his abdomen. Matt's hand reaches over to cusp the back of my neck as we try not to interrupt the stillness of the morning. I gently explore his awaiting body as he jolts to attention with a single touch.

He pulls me in slowly as I roll over onto him and grab him firmly with my hand. The mattress creaks and even our inhalations seem loud; every noise amplified as our faces meet. Matt is more sexual in the morning, the circulation of a horizontal body sends him into an instinctual craving that begins to sweeten as his back arches and a slight dew covers his body against the pure white sheets.

I yearn for him to be inside me, to feel that connection I felt so strongly so long ago. I want him to take the lead, to allow me to be the woman and him the tending man as I forget the roles we carry for the rest of the day, even if only for a moment. Instead, I seem to almost drift away as he takes over with his own hand. He should be pacing himself and ravaging me on this last morning that we will be together for a week. All his pent-up emotion and desire should be thrust inside me repeatedly as we both lose ourselves in the ecstasy of the moment. That is not to be, yet again. The stillness of the morning echoes with just his climax, dirtying the furry trail just below his navel with a crescendo echoed by a guttural moan that carries through our small apartment.

As the only memory of the moment drips from him, stillness returns. He lies motionless on his back as I linger just a moment, and then he slowly pulls me up alongside him with a nudge of my arm. He sexually forgets me once again in this relationship, but I no longer know the words or confidence to let him know it. I return to his side and then edge out just a bit farther as we retreat to our own places and he falls back to sleep. His Midwest upbringing never taught him the reciprocal pleasures of a wife—something I didn't realize until the initial lust and passion of our relationship waned into the malaise of marriage. Then without a moment for my breath to return, the other man in my life beckons. Our son, Billy, calls out in a high-pitched wail, exalting through the air in our tiny apartment as I rush to him during this "only part of the day I have to take care of him," as Matt often reminds me.

Billy is the micro version of Matt, the two-foot wobbly version that has insisted since the delivery room that his needs be satisfied immediately or it's hell to pay for everyone. After he had spent two days in the hospital, the nurses confided that he was one of the few babies they were somewhat happy to see leave. Although they said this with a laugh, we all knew he had a shrill cry that pierced ears and was impossible to quell. In the hospital, I couldn't wait to hand him back after feedings, waiting for that adoration of a mother to set in day after day, only to agonize in a mix of guilt and frustration as I waited for that instinctual bond to initiate.

Billy would cry almost nonstop. We scoured the medical community for answers, from deafness to digestive disorders. Test after test concluded he was simply a fussy child and perhaps I was a hypochondriac. However, life has gotten better; the terrible twos and threes weren't nearly as awful as what came before as Billy becomes more of a mini-man who wanders about our apartment as he wishes in our quest to keep him appeased.

I returned to the office after only thirty days of maternity leave. The day I returned to work, I actually cried in happiness. I finally had a moment of quiet and concentration. Every lunch was a delight, and moments spent working overtime were a reprieve from the chaos that awaited me at home. Matt would hand off Billy and all his demands to me at the door, and then he would check out for the rest of the night. My mother even thought it was too soon to go back to work, but that's just her Jewish-mom mentality. I did have good reasoning and justification. I was the sole breadwinner, and with the magazine performing as it did in the months before the delivery, I felt there would be no job to come back to if I took much more time off.

Now I try to hush Billy back to sleep, but he wakes up ready to eat and cry. His cry is still more of a scream, like a cry you would generate if someone were suddenly to submerge you into ice-cold water in the middle of your deepest sleep. I quickly try to ready a cup of warm milk. This usually soothes his stomach, which may or may not attribute to his acid reflux, making him the way he is. It also may be that this is simply his personality, which I hope is not the case.

"Put some clothes on already," I say as Matt passes by the kitchen to the bathroom, still semi-erect in front of our son.

He insists it's okay among guys as he pees with the toilet seat down in clear view of our entire apartment. I think a level of modesty between parents and a child, especially at this young age, is essential. I don't dare say that or Matt will run naked out on the balcony or come over and slap his dick with its dribble of urine all over the kitchen in a cute, but totally inappropriate rebellion. It often seems he is also a four-year-old, and I am the single adult who makes sure the parental dots are crossed, the bank account isn't empty, and someone doesn't merely wash, but also folds the laundry.

However, this morning isn't about complaining. Even the annoyances seem endearing and essential as we bask in the pre-travel separation that makes this life feel like it's emerging from its arduous phase and more the way I had imagined it would be in the beginning. This morning, he holds my hand a little longer and doesn't run out for the newspaper or for a coffee.

"Today, I'm your personal chef," Matt says, pulling on a pair of oatmeal-gray sweatpants.

"If only I had a bit more time to take you up on that," I reply as I think of warm cinnamon rolls or a complicated tofu scramble.

His attention and affection has me wondering if I should have even agreed to this project in the first place. I didn't have to take it, after all, numerous people in the office are single and better suited for these types of writing assignments, and they have bodies better suited for Rio.

"I can cook under pressure, don't you worry. Today, I'll make you anything you want for breakfast," he says, grabbing me at the waist and pulling me so close that our noses touch. "Anything."

"Anything, you say?"

Just as I say the words, a box of Cheerios falls off the counter and its contents scatter across the floor behind me. It takes but a moment to remember why I essentially begged for the assignment in the first place and how desperately I need a break, a momentary pause for myself, even just for a few days. The monotony of my life needs some shaking up from yet another weekend of pizza dinners, of watching reality TV with a man who falls asleep at 9:00 p.m., and another male who wakes at 5:00 a.m. to inevitably only be pleased by finding his favorite cartoon in these meaningless years of thankless, patient parenting. Having spent these last year's essentially at home, what I really crave is a glimpse of the life I once knew with a little bit of pampering, thinking about something besides my husband and child, and with days that begin with a proper hotel breakfast of crispy toast, complicated eggs, and an intelligent article in the *International Herald Tribune*.

"Yogurt would be lovely, honey," I reply, knowing the mess a good omelet scramble would create and the likelihood that the pan would still be dirty by the time I come home in five days.

I've dreamed for months about having three days of continuous me time, and now just three hours until fruition, I sit somewhat dreading it all. The very process nauseates me as I plan my airplane outfit, double-checking my bag, and virtually fearing the idea of Rio.

Then the guilt sets in as I look at my two men, the ground to my earth without which I would wander through life as one of those working women who never find anything more than another job, never marrying, never belonging to anyone or anything. And instead of holding it with all my heart, here I am grabbing an extra swimsuit and contemplating fedoras, instead of reading to my son at night in his most formative years, or tending to my husband who spends every single waking minute in this apartment being both a mom and dad while I roam the world.

"Honey, your car is here … I think!"

Time trips my step in a crescendo of emotions. Billy screams at the top of his lungs and Matt rushes into the bedroom while I grab my laptop, triple check my passport, and stand at the threshold of our home. I am thinking what if the plane crashes or what if Matt dies of an unexpected heart attack in the middle of the night, or meets a woman at the grocery store who appreciates and has time for him.

Together we stand—this motley crew of former and future dreams—in a group hug. Billy screams in his usual fit of tears, and Matt manages to see through the noise and the speed of the moment to look into my eyes and make it all pass into the periphery for just a moment.

"I love you more than anything else in the world."

His words manage to envelope all, including Billy who is hushed to stillness.

"I love you, too."

"Be safe and come home quickly," he says as I pull away wishing I had never asked for this assignment in the first place.

His words echo in my head as I take the two floors with the staccato-like thud of my over-packed suitcase dropping on every step, and I think of ways to call my editor and explain why I can't go.

From our Williamsburg building and into the street, I look up at my home. It has never seemed more idyllic. The driver undresses me of my luggage, and I sink into the backseat of the bouncy black town car. My hand, sticky with Billy's slobber and various hand lotions, grips the door strap and pulls it tight as my real world and life fade behind me. The car feels like an unfamiliar world, its fresh newspaper tucked behind the driver's seat just for me, and windows free of smudges and stains that transport me to a life I had long ago.

CHAPTER 2

DAVID

RIO'S AIRPORT IS named after the man who sang "The Girl From Ipanema." The aging concrete relic squats on the horizon with spotlights that flood its crumbling facade in almost too much brightness among towering cranes that have been there for years, even though the place has virtually never changed.

A strange airport, built for greatness, is mostly relegated to commuter flights and the spare European and US carrier that manage a few flights a day. There are moments in my life that I crave this city, its visceral mulatto madness of all-night sex and women who will grab guys like me off the street and devour them on their mother's porch. It's the prettiest place your eyes will ever see, even from an airplane window—jagged mountains with shapes as if made by a Vincent van Gogh god.

The benefits of being in seat 2A include being one of the first to disembark this flying bus to speed-walk my way through ramps and roped corridors that ultimately lead to a brutish customs guard. He eyes my passport with crumbled brow under an infrared light and slowly scrolls through an antiquated commuter screen before staring me in the blues and waving me into his land.

As the rest of the plane catches up with me at baggage claim, I try to recognize some of the faces I lingered with before boarding the plane almost eleven hours ago. I am remarkably unable to remember a single person aside from my flight attendant who looks so much better in her full navy uniform and scarf walking the airport with a sexy familiarity that didn't translate while she was stirring my martini or carrying off my dinner tray when I rang the red overhead button for her.

A Tumi bag later, I make my way into the airport's central marketplace, namely the arrivals hall. It's where a country truly begins for me—a place where the institutional airport retreats to be somewhere authentic, where coffee places don't look like Starbucks and cafés don't feel like a Pret a Manger.

Once upon a time in Brazil's poorer past, a visitor would be inundated with pesky cab drivers and porters who would swindle you for as much as they could get before passing you off in a cab where the driver wouldn't turn on the air conditioner and take side streets all the way to your dodgy Copacabana hotel. These days, the Brazilians are rich, their old but immaculate airport with a fleet of cleaning staff and maintenance professionals in crisp shirts and cheerful smiles—truly the new order of a BRIC world.

In fact, it's almost impossible to find a cab at all, which is why the Fasano car is supposed to be here with a sign that read Mr. David Summers. Sometimes the drivers linger to the side or hover in the background, but as I study each sign and look deeper and deeper into the crowd, I see nothing.

Perhaps a strong coffee is in order, and so I meander to the coffee counter. The sounds of American accents slowly catch up with my speediness through customs and make their way into and through the airport.

"*Brigado, un café dople?*" I ask in my best Portuguese accent as the overdressed waitress straddles the register with her too-exposed shoulders and hair that has a stiff sheen that frames her sweaty smirks.

"A-mer-i-can-o?" she asks in a five-syllable sprawl that sounds like there's a period behind every other letter.

"No, *eu sou britânico.*" I look away so as not to lead this hungry, overly flirty woman on for something more.

My gaze returns to the terminal and my lost driver, who is most likely on a cigarette break or tipping off a security guy so he can park at the gate and leave his car idling. Then, among the cab drivers in their best working suits and a cleaning staff in their utilitarian blue uniforms, there she is.

An embroidered white linen shirt suits her, complementing her porcelain complexion as she does everything not to look at me even as she walks in an almost-straight line toward me. All the noise and commotion of the airport seems to descend into silence as with each step she cuts the distance between us like a knife. I finesse her with my own stare, passing over her, and then returning in a direct gaze and yet, nothing.

She holds copies of *Vogue Italia* or some other voluminous magazines tightly under her arm and approaches within a few feet of me without so much as a glance of her iridescent green eyes in my direction. She comes so close that I can actually smell her, a citrusy scent with a hint of jasmine and a smugly robust spice that's noticeable even above an air of coffee beans, fresh-squeezed oranges, and burned toast. As I move just far enough from the register to allow her space, she shoves her roller bag between us and greets the waitress with a neutral semi-smile without teeth or tensing of her eyes or a mere notice of my presence even though I am three feet from her lips.

"*Café com leite, por favor?*" she says with the most un-American of swift dialects and without a single missed syllable.

A stillness washes over me as I listen for more, so much so that the waitress interrupts in a yell of choppy English above their conversation, "Mister, here is your coffee!"

Here I am, revealed as the outsider. I take my coffee and retreat to a standing table near the edge of the café to watch. I watch for a sign of her slipping up that will negate her in my mind and explain her total ignorance of me, maybe pulling out a credit card as if she's at Starbucks instead of the cash these types of places require. Her perfect posture and shiny bag make no mistakes, and I resign myself to calling the hotel to inquire about my car.

As I become involved in conversation with the hotel receptionist, I can feel a single stare fall on my neck. I quickly look and with a swift turn in response, she looks away, perhaps never looking at all, distracted by her coffee and conversation that lingers with the chatty waitress. Despite my attraction to rejection, this proves too much even for me, so I mentally say good-bye to her and that Fasano driver, wherever he might be.

I forget that you actually see more in the back of a taxi. The glass widows clear for viewing Rio's elevated highways that wind around the motionless lagoons with their fabricated beaches by the airport and through two of the now tamed favelas that claw their way atop a hillside. Their poetically crumbling facades are enveloped in a geometric glaze of brick and mortar chaos, capped in satellite dishes and electric wires. There's a long tunnel that you pass through that seems to divide the black-and-whiteness of suburban Rio from the Pantone city itself, a dark and mysterious strip of roadway that in its day was prone to well-publicized robberies, when traffic would be halted by drug lords and bandits targeting passing taxis and buses.

Today, the worst thing that can happen is that traffic might make you late for your dinner in Santa Teresa. It zips along with ethanol-guzzling SUVs and puttering motor scooters with shirtless guys and their girlfriends clinging to their shoulders with penned in colorful tattoos that draw the eye. Together we all emerge at the end of the tunnel that spills onto the famous Lagoa and its incongruent residential high-rises with their first three or so floors trimmed in chain-link balconies facing the holiday Christmas tree that lights up every December and then sits out the rest of the year along the shore. Along the lake, women saunter along the sidewalks in nothing more than a bikini and flip-flops, their chocolaty hair blowing behind to lure chiseled men in those wide-banded Speedos that try to catch up, even to just see her eyes.

Signs point in various directions that define the city, from Leblon to Copacabana. These were once the narrow parameters for tourists in the city that's expanded and thrived under a stronger economy and better management of the police. My bosses insist it's only a cycle, and despair and financial ruin will return to these lands. Rio has a long history of being savaged by us Westerners, who loot it for its minerals and fleshy innocence, only to leave it in ruins and then pick it up again in some sort of whirlwind romance.

Today it's the international conglomerates and private equity companies, like the one I work for, that purge the country of its resources. And really, that's what my job as their risk analyst is all about, finding the prettiest of financial novices who are like those virgins of old who have no idea their value as we write them a check and strip them of most of their business rights. Then we put them in a pretty dress, smear them in the finest make-up, and spritz them in the most intoxicating of fragrances before we parade them on the world's financial markets where the highest bidder wins.

There it is, and it wows me even on the umpteenth time. That most beautiful shore of the Atlantic dotted in numbered lifeguard towers with a long boulevard and promenade of wavy geometric mosaic tiles that almost hypnotize you into this sexually charged trance that lasts every moment in Rio. The beaches are full, even on a Tuesday, a cavalcade of almost naked bodies running, biking, and rollerblading in all shapes of perfect, past the numerous identical kiosks that sell coconuts with a straw and the strongest rum drinks you'll ever taste.

With a swift stop, the door swings open and a line of six or so men in suits and security uniforms line the cobblestone valet of the Fasano with its glassy-steel frontage framed in swags of white drapery and cool chrome signage.

"Are you checking in, sir?" asks a young valet lingering in the doorway in a white shirt and pants far too woolen for this humid February day.

"Welcome back to the Fasano, Mr. Summers," says a suited man, interrupting him from the reception with an apologetic undertone that translates even in his broken English.

"We are so sorry about the car. There was an issue with the driver, and he missed you by ten minutes. Please accept our sincerest apologies. We've upgraded you in hopes that you can forgive."

Sadly, an upgrade at the Fasano usually just means a higher floor.

The luggage flies out of the taxi in a melody of formal Fasano footwork and through a separate entrance from the guests. The taxi driver approaches for his tip, and a few more of the footmen hold the glassy hotel gates open for another visit.

This hotel was supposed to be an Argentine property by Alan Faena, a fashion-guy-turned-hotelier from Buenos Aires who fell on hard times after the opening of his Faena Hotel+Universe, after Argentina's ultimate devaluation. He was partnered with designer Philippe Starck, who stayed on the project once it was sold to Sao Paulo's Fasano family, a three-generation group of Italian restaurateurs who made this their second hotel property, and really their best to date.

The dark lounge, with its futuristic leather chairs and Sérgio Rodrigues sofas, is separated from the lobby by a succession of white drapes that billow with every opening of the glass doors. The front desk is a step back to Rio in late 1950s, but filled with the young and rich in designer linen and complicated straw hats that make the grand trek to this place, which is like the architectural incarnation of sex itself. Silk-screens with folkloric scenes of the Amazon hang from antique glass behind the reception carved of a single fifty-foot piece of timber.

The staff, in their matching vintage khaki uniforms, appears as if cast for a movie, most having been here every year since I started visiting. The same woman, Isabella, tells me the latest restaurant opening, while the chap named Marcello, who looks like a thug version of Antonio Banderas, stands next to the door and assures guests are actually guests and that no call girls or hookers or escorts make it to the rooftop pool, even to the point of his own embarrassment.

The elevator lingers a little too long on the lobby level as a rush of guests make their way in and push me to the back. Fedoras are everywhere in these parts of Rio as the door stutters open again to let in that inevitable sixth guest. There it is again, the spicy citrus scent of the American woman who shunned me in the airport. Now she simply turns her back to everyone, including me, without a "hello" or an "excuse me" as the door shimmies to a close.

Her scent makes immediate friends, even if all remain silent and pretend they're actually alone instead of crushed together in a six-by-six stainless steel box built by construction workers constrained by a tight budget and an almost too-timely contractor. And there on that second floor, which offers either a loud room facing the beach or a dark room facing the rear of an unattractive apartment block with strings of dirty laundry and too-chatty housekeepers, the American leaves me yet again without a glance or an acknowledgment or even a look of the eyes.

The fifth floor is where you want to be at the Fasano. It faces the ocean and is the perfect distance above the beach crowds to still be able to see who has the hot body, but not so close that honking buses or 2:00 a.m. crowds leaving the basement bar wakes you up. The Fasanos were an unlikely pairing for Philippe Starck, the infamous designer of gilded seven-foot wingbacks and acrylic ghost chairs, who suddenly found himself working for a family more familiar with old-school deco styling than slutty baroque. The result was a success, even if the personal relationship was not; a hotel that mixes rich Old World style with abstract artwork and Rio glamour that I always look forward to visiting.

The rooms are the perfect beach crash pad. A head-on silhouette of the Cagarras Islands frames a two-person balcony with teak deck; Eames chairs and mirrored walls make it hard for nosy neighbors to see inside. A king bed like you've never seen straddles the center of the room, with black-and-white images of lifeguards on some sort of massive diving pier in a Brazilian beach Neverland that makes for good daydreaming from a cushy leather chair I'm sure the Fasanos had to plead for Starck to accept.

Traveling for work has its benefits when you're working for the likes of my firm. A chilled bottle of Moët and a whole coconut with a straw poked through its top awaits me in the room, but so does an in-box full of messages that suddenly make my iPhone vibrate like a popcorn machine as I contemplate how many hours I can goof-off without replying and before it becomes obvious that I'm goofing-off.

At different times of my life, I would arrive in Rio only to rush out again to the beach or to the bar or to the gym, but at the Fasano, there is that incredible pool on the rooftop that's like an attraction all its own and like nowhere else in the world.

Etro swim trunks, same shirt—fully unbuttoned of course—and retro sunglasses that make me look like a modern version of Rudolph Valentino or Errol Flynn. Fasano also gives you free flip-flops, which I never want to own until I'm in Rio, and then they never seem to come off unless I'm headed to a meeting, and maybe not even then. It's always an awkward moment standing at a hotel elevator half-naked when someone like a housekeeper scurries by or a man in a business suit on the elevator stares, likely wondering what this grown man is doing at 4:00 p.m. on a Tuesday in beach attire.

Then the elevators open to the Fasano rooftop and its showstopper bar laced in pinewood sectionals with creamy white-striped cushions under a shaded trellis. Endless lounge chairs are strewn with fashionable couples sipping rosé and snacking on tartares, and who scrutinize every person who passes from the elevator to the main pool. One of the prettiest pools I've ever seen, it never ceases to inspire me. Its chunky white marble and infinity design spills over its edges every time someone closes his or her eyes and jumps in.

Paisley-shaped mirrors line the perimeter brick walls and reflect the high-rise horizon and jagged skyline, which I think is actually prettier than Sugarloaf. The mirrors also generate a little-known death ray that I discovered the first time I came here when I got the most excruciating sunburn across a slice of my torso.

Cabana guys, a good decade past being able to call themselves boys, fetch towels and umbrellas as I circle the edge of the pool to glimpse the fish that will be filling my pond for the next week or so. The hotel is incredibly incestuous, as most guests opt for the pool in lieu of the beach and spend most of the day spilling their guts to new friends over endless passion fruit caipirinhas and platters of fries.

I take a spot at the edge of the pool where only a few loungers remain, next to a circle of Russian rich guys in stubby shorts smoking cigars with an entourage of hot Russian models, one of these women tries hard not to look my way. There's an American or Canadian couple with their Four Seasons hats and plastic bottles of water from the room because they're too cheap to buy them at the pool. Then there's the lone gay guy in between visits to the local boy's club baking to the perfect shade of eggplant before he exploits his next victim for as little as he'll accept.

"*É esta espreguiçadeira tomadas?*" I hear a crisp voice encircled by a corona of sun as I pull away my sunglasses and sit up to look.

As I squint, that familiar voice repeats, "*É esta*, I mean, is this sunbed taken?"

Before I have a chance to reply or even mentally connect the translated sentence, a flurry of three cabana guys move her lounge chair a good five feet away below that fateful mirror. Her bag overflows with magazines and a clunky object I assume is a laptop.

"*Não, ele está disponível*," I reply in my gruffest and most manly of Portuguese accents.

"*Muito obrigado*," she replies in a soft voice as she struggles for cash from her purse and slips it to the attendant.

She's more glamorous than I remember. Even at this upward angle, where I see more thigh than I would have expected under a sheer top and colorful bikini cinched so tight to her ass that I could make out her even more personal silhouette. She places all her belongings on the opposite side of the lounge away from me. Her face, now covered by a hat that is fashionably large without being too big, sits above a face fully concealed by a pair of black sunglasses far more South of France than Brazilian beach.

I straddle my lounge to sit up and pull my shorts down from their rolled-up norm that makes them look more like Speedo—the surest way not to land an American chick. The music gets louder into afternoon, a sultry mix of acoustic lounge anthems where you don't know who sings them or even the name of the songs, but they ooze an Ipanema sensuality that makes everyone ready to let loose.

"What brings you to Rio?" I ask in the worst of a scratchy, premeditated voice attempting to rise above the volume of the music and pool, but not so loud that the loungers of Canadians turn around in recognition or join in on the conversation.

She removes her glasses without leaning forward or even moving her head.

"I'm here on business," she says, an aura of mystery that I plunge into headfirst.

She bites the tip of her sunglasses and raises her head to reveal eyes the color of cut kiwi with a beautiful black center.

"There are worse places," I reply.

"It's definitely prettier than sitting in an office back home," she says, her smile soft, and then she lies back under her hat.

Her glasses are too dark to tell what she's looking at, perhaps my legs or my shorts or my chest or maybe nothing but that amazing view that hovers on the horizon and just makes you want to savor such moments of beautiful life.

"Funny enough, I'm here on business as well," I intrude.

Not even a crack of a smile emerges from her increasingly tense face. The music, the kids in the pool and the noise of Ipanema itself seem to come to a long, exaggerated silence as I wait for a reply.

"We were actually on the same flight, I believe," I volunteer, hoping to cut the tension and tease out a response.

She leans forward and adjusts the towel around her waist, partially getting up to readjust her shorts or perhaps flee our conversation.

"Yes, and in the coffee shop as well," she adds with an asymmetrical grin as if surprised by my admission.

"I thought I was going unnoticed as a Brit until you barged through with your perfect Portuguese."

"Hardly perfect, I would say. Just a few too many times not getting the cappuccino I asked for in Lisbon one summer."

She relaxes a moment, and for the first time since I've seen her, she pushes back in her lounge and adjusts the colorful straps of her bikini underneath her cover-up and drawing my eyes, even though I try desperately not to look. Obviously, many beautiful women occupy lounges at this pool, but something about her simply sucks me in and has me watching her every move.

Silence seems to suit her better, perhaps it's the jet lag, or feeling uncomfortable in a corner of the hotel pool to talk so openly with another man. My instincts say she's in a relationship and quite happily. In the moment of granted silence, she relaxes enough to tug on the sleeve of her white cover-up. She lifts it over her head almost in slow motion above two perfectly molded breasts, sculpted masterfully into a bikini that's neither too large nor too small. She tilts her sunglasses just enough to allow me to see her looking at me watching her every move like a ballet.

With a quick push up from her lounge, and without a single word, she walks to the pool, her lower body with more of a curve than I could hope for and legs that make even the Russian models take notice. She ties her hair up without slowing in step, and then sits on the white marble ledge of the pool that retains its chill despite the muggy Rio air and warm water. Without causing much of a wake, she pushes her body into the water with the grace of a woman who wishes to go unnoticed.

Not one to chase too closely, I grab my shirt and make my way past the pool with a single hand wave to that woman who still bears no name. I hope to find the real Rio and its attainable women who lie beyond the hotel. You don't capture the real feel of Rio inside the Fasano; the city comes to life only once you escape the double-glass doors and step onto the cobbled-marble sidewalks and the zippy roadway that runs along the beach.

Rio of today is nothing like it appeared when I first visited a decade ago. Gold-speckled apartment blocks fortified with wrought iron gates no longer have the barbwire-draped ornamentation or multiple armed guards. Today, there are only sleepy guards in security booths crowded with portable TVs. Overgrown trees with branches that reach from the sky to the sidewalk shade the congested streets leading from the beach. I pass the rainbow canopies of gay bars where beady eyes are best avoided, and then the corner café with its orange plastic chairs, shiny Formica tables, and chatty waitresses who serve coffee that jolts the heart and the only sugar-free acia I've found in Rio.

From the leisurely residential streets of Ipanema, grandmothers carry plastic bags of groceries with granddaughters in hand, appears a cluster of hardware stores where workers rush in and out next to grocery conglomerates with flashy logos that mean something to local eyes. Here, Ipanema succumbs to more downtrodden Copacabana that was once the most fashionable part of the city. Here, you'll find the more dated apartment blocks where the elderly linger by propped-open doors, and faded hotel towers disappoint first-timers above a few American bars that are the Brazilian version of a strip club. Back in the day, you could find the most beautiful women in the world literally dancing to eat, but these days, the economy has left these places to aging drunks and drug addicts to operate.

For those who want a little action, the beaches of Copacabana are where to go, especially around the Orothon Palace that's enveloped by the ladies of the night as well as the prettier ones who gravitate by day to the strip of sand directly in front of the hotel. While I'm not one to pay for sex, I always find it fun to go for a swim and take in the sights in these grittier urban parts that remind me of that old Rio I once knew. Ipanema guys are a softer bunch than the steroid-fueled gym Barbie's who preside over the beaches of Copacabana. You don't want to carry much or stand out on this strip of sand than I already do with my English skin and eyes, across the wide sidewalk that's far less congested than the one back near the Fasano. The sand is painfully hot as I tiptoe around the clusters of locals sprawled toward the sun, and I make a direct line for the water.

The crush of people who clog the beaches in late afternoon can be overwhelming, most bringing coolers full of canned drinks and bags full of food to share with friends. Even the water can be crowded, a shoreline packed with those who lack air conditioning at home and clog the entry points. Despite its brownish color this afternoon, the warm water washes my body clean of its sweat, airplane staleness, and a layer of Rio dirt that sticks to you almost any time you walk through the city.

Heads bob in the water as women, men, and even children stare at a white man in these parts, wondering what he's doing in this section of the beach if not for sex. Not for first-timers, this part of Rio can still intimidate those not familiar with the ground rules. First, don't even look at a woman if she's with another man—at least when he can potentially see you doing so. You never, ever make the mistake of chatting up a girl younger than eighteen, even if you and she are thoroughly up for it. Lastly, you never, ever dare bring a woman from the beach back to your hotel.

As I sit on a ledge of sand closest to the water, the beach feels like the grittier Rio I knew of old, with its familiar vendors hawking those puffed peanut-flavored rings, fancy ice cream bars, and mate that are all staples of the Brazilian beach. There, in the distance, our eyes meet over no fewer than three women and a child building a sand castle precariously close to the waves. She stares without so much as a blink walking in my direction with her black swimsuit cinched tight in its wetness to her thighs, which curve in an almost immoral angle making them seem like they were built by God for grabbing.

She inches closer as if blown by the wind. Her black eyes pierce, entrancing mine with her mocha skin and curly exotic hair dripping on the ends. A smile erupts even before a word. She sits next to me passing a touch of her foot over my sandy ankle as wave's crash and crowd's hum around us.

"You Americano?" she secretes from her fleshy pout with glaringly white teeth of which I can see only a trace as I fantasize about the taste of her perfectly drawn lips.

"Englander."

My direct gaze says, I'll fuck you right here on the beach if need be, and it's definitely going to happen; I'm going to get inside you. Her eyes struggle against the sea breeze as a single strand of hair beckoned by my perverse thoughts shoves itself into her mouth; her generous fingers tug at it but only push it in more, deeper, as we gaze into each other's eyes that feel as though we've sunken into each other's souls.

"You sleep at Hotel Copacabana?" She references the posh hotel down the beach where most businessmen stay, and most Brazilian girls like her, only venture into once they are married or rightly dressed for a private client.

Her question gives away her intent, a cash deal negotiated with a guy she would probably do without even being paid.

"No, Marriott, da." I point to the nearby hotel. Her sexy exoticness fades in just a single question as a look of disappointment echoes across her face. She inches a bit farther away and ponders my fallen value.

My instinct is to continue to flirt and watch the salesmanship of a prostitute give way to the more primal desire of a girl who's obviously into a guy. However, I also realize that leaving the situation without a room or intent to seal the deal would have her following me off the beach or causing some sort of commotion that I would not likely win given her home-beach advantage. Despite her knowing she cannot make money off a guy like me, she lingers with her eyes as we savor the passing light of the sun retreating to half-brightness beyond the staggered skyline of Copacabana.

Realizing that our meeting is almost over, she firmly places her soft palm on my upper thigh in a clumsy last-ditch effort. I pull away with the tide and along with it, a fantasy that just isn't meant to be this day.

Then Rio and its women became secondary as the purpose of my trip, and life swept in on my second day that lasted forty-eight hours, thanks to one hellish all-nighter, courtesy of my firm's partners in London. The very purpose of me being in Rio was to sort out quickly whether our venture capital company should continue with our offer to buy out a Brazilian-based advertising company. My partners didn't appreciate that I was three days in and had gained so little insight into the financials of our acquisition prospect so far. Usually, a deal is either good or bad based on things you dig out of financial statements from larger accounting firms well in advance of such a visit, which usually comes shortly before the final deal negotiation.

However, accounting isn't as transparent in Brazil, and sometimes that equates to a better value for buyers. Other times, it's simply a hack deal only discovered once you're on the ground. My job is to sift through the numbers looking for inaccuracies, and then shift to the profit forecasting looking for ways to make even more money. This time, everything was off, from the in-house accounting to the lack of earnestness of the local management. It literally felt as if their last twenty-four months of accounting was made up at the last minute by the owner, who seemed to have second thoughts about bringing on an international partner for what was really a domestic online advertising agency that would never reach outside Portuguese-speaking counties.

When I work, I vanish, in mind and physically, into the job that takes every moment of my attention and makes everything else in life secondary. It's only at the end of the project that I look up, often realizing that life has moved on and sometimes without me. To my inner consolation, I did not miss any beach time, as it had been a hellish two days of Rio weather with almost unbearable heat that made leather loafers and even a thin summer suit unbearable. Add to the equation the wall-unit air conditioner in the accountant's office I was working out of, heaving with an asthmatic wheeze and blowing lukewarm air as I sweat through my white shirt and even my boxers, which began to weep through my suit pants.

As I'd look out of my downtown window, I could see everyone struggle with the heat. Through their windows, I saw bankers working in undershirts and an older woman sitting in only her bra attempting to air out her blouse as her grandmotherly arms waved in the wind. The inside of my own window was constantly wet with humidity even though it was entirely rain-tight. Without a view of the mountain or crashing shoreline to console my thoughts, for a while this inner Rio felt like hell on earth.

It is late evening as I make my way back to the Fasano, and now I'm one of those overdressed businessmen I always scowl at on my first day for interrupting my vacation fantasy. And to the rooftop without interruption, I make my way to the bar, which is as packed as I have ever seen it. It's brimming with tightly packed families eating plates of Brazilian hamburgers, that lonely gay man who now has a similarly tan fellow in tow, and that American woman in full fedora and flip-flops captured in the waning afternoon sun. This is often my frustration with the Fasano, a rooftop with not nearly enough loungers or chairs to accommodate a half-filled hotel, let alone a sold-out one.

"Can I get a passion fruit caipirinha, please?" I say to the barman.

As my lips move, I feel a single bead of sweat unleash from my upper lip as the barman nods. I can tell a thirty-minute wait is inevitable. I walk over to the glassy ledge by my dear American friend who is deep inside her laptop. As I edge closer to look, I see her typing a mile a minute in some sort of software program with a glass of rosé in front of her and a half-eaten bowl of nuts. A single seat sits in front of her, but in all honesty, I'd rather stand than endure the non-conversation we shared on the first day.

Whether it's my mood or not, the crowd seems livelier than on the first day including a gregarious Russian man chewing on his unlit cigar like it's taffy. Next to him is his waif model girlfriend who looks at him only when her wine glass is empty or the bill arrives.

"*Un caipirinha de maracujá,*" the waiter mouths off in a louder-than-expected voice as he holds a full tray of drinks including mine. He sets the drink on the American's table in front of the lone empty chair, which he tries unsuccessfully to turn toward the sea.

"May I take this chair, madam?" he asks.

The American looks up as if startled from mid-thought despite her fingers having been long inactive.

"Of course, no problem at all. Just let me ..."

"Absolutely not, I'm totally okay standing at the bar. I didn't mean to interrupt," I say.

Her gaze rises to meet mine. Her eyes, a mossy green color, and a stare so deep I can't tell if it's interest or disdain.

"No, please, I insist. Plus, I heard you don't want to miss the sunset," she says.

As I maneuver around her back, I try to conceal my back with its long trail of sweat through my white shirt. I quickly plop into the cushioned lounger and attempt to swing it away from her table.

"That's really not necessary," she says in response to my repositioning.

"And not really possible," I joke. "I'm afraid you're now stuck with me."

A giggle emerges as she stares at me, differently today.

"We should really do this again," she says, closing the lid of her computer and setting it on the table before pushing the heavy sunglasses atop her head. "I'm Catherine."

She reaches out her hand as I put my drink back on the table next to her computer. I quickly try to dry my hand on my sleeve before extending it toward her. My full palm, still moist from the iced drink, envelopes her soft flesh while her pinkish nails, perfectly manicured, brush over my wrist.

"I'm David, and it's truly lovely to share a table with you, Catherine."

Her stare is intense. I can see in her eyes the reflection of the setting sun behind me that has enveloped the sky in a fiery orange hue with a reddish tint along the horizon.

"And you're from New York, I take it?"

"Yes, I live in Manhattan. I work in publishing."

"So you're a publisher or in ad sales?" The conversation gains a metronomic beat with each back and forth.

"No, I'm editorial. Actually I'm a bit of everything these days, which includes writing, editor, part-time Photoshopper, and the whole sort."

"Which means you need a vacation?"

"Well, sort of. Actually I'm here on assignment, and I figured it could be a bit of both in lieu of handing it off to one of our freelancers."

"Brilliant, and here you are enjoying the best of both worlds."

At the bottom of my drink, I figure this is where our conversation ends. I lean forward to make my exit trying to conceal my sweaty shirt that's blotchily soaked front and back.

"Sir, *duas bebidas mais, por favor.*"

To my surprise, she abruptly orders a round of drinks.

"I ordered you another drink … I hope that's okay?"

"Actually, I'm a bit embarrassed to even be sitting here like this," I say as she raises her left eyebrow, giving her a teacher-like sexiness that I hadn't noticed before.

"A hot and poorly air-conditioned office got the best of me, and to be honest with you, I wasn't expecting to be up here long without changing."

I point at my shirt, and she lingers in a stare as the waiter places two more drinks in front of us on our table.

"What do you do for work?" she asks.

"Do you want the long or short version?" I ask without pausing for an answer. "I'm essentially a risk analyst for a venture capital company based in London."

"And that means?"

"That means I try to keep my company from making bad acquisitions. When new companies see me, they think I'm part of a group that's buying their company, but really I'm there to determine if it's actually a good deal, and if it's not, how to get out of it as quickly as possible."

I pull my collar looser, and she studies the horizon as an awkward pause lingers. This is usually why I avoid the explanation of what I do to women.

"So you're on the road a lot?"

"Almost constantly, but that's part of what I love about the job. I'm constantly in flux and learning, whether it's about a new client or an entirely new city that I've never visited. Like Mexico City, it's a place you'd never necessarily think about traveling to, and yet, it is a most incredibly vivid and real city."

"What's it like? I've always been fascinated with Aztec history and the whole Cortés conquering Tenochtitlan thing."

Catherine's focus isn't what I'm used to from women; she listens to every word, and then continues the conversation instead of redirecting it to whatever is occupying her own mind.

"Actually, the whole Aztec history is downplayed simply because the colonialists preserved so little. But you find bits of it here and there. Plus, there are these incredible buildings from the seventeenth century. A friend of mine is an architect, and he just converted this building that has these folk art murals on the wall that just humble you, and he lives in this place. Then there's this outrageous food scene you never really hear about and the art."

"Yes, the art is supposed to be amazing. There's that new museum and all, right?"

"Exactly. Wow, you really know your stuff," I say. The remark echoed in my mind as well as in my words. "I hope I'm not boring you with all my stories."

"No, I really enjoy it, actually. I'm a writer, so I love hearing a good story. So you are based in New York?"

"Actually, I'm based in London, but spend most of my time on the road."

She makes me worry whether I'm saying the right things as I feel a droplet of sweat roll down my neck, across my chest, and along my stomach like a marble.

"Just take it off, already. You're in Rio for Christ's sake," she says as if she's said it before. "And Lord knows you're definitely not shy."

The suggestion catches me off guard. She backtracks in a verbal stumble.

"I mean, you're dying, right? It is Rio you know, and you're sitting five feet from a pool, so I would assume queen's etiquette dictates that is acceptable."

I feel a smile of relief widening across my face as I jump to my feet and struggle to remove my white shirt. She looks off in the distance as if to provide me a moment of privacy. The sensation of air on my bare chest makes my nipples tense and sends a bolt of blood to my dick that I try to conceal with my shirt in front of my trousers.

"I must admit, that's like a sentence being lifted," I proclaim, plopping back into my lounge chair.

"You seem the type who's more comfortable with their shirt off anyway," she jabs.

"Actually, I would have kept it on if you hadn't insisted," I deliver back.

Her responses gain a sort of momentum as she inquires on endless superficial details about my life with little contribution about herself. She seems the commitment type even if she doesn't utter a word, but with each sentence, she becomes more attractive to me in her own flirty way, even in this city of more exotic women and easier prospects.

She recites all the lines of a woman who is trying to maintain her distance, even though I know the attraction that must lay just beneath the surface. She's the type of woman who would never waste her conversation. From the glass reflection behind her, I can see the sun falling to a lazy half-mast, just about to plunge behind the clouds off Ipanema.

"Here, grab your drink and come with me," I say abruptly as I point to the glass ledge next to the pool that juts out over the Ipanema horizon.

"What about my stuff?" the American in her interjects.

"You think they want your ten-year-old MacBook Pro? He'll watch it for you," I say, gesturing to the waiter summoned from our sudden movement.

"You'll watch it for her, right?" I nod my head even though the waiter doesn't really appear to understand what I said, and then I grab her drink and take it to the ledge.

She follows hesitantly, positioning herself a safe distance behind me as I pull her to the narrow ledge. The sun's yellow ray's burn to a darker orange with purple and pink edges that feel as if they want to touch the favela of Vidigal that rises on the hilltop behind Leblon.

"Why do I have the feeling you've done this before?" she says, negating the moment. "You in your Gucci loafers and belted dress pants."

The sarcasm interrupts the magic of the moment, and I don't dare deliver a sharper rebuttal or we'll miss the sunset entirely.

"Now, just watch what happens," I whisper as the people sitting behind us rise to their feet and the descending sun slips into the crescent shape that, as a child, I thought looked like my thumbnail. The sun becomes just a sliver and smaller and smaller and then nothing.

Then, in the immediate absence of the sun, she looks into my eyes, pulling away with her lower body but coming closer with her stare that makes her feel inches away.

As if beckoned by the gods, a clamor draws her eyes away and onto the distant horizon. She gazes somewhere far out at sea as the noise comes closer and closer. Obscure but intense, a wave of sound erupts into a more familiar applause that envelopes the far beach and then closer and closer until it passes upon us as the residents of Rio, both temporary and forever, begin clapping as if it was the first or most beautiful sunset they had ever seen.

The sound is so intense it washes both of us away in the moment, and guests behind us applaud in a mixture of whistles and catcalls. Catherine leans in with a push on my shoulder as if to say, "hello" or "thank you" or "you were right." As the sound returns to passing buses and waiters clearing the lounge chairs of the day's towels and glasses, Catherine lingers with me at the glassy ledge.

"I think that was the most incredible sunset I've ever witnessed," she says in humble honesty.

"And even though they see it every day, they appreciate it as if it were the first time."

"Does that happen all the time?" Her forehead is peaked under her long hair blowing in the wind.

"You'll have to come back tomorrow night and see."

"I kind of wish this trip would end right now. I have to say, it's been the best thing I've experienced in Rio so far."

"Are you kidding me?"

"I have to say, I really don't get this city; it's not at all what I was expecting," she continues.

"What were you expecting?" I echo in dismay.

"Maybe it's just the wrong time of year or something, but I expected to find young lovers lost in passion on endless street corners, and the girls from Ipanema lost in this exotic fog of Rio," she says as if looking to fulfill her own romantic fantasy in which I wouldn't mind participating.

"Maybe you just didn't find the right guy to show you until now."

"No, no, no, you're taking it the wrong way." She attempts to backpedal. "I'm just saying that there is supposed to be this primal and exotic utopia where everyone feels sexy and desired, but instead, I found much more of a frenetic city pace and urban grind, albeit mostly in beachwear, but more or less what I face every day in New York."

"Could it be that possibly, and just hear me out, that you were too focused on finding something preconceived, instead of allowing it to evolve around you? I can assure you, there was probably someone who desired you on this very rooftop, let alone while wandering the city the last few days."

"That's very sweet of you," she replies genuinely, "but as a writer, you are really more of a voyeur looking for it at a distance rather than trying to find it for yourself. And then the only good thing I've had to eat was the pasta and orange juice from the room-service menu."

"What about the beach or shopping or the flea market?" I ask.

I want to tell her that she's captivated me since seeing her in the airport, but I realize she's the type to cower under such compliments. She seems entirely unaware of her beauty and a bit uncomfortable even to address it, which makes her even more desirable.

"The beach was kind of dirty, which I hate to even say because it's so incredible from afar. I was just expecting Rio to wow me, to whisk me away right off the bat. I asked about shopping, and they sent me to a horrible mall that's a forty-dollar cab ride away and full of Western stores. And then there's that flea market."

"Yes, it's supposed to be great, right?"

"Wrong. It was some disgusting warehouse called a flea market because it literally has fleas, I think, and is filled with weird eighties office furniture and not nearly the collection of hidden Niemeyer treasures I was expecting."

Catherine seems easily disappointed, or perhaps a woman who wants things exactly as she expects them with little deviation. Our conversation lingers past dusk and into the evening as the bar fills with a dressier clientele and my lack of shirt hidden with a towel begins to look more and more out of place.

"Can I tell you what the best part of my day has been so far?" I say, knowing perhaps that it's going too far.

"What? Do tell," she replies with her near-empty glass in hand.

"It's been sitting here watching you look away from me and at the view behind me. I've watched your eyes gaze to this other place just over my shoulder, and I love seeing your mind get lost between our conversations."

"I hope I haven't been rude; it's just that the colors are so vivid it takes me to another place. I guess it's that side of Rio I do like."

In my mind, I envision sharing room service with her in my room. Then I would bend her over the terrace, or in the living room, and she would straddle me on the Eames chair backward and then forward. But I can tell Catherine is a different sort of woman, one who wants candlelit dinners and handholding on the beach with a man who lives up to whatever is stirring in that always-busy mind of hers.

Before she retreats, and she will, the best plan is to beat her to it.

"So this is where I say good-bye," I say under a Fasano towel in dim light as waiters wait for us to clear away from the table and let them set up for the next guests.

"It is rather late, and I should get some work done," Catherine interjects.

"So do I … I should have started awhile ago."

Catherine rises and extends her hand as I lift from my seat. Something about her makes me crave her more, and it isn't just the physical.

"So, listen," I delay, "I'm not sure how my day is going to unfold tomorrow, but there is a slight, ever slight, chance I could wrap up by lunch."

"That's really not possible, I'm not really—" Catherine attempts to shoot me down before I interrupt her.

"I mean, this is purely on the basis that you're doing this town, and you will be doing your readers a great injustice if you leave here not having been somewhat moved or affected by this truly incredible city."

"I'm not totally negative on Rio; it's just that it hasn't been as I expected," she replies.

"Please, let me have three quick hours to show you some things I truly love, and then we will say our good-byes … no harm done."

"Three hours? You think you can make me love Rio in just three hours?"

"Absolutely, but no more than three hours or my girlfriend will get jealous." I say this like a verbal spike strip, even though I am thoroughly single, to halt her trepidation as I begin to walk away.

"Wait, I haven't agreed to this yet," Catherine sparks.

"Oh, and another thing … all you can wear are shorts, flip-flops, and a T-shirt." I point to her wrists and white linen outfit. "No jewelry, no purse, no fancy stuff … just shorts and flip-flops and we go."

"Shorts and flip-flops?" she muses. "I guess I can sort that out."

"I'll see you tomorrow in the lobby at three o'clock. Don't be late, and don't stand me up."

"Stand you up?"

"Yes, I can see the excuses in your eyes already, Catherine. Spontaneity is part of getting Rio."

I turn away with a fading wave as she returns to her computer and her bag and her American stuff that will probably take her another hour to pull together so she can leave.

Back in my room, I feel a quietness that's reminiscent of my overall life. There are no urgent personal calls to a family or girlfriend to make. There is no rushing for dinner plans or places I'm expected. There's just the work, the room, and me. I roll through the door pulling my clothes off in a single yank and draw open the shades that look over an evening Rio beach still teeming with life even in darkness.

As I stand naked, the small kiosks that sell juices and coffees still perk to life as barefoot businessmen run off their day, grandmothers walk one pace at a time with strollers in tow, and teenagers sludge around attempting to find mischief. I imagine dinner at Sushi Leblon or a drive to Aprazivel in Santa Teresa with someone other than myself, but tonight it's only me at this tiny table and the work—truly the only constant in my life.

Little did I know the next morning would begin my last day in Rio. Most of my work would be in vain, and my time here was going to be cut short, as my company discontinued their plans to acquire Adib, the Rio advertising company, due to "non-transparent accounting practices" that made the value of their operation infeasible to calculate for an outside buyer.

Sadly, my company didn't communicate this to me before yet another all-nighter and a commute to those musty offices that were actually a bit more charming when I knew it was my final day. I used to have a feeling of failure when deals like this would simply collapse after weeks, sometimes months, of working on them. Now, I just see it with excitement for where and what is next to come, providing I get out before having to see the disappointed business owners who don't always greet the news as well as they did in Rio.

A layer of cloud cover blankets the Rio sky, not so much that it's raining, but just enough to shade me on my return to the hotel under the penetrating sun. I had enough time from work to take a quick shower, and promptly at three o'clock, I arrive in the lobby wearing even less than suggested—a spare pair of beach shorts and flip-flops.

"Well, hello there."

Catherine is already there, popping her head up from the lounge with a bag in hand and an asymmetrical T-shirt that dips around her breasts and covers her simple swimsuit. She beams with no lingering hesitation or previous negativity to detract from our day.

"So no," I say even before hello. "This is not what I said you should wear. You want to homogenize with the locals in Rio. So tie that thingy around your waist," I say, pointing to her scarf-like shawl, "and leave your bag here."

"What if I buy something or need money?" she responds as she hands me the bag.

"I got it today; just leave it at the front desk."

With business cleared from my mind, the day is as much about having fun for me as it is showing the American around Rio. In our coordinated Fasano flip-flops, we set out under an uncertain sky along

31

my favorite street just around the corner from the hotel. R. Farme de Amoedo is lined by attractive, yet unassuming apartment blocks from the seventies interspersed with newer construction that blends into the sky of converted balconies, satellite dishes, and outdated antennas. A busier corner approaches with overflowing shops and cafés on all four corners. I wave to the coffee woman who chats at me every morning across from the greasy chicken place with its 3:00 a.m. hamburgers and hangover breakfast platters.

Part of falling in love with Rio is knowing which streets to take when walking and which strips of endless concrete and traffic to avoid. Keeping a speedy pace even in flip-flops, I see Catherine looking at the windows of Osklen with its sexy-surf style, which she's obviously never seen before, and studying each of the passing men in their utilitarian business suits, and teenagers with impossibly perfect skin and edgy hair that suits their skimpy beach outfits. We pause in front of a small kiosk on the park with the words Sushi Cone written in bold neon lights.

"Um, no thank you." Catherine backs away from the window as I step closer.

"Sushi is a big deal in all of Brazil, part of the country's fascination with staying fit," I say with a show of my abs. "And it's so refreshing, even on a hot day."

Catherine wrinkles her face in disagreement.

"They eat it everywhere, including to-go with scoops of tartars and sashimi … that's going to be the best snack you've ever tasted."

She still hesitates.

"Just try it, I promise." I handed Catherine her first cone, a salmon one, which tends to be the safest bet for first-timers.

Catherine goes in for a bite, turning the cone with its sesame seeds and wasabi powder, to find the most approachable side. She goes in with her teeth, demure and tactful, making certain no pieces fall, and making the napkin she took in her hand unnecessary.

"Oh my god," she gushes with a partially full mouth.

"And it's even cold, right?" I say sarcastically, watching for her smile and nod of agreement before I take my first bite.

"The first hour or so I'd stay close to a bathroom just in case," I say in jest.

I like that she's unafraid to try something out of her comfort zone, trusting my guidance as I lead her through the parts of Rio that inspire me so much, and yet I've never really had the chance to share in conversation with anybody.

"So you travel all the time for your job, David. Do you ever get sick of it?" Catherine asks.

"I love it. It takes me to these amazing cities and allows me to feel like I'm a part of them for a few weeks or months. Normally, when people travel, by the time they get to know a place, it's time to leave. This way, I really get to feel like I've lived and felt each place."

"Don't you miss home or your family?"

"You know, it's not for everybody, I guess. But I love it."

"So how much longer will you be here?"

"Actually, you have me on my last day," I say, looking into her eyes to heighten the stakes. "But no pressure, you have all day to fall in love."

"What? To fall in love with you?"

"Rio … all day to fall in love with Rio," I clarify.

"Well, I am quite honored, and I'm already seeing a side of this city I like a lot more."

Catherine's eyes linger on the surfers who pass her way and they linger with their eyes. She studies the small home shops and magazine racks and points out the publication she works for in the United States.

"This is the magazine I work for back home. Have you seen it before?" she asks, pointing to the periodical that's tucked in the back of a second shelf and covered in plastic.

"That would be a negative, but perhaps I'm not really the demographic, am I?"

"You know, it's not *Vogue*, but it pays the bills and allows me to travel a lot."

"So, travel writing, mainly?"

"A mix, but mostly I write the cover stories and stalk celebrities to be on the cover."

"So you meet most of them. That has to be exciting."

"Sadly, most of them don't live up to what you imagine. But I try to remember it's just a job for them, and they're not really trying to be my friend."

"Does anyone live up to what we make him or her out to be in our minds?"

"I'd like to think so, otherwise, that's such a grim outlook on life," she says having pondered the idea deeper and with more emotion than myself.

By late afternoon, the humidity has almost become intolerable, and we tuck into Doce Delicia, a fashionable café along Rua Aníbal de Mendonça with the best salads and generous pours of rosé around. Inside, the honey-colored woods look freshly oiled along the floor with simple rosewood chairs and cheery striped cushions. Catherine and I take a seat in a quiet corner.

"So tell me about you … where is your family from in the states?" I ask as I spread a starched white napkin across my lap.

"My parents live in Albany where I grew up," she says as if starting a longer story.

"And they're still happily married?" I ask as she stays safely on her side of the four-top table, but her legs are so close that I can feel the warmth of her body radiating to my bare knee.

"Well, they're still married, but I'm not sure how happily. They are that couple who stayed together for the kids, and when they were finally empty nesters, they decided that companionship was better than being alone even if they weren't in love with each other anymore."

"That's exactly why I don't believe in marriage. How can you love without passion? That's why I think relationships are only supposed to last for a few years, maybe ten, tops, and then it's simply in our DNA to want more."

"And by more you mean what, exactly?"

"It's that chase, that seeing a woman for the first time and being able to do nothing but think about her and being with her over and over again to the point that you're almost mad. I can't imagine being at a point in life, in a marriage, that you could never look forward to that again."

"And your parents, where are they? In England, I assume?"

"My parents are quite happily married," I say with a pause, "in heaven."

I smile as Catherine chuckles loud enough to draw the attention of the table nearest us with two older Brazilian woman eating triangular slices of white-frosted cake.

"But on earth," I continue, "they couldn't stand each other and divorced when I was at university."

"I'm so sorry. I didn't mean to laugh," Catherine says, covering her mouth with her delicate hand.

"I like seeing you laugh, it's okay."

She has girlishness despite her age. It's refreshing she doesn't talk of children or the desire for them, which is always the elephant in the room with women her age.

The moments in the café sat well with Catherine and I. My one last wow moment in Rio needed to be at the beach, even though our three hours were now in overtime. Setting aside her excuses of not having a towel or sunscreen, we eventually make our way back to the ocean and to the ninth lifeguard stand where it seems every supermodel and sexy resident of Rio was sprawled out on a towel in the sand.

I can tell that Catherine, uncomfortable among the sheer mass of people at the beach, is apprehensive about the whole idea. I take her arm and meander through the crowd to let her see first-hand the microcosm of life that gathers here every day. The various circles defined by conjoined towels offer smart tourists, drag queens, and muscle men who can barely bend their arms, barely notice us as we cut our way through the sand.

"You can almost get lost in the sea of people and noise, able to forget the crashing shore is just a short run away," she says as the thump of house music blares from a speaker and vendors yell their various products.

"Look into their eyes, Catherine, let them penetrate your soul. That is what makes this place Rio," I tell her as she fights past the last few people, and then steps down to the shoreline. She stays close to the slope of sand eroded by the waves. We continue to walk as she maintains her distance from me, avoiding our bodies brushing against each other in the blistering sun and its weighted humidity that might forge us together.

"Brazil is best seen with one foot in the sea watching the kaleidoscope of people who live their lives and do their jobs and earn their money in order to spend as much time as possible at the beach," I say. "It's almost poetic."

Like the Marrakech medina, but on the beach, octogenarians the color of a well-worn saddle, sit inches away from teenagers experimenting with pot for the first time, while kids barely old enough to walk learn that a sandy fortress built at low tide is prone to ruin while their parents make out a few feet away.

"Let's sit for a minute," Catherine gestures as she moves in toward her ledge of sand built by the high tide. Even in her casual clothes, she sticks out with her too-perfect hair and swimsuit far too fashionable.

"No, no, let's go out for a swim," I say, pulling her arm.

"I really don't know if I want to swim in that water," she says emphatically, but without finalizing it with a seat in the sand.

"Suit yourself, but I'm going in, and you'd be wise to follow."

I rip off my shirt, drop it in the sand, and run between the walls of people who look as though they might never leave the sea. The water is a little murky, especially under the cloud cover that strips it of its turquoise hue and allows it to be judged by fickle tourists. The sky seems only to be worsening, darker clouds gathering above us making the humidity worse and giving the illusion that violent weather is approaching.

"Wait for me!" a voice yells from behind as a stripped-down Catherine sheds her clothes and sprints into the water. Whether it's out of fear of lightning, the annoying teenage boys, or a desire to be near me, all her trepidation and thoughts appear to have vanquished as she gently pulls my hand under the water and joins me in a single plunge.

"Is this not perfect?" I say, inches from her fully revealed face. Her wet hair perfectly contours her head and sun-kissed face that makes her eyes even greener.

"I was wrong. It's heaven, really heaven." She releases my hand and swims farther out.

"Although I do like watching all the guys look you up and down as you cross along the sand. That's kind of hot, I must admit."

"What are you talking about, David? No one was looking at me, especially with all the amazing Brazilian women here." Catherine dismisses the idea as if it's something she secretly tells herself all the time. Her modesty is innocent and magnetic.

I swim behind her as the ocean floor vanishes from our footed reach. She spins on her back, and her face and feet float on the water. Just briefly, she emerges with the playfulness of a girl let out of her cage of thoughts and rules and personal judgment.

"Look at that sky ... it looks like a tornado is coming or something," she says in wonderment.

Her marvel turns to a shriek when a lightning bolt ignites the afternoon sky above a cluster of rocks in the distance sending her under and into my arms in fear.

"No worries, we're fine in the water," I reassure her, holding her tight. "And as long as you're not wearing any jewelry that would make you a lightning rod."

Catherine acts as though she doesn't hear my remark, a backhanded question meant to determine whether I make my move or simply remain friends in this incredibly romantic moment.

"You're not in a relationship or anything, are you, Catherine?" I ask as she swims away from me and into deeper waters.

I swim after her and go deep to grab her torso. She squirms as I take her hands and hold them in my own.

"I'd be terribly disappointed to start liking you and then find out I couldn't actually have you."

"Oh, please," she says, wiping the water from her eyes.

"You're not one of those women who leave their wedding rings at home to seduce gentlemen like me in the sea, are you?" I continue sarcastically, but with a note of truthfulness.

"A man like you would never be interested in me, at least for longer than a night." She pulls her hands away. "I left my jewelry at the hotel like you told me. And if you are trying to ask, I'm not serious with anyone right now."

I see the barriers I perceived between us fall away. My view of the day changes in almost an instant. I grab her again from behind, my legs wrapping around hers, and I thrust her with my waist, cradling her as we watch the clouds and storm circle above.

"Don't even start, Mr. Summers," she says without pushing me away.

I pull her closer and feel a thrust of blood shoot through my dick. A sudden rush of thunder unleashes across the sky as the beach crowd quiets in awe. In fear, she envelops my body in hers, and I hold her closer, my arms over her breasts and caressing the soft skin under her arms and alongside her stomach. There's the voluptuous femininity of a real woman to her body as my hands work their way down her thighs.

"Oh my god … is this safe?" she says with a whisper of uncertainty.

"As long as you stay close."

"I'm terribly afraid of thunder," she says as she holds on tighter.

Thoroughly enthralled by the storm, she allows me to explore her body without going beneath her swimsuit or being too aggressive with my desire. Her skin is ridiculously soft. My swimsuit fails to conceal my excitement as I rhythmically begin to test her resistance to me from behind—faster and faster. She does not stop me. I feel a hand slowly caress my leg and then my thigh. I kiss her neck along the rope of her necklace line, ebbing and then intensifying with a proper bite that I felt sent a chill down her spine.

The flatness of the water is suddenly interrupted with drops of rain that grow bigger and bigger, enveloping us in a warm shower. I pull her even closer, more forcefully, as all attempts to conceal my intentions are revealed. I want to pull her swimsuit to the side and slide my dick into what's only a few inches from me, but something tells me not now, even though there would be nothing more perfect, more raw, more Rio as the rain intensifies into a proper downpour that hides us if only momentarily. She turns to me and our lips lock in a kiss that consumes both of us. Time stills, sound stops, and our attempt to stay afloat seem secondary as our heads fall below the water.

My hands can no longer deny what they want. I make my way under her bikini, grab her full, ripe breasts from beneath, and submerge my head to kiss my way down the front of her body. Thunder roars across the sky as swimmers beyond us pass without interrupting our moment. My hands feel the arches and depths of her inner body, and I feel her hand grab me for the first time. I want to be inside her. I want it so bad, but I also know I wouldn't last for more than a second in this moment when she feels so right. I turn her around as my legs wrap around her again, me fully exposed from my swimwear, and our flesh touching skin-to-skin as I increase my forcefulness.

"I want to be inside you, Catherine. I want to fully know you, right here," I say, well aware I may have gone too far.

"David, we can't. I can't."

"Give into it, Catherine."

"I can't, David, really I can't."

"There won't ever be this moment again, right here in this secret … the rain and water and us."

"But David, it's perfect to me already."

I pull back without pushing away realizing Catherine isn't that type of woman who does this sort of thing despite every part of her body saying *take me now*. With a lull in the thunder, she breaks away from my arms and back toward the beach. I follow. There's a momentary coldness to the air as we emerge, and the rain pours on us. I take her hand, and we run in a full sprint down the beach and back toward the hotel.

"It's raining buckets and buckets, David!" she yells above the din of pelting rain. We run side by side, and soon the rooftop of the hotel comes into sight. Barefoot, we make our way onto the warm sidewalk and across the pavement of the busy road dividing the hotel from the beach.

At the end of our frantic run, we stand nearly naked at the valet of the Fasano. The staff rushes to bring us towels without a hint of anything being abnormal about our state of undress. We slip through the side entrance and stand alone under our terrycloth cloaks, staring into each other's eyes.

"So this is where we say good-bye?" I ask.

"David, that was incredible."

"We are not done yet, there's still more to see of Rio. It's just getting started."

"I'd love to, really, but I just can't."

"Will you have dinner with me, please? It's my last night."

Catherine hesitates as if I've cracked her hesitation, and the night to be flashes through my mind.

"David, I have so much work to catch up on. I only have one more day left here too, and I have to get a lot more work accomplished."

"It can be a quick dinner … sushi."

"It won't be a quick dinner."

"It really will, I have to pack. We could order room service in my room if you want." I know it's the wrong thing to say even as it comes out of my mouth.

"Yes, room service in your room. Now I know how that would end up."

"It's not like that. I just want more time with you. You really made my day, and I just want it to last a little longer."

"David, I'm not one of those women who just has sex in hotels. I like you and I liked our day. Let's make that the memory we both take with us."

She grabs my hand with a tenderness I have not felt in years, perhaps ever. Not having her simply makes me want to have her even more. I look deeper into her moss-green eyes that make time tick in half the time and say everything, even when nothing is said.

"So this is where we say good-bye." Catherine says it in a way that makes it clear to me there will be no dinner. This is indeed good-bye.

"I'll leave my information for you at the front desk, and I'll look forward to our paths crossing again," I say, pulling her cold wet skin close against my own under the towel.

"I would very much like that, David."

Catherine seems to hesitate, perhaps reconsidering dinner or thinking of a compromise that might give me just a little longer with her. I know my life and my way with women—if it's not here and now, it will never be again.

"And I really did have a great day, my best day in Rio. You're a terrific guide and a gentleman. I haven't known one of those in a long time. Thank you for that."

CHAPTER 3

PARIS

IO ISN'T A trip up Corcovado or a certain churrascaria or a nightclub where every supermodel in the world has danced until six o'clock in the morning. Rio is what happens in the moments of those sticky afternoons along its wavy mosaic sidewalk. As you're sipping coconut water, an impossibly perfect man in a swimsuit smaller than yours, lingers with his eyes and stands so close you can feel his breath on your moist skin, and the hairs on your neck stiffen as you linger for just a second, and then another more.

My Rio story reads like a love letter to David, even without a mention, comment, or insinuation of his very existence. Since returning, it's been a swath of endless winter in New York; dirty snow is everywhere, and steam clouds envelope the skyline in a dreary constant of concrete and grayness. To think of all the wasted time I sat poolside in Rio wishing to be back and yet, every day since, has been marked by a countdown of the hours since I left it and dream when I can leave again. It's only been three weeks, but it has felt like a three-year sentence for a heart that has been sucked from my cavity.

For me, Rio was really about a single twenty-four-hour period. That one day spent with the man who came and left my life as quickly as we wandered through the city and found ourselves in the middle of the Atlantic only moments from my demise as a wife and mother. In that instant, I was bound to no one, and I knew if I controlled myself, there would be nothing lost in allowing me to go to the brink and no farther. However, in that moment and ever since, it is all I can think about.

David has consumed my thoughts from the moment we hastily parted, and him pleading just a few moments more, took every ounce of me to decline. Everything else in my life seems secondary. He invades my deepest fantasies to the point that thoughts of him corrupt my eating, my sleeping, and my thinking. He is the only man I have ever met who made the idea of my risking everything seems as if I was risking nothing. I lost something of my old self in the water that day, alive under his touch, but trying so hard not to allow the situation to go any farther. How I wanted him inside me as we devoured each other in the water, his manhood alongside my skin that makes me crave to this day that he had actually been inside me, just once, for only me to know and savor in my mind for the rest of my days.

Now I know so much more about David Summers. I hadn't even left Rio before I began researching his background like an interview subject or some sort of stalker, of which I'm sure he has no shortage. He was born in Essex. He gets his strong nose, sculpted profile, and exotic black Anglican looks from a gene pool descendant of Roman soldiers who occupied his ancestral town in the first millennia when it was known as Camulodunum.

His Facebook profile wasn't private, but there's very little of him on it except for a cropped photo of his one eye, which is almost neon blue juxtaposed to his fair white skin and pitch-black hair. I saw images of rescue dogs and an organization for which he volunteers. He also has an occasional check-in at the Groucho Club, Morton's, and Crazy Bear, where posh London guys go to find sex. David Summers has no siblings, just a lone cousin listed on his Facebook profile. Unlike him, I'm too private to admit anything in the social media forum.

Each page of information read like a deeper betrayal of Matt, and yet I delved deeper without hesitation. Before Rio, David was in Shanghai, Tokyo, Sydney, and Paris all within a span of what appears only three months, and likely a woman like me in every one of them. A Twitter profile revealed one status update from six months prior complaining about a barking dog in Moscow, and a lone Twitpic of ballerinas on their way to the Bolshoi Theatre with the caption, Black Swan or White, can I take both?

LinkedIn was perhaps my kindest source with more than thirty-one hundred connections, none of which we share. The site offered a fully updated index of his last five positions in various banking houses, as well as a description of his present job description: I run the team at Alistair of London, which focuses on building relationships with businesses in emerging and developing markets. The site also lists double degrees, one in marketing at the University of Gloucester and a later one from Cambridge.

I returned from the trip in a desperate state. I worried that despite having stopped myself from actually sleeping with David, I had crossed the line. I thought Matt would be able to sense my hesitation with him and us, but as I returned to our dark house that night from Rio, I found nothing but uninterrupted normalcy. All was quiet and excruciatingly the same, despite the glaring change I could feel inside of me. Matt slept peacefully with one leg out of the covers as he always did, and Billy slept well through the morning and awoke at 5:00 a.m. as if I had never left.

The days after that were anything but normal for me, distant and sometimes downright confrontational with Matt to the point of instigating trouble. I avoided kisses, embraces cut short, and bedtimes coordinated. I dreaded the moment when Matt would ultimately initiate sex. How can Matt possibly compete with the likes of David, a man who grabs life by the hand in a way that I haven't felt in years? I'm not sure whether it's something he did to me or simply I have regained my independence, but I am different since Rio.

Then there was the situation I was most dreading. Upon arriving home on the fourteenth evening, I opened the door to a dark house and the worst of my fears. As my eyes adjusted to the darkness, Matt appeared from behind the door dressed in a crisp white shirt and khaki pants, freshly shaved, and hair slicked to the side the way he knows I like.

"Welcome home, honey. I've missed you." He grabbed me fully around my lower waist and kissed for more than just a couple's kiss.

As I looked around the house, I saw the living room lit in a candle path that led to the dining room table. Two chairs sat side by side, and plates were set on the table. My knees seemed to stop the flow of blood to my feet.

"Matt, this is beautiful," I said, despite collapsing inside.

He took my hand, pulled me through the room, and seated me at the table in front of a white plate with a hefty portion of pasta. Two glasses of red wine were at each serving, his only half full.

"I put Billy to bed early, and now it's just you and me." He lifted his chair and placed it awkwardly close to my own. He then lifted the wine glass to my mouth. There was no escape.

There were glimpses of the man I used to know, even if just fleeting. When we met, he was a freelance production assistant with burly biceps that were always showing themselves under his plaid lumberjack shirts on photo shoots. I thought I only wanted to sleep with him, but he made me laugh and feel comfortable in my own skin. He saved me, like the last exit before I became one of those obsessed women who work their entire lives only to discover at thirty-five she passed up love and family.

He makes the best pasta I've ever tasted, adapted with wheat noodles and pine nuts and sweet raisins to make up for the fact we both gave up meat a long time ago, or at least he thinks I did.

"It's delicious," I say, hesitating to eat the entire portion after having lost a fair amount of weight doing my version of the Paleo diet since Brazil.

"You've barely touched it." He takes my fork and drops it on the plate.

He caresses my hand with his soft, thick fingers roughened by years of work, but now has just the lingering scent of baby oil. I know where this is going and it feels so wrong. My heart holds onto the memory of David, the memory of his touch and his kiss that will seem so much farther away once I am with Matt again. There is no resisting without making an even larger issue. I resign myself to get through this, and I hope to come out feeling the way I once did in this relationship.

He stands up at the table, and I can see his erection compressing his khakis, already a bit tight from weeks of no morning runs or jaunts to the gym. We haven't had sex in weeks, and I know this must happen regardless of how I feel. He takes my hand, places it on his dick, and pushes away the plates of food and drinks as if they're token collateral for what is to come. As long as I don't let him inside me, I know everything will be okay.

He stands in front of me and drops his pants around his knees. I imagine David in front of me, his translucent skin soft with a salty sea kiss and those muscular legs wrapped around me. I imagine what he would taste like, how he would control this situation and fill me.

"I've missed you, baby," Matt whispers, as his dick stands almost throbbing in front of me with a dew of pre-cum already emanating from the tip.

I imagine David as I grab him from the shaft and edge closer without actually taking him inside my mouth. Matt drops to his knees. Our lips meet in a deep kiss, not the married kind or the lover kind, but the awkward first-time kind, where our tongues intertwine, and my fully conscious mind can taste the treachery of my adulterous desire.

One of my hands grabs his back, already damp, as the other pulls on the hairs of his upper chest. I imagine my gentler lover, smelling the way he does, as he drops to his knees and devours me in full daylight as my mind casts judgment on this dimly lit apartment and this rushed sex that could be anywhere with anybody.

Matt tends to be quick to ejaculate, but I notice he lasts longer than usual before trying to enter me. He inevitably does, thrusting himself inside me along the brim of our bentwood dining chairs where I sit arched with his fully erect dick that goes in painfully deep the first time. He grabs the back of the chair in a somewhat awkward position, my hand falls into the plate of uneaten pasta, and he rattles me back and forth and back again.

I pull his hair and hold him back like the extended legs of an unwilling rider. The intensity edges on pain as he thankfully nears climax. I feel as though I've left my body and hover above the room in judgment as I moan louder and louder hopeful this will end. Then with a forceful push away, he erupts just outside of me and along the brim of the chair. His brow now fully sweaty, he leans in to kiss me with all his masculine, labored breath. I soften with a sense of relief that this much-needed moment has happened. Afterward, Matt retreats to our bed, and I into our bathroom where I cocoon myself in the noise of running water to finish myself off with recollections of David's touch and as many memories as I could recall of his voice, his smell, and his stare that will soon slip away from me.

The following day in the office, I felt as though my train had been realigned on the rails, even if not in fluid motion again. Perhaps I had quelled this Greek tragedy in the making. There are always distractions in a marriage, but ultimately you return to your husband and realize the reason you committed to a life with him in the first place. This, I hoped, would be my moment where David faded from my mind and Matt returned to my heart.

The office proved to be as trying as my marriage upon returning from Rio. I returned to the office to discover the actress we booked for the June cover wasn't available to shoot in New York, which meant I'd have to source existing images or go with an entirely different person, which was nearly impossible, given the magazine was scheduled to print in less than a week.

These are some problems with a B-list magazine. Neither celebrities nor their publicists ever take their scheduled photo shoots or interview times seriously. When I started at *Rouge*, we were one of the few magazines still to have covers with the occasional non-celebrity model in various sexy-with-a-wink poses and gloomy articles on "Life after Divorce" and "Sex in Your Widow Years." I was one of the drivers of change at the magazine, insisting we stick to a twenty-eight through forty-five demographic and a celeb-only cover, even if it meant not always shooting ourselves.

As the magazine started to improve in sales, I stayed loyal to my editor instead of following everyone else to better titles like *InStyle*, *ELLE*, and *Marie Claire*. Now here I am, almost seven years later at *Rogue*, in the same position with a better title, more money, and a nicer office doing the same daily penance in an economy where it isn't nearly as easy to jump ship.

After a few pushy e-mails and publicist calls, the magazine's unenthused cover star alas surfaced as I tried to figure out the various details of a rushed interview that she would inevitably cancel or want to do over the phone on the day before we're supposed to go to press. The compulsion to spy on my would-be lover was fully suppressed until an hour after lunch. When the morning's work seemed able to be put off until the following day, I found myself hovering over his latest Twitter update, "Wheels-up to CDG, some work, and hopefully a little play."

With little more than his fifty-character status update, I allowed the axis of my reason, my life, and my relationship to tilt on its side once more. I will do the interview in Paris. Typical to my character, the dominoes were set in motion at warp speed from idea to end plan. I aggressively suggested to the publicist that the interview take place in Paris as soon as possible. Surprisingly, it was an easy sell to her as well as to my nervous editor, frantic to wrap up this issue. Matt, still comforted by our night together, appeared caught off guard by the last-minute trip, and to a playful Billy, I promised a very hip French toy on my return home.

That's how I end up here, in my flying 777 sanctuary, even if in economy class. I awaken on the plane somewhere above the Atlantic bound for Paris and knowing full well my mistake in motion. I awake in an Ambien haze to that scurry just before landing when half-eaten trays of breakfast are collected and coffee cups clink as flight attendants pace the aisle looking for those still reclined in their business-class chairs. I wasn't really expecting to sleep on the flight, taut with anxiety about my decision to do this and leave my husband and son yet again.

"Can I get you to lift your shade, ma'am?" asks a flight attendant hovering above with a mom-like French accent. I lift the flap in an instant.

"How long till landing?" I ask the slender and distinguished flight attendant, whose hair was pulled tightly back behind her face.

"Captain says it's about forty-five minutes," she says in her fabulous French accent.

"So I have time to do a quick change once the bathroom frees up?"

"Yes, we'll announce the final call for landing, but you can have a few minutes after that if you want. I won't tell." Her authoritative but considerate manner makes me feel more relaxed as I get up with my makeup bag and line up for the restroom. Through the window, Paris comes into view through the small window in the bulky exit door with its plastic covering.

In February, thick clouds always blanket Europe, the weather rarely letting itself known until that one dip that takes you just below the cloud cover to reveal the sprawling city of Haussmann rooflines and urban perfection where even the outlying suburbs offer some sort of romantic charm. The city seduces my thoughts as much as the possibility of seeing David as I mentally plan my outfits under either a heavy cashmere coat or a Rick Owens trench that justified my checked bag surcharge.

Charles de Gaulle Airport never disappoints with its customs line of exquisitely dressed travelers and epic hallways that feel like a catwalk for my new Giambattista Valli boots. The automatic doors that open to the outside world reveal a platoon of drivers with more signs than I could have ever imagined. Virtually every hotel is represented with a clearly written all-cap nameplate. I spot my name almost immediately. I approach my Parisian driver who has a super-cute pencil mustache and a slender silhouette that makes him look forty and not his youthful twenty-something that almost feels of another time.

"Are you Ms. Catherine Klein?" the driver stutters through a mere sentence of English with secondary syllables that linger an extra beat on his boyish pink lips.

"Yes, indeed. Thank you for being so prompt." I smile as he grabs my bags without attempting another word and quickly walking a few feet ahead.

His suit shows the sign of a long day, or perhaps a few wearings since last pressed—wrinkled in the rear of the pants, at the knees, and just below where his butt should be on his slight torso.

As we get into the car, the scent of cigarette smoke fills the air despite a well-positioned No Smoking sign. The boyish driver enters the car and makes eye contact with me sitting patiently in the backseat, and then again. His thick black hair seems almost stitched to his head like a doll without a bit of flesh or scalp exposed. His pitch-black eyes are deep set with black circles that look like bronze coins but still sexy and mysterious.

He navigates the immaculately paved freeway with the zeal of a boy captivated with driving a car he can't afford, passing and changing lanes with full blinker and right-yielding European vibrato before exiting into the thick sprawl of Paris. And there is that perfect urban landscape that seems planned by Aphrodite herself, from quixotic buildings clad in balconies built for two to cinematic cafés where couples linger over shared lunches and coffee always served with a proper cup and saucer. Bridges are capped in a frosting of gold paint flanked by iron art nouveau lampposts that herald a time when kings paraded with cavalry and princesses traveled by gilded horse-drawn carriages.

It's difficult not to stray into deep fantasy when lost in the shade of the meandering rues and the interconnecting arrondissements of central Paris. I wasn't quite sure where to stay, either, as it was high season and rooms would be tight virtually any place you'd want to stay and even in some you wouldn't. Then there was the question of where David might be staying, and how close I could get without being too close.

With the Plaza Athenee and Le Meurice fully occupied, my choice was between the super-cute but sort of removed Hotel Tremoille or the Ritz in all its aristocratic glamour. Plus, the fact that it was soon closing for renovation made me want to see it one more time in all its fabulousness, especially on someone else's dime. I also figured its close proximity to the Costes, Bristol, and InterContinental increased the chances that I would bump into David.

The driver takes the grand approach to the Ritz from Rue Saint-Honoré before turning into Place Vendôme, which brings a jolt of wheels over cobblestone pavers as the plaza's column comes into view. Built by Napoleon from bronze derived from his enemy's canons, yet it was years before I ever really knew what it was despite seeing it all the time.

It's hard to imagine Place Vendôme being anything but a fashionable square, but under its glittery commercial facade lays a history of almost constant friction and a centuries-old struggle between those who have and those who don't. How unlikely that a working-class girl like me would be staying at its most fabulous hotel just a few centuries later.

Paris is a city truly unafraid to tear down monumental things, whether a landmark to Louis XIV that once stood at the center of this square, or the former Tuileries Palace that burned nearby during the Paris Commune, which I can still hear my college history professor describe in detail. Even this column was a replacement for another destroyed by an angry mob, only to be rebuilt a short time later by Napoléon with a statue of himself secured back on top.

A flurry of activity outside the Ritz has us sitting idle. My eyes are transfixed on its fairy-tale facade with its white canopy awnings and windows that seem to each tell a different story of the guests within, despite their almost identical, symmetrical architecture. By the end of the ride, I'm a bit more charmed by the driver as well—the kind of guy who would take you to an edgy Paris party or nightclub for a long night you would never forget—even though no more than three words and a few more glances have been exchanged between us.

"So if you need anything while you are in Paris, please do not hesitate to call me to be here," he says in his boyish tone, looking through the mirror and into my eyes at the end of the sentence.

I take the card and notice his long fingers that taper between thick knuckles and come to a head at a rounded, well-trimmed nail.

"What hours do you work? I may need a driver for an afternoon or evening depending on my work schedule."

"I work all day and night; you just call and I come."

He looks away as the traffic clears in front of him, and a dapper bellman whistles his attention as the car moves forward. In my mind, this kind of man is who you have an affair with, the type who is attractive and sexy-wild, yet also the type you're eager to leave as soon as you're finished and not linger in a romantic sugar coma that consumes everything that you are.

Staying at the Ritz is a benefit of the journalism world that makes up for years of low wages and long hours. The valet lacks the sexy brutes that line the front of the Costes or the quaff haircuts of the Athenee; these courteous kinsmen have been at the Ritz for more than a generation with eyes that can assess your breeding and social credit score without uttering a single word. Their uniforms have the fit of being worn over years with slight shoulders and stuttered movement that make you hesitate to hand them your heaving luggage.

The driver readies the credit slip as the men rush the car, his left hand gripping the pen in an almost boyish apprehension about the paper of someone who spends very little time writing much of anything.

"Please add twenty percent if possible," I say.

"Thank you very much."

He responds immediately, looking up to gaze through those midnight eyes that have yet to see very much of the world outside this city. However, I guess if you're going to be untraveled, there are worse places than Paris is.

With a pull of the door, the Ritz comes alive as my black Valli boot extends out the car door and struggles just a bit on the cobblestone landing. I look up, staring in the eyes of architectural greatness, the aged masonry details of the square enveloping my soul and washing away any trepidation I had about the trip. The scent of wet Paris asphalt from a morning rain mixed with auto exhaust fills the air. I make my way under a buttoned trench to the plush red carpet and through the revolving Ritz doors that seem to connect to a different era.

I sometimes wonder if Saudi princesses who call the hotel home or better fashion editors are ever as humbled as I am walking through the entrance, each pacing footstep meeting the royal blue Oriental rugs as endless candelabras, scones, and statuary glisten in perfect gold. Ornate Louis XIV furnishings are everywhere, beckoning another time when women would sit for daily tea and businessmen would gather near the largest lighting fixture that was among the first in Paris to be electrified.

You don't stay at the Ritz because you like the endless gold decor that would look garish in almost any other setting, or the crystal chandeliers polished almost daily to give them that impossible luster. You stay because of the people. Since the beginning, scenes have included the likes of Marcel Proust pursuing handsome waiters at grand dinners in the hotel dining room. And Coco Chanel living out the war years in her apartment while taking a Nazi lover. Or modern-day fashion alum like Valentino or Karl Lagerfeld opting for the terrace at lunch or evenings at the lobby bar in lieu of their usual creative isolation.

When it comes to rooms at the Ritz, I've learned it's a bit of a mixed bag given the hotel's history as a one-time private residence turned hotel in the late nineteenth century. Opened in time for the 1900 World's Fair, it was the first hotel in the world to have a private bathroom in every guest room, and you could bring your household staff, which many people did during the rationing war years, storing them away on the hotel's top floor made almost entirely for maids. These days, an ideal room would be on the lower floors. Ideally, the second or third floors are home to the best rooms like the Imperial Suite that Dodi and Princess Diana were living in at the time of their accident, or the Windsor Suite, where Wallis the duchess of Windsor would take many of her arranged interviews while her former king languished over his memoirs.

Hotels upgrade B-list magazine editors like me, even the Ritz. A bellman opens my third-floor room facing Vendôme Garden seen through arched windows hidden behind swags of plush drapery tasseled to an inch of their life next to beds tucked in Wallis blue-quilted coverlets under robust gold headboards. Upon opening the door, I'm usually greeted with a small floral arrangement from the Parisian florist Djordje Varda or a bottle of Moët that's the standard greeting from the manager. The decor is still rooted in pieces from another era, like desktop makeup mirrors in lieu of functioning business desks and boudoir side tables with lighting better for mood than practicality.

"There you go."

A quick €10 tip rids me of my fatherly bellman and casts me alone in the room to prep for my interview. At the beginning of my journalistic career, I would have researched a subject for a good week before ever sitting down for a sixty-minute interview that would lead to a national cover story. These days, however, I'm rarely as prepared. I rely on a quick read of a *Wikipedia* page and a wing-it attitude that relies mostly on my remarkably accurate tabloid knowledge. The results are a more interested interviewer who makes the subject far smarter than the person really is.

That's a funny thing about celebrities; as soon as they become famous, they think the years of lost education and life experience mean nothing. Their words are suddenly valued and opinions so sought that they begin to believe they are actually experts. So there's really no point in researching people who are going to admit to nothing or believe they have an answer for everything.

In lieu of doing my due diligence, I retreat to my emotional lunge back toward David Summers. Before unpacking my carry-on or hanging up my garment bag, I begin a journalistic flush of every five-star luxury hotel and four-star design property in the city center to find him. Plaza Athenee, Le Meurice, and George V are all marked off the list in addition to less obvious places like the Pershing Hall and L'Avenue just in case Oscar Wilde is on my side.

My goal isn't so much to rekindle the moment we had in Rio, as it is to have one more chance to seal the memory of his face into my mind so it sustains me in my own world for just a while longer. I do not intend to talk to him, and I'm still skeptical that I'll even be able to find him, but there is an instinctual need inside of me to know where he is, if only to share the same air in an unknown room or street corner for just a minute more before I return to my old life.

The beauty of the modern front desk personnel is that if you ask, "Is David Summers staying in your hotel?" they would never answer the question. However, if you ask, "Can I have David Summers' room?" the answer is either a "There's no guest by that name," or they simply connect you to his room.

Alas, my answer comes after the tenth or so call—the Park Hyatt— the type of place a top-tier financial firm would put one of their mid-range staff in Paris. The connection catches me off guard, and I hang up the phone with the connecting dial tone. I imagine him sitting in his room working away by the dim winter light, shirt unbuttoned, and boyish scruff under a heavy brow. A redial to the hotel and I discover from the desk clerk that the property is even closer than I imagined, on Rue de la Paix at the north entrance of the Place Vendôme. It's also a perfect location to hold my interview without worrying about paparazzi, and of course, I have a chance of seeing David one last time.

The following morning is a remarkably bleak winter day in Paris; cold winds blow in from the North Sea, and anything taller than a five-story building gets lost in a pewter-colored cloud. Morning coffee at the Ritz isn't quite the same as a fix at a local Starbucks. I linger in my own fog doing a quick read on my interview subject, a well-known host of an American reality competition. She got her start in London at nineteen when she was a Page 3 girl, those scantily clad models in *The Sun*, who inevitably mutate into B-list TV stars. Some, like my interviewee, catch on in the US where some unattractive agent or producer lures them to

LA for a Hollywood dream that ends up on some cable TV network like hers, and she ends up in a magazine like mine.

The weather is so bad the doorman at the Ritz offers me a complimentary lift just the few blocks to the Park Hyatt. I snuggle into the back of an extravagantly large Mercedes sedan not even long enough to warm the black leather seats. My reflection in the window seems unfamiliar; a woman I try not to judge so far from home and in a place she should not be. We pass up the Rue del la Paix, past stores like Bulgari and Van Cleef. There, after only a few short blocks, a Park Hyatt attendant opens my door, and I stand before the demure marquee. I see the hotel's manicured potted shrubs and fleet of black sedans that line the sidewalk. The hotel isn't as grand as I imagined, despite its quaff Haussmann facade that's gotten the American once-over, a mix of Ralph Lauren and sterile Italian modern design.

The bar is busier than I expect on a Saturday morning, an assortment of men in black suits and a handful of thoroughly Parisian-looking women with colorful scarves and all-season black skirts over dark leggings occupy my booth and force me to move to the opposite end of the bar. The phone call to my husband and Billy last night left me less remorseful of this trip than I had anticipated, both of them jovial as ever on their movie night with not a bit of curiosity or jealousy regarding me or Paris or me in Paris.

Something about a chain hotel like the Park Hyatt homogenizes travel, making you feel like you're in a soulless convention center or in an arcade of a cruise ship that could be anywhere. Even the staff is plucked from international hotel schools. Their almost rigid service is heavy on formality, as the twenty-something waitress with her pulled-back blonde hair rushes over with pad in hand. Her accent says Eastern European and a secondary accent that says Swiss or British or German.

Before I have time to order, there she is on point—my elusive interviewee—one of the first ever to arrive exactly on time. She is dressed in some very LA fashion sneakers, likely from Louis Vuitton or Prada, and a smart black trench coat that's likely concealing a pair of Free City sweats or black leggings under her latest rugby boyfriend's sweatshirt.

She makes her way to my table, a studious model, I must admit, who can quickly figure out a room.

"You must be Catherine?" she trumpets from a few tables away as the empty bar echoes her vocal vibrato.

"And you must be the very punctual Kelly?"

"Indeed, and thank you so much for making the trip. I know it's not an easy commute from New York."

"But who in their right mind is going to complain about a weekend in Paris, right?" I respond in a refreshing pace of conversation I wasn't expecting.

"May I sit here?" She tosses her coat on a chair opposite me and plunges on my banquette inches away.

"Do you mind if I tape this?" I ask. "I know some people are weird about that, but it really does keep the story accurate, and I can forward you a digital copy to ensure what you say is written as you said it."

"Certainly, go right ahead."

She settles back without readjusting her hair or the elongated arms of her sweatshirt with its ripped collar and skeleton logo on the arm. She's wearing no makeup despite her thirty-something age, her flawless face glazed in a matte effervescence as singular strands of chocolate locks kissed in crimson explore her temples.

"How is LA treating you?" I ease into the conversation.

In all honesty, I record my interviews because I have a habit of drifting off when it comes to such questions. When it comes to women's magazines, it's trivialities like what she looks like when she walks in and the type of coffee she orders that people really want to know.

"I must admit, I've really been enjoying my time in LA. It's so refreshing to wake up every day and have the sun shining and be able to take a hike or hit the beach for a jog."

The English are always talking about the weather and the ability to exercise outdoors in reference to life in America. Rarely do you hear that they love the people or have made the best of friends.

"And I've been able to finally get a dog, which I've wanted all my life but have never been able to because London life is just so much more of an effort than LA is."

This part of the interview, which either we stay with the pleasantries and I simply later add preexisting quotes to the story regarding her love life and failed marriage with a photo timeline of previous relationships, or I redirect my more intrusive questions with the disclaimer, "My editor would fire me if I didn't ask."

As she explains how she adopted a dog from a rescue group that she discovered near her favorite LA coffee shop, I see a face of scruff and a perfectly groomed head of wavy black hair. My eyes are transfixed, my palms start to sweat (which they never do), and this woman talking about dogs and the coffee shop evaporates from my consciousness.

There is David. David Summers. A man so perfect and yet so unknown I cannot get him out of my mind or stop thinking that he was somehow meant to pass through my life.

As he stands at the edge of the bar, I want to burst from my seat, run up to him and into his arms as if my next breath depends on it. I want the skin of my cheek to rest upon the lapel of his navy blazer as his scent envelops me into love's blinding haze once more. The reality of him exceeds even my fantasy, like a full-color image that before was just a partial etching in my mind.

He's taller than I remember, hovering over the bar with his elbows propping his upper body on the counter as he summons the waitress's attention faster than most with his frosty arctic eyes and Roman face. I contort my head to face Kelly as not to call attention to us, but then I return to my original position. I do not want to miss a single movement. I wonder if he's speaking French. Is he staying in his room alone? Would he even remember me, or know I risked everything in my life to travel around the world to see him just one more time?

"I'm not even certain if we have dog mills in the UK."

I jolt back into my interview to realize the conversation has digressed into one entirely about dogs. Then I change the subject. "What do you think is the difference between American women and British women?"

There is a long pause.

"I mean, in terms of the balance between working and family?" I elaborate.

Kelly's eyes draw a blank stare as if her pupils were tied to the answers at the back of her impossibly beautiful head. Her gaze abruptly shifts to parallel my own across the room as that familiar, godly face crosses this dismal anywhere-lounge and looms closer in our direction. I look away as if not to stare too long into the direct sun. As my stomach sinks, I am fear-stricken and equally eager, and I wait to hear those perfectly set lips utter my name once more.

"David Summers … is that you?" Kelly erupts in a cackle.

She jumps from the table to embrace him in a hug that forces him to take a step back despite his powerful stance.

"I cannot," she says in that utterly London two-syllable-ness, "believe you're in Paris."

David stands directly above her grabbing her hips at an angle that accentuates their difference in size.

"My love, I haven't seen you in ages. You look amazing." His eyes turn to me for agreement only to recognize yet another face.

I remain seated with a courteous smile. I extend my hand as if to notice no more than a stranger would in an unfamiliar city interrupting the flow of my work.

"Indeed," I reply. "I'm Catherine."

"Are you kidding me? Of course, I know you. No fucking way! I can't believe it." David pulls away from Kelly and moves to my edge of the table.

"Do you know who this is?" he says, looking at Kelly and pointing to me.

"Actually, she was just asking me the difference between American women and British women, and you're probably a better one to tell us," Kelly says.

David laughs with a manly vibrato and then retreats from his intended rebuttal.

"You know, this is only the head of the Rio tourism board seated with you in the middle of Paris, and not a very good tourist spokesperson at that, I may add."

"A woman with two jobs … she's after my own heart," Kelly replies with a grin as she throws in her own reference as a host of a US reality show and a UK entertainment news program.

"Well, not exactly," I calmly interject as David sits in a chair opposite us. "David and I stayed in the same hotel while in Rio recently, and he was nice enough to share his favorite local haunts for an article I was working on."

"Oh, yes. David is always one to help a woman in a far-off land who finds herself in distress."

"Are you two staying in this hotel?" David asks.

"No," I say, "but I figured this would be quieter than holding court at the Ritz."

"Quiet? More like dead," he adds.

"Jack keeps an apartment here that he lets me use now and then," Kelly says, referring to her on-again rugby boyfriend who's currently playing for a French team.

"Wow, Jack. Now that takes me back. So wait, how do you two know each other then?" David asks.

"Well, you know I'm back in London doing publicity for the UK show and doing a few press pieces in the states," Kelly answers.

"Ah, I see. So this is a work meeting?"

"Actually, I was just in the middle of our interview," she says, gesturing to the recorder with a red flashing light set between two Diet Cokes.

"So, I'm interrupting?" David grins before leaning forward to stand again.

"Not at all, stay and chat for a minute … oh, please," Kelly insists.

"Really?" David looks at me with those always-lusty eyes that are hard to reject. "Actually, I insist you continue working, and I'll just sit in and listen." His head tilts forward at an angular position that makes his stare appear as cat's eyes.

"Is that allowed?" Kelly asks, and both of them look at me.

"Well, not technically," I say, "but as long as all of this stays at the table, I guess it would be okay."

"Catherine likes to do things by the book, don't let her fool you," David says.

"Don't make me change my mind, Mr. Summers," says Kelly. Then there's a pause before an almost scripted return to our conversation. "So back to the question at hand."

As I focus on Kelly, I can feel David study me from the color of my nails, to my choice in boots, and the way my hair lays along my collar. His focus is intense as Kelly continues with a dissertation of how American women expect all those older than thirty-five to have children and if they don't, there's something wrong with them.

Under other circumstances, I would have been impressed with her answer, but under the penetration of his eyes, I am unable to concentrate on anything but him. Even without looking at him, I see him, I smell him, and that scent of perfect citrusy cologne and a freshly showered man lingers in the air as if you could grab it and taste it in your mouth.

"Are you married, Catherine?"

Kelly comes at me with the interrogative dagger, something that definitely would not have happened if David hadn't joined and all but abandoned her with his attention since sitting.

"I am not." I reply almost instinctually as judgment and deceit indicts my soul. She would not have asked that question if I were a decade younger. I immediately regret the directness of my reply instead of just being vague, opening the door of judgment to be cast on all that I have done to get to where I sit in this very moment. The conversation continues without me, a sign of a good interview but also of a writer trapped in an emotional juggernaut no longer in her narrative.

"Ladies, sadly I must leave this gripping interview to attend to a meeting." David looks at his watch hidden under his French cuffs before rising, as if fleeing the idle conversation that I have lost track of since my revelation.

"Kelly, I hope to see you soon in London, and Catherine," he turns to take my outstretched hand that sits in the nape of his fleshy palm only an instant, "… it's always fun when our paths cross."

Without a mention of connecting while in Paris, exchanging numbers or e-mails, the man I have traveled halfway around the world to get a glimpse of walks slowly across the bar and most likely out of my life forever. Questions scramble through my head like, "How can I let him just walk away?" and "What if I never see him again for the rest of my life?" as I savor every breath until his scent finally leaves, and I'm left with Kelly, an unfinished interview and this life.

As the interview concludes with a hug and a superficial promise to stay in touch, I make my way out of the Park Hyatt. The rain has once more intensified, the early afternoon sky looks like full night. I'm hoping David is at the valet or on the corner waiting for me, but as the Place Vendôme approaches, he is not there, and I'm swept with a sense of disappointment and then immediate relief for having survived the situation and yet accomplished what I aimed to do—to see David one more time.

Yet, there's a whole city to console me on my last twenty-four hours in Paris. I enter that fabulous square, pass the valet, and head into the entrance portico inside my gilded sanctuary that numbs my heart and softens my mood. My sore feet are a bit more at ease on the plush carpeting of the lobby, this golden palace that feels neither tacky nor over-the-top in my tepid mood. The elevator doors open, and I imagine the decades of broken hearts during the 1920s when lovers would part because of society's rigidness and wars, and then today when lovers who will never be draw together and then apart without ever really knowing each other.

Not much will put me in a better mood, but a quick trip to Palais Royal for a little window-shopping and an almandine croissant should do the trick. The elevator doors open to my fourth-floor home for this one last night. Its ornate Wallis blue hallways and gold leaf wood doors soothe my heart and seem to stretch forever before my eyes.

"And before you run and get hotel security, let me explain."

A culmination of my deepest fantasies and darkest fears, there he sits snuggled into the alcove of my doorway, seated on the floor with his bold-striped socks and floppy black locks that catch me in a fright.

"Oh my god … David?" I gasp.

"I didn't get a chance to really talk with you as Kelly was rambling on with all that nonsense," David says, rising to his feet.

His shirt is unbuttoned and jacket collar pitched to reveal a stripe of color beneath his Etro lapel. His scent returns and leaves me spellbound, so intense and intoxicating that I open my door and pull him inside by the cuff of his jacket. He follows without strain as he slams the door shut and pushes me across the room and up against the wall with the force of a man.

"You didn't e-mail me after that incredible afternoon," he whispers in my ear while biting at my neck and thrusting me into the wall again and again.

"What are you talking about?" I insist. "You never gave me your information."

"I left it for you at the hotel in Rio, and you didn't even write to say thank you for that amazing day."

"You have one of me in every port, Mr. Summers. Don't try to fool me."

No information had been left for me at the hotel at the Fasano, but like most of Rio, hotel attendants can tend to be unreliable. I believe David to be a man who fully means what he says.

"I liked that port, and I liked it with you, Catherine."

He kisses me down my neck and on my breasts; his hands caress my lower back, grip the lip of my skirt, and unzips the back. He has the force of a man in control and the passion of a well-practiced boy ravenous for the flesh.

"Do you know I've thought about you every day since Rio, checking my e-mail nonstop, waiting for you to remember that day, recall me holding you in the water?"

"David, I didn't know. I had no way."

Words do not matter at this moment. Within a matter of seconds, I am standing in the middle of the room naked. He kneels before me kissing up and down my legs while in between them I am already wet. All modesty and shyness vanishes as each kiss seals his desire for me. I feel like a goddess under his forceful hands, which explore every inch of my body as though it were the first he's touched.

Without him removing a single article of clothing, not even his jacket, he buries his face beneath me. I arch my back to the wall in a fit of ecstasy as his fingers explore my most private parts. My hand falls on a cold slab of marble surrounding the fireplace as he twists me around and explores every crevice of my body with his tongue, forcing his thumb down the middle of my spine, and then inside me only to pull it out again. His every movement has an intention just for me, finding those spots within me that torment and send me into a fit of ecstasy.

"David, I need you inside me!" I scream.

"Not yet," he replies in a sexy rasp.

"I'm going to explode if you don't."

"We only have this moment once. From now on you will know me completely, but not just yet."

My mouth meets his as I suck on each perfectly drawn lip and touch my tongue to his teeth. He slaps my ass with both hands to thrust me closer. I tug at the buttons of his crisp white shirt to reveal the speckling of hair across his lean chest and his deep muscular stomach framed by his pelvic muscles that I lean down to lick. He pulls me up with a forceful tug and shoves his finger into my mouth jarring it to the back of my mouth as if trying to reach my soul before inserting his tongue.

Like the guilty aware of her impending corruption, I drop to my knees into my crime and pull at the top button of his jeans. I look up at a body that would humble Rodin and an equal face with sweat forming on his brow. David's crafty hands pull his jeans down in one swift movement. His legs and feet coordinate to reveal him standing in his sexy-striped underwear and an erection he can't contain.

He grabs my arm and leads me to the windowsill. The visual of the distant Paris rooftops feels like a dream, and all that matters in life is right here inside this room. His long hair smells of the most intoxicating potion as he wraps his head over my shoulder. I reach behind to get a feel of what is to come.

I turn to face him as he pulls off his boxers to reveal all that is he, long, thick, and rising straight up against his stomach, even when standing with its fleshy uncut head and perfect pinkish-white coloring. I grab it before he takes over again, and he forces his finger into my mouth. I rush down for a taste before he pulls me away. He is all I desire at this moment, and I must taste him. The skin wraps over the entire head, a rubbery perfection that I pull back with my lips with taste that is sweet and sticky to the tongue. He is in control here; he pulls me up again and toward the window in an instinctual force that is irresistible as I lean forward onto the windowsill, and he drops once more to his knees.

David's tongue is as sweet to the touch as it is to the taste, penetrating me ever so gently with soft gyrations as I pull at the walls, grab at his hair, and collapse into and out of ecstasy. He knows no time as he finds every corner of my inhibition and licks it away sending me into my first orgasm with him, but it only increases his resolve to continue exploring me deeper and deeper. He's unlike any lover I've ever had, almost insatiable in his desire for me as I hear my own unrecognizable shrieks of ecstasy echo across the room as if it's someone else entirely.

The window above me fogs up from the heat of our bare bodies. I can no longer separate my eyes from his and I turn to face him. His mouth envelops mine, and I taste my own sweetness on his lips.

"I wanted you in Rio so bad, but this is even more than I imagined."

He holds my chin as he confesses into my eyes. He props me on the windowsill in a single lift as my knees splay to the side and all that I've fantasized and dreamed of in the moments since Rio is plunged to the deepest reaches of my body in a single, exhilarating thrust as I take all of him within me.

"Catherine, you feel even better than I dreamed."

There's an intoxicating rhythm as he fills me over and over again before pulling out, waiting, and then going back again. I can feel him getting harder inside me, conforming to the contour of my body, as his dick gets so thick it feels as though it might explode. His movements are like a dance where his eyes close for only an instant and then return to mine. He doesn't retreat into his own mind, and we connect so deep that for an instant I feel as though we are a single being. As I feel him increase in force, I pull him closer and shatter in ecstasy yet again as he watches in such awe that it pushes him over his own eruptive edge.

David pulls back the sheets of the tightly tucked bed of starched linen and slides me inside before slipping in behind me, still fully erect, as if eager to go again. I still feel among the fog and clouds as I hold David so tight to me that he adjusts himself against my exposed back.

"That was, I mean, wow. I wasn't expecting that, really," he says as his labored breath recedes to normal. I wait for that moment he does the typical male retreat that most men do right after sex.

"I don't think I even know what day it is anymore," I say.

I forgot how good sex could feel, the delectable exploration of an unknown body from the inside with moves that aren't of a familiar routine, but that of an unbridled lover you want over and over and over again. Then, the rabbit hole of guilt takes me away in an instant as I see Matt's face and that of Billy. I will never again be able to call myself faithful to my husband, even if it's something only I know. I will forever be a wife who has cheated, even if this all ends as I plan to do here and now. What is done is done, but now this must end.

"It's the first day, that's what day it is," he says without hesitation.

"The first day of what?" Anger sweeps over me as if he is to blame for all that I have done.

"The first day we ever made love, and in Paris, no less."

David has a way of making things seem permanent, even though I know his type likes anything but. It has to be torture for the women he dates. Perhaps that's why they fall for him so easily, believing he will catch them mid-fall and live happily ever after only to find out otherwise.

"Is this the first time you've had sex in Paris?" I turn over and ask with a tinge of spite as if he is to blame for my infidelity. However, with a single look, I'm taken aback by the brightness and alertness of his perfect blue eyes against the pure white sheets.

"It's the best sex I've had in Paris."

His answer jolts me back to reality and alludes to the broader truth that it's probably just the best sex he's had in Paris today. My eyes return to the city that lies just outside the window. The truth vibrates like a percussion orchestra in my head. You don't leave your husband for a man like this; you cheat with him once and leave.

"So tell me more about the David who lives outside of hotels."

"The David who lives outside of hotels? Well, I don't get to see him very often because of my job. But when he's in London, he likes to see his mates from university and go out to dinner and the likes."

"And in terms of love?"

"I love a lot, I quite like love."

"That's not what I mean," I say as I nudge him in the shoulder. "Have you ever been married?"

"God, no."

"All right then, who was your last girlfriend?"

"Is this what I have to look forward to from a journalist?" he says with a wide smile. "Well, that was awhile ago, but I was dating a woman named Ana who was a model from near my hometown."

"Model named Ana. Got it," I say with sarcasm.

"She wanted something far more serious than I was ready to commit to, so we thought it best to part ways."

"So she moved out?"

David laughs at my question with some dismissal as if I said his skin was purple and not the most aristocratic of pale, perfect alabaster white.

"We definitely didn't live together. I'm home so seldom that I like to keep my house off-limits."

"You mean bachelor pad?"

"So, what about you? How long can I linger in bed with you at the Ritz?" He doesn't seem comfortable with anything that broaches the emotional, so his boyish grin guides me onto another topic.

"I should really get some work done; I have an early flight back."

David jumps to his knees and on top of me with a boyish playfulness that juxtaposes his masculine body and the long silhouette of his dick, which I cannot take my eyes from as it lingers above me.

"Wait! This is your last night in Paris, and we're lying here talking about crazy model Ana?"

"I'm already behind on my work, so I guess this is where we say our good-byes."

"Good-byes?" he says in smug disbelief. "I just found you in the middle of Paris after thinking about you every day since Rio. I believed I would never hear from you again, never."

"Really, you don't have to tell me those kinds of things."

"Well, you're absolutely not getting rid of me so easy, so you better accept it."

"Is that so?" I ask, seduced again with his adolescent tenacity that has probably never had a woman tell him no.

"So listen, I want to take you somewhere, but I don't want to waste time running back to my hotel to change or anything."

"I'm fine just staying here. I mean, it's the Ritz." It's my one last attempt to end this here and now before a careless infidelity becomes a full night or perhaps even more.

David becomes silent thinking a second. He falls back onto the bed next to me and tucks under the sheets with his head against the pillow next to me.

"Listen, if we weren't in Paris, I would say let's just stay in the room and go at it like rabbits all night. But part of me wants to show you off to the world, especially if I only have tonight."

"One night in Paris; it kind of sounds like a movie." I realize there is no retreat.

"Actually, I think it's a sex tape, but I don't know how I know that exactly."

David scurries into the shower as I watch him leave; his athletic torso looks as if it should preside over a rotunda all its own at the Louvre rather than wandering the mortal world with women like me chasing after it. Without moving from the bed, I see him stepping into the shower and turning on the water. He closes his eyes and lets it wash over his face and down his body. He takes my breath away, even after feeling every inch of him inside me.

I struggle under pressure when getting ready, but luckily, I planned this outfit in my head. I throw on my Rick Owens that now fits the way it should and not the way it did when I bought it on sale at Bergdorf's. My makeup goes on sparingly, and I do a quickie blowout with the door closed as not to give away my beauty regimen to a guy who is used to women who can just put on lip-gloss and go. I look in the mirror and see a different person than when I arrived in Paris, ignited within by a passion I haven't felt in years.

"You look incredible in that outfit ... I can't even stand it," David says with an earnestness that has me glowing the minute I step out of the bathroom. He grabs my hand with a gusto that allows me to be the woman for the first time in a long time, and he leads me out of the room as the Ritz comes alive in a different way than I ever imagined. The lobby purrs with a sophisticated buzz of passing diners and hotel guests on their way to or returning from their fabulous adventures. Everyone seems to look at us as we pass. I smile, despite speculating if, perhaps, they wonder what a man like David is doing with a woman like me.

After such an incredible evening, I almost forgot that Paris waits just outside the walls of my room that became the perfect place in the world in those last hours. The lobby looks entirely different by night, as if dressed in the light of its best tuxedo. It dazzles with emblems of gold above grand seating areas illuminated by flickering candlelight. I have such a different feeling inside me as I pass through these revolving doors yet again, as the hotel car idles right at the curb.

"Monsieur Summers, your car is here for you."

The chauffeur opens the door, and I sit once more in the same seat I took in search of David. I held the found treasure in my hand unwilling to let it go for even a second out of fear it might vanish in front of my eyes.

"How did he know you were coming?" I ask.

"I called down while you were in the shower."

"Are you always a step ahead?"

I want to ask where we're going or what's in store for the night, but for once, it feels nice to allow someone else to take care of me. I imagine it will be somewhere modern and trendy, as David seems the type. Maybe he'll take me to a sushi restaurant or somewhere new where it's hard to get a reservation. The tinted windows of the car make it difficult to enjoy Paris by night, but who cares when David is next to me. It's no more than a few minutes when the car comes to a stop and the door pops open in front of a red restaurant called Davé. David grabs my hand and leads me inside.

"Mr. Summers, how good to see you again," says a handsome Chinese man who appears to be the owner. He takes his hand with a successive bow that David mimics in return.

"Davé, this is Catherine Klein."

He extends his hand with a more genteel grip; his hands are as tender as soft butter.

"Miss Klein, welcome to my restaurant. David is a very good customer, and I take very good care of both of you."

The restaurant isn't at all what I was expecting, this retro-chic parlor of Maoist red walls dotted with black and white photographs of Carla Bruni, David Bowie, and the former French *Vogue* editor Carine

Roitfeld dining throughout. There, in one of the photographs, next to a caricature of John Galliano, is a picture of my David in a group of attractive but not famous faces.

"Wow, you're even on the wall. That's impressive."

"He puts all of his friends on the wall. It's less about the people being famous and more about who he connects with."

Dim lights lend the feel of a modern-day opium den. Black lacquer chairs surround closely packed tables of incredibly fashionable guests hovering over quiet, intense conversations, and a backbeat of Charlotte Gainsbourg. Our table is tucked in a corner with a Ming-looking lamp made out of a vase set on a white tablecloth.

"Is this okay?" David asks before sitting down.

"Yes, perfect actually."

We both disrobe of our winter coats that the waiter takes with him without giving a numbered ticket in return. There are no menus. I tuck the overly starched napkin into my lap as my eyes once more return to David, who has long since returned his gaze. He grabs my hand and strokes it with his thumb in a rhythmic motion that's soothing to my heart and tells everyone around us that I am his and he is mine— at least this one night.

"So, this is the type of place that doesn't really have a menu, so I'll just order for both of us, if that's okay."

"No, totally, I love that idea," I reply.

"Is there anything you don't eat?"

"Nope, just order away. I'll try anything once."

"Anything?" he asks with an arched eyebrow as his leg rubs against my inner thigh under the table.

"So, I want to know more about you, David Summers."

"Uh-oh, what do you want to know?"

"Have you ever had your heart broken?"

"Sure, when I returned home from Rio and this woman I met didn't even try to contact me," he says with a sly smile.

"I'm being serious. Have you ever been head-over-heels in love?"

"I'm not sure. But I have to say that I really haven't made it a priority in my life. Marriage has always petrified me, and I always felt like love was a one-way street in that direction. I just can't imagine having to answer to another person or being responsible for keeping another human being happy and fulfilled for the rest of my life. That seems like an incredibly long time."

His words resonate with my own experience, the reality of when passion fades to companionship and that flame of desire simmers into a diminished light leaving you craving so much more.

"But you're on the road so much, don't you get lonely?"

"You can be lonely in a house full of people. My parents were terribly lonely with each other. I have to tell you I really love my freedom. I can do and go wherever life takes me, and I usually find something fascinating and familiar in almost every place. That is with the exception of Zurich … I don't particularly like the Swiss."

My mind returns to my own life back in New York. I realize that David is actually the perfect guy to have a fling with because in real life, he would be entirely unavailable. There's a guilty comfort in knowing that I still have that other life waiting for me in New York instead of chasing this unattainable guy all over again at this stage of my life. Perhaps I'll even be more fulfilled at home with this incredibly intense experience I will now carry with me forever. Yet, something about David draws me in so deep. It's as if he's capable of so much more, but resists it with his swagger that makes me drop to my knees willing to do anything for just a moment more.

"I totally agree with you, forever is a very long time," I echo in agreement.

"And that's kind of what I like about you, Catherine. You're espoused to life, a lot like me, and not chasing this romantic fantasy that all these other women I meet are obsessed with obtaining."

There's a carnal desire for him that perseveres and grows deeper inside me sending a quiver through my body.

The food finally arrives in a series of small oval white plates with a heaping of poached lemon chicken, leafy sautéed greens, and fried brown rice. David pokes his fork into a tender chicken breast. Food is the farthest thing from my mind. With less than twelve hours left in Paris, I study his every move from how he holds the fork and lifts it to his mouth to how he uses his napkin after sipping sparkling water from the glass. He's the closest thing I've known to an addiction in life, and all I can think about is that one last fix, just one more time with him tonight that will have to be my last before our lives part ways, as they must.

CHAPTER 4

LOS ANGELES

THE LATE AFTERNOON Virgin Atlantic flight puts you down at LAX in time for a late power lunch, avoiding the flurry of Asia-originating flights that somehow always take longer at their inefficient customs where everyone, including this British gentleman, is treated like a potential criminal. When you are arriving from gray London, early spring in LA can be as hot as summer. The sunshine lures my eyes away from the baggage carousel illuminating that curious space-age building at the center of the airport that's some sort of restaurant or bar.

As you step into the taxi, the airport has a full-time staff passing out papers that instruct you on how much the cab ride should cost at the end of your trip, even though it somehow always costs a lot more.

"The Chateau Marmont, please!" I yell to the driver, who lets me lift my bag into the trunk shared with a well-used spare tire and crowbar.

"Sunset Boulevard, correct?"

"Yes, please, but take the four-oh-five." It usually has better phone reception than the alternate route, which some say is quicker but is so ugly with its barren oilfields and sixties strip centers that it's not even worth the saved time.

I've never been the fan of LA that all my other Londoners profess to be. Sure, the women are the hottest of any in the states, but with minds like children's paste that struggle with intelligent conversation and only make for good undressing and disappointing sex.

It also took me years to figure out the nuances of the city from street pronunciations like La Cienega, said with a Cee-EN-IGGA, who's a total bullshitter, and who is the real deal, especially in business.

That's probably why I've been sent to LA so much in my career—a mix of private venture funds lured by the cache of Hollywood only to discover that the few people who get rich in this town are the talent and the producers. Then there was the whole advertising movement with major firms buying out the independent design and marketing firms hoping they could better monetize the businesses, and then once they would buy the firms the owners that were bought out would laze out their tenures at the company only to set up the same business again once their non-compete clauses ended.

LA is a land of wizardry and liars, especially when it comes to start-ups looking for their celebrity angel investors who got rich quick and think that the second time will be just as easy. There's no tech start-up this time, luckily, this trip I have a meeting with an Ed Hardy-style entrepreneur who wears flashy baseball caps and drives a Bugatti. He's created a healthy baked potato chip called the Air Chip, which is apparently all the rage in the United States and a good candidate for us to acquire and expand or take public.

The entrance of the Chateau is about as exclusive as you get in LA. A baronial manor towers above the Sunset Strip made even better with its infusion of Hollywood history and revolving door of starlets. There's a doorman even by day, a woman though, who holds a clipboard that she's probably held since her club days. She stands out front to make sure no one who doesn't fit into the milieu of the chateau gets on the front driveway, let alone inside. My taxi arrival causes suspicion. She holds up her hand and approaches the rear window.

"Can I help you?" She leans in and says with more of a statement than a question.

"Hello, my love. Would you mind helping me with my bags?" I dismiss her as the trunk pops open, and she radios a bellman who quickly descends the stone driveway with a bouncing brass trolley in tow.

"Could I have your name, sir, to pass along to the front desk?"

"Absolutely, I'm David Summers." I warm her up with my stare as she loosens up and the clipboard falls to her waist. I see a woman who was once a party girl, but now has morphed into some sort of post-party boho elitist.

"Welcome, Mr. Summers. Where are you coming from?" she asks as though genuinely interested.

"I'm just in from wet and dreary London, and I have to say you shouldn't be smug when greeting me with this type of ill weather." She winces at the now-missing sun. "And would you mind telling me your name again? I see you every time I'm here, and my head is usually so stuck in work that we've never exchanged pleasantries until now."

"I'm Suzy, and I told the front desk to have your room ready by the time you're upstairs."

She turns away with an element of dismissal, perhaps because I didn't know her name, and she should actually have progressed from Suzy to Sue to Susan by her age. Knowing her name will be crucial to getting my guests in quicker come the weekend.

Chateau Marmont is about as old and grand as you get in LA, something I don't usually gravitate to in America with its love of charm and faux-antiqueness, but there's something otherworldly about a place where Hollywood history and pop culture seem to meet at a crossroads. A New York hotelier, who is much more of a socialite than an entrepreneur is, owns it along with his handful of boutique hotels in Miami, Los Angeles, and New York, and it's still the place to be after all these decades.

The first-floor entrance, shaded by massive oak trees, is nothing more than an elevator landing and a staircase trimmed in scrolled wrought iron that I prefer to take up the two flights to the main lobby. It takes a minute for your eyes to adjust to the darkness inside the lobby. Its amber light glows from modish lampshades under a carved beam ceiling that looks as though stenciled by hand. It is equal parts private residence and social club with its stout magazine rack and vintage check-in counter carved out of the wall attended by a girl who defies her model looks with nerdy spectacles and askew pigtails.

"Mr. David Summers," she says in an elongated sigh and tilt of the head.

"Yes, correct, that would be me."

"All the way from jolly old England today?"

"Yes, indeed, and with pale skin to prove it, no less."

"Pale is in; tan people are so … two thousand," she says, looking over her black spectacles. "We've upgraded you to a premier suite. It's usually booked for photo shoots and stuff, but not this weekend."

"That sounds terrific, and I promise not to be even a slightly darker shade of ghost white on checkout." I tilt my head down and grin ear to ear in hopes she would send a bottle of champagne to my room.

"You're pretty fine just the way you are, but I think you know that already."

"I have no idea what you are talking about, but from such a pretty face, I will accept even inaccurate compliments gladly."

"Insert swoon here," she says, elevating a limp wrist to her forehead.

"You're one of those anti-Hollywood realist types, too, I see."

"It doesn't get any realer than working the front desk, baby," she says.

She passes a heavy, old-fashioned key into my hand and lingers a second as I take it without a hint of eye contact.

"It's on the third floor and to the right as you exit the elevator. Dinner reservations can be made through Samantha, and I can help you if you need to know where to go out or to any bars or clubs or tea parlors while in town."

"Yes, indeed, a tea parlor would be quite lovely. I will definitely ring you should I need anything."

A quick cruise past the reception reveals a sleepy lobby this early in the day, a spare assortment of readers, and a writer hovering over an empty coffee mug in a corner who probably looks far more studious and intellectual than in actuality.

Outside, the sun has emerged. Its uniquely LA intensity brims over the terrace dining room, over a menagerie of vintage white canopies concealing rattan banquettes and bistro chairs with old-style bar and waiters in black and white uniforms who manage to be formal and artsy. Unlike other hotels in LA, the Chateau always feels like it's part of the local landscape where people who live in the hills come down for supper, and moneyed starlets mingle over buckets of chilled bottles of rosé.

Back through the lobby, I give my sassy receptionist a nod. She doesn't look quite as snoggable the second go-round. I retreat to the elevator and acknowledge my jet lag for the first time. The four-person elevator feels like a death trap. I hope I'm with someone I want to chat up and not this guy who waits until the doors close before giving me the once-over and then daring me with his eyes even though I never dare make eye contact.

"Bye," he says as I make the exit to my floor, which I don't acknowledge given that gays will chase you harder if you ingratiate their advances with comments or replies in any way.

My room looks like every other on the hall, at least from the outside. I have to study the solid wood door with gothic trim before I recognize a chunky iron handle, which feels overwhelmed by the thick key as I slide it into the hole. There's a smell of another far grander time as I enter the room mixed with nuclear-grade American cleaning products. My shoes echo on the hardwood floors into the charming parlor room. Its sixties decor, a true rock star flop pad, overlooks a long terrace and the glossy marquees of Sunset Strip.

The bedroom exudes a sexy privacy withdrawn from LA's blinding sunlight. There's a queen bed and a type of bathroom you'd expect Marilyn Monroe to waltz out of in a towel. Its original pastel tile floors and porcelain white bathtub is more for overdoses than fucking. There's also a kitchen with almost the same minty tile, a bulky stove, and wheezing refrigerator stocked with every high-priced bottle of alcohol you can imagine and more sweet munchies than you could ever dream of—a sure-fire cure to my jet lag.

My usual check-in ritual ensues as I strip off my LA arrival uniform of navy jacket and white shirt with my most comfy pair of Dior Homme denim. The balcony couldn't look more inviting for a nap under a ray of sun that spotlights a perfect lounge chair. A layer of soot covers almost everything in LA, especially this terrace, but my tiredness wins over my bare back as I sprawl out in my striped Paul Smith boxers that look like a swimsuit if not for the cotton fabric and little logo affixed above the unstitched crotch.

I glance up and see the stoic stone building that looks like it was built for a Sofia Coppola movie with its Biz-ness glamour and aristocratic silhouette in this pretend of democratic colonies. Each visit to the Chateau yields a remarkably similar scene. Whether a Guatemalan housekeeper is dreaming out a window, a starlet is having a photo shoot along the penthouse terrace, or weekend bungalow action where real parties usually take place. There's also something about having sex in the Chateau. It doesn't compare to any other hotel with its bouncy beds and its showers that make for interesting angles against the cold, hard tile.

Then my cell phone chirps with its American ringtone that echoes against the spare white walls of the room.

"This is David."

"Is this my dreamy David?" a raspy voice with a hint of a young girl whispers on the line.

"That would be me, I think."

"I'm so glad you made it back to town. I just want to confirm we are on for tonight at ten?"

"That's a positive. Please address the woman at the door as Suzy upon entering. That will make it a whole lot easier for you guys."

"I know Suzy, babes. What's your room number?"

"Actually, I'll meet you in the lobby for a drink first."

"That sounds sugar; I'll see you in a bit love."

I guess *sugar* is the latest it-word replacing *everything*, *perfection*, and *bananas* as the adjective du jour. I met Jamila when I first arrived in LA and would work out at Crunch, which was sort of the Hollywood gym for starlets back in the day. I'd watch her work the room in those tight black spandex shorts that hugged her ass just below a sports fleece that concealed her perfect shoulders and tits that weren't the usual big and fake ones you see everywhere. She'd saunter over to a treadmill that sat in the perfect natural light, and as she'd step on the deck, she'd slowly undress down to a lone tank and even shorter shorts.

Forever she referred to me as her gay boyfriend, even if I would aver otherwise. I'm not one who takes offense at being called gay, but Jamila would test my limits by introducing me to her gay friends at the gym, which began to grate on me. For some reason, Americans think a guy with an English accent is effeminate and most likely gay. Then one day I had her back to my hotel and she, although insisting she had no real attraction to me, allowed me to show her my true talents. She has the kind of passion and sexuality that you're not prepared for, insatiable, moaning as I devoured her without a single attempt to pull down my own pants or anything. On following trips, we would experiment even more, and afterward I would take her shopping and sometimes even help her out with cash when she had a slow and lean month acting.

The last time I was in LA, I told her I wanted to try something new, preferably with a friend of hers. She laughed it off at first, but surprised me by suggesting the encounter in our last conversation. However, the whirlwind of meeting Catherine and her joining me in LA this weekend has me feeling that seeing Jamila is ill timed. Unfortunately, I think she's relying on it for the financial aspect of it given her prompt call. I figure there's no harm in seeing her and giving her the money if she needs it and leave it at that, not to mention the other part of me who wants to see what could have been and what Jamila has in store for me.

The six weeks since seeing Catherine in Paris has sped by, leaving that weekend feeling something truly special between us. Returning to my day-to-day life made the passion and romance seem farther away with each passing day. Fidelity has never been my strength, and life always seems to present a worthy counteroffer to remaining faithful to the women I adore. I expected Catherine to call me every few days to keep me near, but instead I'd get texts and mostly e-mails that, although lengthy and sincere, had me wanting more of her physically, even if just to hear her voice.

At 10:30 p.m., I contemplate skipping the whole night's activities. Catherine is due in LA the following day, and I really don't want to start the weekend off on the wrong foot. But here I am in the bathroom fully erect and knowing that it's been a good while since I've had sex. Faded jeans, white shirt, and navy jacket, I depart my room leaving on a little mellow hip-hop before making my way to the lobby.

There's a buzz in the Chateau almost any night of the week. A perfectly cast stage of women with their three-color blonde hair and peppy dresses bounce through the lobby as the main hostess separates the pretty people to the outside and everyone else to the inside dining room. Men in LA know how to navigate the competition. The old guys hang to the back, the gays walk heel-to-heel with the girls, and the rest of us circle and stalk in a subtle Darwinian duel until we land our prey.

I do a circle around the main terrace and see that famous pop singer who does the lollypop version of a burlesque show as well as the last Batman, who now thinks he's Cary Grant. As I circle past him, under the overhang sits Jamila dressed in a knockout short black dress that shows her sculpted brown thighs the color of caramel. Her piercing midnight eyes meet mine as I approach.

"David, baby, you look hot." She stands to greet me.

"And you don't look too shabby yourself," I reply as Jamila grabs me in a tight hug and cup of the ass as I scope out what could have been my side dish seated on a rattan lounge next to her. She's not as girly as I expected; more of a womanly face with wispy blonde hair and a careful gaze directed at me and then turns away before looking again. Her breasts crown a flowery white dress that's more English countryside than hot night in a Los Angeles hotel.

"This is my roommate, Amber," Jamila says as Amber tightens the grip she holds on some dude seated next to her who looks like a mix of an indie rocker and an American farm boy. "And her boyfriend, Alex."

Alex stands and extends his hand with a firm shake, younger looking in the direct overhead light that reveals blond freckles and an uneven smile with bottom teeth arranged like an enamel labyrinth.

"Nice to meet you, man, I've heard great things."

I wonder how he can speak such pleasantries when I essentially planned to take his girlfriend. This isn't at all what I signed up for but it's probably for the best. I tepidly resign myself into my seat ready to call it a night and chock the whole thing up to Jamila playing one of her mind games.

"Alex and Amber wanted to join us for a drink, and I thought it could be fun," Jamila eases into the conversation.

Amber reaches for the stem of her white wine glass with the hold of a truck driver, and Alex avoids almost all eye contact with me.

"Lovely to meet both of you really, but I have to say I'm a bit more tired than I thought tonight," I confess.

"Don't get all girly on us, David. We cleared a weekend night for you, and you're not going to douche bag on us."

Jamila doesn't mince words. Amber and Alex look on in growing discomfort.

"The fact is I know you're a total pervert, but you're also a hot pervert, and with the actor's strike, things are a little tight for us this month. We could both use the help."

"Jamila, I'm more than happy to help you out without this."

"Save it, and the fact is Amber and Alex are in a relationship, so Alex will just hang out in the lobby to make sure everything is okay."

Alex motions a sheepish, boyish nod, and then looks away to show a silhouette of a guy who can't be any older than twenty-one or twenty-two. This ruthless city pillages these kids for their only worthy commodity. My stare returns to Jamila who has spread her legs to show off a hint of fresh hair that I once begged her to grow back.

"So you guys are a couple?" I look away but feel my desire growing to see Jamila have her way with Amber.

"Yeah, Amber and I met in Iowa and came here together," Alex says as he sips his tall, malt-colored drink with bubbles running up and away from the under part of the glass.

"Did you meet in college?" I politely oblige the conversation.

"Didn't go to college, just high school, and after that we came here to LA."

"And how long ago was that?" I quickly ask.

"It was about two years ago, sir."

The word *sir* sits in the air and astounds me. The calculator in my head equates the age difference around eleven years, which makes it a lot, but not enough to make it wrong.

"Do you know why Jamila brought you here today?" I look into Amber's eyes with a questioning stare.

"David, don't be a dick," Jamila says.

"No," I say. "I want Alex to know why he's here, and what was going to happen. The last time I fucked with Jamila—" I begin somewhat agitated that she would stage such a spectacle.

"You ate me out; you didn't fuck me, darling," Jamila interrupts.

"I told her whenever I'm in town next, let's do a little experimentation, and get an extra girl to play along."

"Yeah, I kind of gathered that," Alex says with less hesitation than I expected.

"But that extra would have been your girlfriend, just your girlfriend," I say with as much humility as possible, but the cut is obvious.

"Yeah, dude, don't make this harder than it is already." Alex leans forward and sets his malty whiskey-coke-looking drink on the table.

"So, what I'm confused by is why you're here exactly, because I don't play around with other guys, and it just makes it all feel very awkward."

Alex abruptly stands up. I stake my ground and make it apparent that there will be no group experimentation happening for me this night or any night.

"David, I told him he could come and wait outside. I didn't think you were going to come to the lobby, and it all got sort of confusing. He couldn't stay in the car because we valet parked it."

"So you make me see the girl's boyfriend who you want me to fuck," I erupt with a mix of irritability from the time difference that when I look at my watch means about six o'clock in the morning London time.

"Fine, so you don't want it to happen now?" Jamila continues, "You want me to starve and have to work at the mall or go live with my parents or something?"

A motionless stare between us is interrupted as Amber coughs ever so slightly, and I see Alex wrap his hand around her upper thigh. The innocence of his touch returns me to a more sexual feeling as her posture relaxes with the comfort of his hand gripping her soft white skin. A mix of jasmine in the garden lends a virginal aroma to the warm breeze that wobbles the giant white umbrellas and shakes the hanging foliage in an abrupt gust.

"So let's all go back to your room, and we can either say our good-byes with no hard feelings or figure something out. You're making too much of a scene here for me, baby. I live in this town."

My thoughts return to Catherine, scheduled to be here in just twenty-four hours, and what could explode from this minefield of desperate people who could turn unmanageable in an instant. A scene in the Chateau would immediately result in my being banned, meaning that tomorrow I would have to explain why I wasn't allowed in her hotel to visit.

"Okay, one drink and then I'll see you all off."

Amber and Jamila rise from the table but Alex remains seated.

"Come on, mate, nothing is going to happen now anyway so no sense in just sitting here. We're good, right?" I say, hoping to neutralize the night and end it on a positive note for this guy who must truly be having a tough time in life.

Alex rises from the table and pulls up his saggy jeans. "Totally boss, all is cool."

The unlikely quartet makes their way back through the lobby as a flurry of eyes gravitate toward the two women as they pass. Alex isn't as refined as Amber is; his jeans and shirt seem as if they have seen their fair shares of cycles in a public Laundromat, most likely with his trendy sport shoes worn out on the heels. He has an athletic build, one that would be hard to take down should things get messy, but I figure Jamila isn't entirely insane, or at least I hope.

With a turn of the key, we pile into my room. Jamila heads toward the stereo and turns off my Jay-Z remix and connects her iPod without hesitation. I busy myself with a bottle of wine that I open and pour without asking anyone else if they wanted a glass. I am still feeling heavy by the earlier conversation and somewhat hoping this will simply turn into a quiet evening alone.

Jamila puts on some vintage Rolling Stones, one of her personality's more positive but unexpected surprises. Like when I found out her family fled Afghanistan and lived in a refugee camp until she was six before they finally found their way to the states, thanks to an aunt in Florida.

Jamila pulls the drapes and returns to the console. She opens her bag and pulls out a baggie of cocaine that she handles with a chemist's caution while pouring it out over the glossy surface. She then licks her index finger as if it were white chocolate or the final bit of cake batter on a spoon. She cuts the cocaine with an American debit card she has ready, and then divides it in five hulky lines as she snorts the longest of them before saying a word.

Alex and Amber approach Jamila, but with a distance between each other as if knowing what is to come between them. Alex inches in and takes the second line in two snorts, rising a minute, and showing the novice's hesitation of taking the whole line.

"Thank you, that's a rush," Alex mutters before making his way onto the terrace.

"Who's next? This whole night is all going to be a whole lot better with a little blow, babies," she says.

"Wait a minute." I see Amber stop in front of the console. "Come here." I gesture for Amber as she turns to Alex and then walks my way and takes a seat next to me on the sofa.

I look into her pupils and see a color of blue so similar to mine, her hair like summer wheat, and skin marked with a permanent blush that's either from the heat in the room or the intensity of the moment. All I can think about is kissing her just one time, just once, and then I'll stop.

I lean in and begin to kiss her soft lips in a forgiving, gentle rhythm that loosens her jaws and opens her tense mouth. We stand and kiss deeper and deeper. I glide my tongue around the slick edges of her perfect white teeth as she timidly enters my mouth with her own. Jamila joins us on the couch, grabbing me from behind to remove my jacket, and Alex vanishes from my eye line.

My hands work across Amber's face, firmly grabbing her mouth and lip with my fingers. Jamila rushes the moment by pulling off my belt.

"No, leave my pants alone," I say.

I can feel my erection swell as Jamila gropes me like an adolescent girl in a movie theater or school dance. I push her hands away and move closer to Amber.

My lips make it onto Jamila's face; she duels for alpha position sexually, but realizes the desire for the unknown leaves me disinterested in her in this contest she cannot win.

"Kiss her," I say to Jamila in a command.

Jamila looks at me with a mix of desire and surprise.

"Kiss her," I say again.

Amber is faster than Jamila. She takes her lips and plants her hands on Jamila's breasts with an adolescent stumble. Amber pulls off Jamila's top as she stands there in that hot black skirt and her bare breasts that capture the light coming in from an adjacent billboard that also illuminates Alex's eyes watching her through the glass that separates the terrace. I thought he would be watching what happens to his girlfriend, but a voyeur's lust wins as he watches Jamila's every move.

"Take off your clothes, Amber." I step back at a safe distance to watch.

Jamila helps her with each piece down to her pink lace panties, which come off one slender leg after another. Amber stands there perfectly naked, her hips wider than I imagine under a narrow waist. Her nipples are framed in pinkish flesh and rising just toward the end with a silhouette that would humble any woman. The mirror on the wall reflects Alex still watching through the glass behind her.

"Take off the rest of your clothes, Jamila," I insist as she removes her pouf of a skirt with a stripper's flirtation. She next removes her stockings and then her earrings that she carefully places on the table before returning next to Amber. Both women are standing completely naked. Amber is much taller than Jamila, a model's figure next to a woman who gets by with so much in life with her perfectly pretty face and body that doesn't nearly compare with its shorter portions.

Alex doesn't attempt to hide his presence on the balcony, he watches attentively with both women fully revealed to him. Despite Amber being the perfect form—the shape of an elongated pear that's meaty on the sides and contours down to two perfect long legs—it's Jamila that he concentrates on.

"Get down on your knees, Jamila," I say from my seated position. Jamila drops to the ground behind her.

I get up, move closer to the couch, approach Jamila, and guide her head between Amber's thighs. Jamila hesitates as I resist joining Jamila's tongue with my own. She falls onto the couch and I back away again. She spreads her legs in an exotic invite as her eyes open to look at me, and then at Alex, who remains clearly in her eye line. Jamila jumps up, grabs me from behind, and rips open my YSL shirt. A button snaps off, flies across the room, and lands next to the door. I push her away again. I must stop.

I didn't want to be here as I near Amber and straddle from above with my body fully on the precipice. Jamila rises above Amber, forcing her to eat her out in a position of dominance that she took when I positioned myself to enter Amber and not her. I want to stop, but all I can think about is being inside Amber. She squirms in desire moaning for me to take her. She grabs her hair and body as if on stage or performing for an audience.

As Amber begs me to enter her, I push Jamila out of the way. The thing about threesomes, with a third unknown partner, someone is left out in the lust of a couple who wants to be left alone.

Jamila is fully naked and moves across the room and onto the terrace. I stare into Amber's eyes, fully ready to be inside of her. Alas, this must stop before it is too late. An awkward and abrupt halt shivers through my body, and I collapse next to her in a sweated retreat. I stopped. I actually managed to stop. Her breath withdraws from exhaustion as a forgiving stillness engulfs the room, and I immediately know I made the right decision, regardless of how late and the fact that I'm still very much erect.

Neither one of us said a word; both of us are probably relieved this didn't go any farther. My hand reaches to Amber's in a humble, excusing motion in hopes she won't feel rejected or confused that I chose not to go any farther. But before she can gesture in return, the silence is interrupted. Jamila is on the terrace atop Alex and moaning in exaltation, both hidden behind the curtains and the very dark night. As I look at Amber, her peaceful spirit fades to emotion as her hand pulls away and eyes retreat from mine. I take my cue.

There's an echo with the slam of the bathroom door; a cold tiled heaven away from all that remains in the next room. What was I thinking? How did I let this happen? I begin to masturbate voraciously, wanting to rid myself of the poisons that make me ruin every good relationship I've ever known, even when it's not my own. I pull harder and harder, and I finally erupt catapulting me away from that moment and into a solitary place where all I desire is to take back those last two hours. My dick falls limp as my inner regret cyclones. I pull back the shower curtain and pretend for a moment that none of that just happened, that no one still lingered in my room, and these wildly different paths hadn't crossed in the whirlwind of a Chateau night.

The hot water hisses as it labors through the old pipes of the building, and I stand under a cold spray that doesn't have a massager or a rain head, just a simple chrome spout that sprays frigid water that envelops my body. Slowly, the water turns warmer and then almost too hot as the cold moves down my body. A warm, tingling sensation relaxes me to the point of urinating on the perfect white tiles.

To the rear of the bathtub, a long mirror antagonizes me as I look at my bare body with legs beginning to show their oldness around the knees and my chest and shoulders that aren't near as bulky as they were a few years ago. And my face, that face with my anybody eyes that are too spread apart with black circles above my big nose and lines leading down around the mouth that are far too deep for my age. Then there is this, this endless carnage of relationships that gets more and more complicated as my desire becomes ravenous for the unknown pleasure that leaves me here hiding and once again alone.

The following morning I awaken to a city covered in a misty fog that leaves a slick residue on the patio even at the late hour of noon. Its wet cushions and consistent drip fall from the Chateau's roofline, down its rusted gutters, and to the pavement along my terrace. I have a few hours to awaken fully before Catherine arrives from New York. I walk into the living room where the phantoms of last night linger through tossed pillows, ruffled furniture, and smudges on the credenza literally licked clean with not a grain of coke left by Jamila.

"Hello, this is David Summers," I say into the chunky old-fashioned cordless phone.

"Yes, sir, how may we help you this day?" the perky receptionist responds.

"Might I request my maid service as soon as possible?"

"Absolutely, we will send someone straight up."

"And would you mind forwarding my request for a double espresso and dry wheat toast to room service?"

"Right away, sir. It shouldn't be more than ten minutes."

My mix of jet lag and hangover haze has me retreating into bed where I lose myself in the plaster ceiling with its handful of cracks and faint smell of paint that comes across the uninterrupted morning. I imagine all the people before me lying in this very spot, some in the company of the one they love and others like me isolated and wondering if I would have even noticed the intricacies of the ceiling if in the presence of another. I also imagine what it would be like lying here with Catherine with no memories of last night resting heavy on my mind.

A hefty knock on the door has me thinking espresso and not the ungainly Guatemalan housekeeper dressed in white with a smile dotted in metal-capped filling who waits on the other side in the company of her vacuum and cleaning bucket. I, standing there in just my white cotton sleeping shorts, leave me a little embarrassed when her eye line is more to my waist than my head.

"You request housekeeping?"

"Yes, come right in. I'll just stay in the bedroom and out of your way until you're done."

She enters directly into the messy living room and sweeps her gaze before going about the process of reassembling what was the visuals and memories of the previous night fade with each pillow in place, every pull of the drapes back to their check-in position, and moving the couch from where I thrust it while inside that young girl. As I withdraw to the bedroom, the door rings. I swivel back and open it to see a dapper twenty-something room service attendant who stands in a crisp white shirt that perfectly opposes the black espresso in the transparent cup.

"Good morning, we have your espresso for you."

My near-nakedness is overlooked in lieu of direct eye contact with the guy who is likely a model or actor cast with his angular jaw line and James Dean looks that would likely emasculate lesser men in a single glance, especially when standing there in their underwear. He lingers in the doorway as I attempt to grab the tray from him with both hands.

"It's very hot, so just tell me where to put it," he insists.

He surveys the room and sees the lone housekeeper with a spritz bottle in her hand laboring over the glass coffee table and looking at both of us.

"Actually, just follow me and put it in here," I say, turning and retracing the steps to my bedroom well aware of what the housekeeper is thinking.

"You can just put it right there." I gesture toward the side table.

He takes instruction quickly and turns abruptly with a bill to sign.

As he approaches, he studies my body with such severity that his gestural statement takes me aback. He looks at my stomach, my underwear, and then my chest without looking into my eyes again.

"I guess I should sign that," I say, taking the bill from his hand.

His gayness catches me off guard, straight appearing and total-guy acting in almost every way. I'm complimented and almost a bit smug by the attention of someone almost half my age, and twice as attractive as I am. Without a word, he stares into my eyes as I grab the pen, sign, and hand the bill back to him.

"My name is Sam. If there's anything you need or want during your stay, please ask for me directly."

Sam gazes down at me once again, objectifying me just enough to have me backing into the main room and seeing him to the door. Without my replying even a thank you, Sam scampers away to leave me with my espresso and disappointed housekeeper.

After a shower and a morning of work, I make my way down to the lobby. The corridors of the hotel linger in near complete darkness despite the afternoon hour. The city sits under a blanket of gloom that will at least dissipate from my mind with the arrival of Catherine. I crave her conversation, the sight of her face that lights up in a story where my mind doesn't retreat into my own thoughts, and instead hangs on her every word.

My clothes are strategic, a long-sleeve knit polo shirt in sky blue that reflects a husband-like glow in my eyes with arms that are soft to touch and potentially cuddle over black denim jeans, and black sneakers you wouldn't be caught dead wearing in any London hotel. The lobby is empty, just the way I was hoping, a cozy corner facing away from the entrance would allow us some privacy. Despite the soggy weather, the patio still manages a crowd for a late lunch, but I still want the comfort of those bouncy sofas that soothe my hangover.

"Can I get you a drink?" the same waitress with the statuesque shoulders from the previous night inquires.

"Actually, just a hot tea would be lovely."

"Any particular kind? We have Earl Grey and English breakfast and chamomile, I believe."

"A green tea would be perfect if you have it."

"That shouldn't be a problem, but chamomile if not?"

"Actually, an espresso if not," I correct myself.

Without a moment to spare, I see her circling the lobby looking every bit the celebrity with her black sunglasses and impeccably tailored leather jacket over two long legs kissed in flowing black pants of an avant-garde cut above boots that stretch for days in front of her. She's far more glamorous and sexy than even I remember. Her eyes have been on me awhile, our gaze connecting in an instant without her pretending to look around the room or searching as if she hadn't seen me. There's realness to Catherine that's refreshing, she doesn't partake in those typical relationship games. She looks stunning as she nears; her hair is a bit lighter than before. She pulls off her glasses and reignites that feeling I get inside since the first time our paths crossed in that Rio airport.

I remain seated, almost straddling her with my legs apart as she approaches the final few steps. I jump to my feet and grab her around the waist as a whiff of fresh leather lingers on her with an underlayer of that citrusy fragrance. I jostle my nose into the cold flesh of her neck and take a bite with my teeth. She pulls away at the forwardness of my hug.

"David Summers, I've missed you." She gazes into my eyes while holding both my elbows in the cusp of her hand.

"I can't tell you how excited I am that you are here. I'm so excited it all worked out."

"How could I not come see you while visiting my country?"

"You seemed so busy, I wasn't sure it would actually happen."

"Well, I wouldn't have been able to stand the thought of you staying at the Chateau without me."

Her eyes hover over mine like an artist tracing on parchment. My eyes move from her stare to take in her body that's a fair amount thinner than just a month ago, even in her New Yorker winter clothes.

"Are you tired? I always forget what a hefty flight that is from New York."

"I was able to sleep most of the way, with a little work in between."

Our conversation seems to detour almost immediately into small talk, as if what we had in Paris and Rio didn't translate over time and distance. She talks of interviews, office politics, and New York weather before asking the obligatory question of me in each area. She settles into the couch. I scoot in closer catching her off guard as she oddly moves away as if the intimacy makes her uncomfortable.

"I have to tell you, I've really missed you since Paris. I've thought about our time there almost every day since," I say.

"I had such a great time; it was so unexpected."

"I'm so happy you could make this weekend work. I only have some quick work on Monday morning, otherwise, I'm all yours," I say.

"That works fine because I have to be on the red-eye back to New York on Sunday night. So once again, we will have to make the most of the short time we have together."

She loosens up just a bit, delivering bad news and shortening her stay by an entire two days without mentioning it in advance or even offering it in its own sentence.

"No, of course, work comes first. I'm totally keen on making the most of whatever time we have together, whether it's our time here in LA, or elsewhere."

Quietness lingers between our words in a disjointed series of questions and answers that make each of us unsettled. I look around the room wishing the chemistry had ignited as fast as in our previous meetings.

"So why are you here in LA again?" she asks.

"Oh, you'll love this. There's this whole phenomenon here with these popcorn crisps, have you heard of them?"

"Air Chips?"

"Yes, exactly. They are trying to find a partner to fund a few other ventures with the intention of selling or making a public offering somewhere down the road."

"Have you tried them? They're really good. Barbecue is my favorite," she says.

"Yes, although you Americans fancy the weirdest of flavors, like sweet potato, or even worse, cheddar."

Lightness ensues within the conversation. I notice Catherine's manner relax and her arms loosen from her torso.

"You don't seem the type who would eat a lot of chips and junk food," she says.

"I've had a fair amount of crisps in my day, but it's usually when I'm too hungover to venture out of the house."

"So you eat them often?" she jabs.

"Exactly, just had some this morning."

The waitress returns with a silver platter of tea and a white plate stacked with an assortment of American-looking biscuits. The waitress steadies in on my eyes. I feel Catherine follow the direction of my stare that looks away as the waitress leans forward to rest the tray on the table, her white blouse revealing a well-filled, lacy cream-colored bra.

"Just a light afternoon snack, I see," Catherine mutters as her hand drifts to my knee for only a moment, long enough to assert her position over the waitress.

"Actually, I only ordered tea," I say.

"Yes," the waitress says, "but I figured you both might like a little snack, or biscuits as you call them." She smiles pleasantly and removes a pad from the pocket of her white smock.

"And may I get you something, Miss?"

"Um, actually I'm not going to be here long, so I'll just nibble off his."

"Are you sure? Not even a sandwich or salad or something?"

"No, really I'm fine," Catherine insists.

"Great, well let me know if you need anything else."

As she turns away, I can feel Catherine's hand move away from my knee, and the conversation begins again with the waitress now a safe distance away.

"So, what's on the agenda for the weekend?" she asks.

"Well, tonight we have a dinner party my friend is having here at the hotel that should be right good fun."

"Meeting the friends already am I?" she asks.

"No, no, not like that. It's just a fun crew, and I think you'll enjoy meeting them. They're terrific lads and very aware I haven't sunken my teeth into you yet. As far as they know, we are just friends."

"Just friends? Is that what we are?" she asks as if offended.

"Well, friends are usually easier to get a hold of than you are, my dear, but let's just leave it at that."

"No, I'd love to go, and I'm sure it will be a fun time."

"And best of all, the party is here in the hotel, so you can drink like a fish and not have to worry about hiring a car or fetching a taxi."

"And what's the attire? I'm afraid I didn't bring too many options."

"They said royal-chic, but I'm sure anything black will do and will match my outfit splendidly."

The more she relaxes, the more she resembles the woman I fell for in Rio and Paris. Perhaps she seems a little out of her element in this new Hollywood backdrop, or uncertain how to pick up where our incredible chemistry in Paris left off, or if it was just a one-time thing.

"So, I'm going to have to run out for my interview, and you're going to have to keep yourself busy for the next few hours."

"You mean you're doing it today?" I ask.

"Absolutely, the faster it's done the sooner I can enjoy myself."

"And who are you interviewing this time?"

"Jessica Biel. Or is it Jessica Alba? It's the more relevant one of the two who's married to the former boy-band guy."

"I have no idea, but it sounds painful," I say.

"She climbed Kilimanjaro."

"My grandfather did too, and enjoyed nightly buffets and morning massages along the three-day journey."

"Wait, so it's not like Everest where people die and stuff?" she asks.

"It's like going to a top floor of a mall, but taking the stairs instead of the elevator."

"Ouch. I'll be sure to mention it to her. But listen, I really have to run, so let's meet up around seven o'clock for a drink and then head to your party."

"No, don't let me keep you. I'll see you here in a bit, love."

"Perfect, and don't get into too much trouble," she says.

We both rise and face each other in an awkward good-bye that feels to warrant more than a hug but less than a romantic kiss. I, however, grab both of her cheeks with my hand and kiss her on the mouth. My lips wrap almost perfectly around hers as she is caught in the moment, trailing again with her own-mouthed reply that passes in an awkward instant.

"Don't be too long."

She pulls away from the table and leaves in much the rushed pace at which she arrived.

Maybe my residual regret of the previous night or the great expectations that linger from Paris and Rio, but I sense there's something off. I expected her to seize every precious moment we manage to find together, but instead she runs off almost as soon as she arrives. Something feels not quite right between us. Perhaps she met someone else in the meantime, or maybe I'm not as charismatic after the prize has been had.

By evening, the allure of the Chateau is in full swing. Virtually the same glamorous people with different faces make their way up the stairs, through the lobby, and into the garden like a cloned procession of perfectly tight denim jeans, edgy eyewear, and scruffy faces. I opt for a dressier look of a white dress shirt and a Balmain tux-jacket with black jeans given the host's request for imperial attire, which in LA can simply mean a long pair of pants. My skin still smells of chlorine and feels the chill of the poorly heated Chateau pool that I couldn't help but take a dip in despite the gloomy weather and water that hadn't been cleaned since the previous evening's windstorm.

True to form, Catherine makes her entrance at 7:28 p.m., emerging from the dimness of the staircase to the almost-perfect white light of the lobby that reflects off her long legs. Those legs vanish under a voluminous black skirt with a creamy underlayer that collides at her svelte hips and wraps her breasts and arms in a tailored silk armor. Her hair is slicked back as I've never seen before, and without any jewelry, this incredible beauty emerges and everyone around her seems to disappear. Like the only electrified house on a city block of darkness, she arrives to the table without any pretense or awareness of the scene she's just created for me.

"Look at you, all handsome in your suit," she says with a girlish excitement completely unaware of herself.

I rise to look into her eyes for some sense of smugness, impressed that she shows no reaction to my astonishment, and proving that she's either the most modest person I've ever met or the best actress I've ever seen.

"I've long been a student of beautiful women, but I have never in my life been witness to quite such an entrance as you just made looking the way you do tonight."

"What are you talking about?" she gushes and conceals her smile behind the hand she holds in front of her mouth. "Have you been drinking, Mr. Summers?"

"No, stop right there," I say in a hushed tone, placing my long index finger against her mouth. "Please, hear me out. You look absolutely stunning tonight. You make every single thing in this place look better, including me."

Her gaze becomes more serious as she goes from listening to hearing.

"You literally took my breath away."

Catherine leans in with closed eyes to kiss me, a soft gentle kiss from her soft lips the color of coral and flesh that lingers and goes all the way to my heart.

"So should we have a drink here first, or do we need to be on time?" she asks.

Catherine seems uncomfortable with the compliments, shying away with a blush that she conceals by moving away from me as well as the emotion.

"I don't want to be rude, so let's get going. I'm sure we'll have a drink in hand fast enough if I know those guys."

We make our way away from the bar as I begin to tell Catherine the background of Harris and Dudi. They've become my best friends in LA, and probably some of the best people I've ever met. We met while I was working for an investment company that was negotiating the sale of a restaurant group they owned. Harris is a savvy business guy who can smell a distress sale from a mile away. They do incredibly well and continue to buy and sell businesses with incredible rigor even though they are too cheap to use my company.

Dudi is the social one of the two, a dapper and boyish Brazilian who brings his passion for life to everything and manages to attract a legion of friends and fans wherever and whenever he chooses, me now included. They have these legendary Hollywood pool parties in the summer that are like nothing you've ever seen, and then they have theme dinners throughout the colder months of the year. Usually, they take place at their house, but it's currently under construction, so they decided to have it at the Chateau this year.

"And when it comes to Harris and Dudi, only the penthouse will do. After you," I say, guiding Catherine toward the elevator.

The Chateau elevator is faster this evening. I slide my hand down the backside of her dress that unfortunately covers every inch of her upper body and separates my hand from her skin.

"I have to tell you, I'm not sure if I want to stand back and stare at you or just have you here and now," I say as my attention turns from facing forward to hovering right next to her.

"I don't think this is the type of elevator you can stop and not expect it to go crashing into the basement," she says with steady contemplation in her eyes.

"I've inspected your dress without you knowing it, and I have to say I'm not seeing the easiest entrances for sneaking touches throughout the night."

She looks down at her impossibly fashionable dress that seems to cover her body almost entirely, and then she takes my hand. "You'll have to get creative."

She glides my hand up her leg as my mind travels with it to the top of her garter and onto a warm swathe of her perfect skin that makes me want to take her here and now.

"You just gave me hope," I whisper in her ear.

Normally at this moment, I'm worrying about what my date will be like in a social setting of people whom I know and respect. I'll worry that she'll talk too much or too little, or use big words in the wrong way that will result in a flurry of texts asking, "Does she get lost on the catwalk as well?" or "And by fruitation, does she actually mean that her dreams result in an apple or an orange?"

A long corridor leads to a door where a burly guard stands holding a clipboard. He says not a word to Catherine as the door opens behind him and his bulky body shifts to the side. At the end of this checkerboard-floored corridor, stands a fireplace that roars in the middle of a grand parlor accented in powder-blue furnishings and a wide doorway that seems came long before the bejeweled skyline that lurks beyond in a trace of fog just starting to blow in from the ocean.

At the piano sits a shirtless man wearing only a broad fur hat à la Peter the Great and strumming Tchaikovsky on the piano. A glamorous chatter fills the air and waiters dressed as Russian soldiers pace the room with troughs of silver caviar in hand. Then I see Dudi.

"My boyfriend is here! David Summers!" Dudi screams from across the room and makes his way to the parlor dressed as Nicholas II, complete with gold medallions and a white uniform that contrasts his black hair and even darker eyes for a gentlemanly first appearance. "And he's brought a hot woman to make me jealous. How dare he?"

His words linger closer together like the chorus of an Antonio Carlos Jobim song.

"You know how those Summers' like to work," Catherine chimes in and makes her way to my side.

"You must be Catherine, the lion tamer." Dudi touches both of Catherine's hands with his fingertips and kisses her on each cheek.

"More of a dog trainer according to some people," I reply.

"David, you look delicious, you lucky bitch." Dudi grabs me around the hips and lifts me in the air taking a good grope of my nether. "I absolutely love this man, Catherine."

"He is a charmer, isn't he?"

"And not that bad on the eyes, either," Dudi quickly adds.

"We met in Rio, you know, so technically our connection is Brazilian, like you."

"You two are so hot, it makes me sick. But come in and join the rest of imperial St. Petersburg."

As we enter, a towering soldier with a boyish face that struggles to be contained behind his Rasputin beard stands in an imperial cloak.

"That two-headed eagle in the middle of your chest is actually derived from the Romans and adapted by Russians," I say to break the ice, and show Catherine a smarter side, but such trivialities have little interest to an LA crowd and don't even warrant a reply from the waiter or my date.

Dudi is meticulous about his parties to the point of passing out faux jewels to all the women as another cloaked attendant carefully places a canary yellow bracelet on Catherine's wrist. On Catherine, the garishness of the piece actually looks fashionable, even real as her poise and grace elevates the crowd almost immediately.

"This is outrageous … are they always so decadent?" Catherine says, eyeing her bracelet as we approach the bar.

"Indeed. This is actually a little tame, but the night is young."

The bartender, with his rebellious beard and overly gelled hair, gives Catherine the once-over. This staff of straight actor guys trying to pay the bills working for gay guys who will do and say just about anything to get them into bed. The bartenders usually come on hot and heavy with the female guests proving their virility, and letting all know up-front for what team they play. It has to be a tough gig, standing in this iconic setting and so wanting to be part of the action and doing the most menial of jobs standing half-naked in a sparkly frock.

Dudi knows a great group of people who span the world of LA business and the entertainment industry. Catherine seems to come into her own among the crowd, a different side of her than I've seen before. She's emerging herself with full rigor among perfect strangers as I stand and watch in awe. She works this type of crowd better than I do, listening with direct eye contact as this woman named Ana, pronounced ON-uh despite her American accent, goes into a diatribe on how anti-gay Russia has become, and that we shouldn't be celebrating its monstrous history.

Catherine listens politely without adding or differing, mentioning that the current political empowerment is in fact conservative, but that it's simply a matter of time before social reform works its way east from Europe. Her kindness seems an annoyance to those listening, these volatile Americans who will fight for any cause as long as it's illuminated as being good against evil or wrong against right.

I pull on Catherine's sleeve as the conversation shifts to another social war, namely lesbian mothers, and her cue to exit is more obvious for me than her.

"That's about to become another revolution right there," I say, trying to sip out another bit of scotch from my glass that's long been emptied of all but ice.

"They just want to show their support to your friends being gay. I get it," she says as we make our way back to the bar.

As we approach the terrace with our refreshed drinks, we see a long table set with about twenty or so settings with plates stacked one atop another and another as crystal glasses crowd a small name card and mask lying over the plate. Each person is given a designated character from the revolution. Mine is a dapper, blondish man named Grand Duke Dmitri Pavlovich of Russia, which is far better than the Trotsky mask laid to the right of me. A card on the back of the mask reveals his tortured life as one of the instigators behind Rasputin's death and dismissal from Russia that ultimately saved his life during the 1917 revolution that took most all of his relatives left behind.

"At least he was hot," Dudi says from across the table.

As I look next to me for Catherine's mask on my left, I realize she's not seated next to me. I had wanted the dinnertime to connect more with her, delve deeper in her life, and have her close to me since it's almost impossible to make plans to be together. She makes her way around the table looking for her card before taking her place between two empty chairs. She smiles confidently across the table as if to reassure as she holds up her mask to show me a mousy woman who doesn't near compare to her beauty at this moment.

"Catherine, who are you, dear?" Dudi yells across the table as everyone buzzes about their own mask and takes a seat.

The seated crowd quiets a bit around the packed table illuminated in dramatic candelabras with the flickering city skyline beneath.

"I'm the lovely Vera Alexeyevna Karalli." Catherine's voice cracks on the first word but nails the last name like someone oiled in the language.

"Shhh! Everyone, I can't hear Catherine. Baby, stand up!" Dudi yells.

Catherine gazes from one end of the table to the other. Not the quiet deer in headlights I would expect from my usual dates, but in the most girlish of excitement with her seat neighbors, who include a well-known TV star and one of Harris and Dudi's fancier gay friends named Cliff.

"This is the amazing Vera Alexeyevna Karalli, who, unlike so many of her contemporaries in St. Petersburg and Moscow at the time, lived to the ripe old age of eighty-three."

A louder, more confident voice prevails as she continues. "She fled the country following the revolution and was unfortunately linked to a man named Grand Duke Dmitri Pavlovich who was corroborated in the death of Rasputin."

As her delicate hand yields the mask from right to left for all to see, Dudi interrupts. "And that terrible man would be you, David."

Startled while looking at Catherine instead of my mask, I jump to my feet. "Indeed, that lovely lady was involved with this unfortunate chap, who despite his wise looks was implicated in the disappearance of cleric Grigori Rasputin." I mouth a drum roll.

"Now, the empress, wherever she is tonight, loved her witch doctors and didn't take kindly to the loss of her Rasputin, whom I believe is also here tonight. So your dear Dmitri, or I for the time being, had him sent to the Persian front of the war and worst of all, away from my great love." I gesture to Catherine.

"Oh yes, she was also an accomplished ballerina who danced with Mikhail Mordkin," Catherine adds, ignoring my romantic cue.

"Another hot man … that's you, Paul," Dudi interrupts again. He motions to an older gent named Paul, who holds up an image of the famous ballet master and does his best interpretive grande pose with his arms.

"Vera also went on to star in several silent movies as well as assist Russians in exile, but sadly never returned to her home."

Catherine misses her beat to remain silent before retaking her seat in a cackle of table chatter that erupts around her.

My side of the table, however, isn't nearly as amused or amusing. I'm sitting next to a woman named Beth who is also from London, but now works her dream job at a Hollywood agency managing reality TV shows that gets her backstage access; her head of hair is more befitting a European prime minister than an LA creative type. Boring as paint drying but entirely harmless, on my other side is a far more curious character named Mitch. His first sentence revealed he was straight like me, but also an actor and here with an older gentleman named Arthur seated next to him. I'd say Mitch is no older than twenty-five, and likely doing everything he can to get through the night without putting out to Daddy.

"So how did you end up here, Mitch?" I say after taking another sip of my pink rosé that reveals itself as Dom Pérignon. A half-naked Russian soldier fills up my champagne flute even though it wasn't even half-empty.

"Arthur asked me to join him for the night," he answers.

Arthur introduces himself, a well-spoken man whose grayed temples lend an air of sophistication, and his rounded belly shows he's either too old or too successful to try to compete on visual terms.

"We met through work a year or so ago, and we've become really good friends. Arthur and I travel a lot together; actually we just got back from London."

"And how was that for you both?" I ask without really caring.

"It was terrific. We stayed at the Mandarin Oriental, went to Harrods, and saw this great play; I forgot its name, with Jude Law in the West End."

I hate the Mandarin Oriental in London, Harrods is a tourist trap, Jude Law hasn't been good at anything since Sienna Miller, and even that is questionable. The relationship of Arthur and Mitch appears to be something that lingers in friendship and sometimes peaks in situations that are more romantic that Mitch likely fends off, but only so much that he keeps Arthur hopeful and the invites coming.

"My girlfriend was a little weird about it at first, but now she's totally cool."

Cool with what, I wonder. Not wanting to put off my seatmates prior to the appetizers, I defer to more polite conversation and ask what Arthur does for work, but my ears transition to the other side of the room despite my agreeing nods and one-syllable responses that keep the conversation going without actually having to participate.

Catherine is seated next to a famous production designer named Clifford Morris, who's one of the better social litmus tests a person can have in LA, carving the fat from the meat with his slicing words that seemed to have evolved into a natural connection with Catherine as he mouths to me the words "I love her" across the table.

To her other side is some well-known TV actress who chats away with the young boy next to her as if displaced from Cliff and Catherine's more intimate and convivial conversation that I'm sure she'd prefer if not rejected from it almost immediately upon sitting. I'm sure it was Cliff and not Catherine, likely asking her about the day's headlines that she's oblivious to unless it was on some blog or a bold-font TV headline she saw at the gym.

The two women sitting next to each other offer a glimpse of me and my love life in time—one, a woman I would have chased endlessly only to have a short, unfulfilling relationship with, and the other a woman who makes me feel like a better person, a better man. There's more than just the sexual chase to Catherine; there's an emotional component she invests in people that makes you want, actually need, the more you are with her. As I sit here, I'm almost jealous of the people next to her. The more I watch, the more I realize how fortunate I am that a woman such as Catherine would choose to spend time with me, and that I've finally arrived at a point in my life where it means something.

Dinner is perfection, even if I enjoy it for no more than a few bites between the glasses of rosé poured like Diet Coke among a now fully blanketed LA sky. As the waiter clears my dinner plate, I notice the actress next to Catherine rise to her feet. I take the moment to swap spots and rejoin my date.

"Clifford Morris, I cannot believe I was seated away from you. Have they no idea?" I plead to him.

"Tell me about it. I was stuck near Gayzilla over here and your lovely date."

Cliff refers to the overweight gay man next to him as Gayzilla, the man still fully immersed in his dinner but not so much that he didn't hear the comment.

"But this one, this one is sheer perfection," he says, squeezing Catherine's shoulder.

"I hear you; I don't know what she ever finds in me."

"Yeah, just look at you."

"He is a beautiful man, though, isn't he?" Catherine confides.

"But listen, honey, I want you to take my number because I want us to stay in touch once he breaks your heart."

"Cliff, I mean really."

"No, I'm serious. I'm in New York all the time, and I think we have a similar groove ... you and me."

Cliff grabs Catherine's hand as she gazes over at me. She takes the wine goblet in her hand and puts it up to her mouth.

"Cliff, why would you say that?" I say, realizing it likely hurt Catherine.

"Oh, calm down girl. I was just kidding. But in all seriousness, you and I are meant to be friends, Catherine."

"She needs another swallow, and these servers are over waiting on us."

Cliff rises from the table, comes over, and gives me a hug before moving toward the bar.

"He was just kidding. You know that, right?" I try to say to Catherine without her neighbor hearing now that a waiter has cleared his plate.

"David, how can you break my heart when you don't even possess it?" she says with a smirk.

The tone in Catherine's voice makes me realize the sting of Cliff's words was maybe far greater than I realized, or perhaps his candidness simply caught her off guard.

"Now, is that very nice?" I say, attempting to soothe her wound.

Words are like gas on a flame with women at this point. I can plead my case harder, but the fact is I've typically been an unreliable lover who is prone to leave a relationship with little more than a phone call.

The music suddenly changes as a moody Hollywood version of *Bewitched* comes from the parlor sung by a black woman. Built like a fire hydrant, her voice justifies whatever she lacks in looks from her proud perch at the piano. Her voice silences the crowd that circles around the glass doors to watch.

We linger at the table; Catherine appears captivated by the music. I turn to the side of my chair, and from under my napkin, I hesitantly move my hand over to her and softly touch the inside of her thigh. She sits in silence looking around the room and avoiding eye contact with me. I wait for her to pull away or even stand up, but her leg relaxes as I caress it ever so softly.

She continues to look away but moves closer to the table as if to conceal my arm that has inched its way to the top of her knee and slowly up her leg. She doesn't push it away as it continues up, caressing the familiar skin just below the outer lining of her underwear and scratching the lacing that separates us like an animal at the gate to create the softest of vibrations.

"Did you forgive me yet?" I ask as we both continue to look away from each other.

She still doesn't say a word. My hand pulls inside her undergarments and makes its way around her smooth hair and soft lips that are already wet as I slide my index finger in without any tepidness or hesitation. The force sends a jolt up her body that startles her neighbor, but not so much that either of us wants to stop.

Alas, I quickly pull my hand away and her gaze finally returns to me, those greenish eyes that enter my own as we stare in the night. I take my finger and lick it as she watches, salty and sweet to the taste that I take to the depth of my mouth and then again as she watches my every move, that's otherwise indistinguishable to the crowd. As she stands, my hand quietly inches up her skirt again as I reenter with my finger that reveals she's come alive.

A cloak of privacy masked in clattering plates, busied waiters, and a crowd captivated by the piano singer allows me to continue as she repeatedly leans into my hand. I steal glances into her face that struggles to remain calm, intact, and normal. Inside she's anything but as my movement becomes more specific, ebbing the spot that sends her over the edge; her knees buckle and for a moment, I think she might fall to the ground in ecstasy.

Catherine takes me by the hand to the door, and we slip out from the terrace and make our way to the staircase. She grips my hand as she raises it in the air to make the tighter corners between floors. We arrive on my floor, although I was hoping she would take me back to her room and avoid the guilty discomfort of having such a woman as her in a space that Jamila was in just a day ago.

My familiar hotel room door embarrasses me in this instant as regrets of the previous day fill my head. Life is so different with Catherine near, so much more complete, and yet, I would risk everything for the momentary distraction. I have shamed her, even if unknown to her, a feeling I don't ever wish to feel again. There's virtue in being with her. Holding her hand is as comforting as kissing her soft lips; the prospect of entering her is as enticing as imagining waking up softly by her side to smell her morning scent and see her eyes struggling with the day's early light.

There's a harmony between us, like a familiar couple who knows the rhythm of the other even after this short amount of time between us. While some women would have lingered in the doorway of an unknown room, Catherine makes herself comfortable. She roams the space and takes in the neon-lit terrace from a spot at the window that couldn't have been framed any better by the best of artists. I approach her from behind and wrap my hands around her waist, softly kissing the back of her neck and nibbling ever so slightly down the shoulder.

"You know, it was modeled after the royal Château d'Amboise in the Loire Valley where da Vinci died," she says.

"What's that, you mean Sunset Boulevard?"

"No, this hotel, the Chateau, it's really just a knockoff of some palace in France. It's so weird that despite its aristocratic ambitions it became this icon of pop culture and rock and roll."

"That famous comedy guy died here, right?" I say.

"Yes, but even more than that, it's always been a sanctuary for artists who made it to mainstream success, and yet crave this reclusion that looms in these dark and mysterious rooms that you can run away to in the middle of LA."

"So it's kind of an irony, right?" I whisper in Catherine's ear as my hands make it to the front of her still well zippered dress.

Catherine walks to the console and places her slight black bag on it. She opens the bejeweled top to pull out an iPhone that she carefully places in the docking station. She plays an unexpectedly folksy song as she hovers over the stereo a moment to adjust the sound to a perfect 1:00 a.m. volume that's neither too loud nor too soft as her hips sway seductively back and forth to the music.

"In the sixties, this hotel, actually, I think this very room was packed with the most famous rockers who ever lived."

"This one?" I respond in surprise.

"I think Led Zeppelin took a famous picture for their album cover just outside your window. The Mamas and the Papas did a famous magazine cover in your bathtub because they were too high to leave the room."

"And in between, you have people like us who would check in and out, getting to know each other more and more," I add.

"They'd also bring their groupies back to the room and have wild nights, at least until they found the one they liked the most. They all eventually pair off, at least for a little while."

"How do you keep all this information in your pretty little head?" I ask slyly.

"It's just so romantic; it makes you feel like you're part of their story, even after all these years. And then you had the Rolling Stones and the Beatles who would come and go in between weekends, where Jim Morrison would fall in and out of love, while Janis Joplin would wander the halls under a halo of pot smoke."

Catherine slowly unzips her corset-like dress down the side; the black fabric falls to the sides and reveals the blush of her pink skin. The dress cascades to the floor as she steps out from inside its capture. She walks to me in just her creamy pink garter and underwear that raises high on her waist with a lacy bra that attempts to constrain her breasts that erupt over the top. She's more playful than I have seen—part show and part innocent—as she moves to the instrumental sound that rolls across the room.

"Do you know who this is?" she says as she gazes into my eyes looking almost irresistible.

I remain silent and shrug.

"Oh my god, you've got to be kidding." She slaps my rear end.

"I'm sorry, I'm more of the hip-hop generation, I guess."

"That's simply unacceptable, Mr. Summers," she says playfully. "This is one of the greatest love stories ever told in music. When I looked into your eyes, those steely grayish-blue eyes, this song popped into my mind."

"These eyes?" I respond as I peer like an owl closer to her own perfect eyes wide-awake amid her story.

"'Judy Blue Eyes.' Actually, I think it's called 'Suite: Judy Blue Eyes.' It's the very reason the band Crosby, Stills, and Nash came to be in the first place. I think they lived in one of the bungalows for a while."

"Did they all love the same American woman?" I say, duplicating her back-and-forth dance as she slowly unbuttons my shirt down the front and caresses my skin as she progresses to my waist.

"Actually, the main singer was in love with this songwriter named Judy Collins. She has this impossibly angelic voice and intense blue eyes. The two of them had this hopelessly tumultuous relationship during a period of two or three years. And then, like so many other passionate relationships, they broke up, but not before he wrote this song and sang it to her."

"And now just the song remains?"

"'For all of us to feel and love and anguish with through hard times as we partake in the love that was and will always be as long as the song is played.'"

Then the song is interrupted by an incoming-text sound that halts the moment. Catherine seems shocked, concerned even, as she rushes over to her phone. I can see that a dark photo has popped up on her phone screen as she rushes it away with an almost frantic fingering.

"Boyfriend checking in on us, love?" I say in jest with an element of sarcasm.

"No, no, just work, my love," she dismisses.

"Work texting you at three a.m.?"

"I think it was from earlier today. It must have been delayed or something."

The music returns as I let the topic fade. Catherine grabs me by the waist and inserts both her hands into the brim of my trousers.

"Do I sense some jealousy, Mr. Summers?"

"Not at all; I just wanted the music to come back."

"So you like 'Judy Blue Eyes?'" she says slyly, pulling off my belt and unbuttoning my pants, which fall to the floor and leave me standing there naked in front of her.

"The only music I can hear is you, Catherine," I say as my erection rises.

She tries to lead, but this is where I take control. I grab her from behind and pull her in closer, thrusting my dick against her body as our mouths collide to the strum of love-struck rockers singing their wholehearted anthems in a mix of Spanish and English lyrics.

I unhook her bra from the back as it drops to the floor, massaging her delicate shoulders that frame her back and down her spine, working my way to the inside of her skirt that clings to her waist. She pulls me tighter as I scour the garment for its zipper. Her hand reaches back to help mine, and she pulls it loose from her torso, leaving her there in just her stockings. She tries to touch me, but I pull her hands away and place them on her body as she caresses herself. My actions become more aggressive as I lead her into the bedroom, holding her from behind at the waist as I push her down on all fours atop the bed. Her angelic hips round the edges of her garter. I pull it off in slow motion along with her stockings as she arches her back.

"Tell me what you want," I say again, pulling her tight and close into my dick, which intersects her pink flesh.

"I want you as close to me as possible."

She tries to rise to her knees, but I push her down again, dropping to my own knees on the side of the bed and caressing her calves as I make my way up her legs with my tongue. My hands trace the inside of her legs and pelvis. I can feel the heat from inside her against my hand, as I intentionally pass over her perfect pinkness again and again. She's the quick-sex kind of lover, as I try to strip her of years of bad habits that will ultimately have her dripping before I'm even inside her.

She struggles to get out of position, and I push her down again. My face makes its way to her ass, licking it on the outside, wetting it with my tongue before working my thumb up and down, and then penetrating just barely and then again. I want her to say something; I want her wild and begging, uttering words I'd never expect from those polite lips that remain lost in subtle, pleasurable moans. I hear her breath becoming long for what she wants most. I work her deeper and deeper from behind with my hands, as my tongue follows and enters her amid a personal scent that intoxicates me almost to the point of erupting.

"I want you inside me. I want you now!" she screams, squirming to get up as I push her back down and rise to my feet. I pull her up onto her knees and massage her breasts. Her back leans up against me and her head contorts back as our lips violently lock. She rocks harder and harder against me as my hands work their way down her stomach and inside to find her fully wet. I grab her with both of my hands and tip myself inside her ever so gently the first time. She arches back and takes me inside as deep as she can manage in an exhaustive breath, alas quenched as I thrust harder and harder to get deeper and deeper inside her. She exalts a sound so euphoric, so complete that I erupt fully within her and our bodies collapse atop one another.

A potent mix of pink Dom, jet lag, and sex that takes every ounce of you kept me in a deep sleep through morning. My eyes open to do a once-over of the room to recognize where I am. Although the location was unknown, I was thoroughly aware Catherine was no longer by my side. I rubbed my hand across the sheets that had turned cold and the pillow that looked as if it hadn't even been slept on. My thoughts churn as I wonder if perhaps she went back to her own room once I had fallen asleep, or perhaps she had other plans and failed to mention them to me. She's so hot and cold, consumed in the moments we're together and then she whisks away to her work-filled life. I've never had a woman whom I've had to chase, and quite honestly, it's refreshing.

Rain beats on a metal drain that drops onto the terrace just outside the bedroom window. It patters like loose change at the bottom of a rusty tin bowl, and it gives me a clue of what LA has in store for me today. Then a scent seems to arrive in my room out of nowhere, a mix of crispy toast and bacon that must be from a passing room service trolley, but as I listen beyond the sound of the rain, I hear the rattling of pots and pans and wonder if perhaps Catherine is still here.

I throw on my white boxers and wander the wooden planks of the hallway into the living room engulfed in a scent to a sizzling sound. I look through to the little kitchen that until now just seemed an unnecessary architectural addendum to this hotel's history. I see Catherine standing in a fluffy white robe, her hair pulled up over her spectacled morning face studying a frying pan in front of her.

I've never had a woman make breakfast for me aside from my mother, and that was so long ago. I cower and then step back to watch just a minute more. I see her delicate wrist maneuvering the plastic spatula, her elbow in the air, and a concentrated stare. The gas flame glows yellow and blue underneath a metal pan that appears as if it's been around since the hotel opened.

A surge of guilt drives through me as I watch her turn this anonymous hotel room into a home, if only for a moment, that's so contrary to what I allowed to happen with Jamila. My soul shrinks to face such a woman as Catherine with such a memory so fresh in my mind.

"Are you making me breakfast? Do I believe my own eyes?" I peek out from behind the wall; I startle her and she drops the spatula on the floor. She quickly picks it up and rushes to me with a tender, slow kiss.

"You know, it seemed like such a good idea until I actually had to cook it."

I wrap my hand inside her robe and around her back. I feel her gray-flannel sweats and white tank top that's even sexy on her.

"It smells extraordinary. I was lying in bed wondering where you might be, and then it was just this smell."

"I woke up early and got some work done and thought it might be nice to actually cook breakfast. I mean, how often is it that you have an actual kitchen in your hotel room?"

"I'd always just looked at it as a really large minibar." I laugh. "So, let's see what you have here … there's bacon and fancy eggs and some sort of fruit concoction."

"I know it's not much, but that's all I could bribe room service to bring me. They couldn't really understand why I would want to cook when they could just bring it already made."

"Well, I get it, and I love it. Is this a perk I can expect in the future?" I ask as I kiss her again on the back of the neck, pulling back her hair that smells of summer berries and cream.

"I always thought it was beneath a successful woman to want to cook, but to be honest with you, I find it really soothing and even fulfilling," she says. "I mean, how many things in life can you work on and at the end of it you actually put it in your mouth and savor?"

"Well, I can think of a few things," I say as I snuggle her in closer.

She slaps my hand away from the plate of bacon spread out on a paper towel blotted in oil.

"What can I do?" I ask as Catherine's attention turns back to what looks like some sort of frittata on the burner nearest the bacon. Toast sits ready on small square plates as well as a pot of French press coffee that's yet to be strained.

"You go sit over there, and I'll be there in two seconds."

Catherine has already set up a small seating area on the floor next to the terrace doors: a blanket lay out over the carpet with pillows tossed from the couch and a chunky candle she might have pulled from the bathroom. It somehow completes her entire fashionable breakfast scene.

"How do you take your coffee, David?" Catherine hollers from the kitchen.

"Strong and black, please." I like that she knows how I take my coffee now.

"How do you take your coffee?" I yell back at her, wanting to know every detail of her morning ritual.

"A little milk, but not much. Why do you ask?" She peers out from the kitchen for the answer.

"Just want to know, that's all."

Catherine emerges from the kitchen with a tray full of breakfast that frames her face in a zigzag vapor. She eases it onto the floor and an aroma of coffee, toast, fruit, and bacon envelops me. She firmly plants a kiss on my face before she snuggles next to me on the blanket.

"Go ahead, eat; it's going to get cold."

"What about you, aren't you going to join me? Oh, wow, this bacon is delicious. What's on it?"

"A little maple syrup and some pepper. It's in the magazine this month."

"I mean, does life get better than this?"

"You mean the girls don't cook for you in every port?"

"Ha-ha, very funny. Just you and my mom, actually," I say, fully consumed by my food.

"Was your mom a good cook?" Catherine asks innocently.

"She actually was. She would make me eggs in toast every morning before school and let me pretend they were eyeballs."

There's a nurturing side to Catherine that I actually haven't known since my mother passed away; she lingers with her stare to listen as I speak instead of looking away or getting lost in her own mind.

"When did your mother pass away?"

"She died two years after my parents divorced. She had lung cancer, and it was a truly agonizing six-month decline. In the end, I wished for her death. It was a very intense time for me. She died alone."

As I look down at the food, I realize the conversation has taken me back to a place I rarely speak about, but it comes natural with Catherine. She takes my hand gently, but not so tight that the moment feels forced.

"And why did your parents' divorce again?"

"Oh, you know how it goes. My father was a philanderer. We all kind of knew. It would creep up now and then as a kid; hints that I would catch in conversations between them. When I was at university, he got sloppier and finally found a woman he wanted for more than a night. It didn't last long, either; he did the same thing to her."

I take another slice of bacon that I eat with a wide, forced smile, somewhat surprised I confessed so much when I generally choose to avoid such a subject.

"Did he visit your mother while she was sick?"

"Let's change the topic; this is still a hard subject for me. The fact is they're both gone, and there's really no reason to discuss it and replay the whole thing in my mind."

"I'm sorry, I was just ..."

"No, and I want you to know. It just feels treacherous to judge the dead. I do love my father; it's just that his actions were so ghastly."

Catherine rises to take the tray back to the kitchen, perhaps a reaction to my pulling away emotionally. She holds eye contact with me in a solemn stare, retreating to a soft and soothing smile that looks down at me from above, as my mom would have given me as a child.

"Do you want some more coffee? I can go grab you some."

"Yes, please, that would be lovely."

CHAPTER 5

LONDOLOZI

I TELL MYSELF this is where it ends. This is where I stop before it goes too far. It will ruin my marriage and everyone, including David, when they find out about the incredible lie I've been living for almost six months. LA was supposed to be the end, the place where I told him I started seeing someone else or that I simply cannot continue this relationship. Then comes the long afternoons and lonely nights where I dream of him, his touch, and the endless conversations that leave me intertwined in emotion, unable to imagine my world without him. Then I tell myself just one more time, I'll give myself one more hit, just one more plunge into this hedonist fantasy that our relationship has become.

Shortly after returning from LA, I learned *Rogue* would be cutting back on travel stories and limiting budgets for travel even for interviews. The news sent my heart to a full stop. While they promised it was only temporary, it immediately deflated any hope I had of being able to sneak a weekend away to be with David. I resorted to seeking out freelance assignments like this one I've taken with *Departures*, the private American Express member's monthly. It's normally a gig when you're between magazines or building a résumé early on in your career, given the poor rates most publications pay and the amount of work you have go through to get an assignment.

And that is how I got here once more, this time packed into seat 32A on an eighteen-hour flight to Johannesburg, and using money that was tough to siphon from our monthly expenses and school savings. Freelance jobs like *Departures* pay a flat rate for a story, but reimburse for airfare and accommodations that are usually in some spectacular places. Being that it's a freelance assignment, it means economy-class airfare, unless someone at the airline is kind enough to upgrade you, which in my case didn't happen because the flight was full.

It's an odd assortment of travelers in the mid-plane en route from JFK to JoBurg. A mix of dapper African men in business suits who seem uncomfortable sitting next to their wives in traditional headdress, and American couples in their most casual of fleece, clinching their iPads, streaming flashing images that keeps the top of the cabin in permanent northern lights.

There's a refueling stop in Senegal on this flight, when at about eight hours after boarding, a flight attendant awakens me to realize I actually did the unthinkable and crossing halfway around the world to continue the affair I never should have begun in the first place.

"Ma'am, you'll have to raise your seatback to its upright position." She says in a soft voice while leaning across me to lift the window shade that lets in a blinding sunshine.

"I'm sorry, how long is the stop?"

"It's around forty-five minutes; we just stay on the plane and then continue as soon as refueling is concluded," her South African accent intones.

The preparation for landing feels as though you're at the end of your journey, only to land, linger, and then begin the whole takeoff ritual again. It's here, midway to South Africa that I want to fake an illness or stand up and scream. I know that upon takeoff I'm well past my halfway point on this journey and fast approaching the point of no return. But this is really the last time, even if I've tried before.

I'd managed three long months since the weekend in LA that brought us so close that I swore before both of us were irrevocably destroyed I would cut it off. I'd managed to get through the first few days, but by the end of the first week, I could do little to resist the urge of replying to his e-mails. Even in correspondence, he's able to rapture my heart like a schoolgirl waiting on the endless love letters from a late-day postman. He's able to lay out his daily rituals and things like running into an old university friend or disappointment in people at work that carry me away and back to him all over again. It doesn't take long before the e-mails are no longer enough as we evolve in a texted banter that inevitably turns sexual and ends up on Skype behind a locked office or a bathroom door and staring into his eyes and willing to do anything to have just a day more with him in the flesh.

Then there is my reality that I free fall back down into at home. The daily routine of cleaning house, grocery shopping after a ten-hour day, and making sure I get those daily hours with Billy after I'm home to read a Grimm's classic together or work on our drawing journal that takes us both away. I tell Matt he should use the time to do something for himself, whether it's enrolling in a carpentry class or taking up karate, as he's always wanted. All I crave is for a bit of conversation or experiences from him that include places outside of this apartment. Instead, Matt gets lost in his nightly television shows and always plans for the next day of nursery school and errands that inevitably looks exactly like the one before.

From Senegal, it's another numbing eight hours before the plane drops below the murky cloud cover to reveal an arid bush landscape dotted by soot-blowing smokestacks rising from humble stone buildings, clustered denser and denser as we approach the city. Joburg is urban and vertical, a Western capital, at least visually. I sit and feel this steel bird turn up her chin and land her underbelly with a gentle thud along the smooth landing strip so far from home.

Staring at the landing strip, I allow my mind to wander and imagine what a married life with David might look like, a more evolved existence with a man who gets me emotionally, physically, and intellectually. However, I usually don't get much farther than picturing myself waiting for him to come home from work or a business trip, as I realize he simply wouldn't be satisfied with a steady, consistent, somewhat boring family life where you don't go to glamorous dinner parties, fabulous hotels, or fashionable restaurants night after night.

The customs line in South Africa is different from other countries; an X-ray thermometer watches for those traveling with possible undetected viruses and makes even a healthy person wonder what happens if such a thing is detected. This is the point in my travels that fills me with regret; inward-pointed daggers insist that I never should have come on this trip to further this elaborate lie that's going to end in compound heartbreak. The proud faces of the African civil servants don't catch my inner doubt as they stamp my passport and declare me fit to enter and continue with this cycle of infidelity and moral lawlessness that despite all my will, I cannot quit.

Then the gates open to the madness that is an African airport. Legitimate drivers stand among tourist wranglers who look to make a penny off any service you'll go along with while simply making your way through the terminal. I try to face the annoyance with a patient mind; it takes all my will to remember the cruel life so many of these locals endure among the brutal townships of JoBurg.

"Ma'am, let me help you with that," says a young boy of no more than twenty with a metal-speckled smile. He rushes toward me and grabs the handle of my roller bag.

"Thank you, but I'm only connecting to another flight."

"Which one? Let me help you to the gate. I will find it for you."

A simple no is eagerly taken in these parts, and I hold a firm grip and force my way deeper into the chaos that is no more than a few steps from the customs area.

"Actually, there is my driver right there." I gesture to a man holding a handwritten sign with my name accompanied by the words Federal Air that will take me onto Sabi Sands and Londolozi.

"Are you Catherine Klein?" he asks.

"Yes, that's me." The young boy yields abruptly.

"Here, let me take your bag. We have quite a walk in front of us."

"Are you sure? I don't mind carrying it."

"No, please, I am happy to help. Where are you coming from, my lady?"

"I'm in from New York."

"That's quite a flight, isn't it?"

"Yes, indeed."

"Have you been on safari before?" he says as the crowds yield to empty linoleum floors and the endless ramps and people movers of the outer airport.

"No, this is my first time, actually."

"You have a wonderful treat in front of you. Londolozi is an incredible place."

"Yes, the pictures look incredible."

"And the Steyn family, they are very well known in South Africa, you know?"

"You mean the owners?" I reply, trying my best to keep up in my deconstructed hiking boots.

"Yes, the current owner's grandfather was one of the most famous men in the bush," he says with a disjointed accent. "He made very important documentaries about the lions around the family's farm where you go."

"Yes, I think I read a bit about that," I reply, even though this is the first I've heard of the Steyns other than to coordinate the booking.

"And then Madiba, you know we call Nelson Mandela, our former president, Madiba, yes?"

"Oh, yes, yes I do."

"Well, when he was finally released under de Klerk, he went to stay with the Steyn family in his first days outside of prison. Madiba recuperated there, breathed the free air, and watched the animals. It is at Londolozi that he dreamed of what would become of South Africa."

I feel like there is more to know from my tender as he drops me off in a kitschy safari-themed waiting lounge where clusters of older Americans gather around *CNN* on the television and eat from a table spread of morning pastries. A light rain falls on the window outside as a series of propeller planes, one smaller than the other, dots the tarmac. I barely have time to get out of my seat before I hear my name called. I am rolled out of the waiting area and onto the airfields where I am led to a plane in full gusto. My hair fights the wind, and I pull out my puffy jacket and climb into the rear of the four-seat plane.

I was expecting other passengers or maybe even David to surprise me on the flight, but alas, I am alone at the rear of the plane with two pilots hidden in the forward cockpit. The the door next to me is slammed shut, and I am left with just my thoughts. The pilot looks behind and then at his co-pilot, just for a glance, as if something was said between them. He gives a thumbs-up, and the plane shimmies to a roll along the tarmac and onto the runway. I think of Matt and Billy at home, and what they're likely doing at this early hour while I get farther lost from them this time, somewhere in sub-Saharan Africa.

The rain intensifies with the crescendo of the plane's baritone rumble as it approaches the end of the runway and comes to a full stop on a patch of gravel. The distance from New York feels overwhelming as I think of entire days passing in Billy's life without me; it's yet another plane ride that will simply take me farther away from the life I once knew. A lull in the engine sends the plane down the airstrip as if released by a slingshot. It propels faster and faster as the horizon shoots by, and the pilot pulls on the throttle and the plane lifts into the air. A horizon of smoke plumes rising from tented villages expands until the clouds intervene and a pause of gray erupts into a clear sun-filled blue sky.

My eyes close and thoughts drift upon arriving at Londolozi. I'll do a quick run-through of the property as well as an interview with one of the original family members before meeting up with David, who should arrive in the evening.

A mountain range outside my window seems to divide urban Africa from the wild bush as the cloud cover yields to an arid landscape of yellowish-brown shrubbery uninterrupted by man or roads or development of any kind. My eyes comb the land to see elephants or giraffes roaming through the bush, but from even this low altitude you truly just see the infinite vegetation and endless horizon.

In the distance a landing strip appears, forged from the dirt and dotted with a thatched hut where a lone truck sits. The plane circles with an abrupt tilt that offers a closer view of the airstrip and two rangers who watch our steep descent and wobbly landing. The plane circles back at the end of the runway to meet two men who sit atop a vintage Land Rover. The plane's engine comes to an idle and the hatch door is opened. I see a thick hand with a veiny, ebony-sheen arm, followed by a youthful face with flawless skin and an equaled smile. He reaches into the plane and meets my own.

"Welcome to Londolozi," he says with a husky voice and an African accent that vibrates high and low.

"Thank you, what an arrival," I reply, as my hand gets lost in his. I jump from the cabin and onto the fragrant land that smells a dusty mix of sage and eucalyptus that is Africa.

"Catherine, I am Nogo, and I am your trekker during your visit at Londolozi," he yells above the engine noise. "Over there is Duarte, he will be your game driver. If there is anything you need during your stay, please feel free to let us know, and we will take care of it for you."

"Thank you," I say as he strips me of my carry-on and loads it into the back of a glossy Land Rover with three rows of seating that rise in height toward the back.

"I am Duarte, lovely to meet you, Catherine."

Duarte is a brutish South African with an unabashed accent and fluffy blond hair that he shoves to the back of his head after every other gust of wind. His face, hidden behind a scratchy beard and a glazed stare, seems to see only the land in front of him.

"Catherine, we will be taking care of you while you are here at Londolozi. It is a very special place. You will always remember it. In fact, I am a bit jealous of those who come here and get to see it for the first time all over again. Each morning, we will come to wake you up at five-thirty, and we will go on a sunrise drive before breakfast. The rest of the day is for you to spend as you choose. Then, in the late afternoon, you will meet us in the main lodge at four o'clock for an evening drive that precedes dinner."

There's a rushed, rugged manner to his tone as his eyes wander the horizon and into the depths of the bush where it seems his true interests lurk.

"What are you looking for?" I ask.

"Well, we saw a female leopard wandering the area on our way to see you. She is the same one we saw last week but lost track. And now it appears she is back."

My eyes join their own looking through the dense foliage hoping to identify the cluster of spots or piercing eyes of the poetic predator. The trekker dangles off the front of the vehicle like a piece of chum perched precariously on a seat suspended off the front bumper. The vehicle stops as talk turns to a whisper, and the trekker takes a few steps before kneeling and poking at the dirt.

"He is looking for fresh tracks to see what direction she has gone," Duarte whispers before talking into a radio to share the details of the find.

Nogo points into the bush as he returns to his seat and grips his rifle secured at his side. The truck turns off the road and into thick shrubbery as the wheels that devour each tree and stump make a crackling sound before finding our way to smoother terrain.

"There, there," the trekker says to Duarte as the vehicle changes direction and the lone leopardess makes her way across the grassy savannah like a displaced phantom in search of home. The truck inches closer, and then he turns off the engine as we move to a silent stop. The leopardess moves uninterrupted on a path that will seemingly collide with us. She stares us down with her magnetic eyes that don't stray from the horizon. She only occasionally takes in a passing sound of baboons that play in the branches above.

"Does she not see us?" I ask in slight discomfort, worrying of our position. Sometimes guys like this will try to impress a visiting journalist.

"She knows we are here, but she does not associate us with anything more than a rock or tree."

Then she vanishes under the eye line of the truck. Nogo grips his rifle, and Duarte moves back to give me a better view as the leopardess makes her pass by only inches from my foot that sits unprotected in the open vehicle. I can hear her breath as she passes, unbothered by her solitude or her admirers who absorb the godly sight without a single camera or a word as our eyes meet. Her magnificent coat seems close enough to touch as she comes and goes without changing in pace or purpose.

"Not bad for the first ten minutes," Duarte says in a whispered voice. He starts the truck again and follows the leopard.

My adrenaline has made me forget my jet lag and even seeing David again. The bush makes everything in that world seem so inconsequential and far away.

"We will just follow her a little more to see where she is going. There is a pride of lionesses nearby, and it is very peculiar that she would travel in that direction."

The leopardess continues uninterrupted on her singular journey, a focus unyielding as if where she is going has long come into view and the miles between are conquered with each enduring step. She is otherworldly; her luminescent coat looks almost oily to the touch as it reflects the African sun. The truck trails a few feet behind with the wake of a bulldozer taking down small trees and shrubs that come between us as the leopardess weaves her way through the brush in near silence with an unapologetic elegance.

"So we need to get you back to camp in order to meet up with Tamaryn and get you sorted before the evening game drive," Duarte says.

"No worries, but that was truly incredible," I say as my leopardess vanishes from view into the thick brush and beyond.

"Please remember to wear warm clothes. Don't let this sun fool you; African winter is felt loud and clear come sundown," Duarte warns. "Will you be alone for the evening?"

"Actually, I'm meeting up with a friend who should be arriving later this afternoon," I reply, uncomfortable using words like boyfriend in regards to David.

"Well, we haven't had word of any incoming flights, but I will double check for you," Duarte continues. "If it's just the two of you this evening, we can seek the game as you and your mate wish."

Duarte hollers over the crackling sound of his radio to announce our arrival as ten minutes out as the downshifted engine collides with the smoother gravel road leading into Londolozi.

On the road, I see animals I don't even know the names of living in this sublime utopia. A group of warthogs grunts across the dry terrain, and in the background, a lone giant elephant tears limbs off a eucalyptus tree.

Upon approach to the camp, a circular dirt driveway is lined with two men standing with trays as the vehicle comes to a stop. A tall, stately woman with an air beyond her young age grabs the handrail.

"Catherine, alas, you're here. It's so nice to welcome you to Londolozi."

A flurry of staff rushes the vehicle as they hoist my bags over the metal sides, into the air, and onto a nearby ramp to avoid getting dirty. Her voice becomes softer as the motor stops.

"I am Tamaryn Steyn," she says, extending her arm as we exchange a genteel shake. My own hand is still damp from the welcome towel as an attendant offers me a Pimm's cup.

As I walk behind Tamaryn, the welcome chitchat is in full gusto. She asks me about my trip and my first game drive; I reply with curiosity as to the weather and game viewing ahead. My eyes, however, are transfixed on Tree Camp that will be my home. One of the reserve's luxurious lodges impresses my already wide eyes. The entrance of carved raw stone supports a towering thatched canopy suspended among hundred-year-old trees conjoined by a cantilevered wooden terrace.

A sprawling living room open on all sides is exposed to all the elements of the African wild, both good and bad. The room is clothed in a glamorous mix of exotic animal print rugs and zebra fabrics muted by pristine white sofas and chocolate leather club chairs dotted in whimsical pillows, and tables clustered with stone bowls filled with curiosities that lure my eyes closer. Tamaryn leads me to a small reception desk that feels like her own where formalities of safari check-in include signing away any responsibility should things go bleak, agreeing not to walk around after dark, and apparently taking the flirtation of the game drivers with a grain of salt.

As Tamaryn continues to explain nuances of communal meals, bush yoga, and daily laundry service during my three-day stay, all I can think about is when that manly silhouette who inhabits my deepest desire is going to walk up that stairway and make this incredible place even more special. Londolozi isn't the type of place the heart should be left alone; the generational glamour is truly of another time and exudes a romance I wasn't expecting, complete with roaring fireplaces and a panorama of trees that frame families of elephants playing along the horizon.

"And as for David, any idea as to when his flight arrives?" I ask.

"Actually, he should be joining you in time for the game drive at four o'clock. I believe he was due to takeoff from Joburg around now, and then it's about two hours to the lodge."

"And that's before dinner, correct?"

"Indeed, after the game drive, you'll have near half an hour to freshen up before returning here for dinner with us and the other guests. Tonight it will be dinner in the lodge, perhaps on the terrace, depending on the weather."

Tamaryn seems an unlikely candidate to be running the check-in at her family's lodge, given her position now as the main point of contact for outside journalists like myself. She seems to rotate between shifts in the bush to assist with lodge management and various marketing duties that seem to suit her well. Her makeup is slight, and her hair is unfussy and windblown that could be the result of a cold ride in on an open jeep. Her clothes are rugged and masculine but of impeccable quality giving her long torso a feminine silhouette despite their bulkiness. She seems relaxed in the lodge setting as if it were an extension of her own home supposedly attached to the existing property.

"Where do you live when in camp?" I ask, interrupting her description of the neighboring camps of Londolozi that are more family-minded than this luxury property.

"Actually, my parents have a house that's part of the main compound that also includes my grandparents' home."

"So there's a whole hidden life other than what guests see?"

"Yes, you can see the house on the ride in and out of camp, but other than that most guests never really know we are there."

"And where does the rest of the staff live?"

"There is staff housing at the perimeter of the main reserve, a good ways away from guests to avoid all their wild late-night antics being heard."

"But close enough to save us if need be in the night?"

"Exactly. Elephant wire surrounds the entire camp because elephants are so destructive, but any of the other predators can walk freely through camp and do. That's why you must stay inside after dark."

Once Tamaryn gets away from business talk, we enjoy a great conversation as we make the short walk along an elevated walkway to a row of cabins along a series of private footpaths. She discusses her younger brother's various bad-boy antics and her mother's classic cake served for high tea. She picks back up on shoptalk as she approaches my room and turns to details about its recent refurbishment by one of Cape Town's top designers.

My mind drifts as I notice I don't need a key or swipe card to get inside my room. A pull of the wooden latch called a baboon-lock opens a solid wood door revealing a large living room similar to the main lodge with fluffy couches, animal print rugs, and wooden tables stacked with glossy books and local artifacts. Timber screens conceal floor-to-ceiling sliding windows that open to a private veranda the overlooks the vast bush land and a small circular pool punctuated with double chrome lanterns and two chaise lounges. Tamaryn continues on a step-by-step tour that doesn't miss a closet description or explanation regarding the Charlotte Rhys toiletries. Every window is open and she describes every nuance in detail.

After explaining the exact time my trekker will come to the room to gather me for the evening game drive, she leaves me be with little enough time for a clothing change, let alone a proper bath and freshening up. Hunger has the best of me as well. I check out the minibar that's well stocked with every liquor imaginable, complete with chunky crystal stemware and fresh ice, but only a lone tin bucket of freshly baked chocolate cookies are left for satiating my enormous hunger. Nerves have me about half a tin deep in the cookies before the ranger arrives with a hefty knock on the door, and I realize nothing stands between him and me in my underwear other than a pull of that lever.

David didn't arrive in time for the evening's game drive, which meant it would just be Nogo, Duarte, and me roaming the vast terrain. I couldn't help but wonder if maybe something had delayed David or maybe a change in plans had him staying behind for business. Or maybe, just maybe, he met someone else.

I am the last to arrive back to the lodge for the evening game drive, and we make our way to the Land Rover where Duarte waits with the engine running. I stumble up the side of the truck and choose between three empty rows to settle inside the middle one.

"There's a hot water bottle under the seat for you as well as blankets to your side should you get cold," Duarte says as we pull out of camp and back on the now-familiar road we drove in on from the airport.

My mind concentrates on the sky, hoping to see any sign of an arriving airplane at the airfield, but there's only perfect blue and a sun toward the far corner looking to make its daily exit. I can't help but wonder what's become of David. Perhaps he found out about this great lie I've been living, or maybe he no longer feels the same as he did in LA or Paris. The driver and trekker are silent, concentrating on the terrain and allowing me to get lost in the landscape of my own mind. The gravel road retreats to a bumpier ride as our truck thumps by groups of impala that jitter with their heads as we approach and then disperse with an almost harmonic trot.

"Do you hear that, Catherine?" Duarte says of the baboons trumpeting overhead in a playful herald. "That is the male baboon calling alarm. There is something they don't like lurking in the area."

Duarte really needs no response to his question, just silence that he interprets as agreement, query, or confusion for which he elaborates further in all cases before jolting the truck in the direction of his own intrigue.

Evening turns to night without me noticing, and a biting coldness sets in, which isn't easily displaced with a now-cold water bottle or fleece blanket. As we drive over the bush, areas of the land are suddenly warm for no reason.

"The subterranean floor of granite that sits just under the dirt stays warm like a hot plate once the sun has set and into most of the night," Duarte explains. "It is here that many larger animals congregate in colder months and—"

Suddenly Duarte's explanation stops; the Land Rover erupts in silence before gliding to a stop above the crackling branches below us.

"Listen to that sound … it's the lioness."

In the night sky, a cry erupts that ricochets from the far reaches of the horizon like a high-pitched whale released from her soul that aches in its tone before coming to a desperate guttural surge she repeats into the night sky as she comes into view.

"Her call reaches out over the darkness over and over again in hopes the male lion will hear it somewhere in this great vastness and will return to her and her cub."

"Her cub? Where is it?" I say in a whisper that carries, despite my low voice.

"He's somewhere near, but what the lioness doesn't know is that the male she is calling was killed by the Ferocious Five, a group of five male lions that traveled in from the neighboring reserve and have killed all the male lions in the area except this one last cub."

"So what will she do?"

"She will eventually catch a whiff of their scent and realize she is in great danger, but we hope not before they hear her own call and come looking with a vengeance."

"Will they kill her as well?"

"That is yet to be determined; she most certainly will fight to protect her young cub," Duarte says with the most direct of eye contact, now fully engaged in this story of life and death.

"But the male lions want to mate with her and produce their own cubs," says Nogo. "So they will most likely distract her before killing the cub swiftly."

"It will be no match, as the cub is still very young, which is why she has fallen behind from her own pride," Duarte says.

"But that is lucky for her, as her own pride has already lost all their own male cubs," Nogo clarifies. "That is why the males are not hearing her call now; they are too busy with the new ladies."

"Don't the lionesses resist after their cubs are killed?"

"The lioness realizes that she must yield to the most powerful of the lions or die herself. She has no choice," Nogo says.

"But she also enjoys the instinctual mating she knows will produce another cub with a more powerful mate that won't let his offspring be killed by a more powerful male," Duarte clarifies.

From the shadows of an African sage bush, a fluffy young cub playfully bounces into view, completely unaware of his universe of danger as the mother sits well aware of the unknown that lies before her. Her two paws fully extended in front of her upright torso lay parallel to one another as her eyes slowly drift into a soft sleep only to reopen swiftly to complete awareness, without any motion, and then closing again to the deepest of momentary rest.

Our vehicle and its three occupants sit motionless as well, imagining the enormous burden this mother faces and the almost certain tragedy that lies ahead of her. My thoughts turn to Nogo and Duarte, who follow these sagas like a sort of wildlife soap opera that lives in a surreal dimension only feet from their touch and yet always beyond their control.

Perhaps my own fate is as clear to those that hover around me. Brutal answers to all my troubles and concern lurking so obviously on the horizon as my each step betrays those I most love to build a relationship of lies with David. My own tragedy seems as unavoidable as that of the lioness, and yet we continue into the unknown and inch closer and closer to danger.

The moment grows stiller as the cub lies down next to its mother, and the encroaching night settles into a quiet lull. I wonder if David has settled into our room, and speculate what our conversation will be during dinner. A crescent moon hovers in the distance, unassuming but made incredible by the setting of treetop silhouettes and infinite African bush etched in darkness.

"Should we get going?" I ask.

Suddenly, without waiting for a response, the roar of the engine interrupts the stillness. Duarte reverses away from this mother and son scene and back along the fallen path from which we arrived. The path looks unfamiliar in the pitch-black night, the front trekker illuminating our way as well as scanning the landscape for other predators that come alive by night.

Duarte finds his way back to the gravel road and then increases speed as we wind our way through the bush and along a plateau overlooking a meandering watering hole. Suddenly, we come upon a massive tree surrounded in illuminated hurricane lanterns wincing with candlelight, and a small bar arranged in the bush with a collection of antique liquor bottles and cut-crystal glasses that magnify the light of the tapered candles glinting above.

"This is incredibly truly incredible," I say as the engine stops once more, and Nogo rushes off the front of the truck to attend the awaiting bar.

"Your sundowner comes a little late, but also a little more magical on your first day," Duarte says as Nogo pours him a whisky straight up and my usual gin and tonic that I didn't even have to request verbally.

"If you look to the horizon, you'll see three hippos in the water. Normally, we would sit along the lakefront, but as it is night, we want to stay a bit farther away should they go on the move."

"They're such loveable creatures," I say with a sip from the thick glass that instantly soothes my chapped lips.

"They are the most dangerous animal in Africa," Duarte counters. "They kill more people than lions and snakes combined."

"While people are swimming or near the water?"

"No, it is during the night that they travel, and they will kill any person they come across with such a ferociousness you cannot imagine."

"Do they crush them or eat them?" I ask.

"When we get back to the lodge I will show you a picture of their mouth; it is incredible. You'd rightly take on a shark versus the bite of a hippo, I assure you."

Nogo unpacks a series of five round metal containers from his sack and puts them onto a silver tray with a wooden inlay that reveals a presentation of South African jerky known as biltong and fluffy meatballs with a name that doesn't make it any more familiar.

"And now we will leave you be for a few moments to enjoy and be at one with the sounds of the bush," Duarte remarks as he and Nogo take leave from the makeshift bar.

"You mean you're just going to leave me here, alone, with the Furious Five on the prowl?"

"The Ferocious Five. And no, ma'am, we will just be over there, but it is important that you hear and feel how it is to be one with the wild. Humans are the most feared of predators; trust me, you will be fine, even if we did leave." Nogo's accent calms my nerves as the men make their way to the back of the truck and out of my sight.

The quietness of the makeshift camp reveals itself much louder than I imagined. The bush lets itself be heard by the faded cackles of a distant hyena between the interspersed splashing of my hippos becoming more and more playful or agitated. It's hard to tell the mood of the wild, such a tenuous line between harmless and deadly that leaves those unfamiliar with the landscape always verging on the fearful.

The space feels entirely different on the ground outside of the insulated truck, away from the guides, and the safety that they provide. I can hear my breath and see it meet the air engulfed in a warm fog that vanishes into the night air. Each of my steps stirs the blotting of dried leaves on the ground, and the scent of Africa lingers in the air as if for me alone. The isolation is intoxicating and such a juxtaposition to the old me. I used to avoid being alone; I always filled my nights with dinners and dates with friends or anyone. I worried I would always be alone. The older I got, the more I started to think there was something wrong with me, something unlovable or unworthy.

I could almost imagine living here; getting lost in the wild and the animals in the bush that fill the lives of these people. Upon arriving, I thought it too isolated and too removed, but I actually feel closer and more engaged in life than I've felt in a long time. For the few moments on that ride, my mind actually drifted from thoughts of Matt and David to see what is directly in front of me. To be here and not become lost in Africa would be a feat that's impossible even for me.

The longer the men are gone, the more wild the sounds became. Although I'm unsure whether it's because the night is ripening and the wild is awaking, or because I am paying attention to all that is around me, and not that which lingers outside the scope of my immediate attention. The sounds are intense as the rustling in the nearby bushes gives me pause for a minute, unsure if I should get into the truck or run back to join the men.

Suddenly, the bush quiets and I can hear the voices of Duarte and Nogo returning to my side. "How did you do? No lions, I take it."

"You're so right. It's an entirely different experience being alone."

"It's like your mind's version of the eyes adjusting to brightness or dark light. After a minute, it's an entirely different world," Duarte replies as the men pack up the makeshift bar and load it onto a platform along the front of the truck.

"We should be heading back, as you'll be a bit short on time before supper." And with Nogo's words, I am reminded that David is somewhere in this great place, likely showering in preparation for dinner or sitting in the lobby waiting for me and all my khakis and linens to arrive.

As we make our way back to camp, the night is still. Nogo and his flashlight search in vain for our criminal lions, another leopard, or wild dogs that seem to be the most elusive to find. Near the road that leads back to camp, a lone elephant stands dazed under a tree as if waiting for a group to catch up.

"What is he doing?" I ask pointing to the elephant as the truck passes by, as if deeming it unworthy of stopping.

"Oh, that is a sad old man, that one," Nogo laughs. "He is an older bull, and when a male elephant is chased out of a herd, he usually lives the rest of his life alone. They don't take him back."

"Never? You mean he is forever isolated from his group."

"Yes, except the occasional mating he steals from other herds. Maybe he makes another family, but very rarely, as once they are the bull they don't play well with other bulls and are too old to win a fight for dominance. So they are alone."

As we approach the camp, Tamaryn stands there again with her attendants ready with water and a refreshment towel. They are illuminated by a row of flickering candles that line the stairway to the main lodge.

"Welcome back. How was the game drive?"

"Still no sign of the Ferocious Five, but we saw the mum and cub that seem to be doing all right."

"Has she gotten wind of them yet?" Tamaryn asks.

"No, but it can't be far off," Duarte replies.

My focus is now on my own primal desire and wonder whether David has made it to camp.

As their animal conversations continue, I make my way alongside Nogo into the main lodge hoping for my first glimpse that lingers in my mind when David is away.

"Um, Catherine!" Tamaryn yells from behind.

"I'm afraid David didn't make it in on the last flight, so I assume he must have missed his flight or has been delayed."

Her words echo through me as a cloud of uncertainty blocks all the serenity and clarity I felt just moments ago.

"He didn't leave a message or call the office in JoBurg, so I would think he's simply delayed and will be here in the morning," she continues.

She handles me with the finesse my mother would use when my high school boyfriends would break up with me. My mind prepares my heart for the worst; David may not come at all. A sense of embarrassment overwhelms me, reddening my cheeks. Here I am, a grown woman with a family, leading this secret relationship with a man who probably has little more interest in me than a passing fling. Even worse, I'm willing to risk everything just to have a few minutes more with him.

"We don't have a lot of time before dinner, Catherine, so just a freshen-up and Nogo will accompany you back to the lodge."

I didn't even respond to Tamaryn. I was afraid my voice would crack or she would read my morose face fraught with disappointment. All that is magical of Africa is wiped from my mind, and thoughts of David not even having the decency to e-mail or call the lodge to let me know his decision not to join or need to cancel. There was a silent, sullen melody that accompanied Nogo and me on our walk to my cabin, a journey I was reassured once again that I could not make on my own.

I collapse behind the door with the baboon lock pulled shut behind me. A feeling of nausea and doom coupled with my lack of sleep and jet lag overwhelm me. I get up and check the room, opening the closets and even looking inside the shower and along the terrace to make sure he wasn't hiding as a joke or a wonderful surprise. Reason and sanity slip away as tears erupt. I think of his face, the scent that lingers in the nape of his neck, and then I imagine someone else holding her head close to his. Perhaps he's met someone else; why wouldn't he? A guy like that would have so many more options than with just someone like me.

My tears defy my mind's attempt to insert reason into this moment. My chest echoes in a sullen melody. I imagine never again feeling the caress of his hand, hearing the gentleness of his words, and seeing his eyes that hold me even when weeks and weeks force us apart. My mind lurches back into the moments swimming in Rio, seeing him in the hallway of my Paris hotel, and that blissful, long night in LA. I quickly come to the realization it all may be over.

Although I search for reasons to believe, the simpler explanation seems the more obvious one. He must have met someone; he must have found someone who better fits him and his lifestyle. My mind cannot comprehend the thought of never seeing him again, never looking forward to the next e-mail, or never feeling the touch of his hand. This must be his parting routine, a vanishing act with no notice or explanation. Still, I hold onto the belief that he's simply not that kind of man. I pull out my phone to double check if perhaps an e-mail or text has come through. But there truly is no service in this desolate span of southern Africa.

As I sit collapsed on the floor, I hear Nogo along the walkway gathering other guests and escorting them to dinner. Quickly, I rush to the bathroom mirror. I see this tired, dry, mascara-streaked face glowering behind a wrinkled brow and withered eyes drawn exactly as a woman my age, riddled with pain and loss of that godly vice she can no longer imagine life without. I hear a sturdy knock to which I consider saying I'm too ill or too tired to make it to dinner. I struggle to throw on a fresh shirt and chunky cashmere knit to emerge to a recently showered Nogo who beams as bright as the moon.

The walk to the lodge feels longer than on the way to my room. My eyes peer up and see magnificent trees that line its terrace ignited in lanterns and a fireplace erupting in bluish flames as we take the few steps up the main staircase. A group of well-dressed guests huddles at a small bar in a corner of the room. Nogo leaves my side, and I make my way to join them given the lack of any other option. Their American voices coupled with a few non-native accents sound crisp in the air as I approach the back of a younger woman with silky black hair and wearing an oatmeal wrap-coat that looks like a woolen macramé.

My mind doesn't accompany me to dinner, it remains back in the room scattered on the floor looking for pieces of my life to hold to my heart in an attempt to get through the first of many unimaginable nights. The well-dressed American is Heidi, and her husband is Justin, both of whom are on the second leg of their two-week honeymoon. I meet a Midwest-type couple whose names I can't recall. They are on their trip of a lifetime that they sacrificed most of their working lives to afford. An older South African couple, who considers this a long-weekend trip from their Cape Town home, shares idle conversation of the other lodges in the region. Then there's me.

Luckily, a late arrival for dinner meant cocktail conversation stuck mainly to pleasantries before making my way to one of four tables arranged on the terrace. Mine is the one closest to the edge lit by candlelight with two plates facing each other a good distance from any other guests. Trees reach out over the tables touching each other longer and more gently than any humans do. Candles flicker everywhere, and the sound of the infinite African night plays like a soundtrack that couldn't be more dramatic and vibrant. I had envisioned more of a communal table, but alas, I will sit alone in perhaps the most romantic dinner setting I have ever witnessed.

Tamaryn approaches through the lodge, by the bar, and onto the terrace in my direction. She looks even more regal in her dark, still-wilderness-minded clothes with a fashionable scarf tied meticulously around her neck.

"Catherine, I thought I would join you for dinner if that's okay?"

"That would be lovely, truly lovely," I say, despite wishing for the solitude as I do everything to avoid erupting into tears.

Tamaryn takes her seat opposite me and undoes her scarf with a regal, circular movement. Staff rushes to her side to pour the water, place the bread, arrange the butters, and pour the wine she selected before arriving. She lives up to pictures of the proud and adventurous relatives who precede her and lay a foundation for family and legacy that I am sure will endure longer than any of my own will.

"So tell me about your glamorous life in New York. I always dreamed of living there," she says as she leans into the table and grabs her glass of crisp white wine.

"New York? Well, it definitely lives up to all your expectations, but somehow you still find yourself complaining about it at every opportunity," I laugh.

"Oh dear, but isn't that with any place?"

"I guess. Sometimes I find that the parts of life like getting to work or going shopping or running to a doctor's appointment is an afterthought in most places, but in New York, it's almost a job in of itself. I mean life in New York is truly hard, and you do have to stay a pace ahead to just get by, let alone hopes to one day thrive."

"From the outside, it seems so glamorous. It's really a dream for so many kids I know. However, I see what you're saying. I mean, as a child, I would beg my parents to take us to Cape Town of Joburg and now here I am as an adult continuing the life that was laid for them by our grandparents."

"There's an intimacy here that surprises me. I thought that with so few people in such a large space, you would feel isolated. But really, it forces you to connect with everything around you; even your staff is incredibly engaged with one other."

"Yes, I guess it's the legacy of the African tribes, they forge incredible bonds that I assume we've picked up on and continued with our own traditions," she says in a hushed, soothing tone.

"It's really an incredibly special place," I reply.

"And tell me about David, have you been together long?"

"In all honesty, I'm not even sure if we're really together." I pause, shocked by my truthfulness and hoping to restrain myself from exploding into tears.

"You know, it's a long-distance thing," I continue. "It's intense when we're together, and when we're apart, we attempt to keep that memory alive through e-mails and text. But really, David likes being single, and I know that in the end, it will be my heart that's going to break, not his."

"Isn't it always the story though, as women?"

"I would have thought it was a little different here."

"You know, I struggle here with all these single men who pass through the bush looking for fun and adventure. I watch them all pass and wonder when one of them will stop and say, 'You're worth it, you're worth stopping and getting to know better and maybe, just maybe, having a life together.'"

"And it's coming for you, I can feel it. You have such a wonderful energy inside that it's just a matter of time. You're also still very young," I insist, noting the slight age difference between us.

"Not that young, trust me," she replies.

There's fragility to Tamaryn that I had not previously noticed, tippy-toeing through a maze of emotions that leaves me forgetting my own woes and remembering similar thoughts that plagued so much of my own life.

"You must be patient; he's out there somewhere, I assure you."

"There was one guy I dated for about a year, and I thought everything was going really well. He met my parents, got along with my brother, and we'd talk about our future all the time."

"And what happened?" I ask.

"One day we woke up, he turned over, and told me he wasn't in love with me. It was if he stated a fact he knew all along, he had tried to make it work, he really did. Then one day, he simply had enough … of me, that is. He said he loved my family and loved the life, but he didn't love me."

"But hear this, it is better to wait until you find the right guy and not just the one who stops, and you worry that another one won't come along in time."

"Yes, but I very much want a family. I can't imagine growing old here alone, watching everyone else have what I want as I pass through life completely alone." She muffles a choke while taking a slow sip of the wine.

"You won't be. You must be patient and wait until love finds you, please believe me. You don't want to marry someone who only meets most of what you want."

"I try to reassure myself of that, but it's a story I've been retelling inside over and over again. At a certain point, you have to prepare for the alternative."

I see a younger version of myself in Tamaryn as the intensity of the conversation dead ends in silence. The only resolution to our questions is a story that only time can tell, and we are both smart enough to know it. I could see we were eating faster than the other guests who were just taking their entrees as we progressed with dessert. In mutually resigned smiles, we ate a caramel-laden dollop of ice cream before she invited me back to the bar for an after-dinner drink. Citing jet lag, I excused myself to return to my room. We separated with a long, comforting embrace knowing the emotions that stirred within both of us.

A different guard walked me back to the room. He remained silent as we exited the lodge and made our way with a torch to the elevated walkway. Shortly before we arrived at my room, he grabbed my arm and hesitated. A rustling in the bushes revealed itself as a charming warthog that had wandered into camp. With a soft laugh, we parted ways. I rejoined my misery, and he made his way back to whatever it was the guards and staff members do come nightfall and freedom.

With the closing of the lock, I was immediately grief-stricken again, falling on my bed and imagining what could have been with David if we had just one more time. I imagine us lingering in the morning, watching the bush ignite in sunrise, or waking in the middle of the night to feel his warm naked body against mine. I felt the need to talk to him, but suffocated from the lack of cell phone or e-mail communication that might have kept me from knowing what actually happened. My deepest fears taunt. I resign myself that he met another woman, one who's closer to his age and life in London, who's more available than my life allowed.

My thoughts return to Billy and Matt, who sit at home with hearts full of love, unknowing what I have become. Ultimately, I tell myself that David not arriving could actually be for the best. I still love my husband and really don't know when I would have ever found the strength to tear myself away from David or found the courage to end my marriage. I can't imagine being a single mom explaining years later to my son what happened to his father and me, and why I was willing to give up so quickly on him and us. I'll give my version of how I imagined everything so differently in the beginning, the way all other divorced women do. This wasn't what was to become of any of us.

Maybe life can still be different with Matt. Everything was more passionate between us prior to having Billy; we were social, and he was motivated to do so much more than just be a stay-at-home dad. I wonder how we can ever get back to that place, how I can ever look at him and not think of my enormous betrayal. How do I learn to love his touch again, to look in his eyes, and not imagine that it is David's hands and body that I so crave? When do the memories of David's body and scent retreat from my soul and allow me to be the wife and mother I have failed to be? I can't help but think that despite my heart's utter pain, David not arriving is the universe's way of saving my soul before it is all too late.

Without taking off my clothes or even my makeup, I turn off the lights and allow the darkness to cradle my lost heart. As the tears ease, the sounds of the outside penetrate and release me from the inward consumption that has left me with nowhere to go or think or feel. After I pull off my shoes, I stand and make my way to the well-secured door and push it open to leave only thin netting between the wild and me. *Come have me*, I think, and with it all this misery. I run back to bed and hide under the covers. The sounds magnify so much more with the open door. The chill sets in immediately, forcing me to find that warm spot in the bed again left by my prone body.

My mind drifts back to the first time I actually allowed myself to talk to David in Rio, thinking that just one conversation would be harmless. Then the reassuring promise that a day together would mean nothing and that a simple kiss wouldn't lead to anything else. Then there's that moment you fall face first and head into this place where every fantasy you ever dreamed, and even some you didn't, are fulfilled by the flesh. You tell yourself that this man can only live in this compartmentalized world of sporadic weekends, and that if shown the real you, he would vanish before your eyes, but you continue to dream of only him.

I hear once again that faint call from earlier in the evening, the incredible call of the lioness that she sends to search the night for her fallen mate, not knowing he is gone, and that daunting misery that lies in her path. She calls again and again and again with a rhythmic precision unyielding to time or sleep or hunger. Her anguished lullaby comforts my pain, tempers my loss, and helps me to want to live. It hushes me to sleep, knowing that despite the enormous defeat, I will ultimately survive and be again.

A thump on the door at 5:00 a.m. sends me into a state of terror, a combination of my eyes not adjusting to the darkness and lack of remembering exactly where I was this morning. An African accent is indistinguishable except the word coffee that alerts me of my surroundings and the numbing cold that has penetrated me to the bone.

"We will meet you at five-thirty," says the man. I hear a series of heavy footsteps that follow and slowly fade to silence on the outside walkway.

Reality of the place, the situation, and the new day taunts me as I pull the door open and take my tray of coffee steaming inside a tall French press. There are two cups next to a plate of sugar-topped cookies the texture of biscuits that crumble at a poke of my index finger.

As I sit on the bed looking at my watch with only ten minutes left before I am due on the truck, I am tempted to ditch this place altogether, but the lack of communication with the outside world makes it hard to justify a family emergency, or at least knowledge of one. I consider saying I'm sick, but then they'll summon their own doctor. With no escape, I must slip on my jeans, pull on my coat, and tie my scarf around my neck as I go out this door and begin my old life again, as it should be, in this post-David world that I now face.

As I make my way down to the lodge, I can see other guests making their way out and into the trucks. Duarte lingers at the bottom of the stairway, most likely wondering if I would show or choose to spend my day with eyes closed in what could be the most majestic place on earth. Even I, in all my despair, can see it would be a great tragedy not to let this place affect me and see as much as my eyes can take and my heart can bear this day.

"Good morning, Catherine. Good night's sleep, I hope?" Duarte says, looking more handsome this day than the last, his beard, and wavy blond hair groomed.

"Yes, wonderful, actually. I could hear the lioness all night."

"Good memory. Yes, we all did, actually, until around three o'clock when she stopped or moved along the riverbed where sound doesn't travel as well."

"Do you think the cub is still with her?" I ask.

"Well, he would have been fine as long as she was calling. After the interruption, it's anyone's guess. But before we head out, did you want to grab a bite of food?"

"No, I'm not much of a morning eater, so let's be on our way, as I don't want to hold you guys up."

"Well, it's just you in the truck again, so there's no problem, really. Also, I wanted to let you know that Tamaryn checked with the Joburg office, and all flights were on time from London yesterday. There was no word from David. But communication is very slow in the bush, so perhaps something kept him back in London?"

"Yes, perhaps. His work is very busy, so who's to tell, really."

"So let's be on our way and see if we can track down some of those male lions. Also, there was a rhino spotted nearby last night, so we'll try to see if we can catch up with her."

With an unyielding gusto, the truck roars away from the lodge and temporarily from all my angst and sadness. The morning air is alive; the naive precursor of a harsh day for all that inhabits this magical place and may likely face its death.

It's a short drive before we arrive to our first idle of the truck—a family of twenty or so elephants are en route to the local riverbed. The agitated bull is the first to trumpet our arrival. He turns to face us and puffs his ears with a siren that startles even Duarte, if I'm to read his hand placed tightly on the ignition key. The bull's front foot kicks up a plume of sand visible in our headlights as he jolts forward and then to the side as if to test our vigilance. He trumpets again, and suddenly Duarte flips on the motor and speeds a few yards up sending the bull after us just a few steps and then retreating to the rest of his family and away from our truck.

"That was a testy one," Duarte whispers.

"Do they ever actually hit your vehicle?" I ask.

"Not only will they hit your truck, they will trample you and everyone inside it without hesitation." Duarte continues, "It's a new bull for the group, and he's just proving to the ladies that he won't take any shit."

We linger on the elephants for a good while, trailing them as they round the path leading to the river with its own share of toothed demons, but also the elephants' source of replenishment. The younger elephants emerge from the shadows of their mothers and cautiously test the water before indulging in a sunrise drink. Stillness lingers everywhere as if life isn't quite ready to take a breath from the daunting night and all its deadly dangers.

"Should we try to find that rhino?" Duarte asks while restarting the motor and pulling away. The elephants barely even notice our departure. My eyes linger on the moms and their doting stare under those long eyelashes and gentle gaze that never seem to leave their children. It makes me think of my child, long removed from my own watch as I sit in this otherworldly place doing that which I now regret having done.

We drive endlessly without seeing much more than another grouping of impala that shudder with an ominous noise negated by their delicate appearance each time we pass. Duarte seems frustrated and stops the vehicle in the middle of the road. Nogo jumps from his seat and looks at the tracks in the dirt that pace down the road.

"It's the brothers; I can count four different paws." He continues up the road, "And I also see the older paw prints from a young cub that's probably with our lioness."

Nogo looks farther down the road as Duarte turns shaking his head.

"That's not a good sign for your cub," Duarte says in a soothing tone, diminished from his matter-of-fact ways of the previous evening.

"But unfortunately, we need to get you back to camp to meet everyone for breakfast. We've already been late two days in a row, and I don't want Tamaryn to get angry with Nogo."

Nogo looks up from the road and returns to the truck, leaving his scattering of tracks in lieu of Americans who hardly need another meal, and me, who will sit through it counting the minutes until this entire experience is behind me.

As we round the bend, the lodge comes into sight. Once more, the familiar welcoming procession lines the circle outside the lodge and the black faces chime with a smile even at this early hour. As we approach, I realize a new group must have arrived at the lodge. I see a genteel older couple standing at the stairs next to a tall and elegantly familiar man with jet-black hair and a smart blazer with its lapel pulled high under a chunky knit scarf that blows behind him with the wind.

As the truck stops, I forgo the pleasantries and towels and make my way to the man, who with a single shift in weight from his right to left leg, drains all the hurt and loss I have felt in the last day. It is replaced with complete and utter exultation upon seeing those familiar arctic blue eyes that pierce through my hurt and anger among his fogged breath and making his pink lips even rosier against his fair skin.

"David? David, is that you?" I yell out, as if disbelieving what my mind attempts to process in front of me.

"Catherine, my dear, get over here."

My eyes and heart cannot believe that it is he and this is not some sort of dream. He pulls my hand and I grab his sleeve with my other. I remove his soft calfskin glove, touch that familiar flesh of his inner palm, and hold it against my own. His smell returns as I touch his warm hand to my lips. He looks at me, and I realize I have collapsed into a sea of tears despite my smiling face and concentrated expression, trying not to interrupt their conversation at hand.

"Catherine, are you all right? You're flush. My dear, are you crying?" David pulls me in front of him and wraps his arms around me.

"No, I'm just so happy to see you. I'm so terribly happy to see you."

"Babe, I'm so sorry. It ended up that my ticket was booked on the wrong day, and it was impossible to change," he says as his brow furls. "Unless I was willing to sit ten hours in coach. I hope you don't mind, I just wasn't in the mood to do that after the week I had."

"We rode almost twenty hours in coach from Atlanta, so you're not going to get very much sympathy from us, mister," the motherly woman says as she grabs her husband by the arm in a torque of seasoned affection.

"But I have to tell you, it's so little that we see each other that I was tempted to just rough it."

His hands grip me tighter, and his body envelops me in a warm cocoon that makes all my pain and fear slip away, as well as any thought of ever being able to walk away from this man.

I would trade decades off my life for one moment with David; his scent makes everything else in my world seem secondary. I thought I would never know what it is to touch him again, to feel his hand on me, and know the stare of his eyes into mine. There is no turning back in this moment. Paralyzed in love, I cannot imagine for a second not having him in my life.

"So what's the plan, exactly?" David ejects me from my thoughts. "Is it breakfast time or the time we go on the road to look at animals?"

"Actually, I believe they are just coming from the drive, so you can freshen up and then meet everyone back in the lodge," says the older woman again, lending her guidance even though she's barely just arrived.

"I really would like to change shirts and get sorted, do you mind?" David asks as if there was anything else I wish to do in this moment, be near him flesh to flesh.

"So, we are going to the room and will be down in a few minutes," I insert, pulling him away before even finishing the sentence.

A guide joins us on the short walk to our room despite it being safely daylight out. The accompaniment simply prolongs my agony of us being so far apart, not conjoined to chase away the inner fears that filled my night and had me believe all was over between us.

The guide remains on the walkway as we make our way to the door, me first and then pulling David in behind me.

Then the world stops and outside can be anywhere and everywhere at the same time. I tuck my hand under his shirt and feel his skin that's warm from the soft lining. I snuggle my nose under his collar, collecting the concentrated scent of which I simply cannot get enough. He nudges my head with his, tipping me up as our lips meet and mine devours his lower lip and my tongue ventures to touch his top teeth and have just a little bit more of him. My tears amplify when he interrupts our kissing.

"My dear, look at you," he says. "I hope you can forgive me for being a day late. I tried calling you, even at your work to leave you word that I wouldn't make it in time. It's virtually impossible to get a hold of people out here; even the reservation personnel were helpless."

His words send a jolt through me as he backs away and moves closer to the window that still frames a panorama of mist blanketing the bush.

"Did you talk to my assistant?" I ask casually that disguises the urgency.

"I'm not sure who I talked to, actually. They asked if I was your husband and I said no." He takes an excruciatingly long pause and turns to me. "But then I thought, maybe she means boyfriend? They passed my call from one nonresponsive, flippant person to the next, and then I sort of just gave up."

The closer David comes to my real world, the more I sense the impending doom of this situation. I know there are but two choices in this: one is to stay and continue this hedonist fantasy until the truth prevails, or cut it off cold here and now. Having endured an entire night believing he was gone from my life, I am tempted to tell him the truth. I can't imagine suffering the previous night twice, even if that means forfeiting all that could have been until the very end.

"I just want to talk to you and feel your touch," I say, pulling him from the window and back to me.

"Sometimes, I feel as if you're only half interested in this, and other times, I feel as though it means everything in the world to you," he says questioningly.

"I'm here now. Last night I lay here thinking you weren't coming, that maybe you had met someone else."

"Do you think I'm the kind of guy who would do that to you … that I would simply not show up?" he says with a truthful gaze.

"No, well, I don't know. People are always unpredictable when they lose interest in someone; I didn't know how you would behave. You don't really know how people will act until it's actually happening, and it's ultimately much more awful than you could ever have imagined. The aftermath of relationships is always such an ugly place."

"Well, let me assure you, there will be a proper discussion, regardless if you want it or not, when and if things aren't working. And anyway, why would I toss it all in the bag, we are getting along quite nice, I think, or not?"

"No … yes, of course. I just want you to know that you mean a lot to me, and I don't want that to go away."

"I feel the exact same way, Catherine. Do you think I would travel all this way to be with someone I wasn't keen on?"

"I hear you. It's just, no matter what, you must promise me that no matter what happens, you'll talk it through with me and not just vanish from my life."

"You're not going to get rid of me that easily, I can assure you of that, Catherine."

I begin unbuttoning his shirt, craving him even closer to me. I can sense his sincerity growing with my vulnerability, which I camouflage in passion as I pull off his shirt and throw it to the ground. He kicks off his shoes as I unbutton his snug jeans from around his waist, tugging them with my hands while grabbing the inseam of his white boxers that slowly leaves him standing in front of me nude. He looks as though drawn by Michelangelo, his broad shoulders taper down his back to a narrow waist with its veins that tuck around the side of his prominent hipbones that I kiss once on each side.

As he stands in front of me, his dick is swollen and elongated under its fleshy covering like some sort of Italian god carved of marble. His perfection is irresistible. My lips make their way down his thighs and his muscular hamstrings where the furry black hair thickens toward his prominent kneecaps that protrude out above his muscular calves. I look up at his body, his dick now fully erect and tilting up toward his abdomen, pulling him forward enough to reveal an underside of coarse, rosy skin. The hair thickens as it intersects his perfect front and rear body, and he pulls me up with a single tug and our faces once again meet.

There is compassion to David that I haven't seen before; perhaps he's reacting to my sadness, as he slowly erases my fears. Then that incredible dance ensues; he pulls me through the doorway and onto the terrace where an outdoor shower sits concealed behind a small plunge pool. His upright body and protruding manhood makes no notice of perhaps those able to see in from beyond, and he takes me in tow thoroughly in awe of his immodesty. He turns on the water and tucks his head under the spout that erupts with piercing cold water.

The sun warms the flesh as splatters of coldness dot my naked body. My nipples awaken to full arousal, and I drop to my knees. David pulls me back up by my arms, into the air, and onto the railing, that surrounds the small stone shower. My legs straddle the side with wood prone to splintering as I perilously dangle from the edge and all insecurity falls far away. The cold water pours down my body, and I forget that I am anything but the most desired object in his world. David says nothing; he simply drops to his knees and between my legs, allowing the water to roll off my body and into his warm mouth that he spills back on and inside me. The sensation is almost surreal, sending me arching in ecstasy as I hear the trumpet of elephants in the close background.

His thumbs work my flesh, delicately tracing me fully from both ends before rising above me and thrusting inside with a force that almost sends me over the edge. There is a primal magnificence to his sheer strength; it's almost like the instinctual rhapsody of two creatures consumed in a mating ritual. The cold water chills his skin. I kiss and then bite his neck with full force. He responds by grabbing my face and forcing his thumbs inside my mouth as far as he can reach, then he kisses me, and then thumbing me again as I struggle for breath. His rhythm intensifies to where I lose all control in climax, and I feel him explode inside me as he holds firmly with two hands on my back. He's drained of all passion and emotion, falls limp, out of me, and onto the chaise next to the pool. His long torso glistens with water under the winter African sun. As he lies there, I pull myself under the shower and savor what remains of him still inside me. I feel as though the world could not be any more complete even if it's only in this moment and only in this instant. He is a perfect sight, his eyes closed and legs rolled out to the side in vulnerable dominance.

There is a glamorous malaise to afternoons in Africa. David slept on the terrace through most of the day, and I worked on my own story of Londolozi. Time ticks slower and life is more about actual living in this wildly magical place that transports you to a bygone time as giraffes, elephants, and hippos head across along the horizon. In between, we would meet for a kiss in the doorway or outside on his chaise, and I would tuck myself next to him and bask in the winter sun that felt as hot as any summer day. He enjoys his silence, taking to whatever book or magazine he can find in the room and settling in for a good hour before making his way over to me with another kiss. By the time of the evening safari drive, I had pretty much convinced myself that I could live in Africa, or anywhere, as long as he is by my side.

David emerged from the bathroom bundled in his quilted plaid Moncler and I in a heavy sweater as we made our way together, hand in hand, out of the room and back to the main lodge.

"So, he finally showed up," Duarte says to David as they exchange firm handshakes.

"I was polishing up on my lion tracking skills, that's all," David playfully replies as he climbs into the truck and onto the front-most seat behind the driver, closer than I would have preferred.

"That's what they all say until they come face-to-face."

"So, what will we be following tonight, gentlemen?" David says to Nogo. All three men, now fully in conversation, left me the doting woman to enjoy their back-and-forth dialogue. The talking elevates to new heights as they tell the story of the male lions. They talk about how the mother has tried to stay away from them after catching their scent. David encourages Duarte with more questions about the flora and fauna as well as tracking techniques used by the natives. Between pauses and dramatic tales, David turns to me with a kiss and holds my hand tight under the warm blanket as my mind and heart exhale in happiness.

The chatter comes to an abrupt halt as our truck rolls to a stop, and we can hear rustling in the bushes as well as the thumped heartbeats of our guide and tracker. David grips my hand as I slide closer to him for a better look.

The sun has fallen and the night settles between twilight and darkness; a deep chill has set into the bush. And there, in a close pack of four, the lions encircle the lioness. She is the color of sunlit wheat with a mane of cleverly soft hair and ferociousness that reveals itself through a series of trebling roars that rattle the nerves and make even the brave feel just a bit fearful. Their heightened purrs are aggressively amplified with one of the four males showing scrapes of a fight not won. The wounded mother limps under a tree, and up in it, a lone cub holds tight to a limb.

Life stands still in that moment, lost in the noise of an unbalanced fight where the innocent will lose, and life will continue and forget this story of the unfair. The men look on as if disconnected through television or distance, while literally five feet from us a lioness's baby will die and maybe even she will too on this horrible night. The lions begin to circle her as one by one they lunge for the cub in the tree, and one by one, she takes them down. They have the eyes of blood-hungry warriors, hungry to expunge any genetic trace of their rival male and its offspring. The fact it's an innocent cub makes no difference to them.

It's a perilous fight of the truly ferocious, but one the lioness knows is about each minute she can prolong the inevitable. The lioness continues despite knowing it is a battle she will lose. I see myself in her determined eyes, knowing my own journey is about having as many moments with David that I can create, even though I can clearly see what the future holds for both of us.

We sit still for a good hour watching their endless attempts as the cub sits high above in the tree. Each one of us whispers the narrative of the struggle, while inside, I wish somehow we could just chase away the males or somehow intervene. Before I have the courage to utter such a suggestion, the stronger of the male lions attacks the neck of the lioness with full force. The three other males circle her and one climbs the tree toward the cub. The cub struggles on the limb, weighed down with the heavy lion on it, pushing him closer to the edge.

The mother lioness struggles under the mouthed grip of the largest male lion; the sound of a ravaged virgin as if heard from her soul. Then her cub falls to the side clinging for its life on the dangling branch before dropping to the ground in an innocent thump as the three male lions pounce on him. The ferocious vibrato of the warring lions reaches its peak above the shrieks of the ravaged cub in his final agony. Among the victorious feeding frenzy of the male lions, in the distance, the distraught lioness retreats before our eyes in a solitary pace into the wild without even a single look behind her in fear or grief; she returns into the bush to face life on her own once more.

CHAPTER 6

IBIZA

*I*T'S BEEN ALMOST of week of Berlin, and I couldn't be happier to get away, even if just for a quick trip. First, from a business perspective, there's nothing worse than dealing with Germans who seem to get lost in an endless cycle of meetings and pointless deliberation that's surprisingly inefficient, at least on an executive level. What could have been accomplished in a matter of hours in the US or even in a day in London requires an unyielding cycle of conversations about an online art auction website that's neither profitable nor very good.

Then there's the hotel I had the unfortunate experience of booking during one of early summer's first true heat waves when the humidity in Berlin is unyielding and accommodations are best booked based on who has air conditioning. A series of sleepless nights made me more and more nostalgic for Catherine, someone who has been all but missing in the flesh but comes to life via her e-mailed banter that keeps my heart warm since seeing each other in South Africa.

Catherine is inconsistent with calling though, totally detached when it comes to her day-to-day life and has a schedule almost as busy as mine is, which most times has me outright begging to see her. Between the occasional Skype sessions and texts, the time we spend together in these incredible places and the intensity she brings to each moment is what glues us tighter and tighter together as the time between our visits seems to deepen the passion I feel and lengths I'll go to have her near me.

This emotion led me to drop off the work grid for a few extra days and make the usual summer pilgrimage to visit my friends Alejandro and his wife, Chrissie, in Ibiza for a party weekend in which I still indulge to this day. I wasn't sure how to handle the trip or if to avoid it altogether, but I needed an escape from all that is Berlin right now.

When I initially told Catherine of the idea, she scoffed and idled off some comment about not being seventeen anymore, or that there are far more glamorous destinations than the packed Balearics in which to spend a July weekend. I understand her need to be dedicated to work, but we also have something good going that can only last as long as we make time to see each other. I managed to convince her to join me through a mix of first-class airfare and bribed sexting, in which I almost never engage. Plus, my attempt to be fully faithful to Catherine, despite our lack of conversation about monogamy, has led me to an almost two-month dry spell that I know can only last for so long, even in Berlin.

So life plants me at an airport once more, this time at a relic of the DDR known as Berlin-Schönefeld that's in the process of being replaced with a far more modern terminal, which will finally phase out all the Berlin airports that had anything to do with the Cold War or Third Reich. Yet, I've never been so happy to see an airport, the gateway to my escape from the rigidity of Germany. The cab driver almost seems embarrassed by such an icon of the past as he unloads my luggage and sends me on my way into commuter aviation hell. Sadly, the only nonstop flight today is one on Ryanair, the be-all and end-all of flying and the absolute antonym of first class.

Despite it being the middle of summer, the airport is surprisingly dead; a security line took little more than a few steps to get through. On the other side, a duty-free shop of international logos pushed like airport heroin by German fragrance models, line the entrance of the terminal. Among a mix of Eastern European girls looking for any job they can get in this regimented society, one in particular stands out like a bombshell, and she is holding a pitcher of Pimm's. Her short navy work dress and natural platinum blonde hair with pieces that fall perfectly in her pouty face.

Our paths connect as I walk directly for her. I notice our remarkably similar electric-blue eyes and pale skin that could almost make us siblings if not for the ten or so years of age difference. She rattles off something in German, the only word being *bitte* that's at all recognizable to my English ears; it hurt somewhat to see her subtle lips mouth this treacherous language.

"I'm not German."

"You Englander?" she says with a shy smile, but with the gape of a seasoned seductress who doesn't lose a moment of eye contact as I stand two feet in front of her.

"Yes, British, actually. And you? Where are you from?" I say while stressing each syllable of my question, given what I imagine to be her rudimentary English skills.

"I am from Poland," she says as if the answer would be a disappointment upon speaking. I can imagine the judgment such a reply conjures up in her everyday German life where foreigners are lumped together whether from a country a hundred miles or a thousand miles away.

"Do they drink Pimm's in Poland?" I say with a smile bigger than usual, hoping to lessen the load of her day.

"No, not really. In Poland, we drink vodka, not Pimm's. It is too sweet for Poland," she stutters, reciprocating my smile.

I imagine her naked, her tiny breasts that likely curve up at the end with tight pink nipples and a perfectly toned body that's agile in bed as she begs for it again and again.

"Krakow?" I ask as a compliment, alluding to the more progressive of the Polish cities, even though I would imagine an immigrant would more likely come from the rural areas of the country.

"Bromberg, small town in north of country where many Germans."

Her scent is a mix of fruity German shampoo and Pimm's, her eyes inciting an erection not easily concealed in my jeans as I shift to one leg. My mind immediately goes to eating her out from front to back, tasting her as I imagine her to be, even though I know I must restrain myself. It seems at all moments of the day all I do is think about sex. Even though I do a sort of preemptive masturbation almost every morning and night to avoid these moments that arise on a daily basis. I simply won't allow myself to assume the role of my father. I've told myself I won't fuck up what's evolving with this relationship by searching out endless sex that simply dilutes the passion I have with Catherine.

"Do you have children?" I ask, hoping to douse the situation with verbal cold water as various places where two adults can explore each better in an airport terminal flash through my mind.

"Child, me? I am only twenty-one and still in university," she giggles, a reaction that makes her all the sexier.

"Well, I need to get to my gate. But thanks for the Pimm's cup."

I make my way away from her and her leggy entourage before I do or suggest something I might regret. I think of all that could be ruined with Catherine if I pander to the momentary indulgences that will eventually mount and lead to me succumbing to my own instinct. And without a lingering stare or a quick look behind me to see if she's watching, I escape to my gate and into the impossible scene of crying children, teenagers lost in their iPhones, and bickering couples trying to put on a happy face prior to boarding for their two-week romp on Ibiza.

It's amazing to me how such a short flight can connect a place like Germany to a wonderland like Ibiza. However, the near three-hour flight is often the worst part of Ibiza, a flying dormitory of teenagers who catcall on takeoff and deejay a techno dance party through their headphones for much of the flight. Germans clap when planes land; they also run through the arrivals area to be first in the passport control. I attempt to keep pace with those too old for such a spectacle but too young to trail in the back with their parents.

Ibiza shouldn't be judged on the road leading from the airport: a mix of Germanic mid-rise apartment blocks and a distant silhouette of its walled city that looks like so many other fortified Mediterranean towns of old that today serve no other purpose than hawking wares to tourists and framing the photos of those who come once and never again. The road turns to highway and then a series of elevated bypasses where first-timers begin to judge the overdevelopment and congestion.

Shirtless motor-scooterists weave in and out of roundabouts before the six lanes turn to four, and then to three, and then to two as the perfect pavement turns to a darker tar and then to a mix of asphalt and rock before the evening horizon clears into the island's incredible rural interior.

Rural Ibiza is a bohemian paradise for those who arrived, like myself, in their late teens and continued coming every summer, even as their peers canceled one by one due to new families or relationships, only to be replaced by those locals you find who share your passion for this incredible place.

I met Alejandro and Chrissie, two fellow Londoners whom I met at a beach club one afternoon when I was fighting with a girlfriend du jour. They interrupted, or intervened, to share their own fight that evolved into all of us enjoying the next few days in a mix of drug-induced beach dancing and late night partying. The girlfriend didn't last much longer than the trip, but Alejandro and Chrissie remained and have been a part of my every summer since. I'm not quite sure how Catherine will take to the two of them, which is why I opted for us to stay in a hotel this time, versus my usual room at their farm near where we're booked.

Since Catherine does this for a living, I let her select the property, even though I'm a full day early. Rural roads in Ibiza have few markers, no signs, and almost no house number, which means come nightfall, you had better know where you're going, or you'll probably end up somewhere else. Most people don't know this side of the island, or at least don't pay attention to it as much as towns like Santa Eulalia and San Antonio with their big dance clubs and mega-hotels. It's here the bass and boom beats a little lower, at a more livable volume, where lifetimes are abandoned in places like Hamburg, London, or Paris to bet everything on a simpler life with like-minded people who want nothing else than to have fun and live out their dreams. Some of these dreams come to fruition through yoga compounds, hippie art stores, or boutique hotels like the Cas Gasi that comes into view as the evening claws onto its last few moments before night.

A peat gravel drive meanders up to a farmhouse compound of white stucco buildings with glossy green-painted shutters and wrought iron railings that overflow in lush ivy in front of arched windows and terraces. The smell of wet grass is cocooned by pure night as crickets already chime and a young bellman emerges from the double doors.

"Good evening, we've been expecting you, Mr. Summers," he says. I feel ever so slighted when someone doesn't address me in the native language, as if I don't blend in with the locals.

"*Si, buenos noches,*" I reply as he takes my roller bag.

A sturdy olive tree with a twisted trunk looms over the walkway in between squatty palms and terra-cotta pots overflowing with demure blue, yellow, and red daisies. The inside of the hotel is more traditional than I expected, a two-story lobby of three-hundred-year-old stone walls and Spanish tile floors with a fireplace blazing as though it were Christmas and not the beginning of summer. An older crowd clusters in a mustard-painted lobby, their hands cradling goblets of red wine as the interruption of my footsteps is greeted with silent stares.

A tall, attractive woman nears with a tablet in hand; her other hand extends several feet before she's even reached me.

"I'm Barbara, Mr. Summers. It is very nice to have you in my hotel."

I sense a German accent in her authoritative manner as she sweeps me along her side and into a dining room where diners hover over wedges of elaborate fruit tarts at the tail end of dinner, despite the relatively young nine o'clock hour.

"So you will be here for five nights, Mr. Summers," she said more as a proclamation than a question.

"Breakfast is in your room until eleven o'clock or as you desire, as long as you let us know the night before. Also, please let us know if you would like to join for evening canapés in the lounge each night. They are quite delicious and it's fun to meet other guests."

I catch the roaming eye of an older woman forking her last heave of pie. She is wearing stylishly retro eyeglasses. Her wink alludes to what lies beneath and what draws her not to Mallorca or Minorca, but Ibiza.

There's a uniquely Ibiza dream realized through the individual details of the hotel from the restaurant that utilizes all its own garden ingredients to an on-site spa with a staff of yogis and body healers who "are the best on the island," as claimed by Barbara. I can't imagine the profitability of such a property only desirable during June through September and then purely beholden to local patronage. I assume money from other sources keep it alive, much like everyone else in Ibiza who made it elsewhere and come to live off it the way they always wanted for as long as they can.

Barbara gives me a full tour of the property from the kitchen to the individual massage rooms in the spa that she added a few seasons ago. Finally, we make our way to the room arranged within a former barn that's been converted into upper-level accommodations that aren't suites but also aren't standard rooms. Whether this is her usual check-in procedure or she's trying to procure good press, the lengthy narration adds suspense as my eyes absorb the charming space of our room with its canopy bed centered in the middle of the room with soft floral fabric that matches the drapes concealing a wall of French doors.

I want to make Catherine proud with minutiae learned from the owner, but I also want to freshen up and make it over to Chrissie and Alejandro's place before it gets too late. And with Barbara's wordy departure that lingers out onto the terrace a bit longer, she relinquishes me to a quick drop of clothes and a shower in a surprisingly alluring bathroom with its perfumed soaps made on site, and toiletries wrapped in a single twist of ribbon that I know Catherine will love.

I settle into my Ibiza uniform of white pants and my barely buttoned white linen shirt that billows in the whistling wind of the road as I pull into the driveway of Alejandro's farm, or enormous plot of land that will be a farm whenever they get around to planting something. Alejandro is an ad executive from Spain but lives in London, and she is a former something-or-other who may include trust funder or call girl or model, but today she is simply Chrissie. As the headlights draw parallel lines through the misty evening, I see wobbly legs in a black dress dart across the yard and to the side of my car.

"David, David, David!" she pounds on the car windows as I stop the car, fearing I'll run her over.

"Let him get a foot out the door, Chrissie!" Alejandro yells from the porch. He's in all white, his usual uniform, with a fading tribal tattoo around his upper arm that shows his commitment to another time.

"David, I'm so, so, so happy you are finally here! Summer is not the same without you, darling."

Chrissie speaks with a posh London accent that likely conceals her true heritage in the Midlands or Manchester.

"David, my man, where's this lovely lady we have heard about?" Alejandro shouts out.

"Oh, she doesn't arrive until tomorrow, so you'll have to settle with just me for the night."

Stepping up to their porch, the interior house comes into view much as it did last year; a few all-white chairs and a new cluster of über-modern art sits in the corner, likely acquired on the island.

"Well, I see your farm has grown in quite nicely," I say, referring to the barren land that surrounds the house that's supposed to be overgrowing with organic vegetables and fruit trees by now.

"It's coming, it's coming, I swear. We are going to start next season; this year we wanted to focus on the house," Alejandro says, even though the house hasn't changed at all since last year.

So many people come to Ibiza with lofty dreams only to find themselves lost in a sort of hedonist party scene that envelops the island in June and then comes crashing to a halt toward the end of September.

"Plus, we've started thinking it's a yoga center and restaurant we really want, so the farm can come later," Chrissie chimes in.

"Oh, so is that the latest plan?" I say with a laugh.

"Well, sort of. I know it sounds mad, but it's amazing how busy you can be in a place where you really have nothing to do but have fun."

"We don't care really, David; one summer you'll arrive and we'll probably be drinking our own wine. You'll see," Chrissie says with a wave of the wrist.

"But at least you're living your dream; I have to hand it to you. As I was sitting in Berlin, all I could think about was our long lunches at Blue Marlin and sitting on the porch until four a.m., talking about whatever it is we seem to ponder endlessly at that hour."

"And now, we'll have Catherine to make it all the more interesting. We are dying to meet her, David. Am I going to like her?" Chrissie pouts, with lip out like a small child.

"I think you'll love her as much as I do."

However, I also realize the connection between the two women won't be an obvious one, Catherine an intelligent modern woman and Chrissie a runaway party girl fully immersed in the Ibiza lifestyle.

"We've never really known you all settled and loved-up."

"Well, do I seem any different to you now?"

Chrissie circles and studies me from head to toe in a stare before returning in front of me.

"I can't really tell, the outfit still very much says fun David though."

Behind her, I can see I'm interrupting the evening. Wine bottles emptied on a glass table surrounded by burnt black chairs by Maarten Baas that look like they were hauled off the set of a Tim Burton movie.

"You mean you started drinking without me?"

I downplay her jested observation. After all, I'm incredibly different since meeting Catherine, even if it's not obvious on the outside.

Chrissie grabs a bottle of Rioja and gives a hefty pour before handing me a heavy black-crystal goblet.

"So, tell us more about this Catherine," Alejandro adds from across the living room.

"She's smart, sophisticated, and beautiful. I have no idea why she'd ever be interested in a man like me," I say with a smile as I settle onto the white leather sofa.

"But Davey, you always have so much fun here. I don't want you to get all *daddy* on us. She's fun, right? We'll still be able to party and be crazy with her, right?" Chrissie asks before plopping on the sofa next to Alejandro.

"I was totally honest with Catherine and told her Ibiza is wild and crazy. But to be truthful, whomever I meet is going to have to enjoy letting loose and having a good time as much as I do. So it's sort of an Ibiza crash course to see how she does, and I think she'll absolutely love it. Or at least I hope she'll love it."

As I talk, Alejandro caresses Chrissie's hair with a tenderness you wouldn't expect of two people after so many years of being together. They're the type of couple who's constantly together and never more than a few feet apart, always close enough to grab the other's hand or let the other know they are right there.

"So, what's the plan, are we staying here or going out?" chirps Chrissie before I've even finished my glass of wine.

"You know, I'm sort of knackered. So if you don't mind, let's just have another glass, and then I'm probably going to call it an early night."

Chrissie and Alejandro pause before looking at each other.

"Oh no, it's happened. She's ruined him already," Chrissie sighs.

"What? What are you talking about?" I ask.

"You've gone all soft and squishy in love on us. Is this the David we have to look forward to in the future? You would never, ever have wanted to go to bed early on your first night in Ibiza."

"Really? I'm just tired. Plus, I kind of just want to catch up with you guys. I haven't seen you in almost a year."

"Has it really been a year?" Chrissie asks.

"Well, almost; it was last September for the closing parties."

"Ah yes, that was quite a way to shutdown the season," Alejandro adds, alluding to the day I overslept, missing my flight back to London that had me knee-deep in trouble at the office.

"And my liver, I must say," Chrissie laughs.

"We really are happy to hear you found someone you really like. We were starting to worry for you, man," Alejandro says in unexpected earnestness.

"Worry? Why would you worry about me?"

"I mean, at a certain age you pretty much have seen all the women you're going to see in life, and if you can't make it work with one of them, you're probably not going to make it work. You know what I mean, man?"

The clarity and simple directness of Alejandro's words make me feel like it's a thought he's honed over time.

"I don't know if I quite see it that way; I simply do what feels good, and for most of my life, that's meant dating a lot of different people. Right now, it's about getting to know one person, getting to know Catherine better without any distractions."

"So you're telling us that you've been totally faithful to this woman?"

Chrissie and Alejandro are the type of friends I can be completely open with; laying out every truth of the relationship without having to worry one of them will slip up with Catherine or judge me in anyway.

155

"Yes, well, mostly faithful," I say.

"Now, that's the David I feared ... so you haven't been faithful?" Chrissie asks, staring dead into my eyes with a certain disappointment.

"No, well, there was this time in LA that I came very close to messing up, but then I walked away from the situation. So yes, in essence, I've been faithful."

Chrissie lingers in thought as Alejandro speaks, as if for both of them.

"Okay, okay, that's fair. I mean, you're talking to a man who isn't even sure he can get hard for another woman; I've been with Chrissie for so long. I mean, at first, you smell every girl who goes by, and then over the years it just feels natural to be with only one woman. And I'm Spanish, man ... we fuck anything."

"But that's also why I wanted to bring Catherine here. She needs to see the world you live in and know it's still fun and exciting after all these years. You aren't that boring married couple; you're living life to its fullest every day with and for each other. I want her to see how fun life can truly be."

"Well, I'm not sure if it's that idyllic, but it's a compliment all the same," Chrissie says. "But you know, our life isn't all party, there's an equal amount of quiet nights at home when it's just us making dinner and talking in front of the telly."

"Yes," adds Alejandro. "There are always loads and loads of talking with my baby."

Chrissie scowls at Alejandro. "Someone once told me the best relationships are kind of boring. They simply work and life follows," she says.

"But David, you have to lighten up on the whole work and travel thing if it's ever going to work. Long distance just doesn't work."

"Then I need to change professions, Alejandro, because that's impossible in my line of work."

"But David, there are other options. You could do anything your heart desires, so it's a sort of choice you're making," he continues.

"You make it sound so easy, living for the day and just doing exactly what your heart's desire," I contend.

"I love this woman, man; I would rather be homeless with her than the king of any castle without her," Alejandro says, placing a kiss on Chrissie's lips that leaves me missing Catherine even more.

On the drive back to the hotel, their words linger in my mind, but I also feel that Catherine and I are more evolved, and we can handle the demands of a long-distance relationship.

The hotel feels better on my second approach, like a welcoming home that I'm more emotionally ready for after the evening's conversation. Candlelit lanterns line the path to my room even at this late hour that makes me feel as if there's someone out there watching, thinking, and looking out for me. The room door opens to a familiar space. My clothes I had tossed on the floor perfectly folded on the chair, the bed turned down, and pillows tucked with a lavender sprig that I hold to my nose. Without brushing my teeth or even going to the bathroom, I tug off my clothes and dive into the cold linen sheets still stiff and aromatic.

The night is longer than I hoped, awaking throughout the night, but appreciative to take in the sounds of the country and smells of the room, fragrant from the blossoming rosemary in full bloom. At 8:00 a.m., I do what I've never done in Ibiza. I pull on my running shoes and hit the roads for a long run that I hope will fill the time ahead of Catherine's arrival in two hours.

Ibiza is the kind of place where locals sometime stop and ask you if you need a ride if they see you running along the side of the road, so with no shirt and a mind for a sprint, I take to the road for a sweaty, exhaustive jaunt.

Normally in Ibiza, people are going to sleep at this hour, not waking up to take advantage of the early day. There is no one on the roads at 8:00 a.m., and you want to be wary of those who are, as they are most likely returning from Pacha or Space, fully loaded.

The area is teeming with new farms, more obvious on foot than in a car. Families are growing their own vegetables and raising their own livestock in a human experiment that's intoxicating to dream about. Young, glamorous women are out hanging laundry while guys younger and more in shape than even I am, work on fences and houses, chores that seem to never be done.

I round back to the hotel by 9:00 a.m. I notice my terrace has come to life with one of the most spectacular breakfast settings I've ever seen. Not one to indulge in food, I can't help but sit and pour coffee from a silver-plated carafe and nibble on hand-formed scones with marmalades made from fruit trees that line the property. There's also a small note from the owner's cousin who operates a new farm up the road about the selection of meats and cheeses. Birds chirp, lavender lingers on the wind and best of all, Catherine arrives in less than an hour.

I'm dressier than I'd normally be for Ibiza, making my way to the airport a full hour early not wanting to be late and corrupt her first moments here, this place I've beckoned her nearly halfway across the world for a mere few days. It takes less than twenty minutes to get to the airport, a clear blue sky with a temperature that's already hot for our first day at the beach. Radio on Ibiza is a nonstop mix of techno that in recent years has gone away from the hard-core, all-electronic sounds to a more a pop scene with djs like David Guetta and Bob Sinclair who have exploded across the globe. These days, it's not only the nightclubs that lure the top djs, but also the new day clubs at hotels like Ushuaia that host weekly summer parties by Swedish House Mafia and Luciano, along with David and his wife Cathy, who are currently the hottest Ibiza music export on the scene.

And with a hum that drops in from the sea, I see a reflection of steel wings on an approaching plane, and I imagine somewhere inside Catherine sitting, looking out the window, and not knowing what to expect. She might be nervous; I hope she's excited, or maybe she's sleeping, but shortly she will be in my arms again. The British Airways planes are never the new ones of the budget competition—no fancy winglets or jetted noses. The old carcass thumps to a landing and then vanishes from my sight behind the terminal. It is quiet at the airport; only a handful of taxis pull in queue as sliding doors stay shut, almost appearing locked with their mirrored coating.

A solo traveler emerges with a rolling bag trailing, followed by a uniformed pilot or cabin crew with an even bulkier bag. Next, are the London kids ready for their Ibiza party, who were likely rowdy on the plane the entire way here, followed by a woman in a virginal white linen dress, familiar oversize black sunglasses, and hair blowing in the perfect amount of wind. She turns and our eyes meet again. She looks different from before and far different from the woman I met in Rio. She's thinner and has a look that takes my breath away. Despite my loading zone parking place, I jump out of the car and swoop in to grab her. Our lips meet, a more familiar feeling than the last time, and then she grabs my face and stares into my eyes before kissing me again and then again. This is as perfect as love has ever been in my life.

"My David, my David. You are a sight for sore, tired eyes."

She grabs my arm with familiarity, I take her luggage, and we rush back to the car.

"How was your flight? Did you get into London all right?"

"Yes, it was a very short layover, luckily," she says, grabbing my hand and holding it with her own.

"I don't like that you were in my city without me," I scoff.

"Just like you to skip town right when I'm coming through."

"Too bad you can't come home with me after this trip," I say, hoping she'd surprise me with a different answer.

"I know, things are so busy, and I've been traveling so much as it is, you know."

"I get it. Work first. But we must really try to make that work sometime soon."

I try to rush those first moments between long-distance lovers when we talk like strangers, the touch feels unfamiliar, and all the intimate moments we've had before seem so long ago. However, I look in her eyes and see all my emotions rekindled; just holding her in the flesh allows all the feelings to come over me once more and connect to where we are today. I sometimes worry that we are a relationship of vacations, of interconnected summer romances, never really getting a sense of one or the other in real life. However, she's here now, and that's all I want to think about and enjoy.

"So, let me tell you. My friends are a bit of a handful, but I think you'll totally love them as much as I do," I say, tempering her expectations a bit in advance of the scene I'm sure is yet to unfold this day.

"It's Alex and Chrissie, right?"

"Alejandro and Chrissie, and they are very excited to meet you today. I'm thinking we'll run by the hotel and freshen up first, and then we'll meet them for lunch at the beach. That's as long as you're not too tired."

"No, I feel great. But how are you? How are you feeling after Berlin? I've never heard you so glum."

"Actually, it feels like a lifetime ago, now that you are here," I say, realizing she's one of the few people ever to remember what I tell them about my work life.

"And thank you for the flight, Mr. Summers," she perks. "British Airways First is ridiculous, and I slept like a baby and should be fine after a quick shower."

"Terrific."

"Oh, how do you like the hotel? Was Barbara nice to you on check-in?"

"No, it was great; a little different than what I was expecting, but very charming and totally up your alley."

"What? No, now, tell me what you really thought?" she counters with curiosity.

"Well, the location is spectacular, but it's a little old for me," I say, without sounding unappreciative of her work booking the hotel.

"You mean the room is old? I thought they just renovated."

"No, the room is beautiful, and so is the rest of it. It's just the crowd is older than you'd expect on Ibiza."

"Oh, was the pool not stocked with bathing beauties like David Summers likes?" she says with a note of agitation.

"Forget it, I was just saying Ibiza is very young, and the crowd at this hotel is not. As a travel writer, I thought you would want to know that," I say as kindly as I could possibly express.

"Well, I'm not all that young either, David, in case you haven't noticed."

"Okay, the hotel is lovely, and you are lovelier, so let's not turn this very happy day into something it's not meant to be."

"I'm sorry. I just want you to like it. I want it to be as perfect as you are."

"That's more like it. You know I appreciate anything you do," I say.

As we round back to the hotel, Catherine insists on going straight to the room versus through the lobby or taking a quick look at the spa or pool. She's hesitant with her affection with no more than a kiss before going into the bathroom fully clothed with her bathing suit in hand. She emerges ready to go to the beach without any flirtation, lingering touch, or caressing. She's incorrigibly sensitive, and I soon realize things are sometimes best left unsaid.

Icy or not, she looks like a knockout in a lacy cover-up and heels that look as if they're made out of some sort of arty straw, and legs that are far more slender than the day I met her. Maybe it's a new diet or workout, but there's a definite transformation. I dare not ask as I quickly swap shorts, throw on a white shirt, and join her on the terrace.

"It's so much prettier than I imagined, and rustic," she says.

"What were you expecting?"

"Honestly? I was thinking it would be high-rise hotels and loud beach bars, like Fort Lauderdale."

"Well, there is that side of Ibiza too, but we don't go there much. Do you think I'd make you fly halfway around the world for that?"

"You know I would have, in a minute, but this is so much prettier. I never expected there to be this entire agrarian side to it with these old houses and villas hidden in olive trees."

"We could be farmers; that's if we ever got out of bed."

"You'd be one hot farmer, David Summers."

I can tell she's enthralled with the landscape of inner Ibiza as her eyes look beyond each turn and savor the sights outside the car. We pass a series of gated houses on the road to Cala Jondal where along a grassy promenade the white stucco Blue Marlin beach club sits for another season. It's a who's who of cars in the parking lot from reconfigured convertibles made from old Range Rovers to 1970s BMWs with a heavy dusting.

"Is this it? It's called Blue Marlin?" Catherine attempts to get past the earlier emotional hiccup and proceed into a better day.

"Yes, this would be the ever-famous Blue Marlin. It's one of the most fun beach clubs on the island, and it has a great crowd where you always run into someone you know."

"So exciting! I can't wait to touch the water."

"It's a beautiful beach, too, with a swim jetty where you can just jump in the water. I was thinking we'll lie out for a while and then join my friends for lunch as soon as they arrive."

"Are they here already?"

"No. They are on Ibiza time and arrive when they arrive and are usually always the last to leave. That's how they do it."

Before we even make it to the door, I can feel the beat of techno. Catherine walks in front of me carrying a colorful beach bag. She begins to tell a story about how Ibiza was actually once a Phoenician outpost, and all along the shore, you can supposedly see these incredible old ruins that simply lie in the crashing sea.

There's a door attendant, even at one o'clock in the afternoon, who takes our name twice, the second time with spelling, before leading us to the edge of the water two rows in and to a line of four chaise lounges. Catherine demurely settles in, and I take in the surroundings that include a gaggle of loud Irish girls and a group of incredibly hot Russians in the next row who got even better seating than we did.

One Russian in particular takes note of our arrival through her dark-tinted glasses. I slowly undress behind Catherine, first my shirt, and then my shorts and shoes. She watches, not knowing I can see every blink, every glance at and away, and back at me.

Catherine pulls out a book, thick and cumbersome, and lies back on her chaise placed in the second highest notch that gives her a full view of the sea as well as a group of football players clustered around the jetty. I'm sure she doesn't recognize more than their edgy hair and looks. Despite the two months' time between our visits, she sits in silence tending to her book between glances at all that surrounds us including the morning-trance music that's so Ibiza. She doesn't hate it, but I'm also unsure if this was what she was expecting. The waitress approaches, and I order a full bottle of rosé for the two of us. If there's anything that will loosen Catherine up, it's some bubbly.

A bucket of ice later and Catherine is in her full glory chatting with the Russian models in front of her about the football player they fancy and the various parties happening around the island this weekend. She is another person in this moment—flirty and expressive—her touch claiming me as her own and making me not even want to look at anyone else but her. She kisses me while passing a chunk of ice mouth to mouth. It falls into my lap and her new friends laugh in delight. Another bottle is killed with a pop, pouring for all those around us, and alas, Alejandro and Chrissie arrive in a cluster of entourage and my ovation.

"Darling David, introduce us to the new missus!" Chrissie booms across the beach as Catherine jumps to attention and courtesies a hello.

Alejandro swoops in with a more affectionate hug and kiss atop my head. They're both in full fedora-and-linen Ibiza regalia, taking their seats, and introducing themselves to the wider new group as is always done in these parts. Chrissie wastes no time, and before I know it, the question and answer period ensues between the dueling females.

"So you dated him for how long?" I hear Chrissie ask of Catherine. I realized long ago that it was best not to intrude in such girly conversations, especially with Chrissie.

I thought it also an ideal minute to take a momentary leave. I pull up from the chaise and make my way across the now fully packed terrace, past the Russians no longer even remotely interested in me, alongside the footballer players ten years my junior, and onto the jetty among the thump of music and hum of distant boat motors attempting to moor. As I stand there, my black Orlebar trunks falling off my hips, summer in Ibiza is as it has always been, and with a dip in the hips and tip of the toes, I dive into the slightly chilled water and plunge into the deep.

Two hours later, the party has reached its daytime cruising altitude as we migrate to the dining room with our new cluster of friends. Catherine alas, appears comfortable enough not to be the only one still in a cover-up and crunched ass-to-ass with the Russians along the banquette. Alejandro and I bask in a sea of females, including Chrissie, who manages to be the center of the conversation with her antics and stories. I watch as Catherine slowly awakens to me, caressing my inner thigh ever so subtly, but enough to exude her ownership over me in the sea of sexual attention that lurks among the bass of techno and clinking rosé bottles hitting chrome buckets dripping in condensation.

"Catherine is great, my man. Truly tops," Alejandro says to me in the privacy of a smoke plume between puffs from a cigarette that he barely holds between his limp fingertips.

"Thank you. It's amazing that you are able to meet her. It's such a weird relationship, totally different than I've ever had before, but every time I'm around her, it just feels right."

"Man, I totally get it. I can see it in both your eyes when I look at you two."

"I just wish we didn't live so far away and have jobs that are near to impossible to break free from."

"Listen, one of you is going to have to make the move if it's going to work long-term, you know, long distance doesn't work forever especially for a guy like you," he advises in a serious Spanish intonation.

"But I have to tell you, there's something incredibly hot about thinking about her for weeks and going without, and then all of sudden, she's there, and it's so wild and intense."

"Yes, but that can't sustain itself forever, man, that is not real."

"But we both like our lives and it actually works, especially for me. We seem to pick up right where we were every time."

"Until she meets someone who can give her what she wants and is in New York then see how it works, man."

"I think we have something special, though. I'm not worried, Al. Plus, she's not hung up on kids and all that marriage stuff; she's like the female version of me. There's no pressure from her, something I've never experienced with a woman."

Alejandro leans in with a whisper. "At least that's what she's showing you; inside, they all want babies and big fat weddings. It's simply their species."

"Not her though, I'm telling you. I just wish my job took me to the states more, so we could see what real life could be like."

"You've just got to end being a slave to them, man. Just tell them that this is the way it is, and if they want you, they have to accept it under these terms."

"Sadly, Al, business doesn't work like that."

"You need to make it work like that or you are never going to have a relationship, man."

Alejandro has gone to that place in drinking where every dream is simply a matter of wanting it bad enough, and his life is about as ideal as one can attain. As I continue to nod in agreement, my concentration shifts to Chrissie. I hear her explaining to Catherine in a similar tone how exactly to make me finally commit without ever having to have children.

The Russians have switched back to their native language, and joined onto the soccer player in addition to a painfully stylish gay guy wearing floral trunks a fashionable size too small. His attention, as well as the cluster collected at the end of the table, turns to me and points between Catherine and me.

"I just had to come over here and tell you that you are possibly the most attractive man on the entire island," says the bold gay guy who is hovering over Alejandro and me. The entire table falls silent.

Catherine grins from ear to ear. "Isn't he though? He's just perfection," she booms, halting her conversation from Chrissie and kisses me.

"And you must be the lucky missus, I assume?"

"Missus? Not. But I'm the lucky bitch who gets to look at him every day in the shower."

"Oh, I love her. What is your name, darling?" he says with hand on hip.

"Catherine, Catherine Klein."

"I'm Dave Dan, and I think I've found my new summer friends."

"I know exactly who you are, as a matter of fact, I'm wearing a pair of your shoes right now," Catherine says.

"Girl, you are everything. Look at those mules. Spring/summer 2011 was a hit, girl."

"Thank you; it was one of your best collections ever."

"I like to think my next collection is always the best, but thank you just the same," he says, hovering above me.

"So I take it you're in the fashion business," I say.

"Dave Dan is a CDFA nominee for the past three years," Catherine says.

"I like you more and more. Just look at your eyes; they are absolutely divine," he says to me, the skin of his exposed leg now touching my arm as I lean away.

"You know, Catherine is also in the fashion business," I say to divert the attention.

"I did not. Are you a designer as well with your Hermés sunglasses and glamorous vintage cover-up?"

"No, I am just a journalist."

"*Vogue? ELLE? Women's Wear Daily?*" Dave plops on the seat next to me, his wet skin, and leg hair so trimmed it scratches my leg. I push closer to Catherine.

"No, nothing that prestigious or relevant. I'm the associate editor of a Hachette title," she says, oddly vague.

"Which one, my dear?"

"I'd rather not say, as I'm trying not to think about work. Anyway, it's a magazine many designers won't even show in … like yourself," she says.

"Oh dear. You know that's not my fault exactly. It started with Alex McQueen, and I just continued the practice because I thought it was chic to say no to anyone but *Vogue*."

"And anyway, that really has nothing to do with me; I only plan the covers."

"And she does a lot of travel writing now. As a matter of fact, this is sort of a work trip for her," I add.

"In addition to being another opportunity to see David," Catherine says.

"Well, who could blame her for that? Girl, I feel all tingly down there just sitting next to the man," Dave says in his most campy voice. His tone makes me uncomfortable negating everything I am or have to say as a person and treating me like some bimbo he'd meet at a bar.

"Will you stand up for me and just let me look at you already? I promised the ladies down there that if I could touch your abs, I would put them in my next runway show. Ready to wear, not couture, of course. We don't do Russians in the couture shows," he continues.

"I'm sorry, I'm going to excuse myself from this banter, and make my way to the loo, if that's all right." I push myself up and out of the banquette trying not to touch him. I pull away from the table taking his eyes with me, hopeful to lose them at the bathroom.

"Davey, wait a minute." Chrissie pulls at my arm before I enter the men's room.

"We need to find some Charlie, like, pronto," she whispers in my ear.

Chrissie stumbles down a step separating the kitchen from the dining room, one of those short inexplicable steps only found in Spain that Chrissie manages without a fall as Alejandro approaches.

"David, since we left London, it's been impossible to find. I used to call it in like a taxi, and here, it's all of a sudden impossible to find."

Chrissie refers to cocaine as Charlie, something she does with a girlish whine that's endearing, even to those who don't have a clue as to what she's saying.

"So you can't find it anywhere?" I ask.

"Like a hooker at eight a.m., it's nowhere to be found, my friend. Get over it, Chrissie." Alejandro nods his head as a thump of an electronic lounge anthem plays in the background.

"No, wait," Chrissie says. "The girl in the bathroom says there is another dj working the bar at Las Salinas Beach who has some. What do you say we leave here and head over there for sunset?"

Alejandro defers to me and returns to the dining room. In my mind, I worry how Catherine might react, but at the same time, this is part of the Ibiza world and very much a part of Chrissie and Alejandro.

"I'm not sure, aren't we having a good time?"

"Oh, come on, it will be fun. And think of how wild Catherine will get on it."

"I'm not sure she even does it, Chrissie. Not everyone is a fan of Charlie."

"Darling, everyone likes Charlie. Whether they want to admit it or not is another question," she says. "I can't believe how fucking hard it is to score some here. Normally, it's falling out of the fucking sky."

"I mean, we don't have to find it to still have a great time," I say, despite knowing once an idea is in her head there's no getting it out.

"Going to Ibiza and not finding coke is like going to Italy and not finding pizza. It's fucking ridiculous."

"So listen, let's finish off this bottle, and then close out. I'll drive us over there," I say, eager to lose the current crowd we've amassed and willing to accept whatever the afternoon might bring.

"Darling, you're everything. I adore you."

I return to the table to find Dave and Catherine fully engrossed in conversation. He is hovering over a photo series while Catherine holds her own phone close to her chest.

"David, David, come here," Catherine calls me as I make my way to the table.

"David, darling," Dave says across the table, "Your lovely lady and I have an agreement. If she shows me her naughty picture of you, I will send her a gift from my next collection."

"And …" Catherine interjects.

"Wait, she doesn't have such a photo of me, as far as I know."

"What? Wait, you said—"

"Actually, I do, David; not super naughty, but enough of one. He sends them to keep me warm at night when I'm home in New York."

The group laughs, and I get back up and summon the waitress for the check. Catherine obviously enters into the agreement that makes Dave even more annoying and sleazy. I stay at the opposite end of the table with the Russians; their interest in me fully quelled by Catherine. Dave stares me down and then grabs the phone out of Catherine's hands. Chrissie returns just in time, hovering behind Alejandro and massaging his shoulders as Dave tries to hand Catherine's phone to them. They both decline in disgust and interrupt the merriment.

I mouth the words, "Are you ready?" across the table as Chrissie smiles ear to ear and Catherine looks confused. I motion a steering wheel with my hands and make my way toward the door. Catherine jumps up and joins me at the exit of the dining room.

"What's wrong? Are we done here already?"

"Yes, we are going to another party. Are you coming or staying with your new friend?"

"Are you upset with me?"

"Why would you show that awful man a picture that's meant to be between you and me?"

"I'm sorry, it's not like it showed you naked or anything. You're just so confident about your body that I didn't think you'd care," she says with a tone of humiliation.

"Well, I do care, and I think you would as well."

"It's just … you're almost unnaturally beautiful. I figured sharing a picture would be harmless. I had no idea you would even mind, David. I didn't mean to upset you."

It's the most stern I've been with Catherine. She returns to the table, grabs her bag, and plants a single kiss on Dave's head, who looks on completely confused at a now empty table end. I walk ahead of the group on our way to the car; Alejandro and Chrissie linger behind with Catherine.

It's a longer, quieter drive than I expected to the other beach, a somber foursome in a late afternoon shift of mood that's a mix of rosé after burn, and too much sun. Catherine's hand makes its way to mine on the gearshift; my hand struggles between second and third gear on narrow rural roads that feel miles away from the sea. Las Salinas, the beach we are heading to, is one of the fancier ones on the island. It gets its name from the salt flats located along its perimeter. It's a tranquil scene of workers manning the flats as a parade of revelers pass by on their way to posh eateries like Jockey Club and Sa Trinxa, as well as another beach club I've never heard of where Chrissie will alas meet Charlie.

We drive to a gravel parking lot and follow the directions of a pushy attendant who shoves our car in tightly with a line of similarly deplorably subcompacts. We pass a series of bohemian beach boutiques where Catherine's fingers linger between colorful caftans and floral fabrics. Chrissie plows ahead of the group and inside a small bar that sits on the edge of the sand. She vanishes for no more than a minute before emerging and walking farther onto the beach and along the water in the direction of a grassy bluff.

"We have to go to the next beach where the guy is; it's only a five-minute walk," she says, only partially turning around as her voice fades in a forward motion.

"Where exactly are we going?" Catherine finally asks. The sand turns to more of a gravel hillside and cool beach drifts farther away into the warmer hillside.

"We are going to get Charlie. David will never straight up tell you because he's too much of a gentleman."

"Charlie, what's Charlie?" Catherine calls out to the crowd.

Chrissie stops dead in her tracks, turns around, and yells, "Don't act coy! Charlie, darling. You know, cocaine, my dear." She repeats even louder, "Charlie! Please tell me you've heard it called that?"

"That's so funny. Why do you call it Charlie?" Catherine laughs as Chrissie continues on her forward march.

"I think it's because of the consonant it starts with, C as in Charlie," I interject, my voice cleared of any annoyance that may have lingered before.

"Or maybe it was the good man who discovered the stuff, god bless his soul," Chrissie yells from ahead. Her heels tuck under shaky ankles that struggle among the rocky terrain.

The walk is longer than anyone expects, on a dusty trail that weaves along the beach with dramatic rock formations along the shore.

Catherine stops for a moment. "Look at these ruins. Oh my god, I think these are the ones I was telling you about earlier." She points to a massive chunk of ruin with detailed decoration on its side that looks as if it was part of an elaborate temple or column.

"I think these are part of the Phoenician ruins I mentioned to you. I can't believe we just stumbled upon them." Catherine pulls out her phone to snap a picture.

"Darling, those aren't the rocks we are looking for," Chrissie says as the group laughs.

"They'd be far too difficult to chop, although I guess we could just nibble at them until pieces fell off," Chrissie continues.

"Did you know these were here?" Catherine asks. "That's just so weird."

"Really, I had no idea. But I'm really happy you got to see it because I'm a horrible tour guide. It's one of the things you discover when looking for Charlie. I even think that's how I met my Alejandro."

"Not exactly," Alejandro brushes off, lingering behind in a plume of cigarette smoke.

Catherine runs down the hill and onto a small private beach next to the boulder-shaped ruin with its wavy-carved details that I wouldn't even have noticed if not for Catherine. It's isolated perfection as Alejandro and Chrissie walk ahead, and I follow her down to the water.

She carefully removes her shoes and walks a foot into the water. I approach from behind stripping off all my clothes and running head-first into the water. The water is perfection; warmish but still cool enough to be refreshing as my run turns into a full swim. I stop and see if Catherine follows.

"Wait for me!" she screams, and she strips to her underwear and follows in after me. Looking like an alabaster figurine, she rushes to my side, and the wave's crash against us higher and higher.

"You're not going to take another picture, I hope," I say, referring to the earlier situation at the restaurant. I pummel my head in her neck with a series of kisses around her collarbone. "I think I may have to get my own. If only you weren't always so quick to get dressed again."

"Instead of always naked like you, Mr. Summers?"

"Exactly."

"Ibiza is amazing," Catherine says. "No wonder you love it so much. I can see why it's always passed from one conqueror to the next. I think the Phoenicians were the first; they found a port here that was eventually controlled by Carthage and later the Romans who raped it of its minerals." She tugs me closer and loses herself in the ruins, and one of those stories that enthralls her writer's mind and me with it.

"How do you know all these things?"

"You know, I'm always reading something or other. It's so nice to finally have someone who even cares about that kind of stuff," she replies.

"I love all your stories. It sort of soothes me and makes my blood pressure drop. No one's ever told me stories like you do."

"The locals were almost constantly being attacked by pirates," she says with a playful plundering of my stomach.

"Even with their city walls?"

"Even with their fortified city, so they built all those lookout towers that you see there on the hill." She gestures to an abandoned stone structure that looks like a half-built lighthouse on the hill.

"The ones there," I point, caressing her arm suspended in the air.

"What were they used for?"

My naked body holds her from behind in the sea, exploring her with my hands as her story continues.

"They were built so that when the guards were atop the tower, they could watch far into the horizon for phantom pirate ships making their way to the shore. Imagine being there in the middle of the night, all alone, and then seeing the ships approaching in the distance with only hours to save your family, your city … everything. The towers were built in a chain within sight of the next tower, which they would ignite one after another in a fiery circle around the island when trouble was nearing."

"Do you know I've been on this island every year for the last two decades, and no one has ever told me what those were all about?"

"Well, now, you haven't been here with me, have you?"

The moment lulls into a soothing silence. We hold each other in the sea until a group of strangers approach in the distance. Alas, we gather our clothes and scurry farther down the beach to join Alejandro and Chrissie. It's been more than thirty minutes of walking, but neither of us notices as we continue to get lost in each other.

The rocky hill retreats down to the lower beach crowded with sunset revelers along a strip of sand dotted with a pure white beach club and a swath of sunbathers. Our walking increases in pace to a full run as we near the beach. We make our way to a row of loungers where we recognize Alejandro sitting in a sea of smoke.

"I thought maybe you guys had a change of heart and left us," Alejandro says.

"Do you really think after all these years I would do that to you? Plus, I'm curious if she can even find it at this point," I say.

The music is louder and the crowd far younger than at the other beach, more of a university crowd of surfer-type guys and party girls arranged along a long and wide strip of sand around the edge of the hill. Then Chrissie emerges from the crowd of people queued up at the bar. She's walking with a lumbering, confident stride that's no longer hurried.

"Guess who I found?" she says as she comes closer to us waving a small baggy in the air as if a child with forbidden candy.

"You didn't?" Alejandro says with a cigarette in his mouth.

"I did. I told you I would find some, but I just didn't think it would take so long. And I have to say, it looks like pretty good stuff to me," she says with a childish excitement.

"And she's like a horse whisperer of crack," Alejandro says.

"Where did you get it from, my dear?" I ask.

"The dj had it, just like I was told. He was really nice and totally played great music. Now, who is going to come with me?"

"I will. I have to use the bathroom, anyway," Catherine says, much to my surprise.

"I'll join you, too, for the walk," I say as we take the short hike to the two lone portable toilets that sit at the edge of the beach with a queue of about fifteen or so women standing outside.

"How are you going to do this, my dear?" I ask Chrissie.

"I'm just going to walk in and do my thing … won't be long at all," Catherine says, choosing to ignore the two cleaning ladies who stand guard outside each toilet cleaning between each use with the efficiency of Swiss guards.

"Here you go, and under no means drop it because we don't have that much, and I won't be sharing my baggie given the dire drug drought on the island," Chrissie warns and hands a small plastic bag to Catherine. "And don't forget to share it with my David. He's trying to impress you, but back in the day, he was known as a real hoover."

As we get down to two people, and then one remaining person in front of us, my stomach begins to get nervous. The sturdy-shaped maid takes her dripping brush inside the outhouse and does a quick once-over of the seat and floor as the previous occupant lingers with tip in hand until she is done before making her way back to the beach. The cleaning lady barks something off in Spanish as if to motion that it's now available, and Chrissie eagerly steps forward.

"Thank you, Mom," Chrissie says as she enters the portable toilet, handing the cleaning lady her hand as she takes the step up.

The process repeats itself in the neighboring loo. Catherine steps forward hesitantly with a smile and firm grip on the bag of cocaine that Chrissie gave her. She turns to look up at the line of now twenty people swelling behind us. Catherine quickly enters and locks the door loudly behind her. She's no more than a minute before exiting and then motioning for me to take her spot. She quickly hands me the baggy and gives me a kiss. We linger in front of each other and the maid cleans away once more.

"Did you do some?" I ask Catherine.

"I was going to, but I just landed and don't want to overdo it on my first day. Plus, you're here and that's enough of a high for me today."

There's stillness inside the toilet, and I stare at the small baggie with pink dwarfs running around its zip lock top. I imagine the immediate metallic rush that lingers in the back of my throat, instantly replacing any tiredness with an adrenaline rush that's palatable in my teeth and fingertips. I imagine Catherine seeing me high for the first time, what she'll feel, and how she'll maybe think different of me, or see me in an altered, lesser light. Then I stuff the baggie back into the pouch of my inner shorts. I chose to stay present and focused on Catherine in lieu of a momentary rush that would have far too many consequences this day. Outside, I notice both maids knocking on the neighboring cubicle and rattling off something in noticeably agitated Spanish.

"Baby, Chrissie hasn't come out yet, and they are getting very mad," Catherine says as she grabs my hand.

"What? You mean she's still in there?" I take Catherine to the back of the line now abuzz with heckling for Chrissie to emerge from the outhouse.

The knocking intensifies as the word cocaine is muttered from multiple, foreign tongues. Chrissie can be heard trying to fend off the masses without actually having to come out. As the maids bang on the door, Chrissie finally emerges unflustered by the complaints. She is perfectly composed and heads on through the angry crowd to rejoin us.

"What's wrong, darlings? Are you all right?" she says to us, unknowing.

"We were just worried about you, my dear. Was everything okay?" I ask.

"Oh, you know those women, always barking at the English woman. I gave her a tip; what more does she want?"

We return to Alejandro, who's enjoying his own buzz, too bothered with trying to hide his habit in an outhouse, claiming Spain is his native country, and everyone else can just go fuck off. Catherine acts as if enjoying her own high not to disappoint Chrissie. Catherine is more attentive to me with the touch of her hand that lingers on my lower back and just inside the waistband of my pants. She's fully into the music in a euphoria all her own and grabbing the moment in a way I've never seen in a woman.

Along the beach, the daytime laze has emerged into a full-on dance party surrounding the small dj booth where a cluster of maniac Spaniards does their own version of a mosh pit to pop-techno anthems. We watch in a party haze, pawing each other in blissful ecstasy. Catherine kisses my dry mouth forcing her tongue inside while grabbing my lip with her teeth and sending me into an immediate erection that I try to conceal under my thin shorts. We wander away from the dance floor to our own chaises. She straddles me on my back as I slip my fingers under her skirt and inside her panties to warm my hands still slick with suntan oil sheen.

Alejandro and Chrissie are in their own moment, Chrissie dancing around as Alejandro lingers on the ground in a plume of pot smoke. He is staring at her in awe and enjoying the middle of an early evening high that engulfs us all.

"Do you guys want a puff?" Alejandro turns and asks us.

"I don't usually smoke, but thank you," I say.

"I'll take a hit," Catherine says, turning and grabbing the rolled joint from Alejandro. She takes a deep inhalation as Chrissie lingers above waiting for her own puff.

"Come on, David, don't be a stick in the mud," Catherine says as she hands me the joint. I take a long hit that's smoother and more abrupt than I remember. It also immediately makes me even hornier, as my fingers find their way back up inside Catherine's skirt as she sits in my lap again.

"Let's dance, you guys." Chrissie says while making her way, high heels in hand, across the sand to the dance floor that's been created since we arrived.

The sun lingers behind the clouds in its final stages of sunset, and a chill sets in as I get up and try to conceal my complete erection behind Catherine.

We are the youngest people dancing by at least a decade, jumping up and down as if it were the last night of our lives to tracks of Nirvana mixed with Rihanna and The Clash. I try to keep my distance from Catherine knowing I won't easily conceal my excitement standing in this crowded group. Drinks come and go between plastic cup toasts; Chrissie and then Alejandro make their way back to the bathroom. The scene repeats itself through the onset of darkness as slowly, one by one, the beach empties of people and we are left on a barren strip of sand far away from our car, high as kites.

It takes a good hour before we're sober enough to make our way back to the car; we have a long drive ahead of us back to Alejandro's house and then to our hotel. With promises to meet up later in the night at Space, I was well aware neither of us intended to keep those plans. After dropping off Alejandro and Chrissie, we make our way away from their house just far enough that they could no longer see our car lights. Suddenly, I stop the car and make my way to the passenger side. I pull Catherine by the hand and into the dusty pasture under a perfect three-quarter moon that ignites the northern sky.

"Where are you taking me now?" she asks.

"You'll see. Just come."

We walk a good ten minutes in the dark before coming to an elevated clearing next to a wise old tree where I take off my shirt and lay it on the ground. I pull Catherine in front of me and slowly remove her blouse and bikini top that fall to the ground as her bare breasts sit in the moonlight. Then with a single pull, I remove her skirt and underwear leaving her completely nude in front of me.

"What are you doing? What if we get caught?"

"Then we get caught, my love." I kneel in front of her, kissing her from her foot up, and every few seconds stealing glances at her perfect body that rises above my own as her eyes reflect the moonlight. There's a gritty smell to the air as I pull off my clothes and parallel her from behind with my bare body. She shivers a moment as I bite her neck and attempt to find a decent resting place on the ground before my tongue finds its way inside her to a cricket chorus that fills the midnight sky.

She pulls away as if vying for control before standing above me. She dances in a playful, carefree delirium that I've never seen from her before. Gone are all the inhibitions and shyness that plagued her in Rio and kept her from fully falling into these incredibly passionate moments. She gives me a seductive show that has me begging for her, hovering above me with glimpses of all that I desire in the backdrop of a perfect night sky. She drops to her knees and allows her body to gently glide against mine, sending me into a shiver of raging delight as I get harder and harder. In this instant, her mind has muted and her body has taken over.

I try everything to make the moment last as long as possible. I flip her under me onto the ground as I find my erotic home back inside her. I pace myself with a melodic movement, savoring every incredible moment inside her as she stares into my eyes. She moans louder and louder before erupting into the most angelic sound of desire my ears have ever heard. The mere sound sends me into my own exquisite eruption inside her as that poetic motion slows to stillness, and she collapses on top of me as I linger as long as I can inside her.

"I almost don't want to speak because I worry I might wake up," she says with a whisper in my ear.

"Are you cold? Let me put my shirt over you."

I cover her exposed body with a swathe of my white shirt and we linger in total darkness. I'm taken aback by the intensity of our sex; it seems to become only more powerful even though we've past the time in a relationship when it would normally become more familiar and routine between us.

"David, I feel as if the entire world goes away when I'm near you. I just can't get enough of you; you're like my own version of Charlie." She laughs.

"I'm not going anywhere, so enjoy it."

"I know. This place is like nowhere I've ever been. It's nothing I imagined it would be. It's like a hedonist's garden of Eden."

"But that's only because you are here in it," I say as the sweat on my body chills in the night air.

She's able to take a place I already love and make me feel even closer to it by just being herself. It's like there's this entire new dimension to life when she's near.

"I wish we could just stay here forever. Let our worlds simply go on without us and stake out our future on this land. I'll cook and you can just sit there and let me take care of you day after day."

"The real world wouldn't be so bad either, you know, maybe learning what real life would be like together." The very words shock me, as it's typically been the last thing I want at this point with a woman.

"Who wants the real world when there's this though?"

"But you know maybe a weekend in New York every so often or you in London. It wouldn't be so bad, would it?"

A silence ensues with Catherine as her breath lingers on my neck. I can feel her heart beat against my bare chest.

"Would it?" I say again. She looks up and the green of her eyes strokes my heart.

"How could New York ever compete with this?"

Some ten hours later, I find myself lying in the hotel room I had so judged just two days previous, immersed in a sea of creamy linen, laying so close to Catherine's face I can feel each warm exhale drift away from her. She lies in stillness like a woman adrift in the world having found her perfect place to spend a lifetime. Her hairs lie like cut stone, molded perfectly over her arm with an open palm under her face. This grandmotherly room has segued into a cocoon of passion, like the boudoir of an experienced concubine camouflaged as a floral lair.

The room sits with windows wide open and the bright, sunny island alive in full bloom outside. Although the owner brought the breakfast almost an hour ago, I don't dare wake Catherine from this most perfect state as birds chirp, and the sun strikes her bare body just perfectly. In a time when I'm normally strung out from the previous day of partying, at this moment, I'm so enamored that I don't want it to end.

This is what I want life to be—no more Jamila's, no more Russian party girls, no more flyby relationships. I desire Catherine, and I am ready to do what it takes to be with her. I dream of what is yet to come of the morning as I wake her with a soft caress or deep penetration that enters her right from sleep as we begin all over again in this perfect morning with a day still fully in front of us in this summer heaven.

CHAPTER 7

LONDON

I HAVE TEETERED past the point of no return. I have crossed the line and beyond the point of knowing my limits, holding my ground, or knowing anything other than my own unquenchable desire for more and more, and then more of this fantasy. I have with full meditation, compromised the vows I have sworn to uphold, denied the very existence of my own child, and now metamorphosed into a third person who is unrecognizable even to myself most of the time.

This compulsion to see, feel, and touch him leads me away again, head-on, and to London, camouflaged in work that I seek out in order to see him once more. With two days reviewing a hotel in London and a weekend in the countryside for a wedding he's asked me to attend, I contemplated telling him about Billy. I could plead from my heart explaining that he meant so much to me that I didn't want to risk these special times with him for fear he would run like so many other men at the thought of dating a woman with a child. I'll explain that I love him more than anything imaginable, and that I am separating from my husband.

Then reality crashes on me that David won't want what I have to offer, he would never love the real me. Even if he got past the lies and betrayal, he's not the type to settle into a life where passion and adventure are second to obligation and responsibility. I confuse his

179

desire for our relationship with his ability to commit to something far more serious and long-term. It's these thoughts that put me back at square one, trying to squeeze as much time out of this delirious euphoria before the truths of our worlds realign us back away from each other and where it is we both belong.

As much as I'm running to see David, I'm also fleeing everything I face back in New York. I rush to the office in the morning and linger in the evening to avoid the vacuous stares of my husband who doesn't know what I've become, only that the person he's known and loved is absent. In my mind, I justify this treachery, believing that I deserve to be loved and desired regardless. It has been almost a month since Matt has touched me; I fend him off with a mixture of excuses. I blame a delayed postpartum depression, I claim resentment toward a husband unable to support his family, I fault a work environment that only gets more stressful as even I seem to lose track of what is true and untrue in this haze of lust and lies and love.

Arriving on a Wednesday, I didn't expect David to pick me up from Heathrow, and in fact, had said my work had organized a driver, even though I'm doing this whole trip on a tight, personal budget and with the masses on the Heathrow Express. It's not such a bad means of transportation. I enter the familiar train with its TVs that roll prerecorded advertisements as young teenagers with packs slung on their backs pass in front of old women who struggle to their seats among a swarm of businessmen. The doors slide shut in unison with a hiss of air jetting through the springs, and the train slowly shimmies toward full speed. The windows light up to a scene of London done backward, from the midrise suburbs with their busy balconies and rooftop satellites tipped to the sky, interrupted by tunnel darkness and indiscriminate rail stations that we will never get to know or stop at.

London seems to arrive without announcement; a succession of old brick crossings and church steeples of a different age as the rail tracks become more removed and the buildings facing them encroach closer and closer with their graffiti faces seeming to cry in forgotten laundry and barbed wire. Paddington Station seems to always be bathed in half daylight; a five-minute rolling stop as the flurry of readied travelers repeat itself through the opening glass doors that let in the crisp smell of London that infiltrates even the depths of its busiest rail station. It's impossible not to feel more alive for those first few strides in this familiar town. A coffee shop beckons you just next to the doorways that lead to the taxi line that will inevitably be twenty people deep with pushy sorters who tell you which of the six stopped cabbies to get into.

"Two feet planted square in your city. Can't wait to see you." I send David a text and a photo of my bare legs propped up in the back of a city cab with its bulky passenger area and flop-down suicide seat behind the driver.

Despite the calendar that says August, London has a mind of its own when it comes to weather; the sun attempts to fight back the dark thunderclouds that seem to say, "Don't go rushing out of the house just yet this day." The taxi zips through various side streets and alleyways that make this part of London so confusing to navigate, even after all these years. Just when I think I know an area, I'll inevitably get lost on my return from shopping or from a late dinner. I used to be a Soho girl, but recently, the literary side of me has gravitated to the more gentle hum of Covent Garden with its fairytale bookstores around Seven Dials and ten-person restaurants that lend themselves more to discussion versus yelling across a bar.

Though today, it is mostly known as the hub of the West End and London theater district, it's hard to believe that Covent Garden was once an agricultural area tended to by Westminster Abbey. This before being annexed by King Henry VIII and gifted to the earls of Bedford, who built streets of exquisite mansions that surround a central commercial square that eventually became the urban model for the wider city. It's along the narrow Monmouth Street that the taxi tires squeak to a halt on the cobblestone street in front of the red brick sarcophagus of this former French hospital now known as the Covent Garden Hotel, its glossy black windows covered in a moss-gray striped awning.

It's one of several London hotels owned and designed by Kit Kemp, but this one is my favorite. My eyes adjust to the darker interiors as the clank of my heel reverberates over the ashy wide-plank wood floors. Glossy black thresholds evoke a Victorian moodiness as an elaborate iron and stone staircase rises above the carved wood reception counter exuding British countryside glamour. A clock ticks above an old bookcase with numbered slots that refer to another time of forged keys, delivered telegrams, and handwritten notes.

The lobby is quiet in this hour between lunch and happy hour, and a downpour of rain engulfs my wake as a gentlemanly bellman grabs my one bag and the cheery receptionist disrupts her busied idle.

"Welcome to Covent Garden Hotel. Could I please have your last name?" she says with a faint Eastern European accent.

Our conversation is brief as she swipes my debit card that always has me concerned my bank will decline it with a too-hefty deposit, but my own credit card is still unpaid from my last trip that's awaiting reimbursement from work. Without a word, the receptionist hands my bellman a metal key with chunky chain, and we make our way to the elevator among a conclave of floral swag drapery with lazy pleat and a circular wooden settee with subtle satin pillows and a precious rattan back.

A series of private drawing rooms offer a communal living space for guests with an intricate French stone fireplace against a wall of carved wood paneling and an open bar where honesty isn't questioned. Fashionable women sit hunched over metallic laptops and a cluster of gays watch my footwork as we vanish behind the accordion double doors of the elevator; the bellman with his heated breath exhaled on my bare arm. A quick glance at my phone reveals no reply from David; I even double-check to make sure I sent it, which I did. I assume he's neck-deep in work, which is refreshing in a man, but at the same time, a burden not to read into his silence.

With a sort of vibrato, the bellman pushes open the heavy wood door that seems to keep out as much as it secures from within. There's tranquility to the room despite the commotion that waits just beyond the heavily sash windows and drapes that have their own woven sunshine against the gloominess that looms from the sky. A coin tip would be greeted with a scowl in the states, but a small £2 currency still jingles happily between hands in the UK as the bellman backs away without turning around, in old servant style, and he exits the room.

I contemplate opening the computer and checking on work, or even beginning the quick London writing job I took for an online travel magazine that will at least partly make up for the cost of the trip. Instead, I make my way into the comfort of my speckled gray bathroom. Its uniform granite soothes my bare feet and eases my eyes as it rises along the walls; the scent of lemon leaves hangs in the air from the Miller Harris toiletries that are like an aromatic postcard of my London. The simple white sink comforts both my hands as I lean in to take a close look at my tired face, bordering old with fading eyes from a long flight and incongruent life that leaves me sleepless most nights and restless throughout my days. Yet, here I am again.

A warm bath soothes my nerves enough to nap for an hour or two in the complete darkness of a drawn hotel room. I am awakened by a text that jumps me out of bed and to the desk.

"Hey sexy, welcome. Can't wait to see you tonight."

His text relinquishes any hope I had for an earlier rendezvous with no attempt to be spontaneous or impulsive for a hotel drive-by that I yearn for so desperately. I imagine his warm body next to mine in this terribly large bed; its perfect pillows and sheets tucked and topped with a fluffy quilt that hugs my body. The room is built for a woman; its pastel accents and soft floral prints lift my mood with an adoring female dress form that watches me from afar, as in all of Kit Kemp's rooms.

In lieu of lingering in the hotel room and waiting for David to break free of his work, I suit up in my London street clothes and emerge from my jet lag coma and into the roaring after-work scene of packed corner pubs and suited workers. On the path, I weave through Soho, along Carnaby Street, across Oxford and onto Conduit Street where the shops like Vivienne Westwood and Nicole Farhi are still alive in the early evening, and a lingering cloud cover makes it feel far later than it actually is.

I pop into the first-floor tearoom of Sketch, with its white townhouse facade and posh Alice in Wonderland decor, where teacakes are stacked like returned library books on perfect white platters and waif-thin women sit on whimsical rattan chairs.

"A table for one, please."

"Are you here for high tea?" the hostess inquires. She's in a black turtleneck that defies the season but accentuates her already flawless figure.

"Actually, I'll just have a drink at the bar."

I change my mind from cakes and sandwiches in lieu of singular vodka cocktails that will keep me from packing on the pounds while away. I'm the only one at the bar with the lone bartender who looks me over with pity or annoyance upon his approach.

"A woman who snubs high tea, she must be American," he says, grabbing a wine glass from under the bar.

"That obvious?" I say.

"Let me guess, glass of Pinot grigio?" he says instinctively.

"Ouch. Actually, I'll have a Ketel One martini on the rocks."

"Even better, a New York girl," he says in a forced American accent while grabbing an ice pick with his thick veiny hands. I notice an indistinguishable tattoo that begins at the wrist and vanishes up under his starched white shirt.

"Do you work over all your patrons this way?" I ask.

"Only the pretty ones, my lady," he says. His deep brown eyes and tossed hair falls over his ears; the kind of guy you could get into a lot of trouble.

The busyness of the café makes the isolation of just us two at the bar more intense. I restrain myself just a moment as my hand touches the stem of the martini glass, its opaque edge dripping in condensation that falls down my cheek. His stare lingers in front of me.

"How is it?" he asks.

"Refreshing, and just the right amount of dirty."

"Oh, I can make it dirtier," he leans in with a smug smile.

"Do you kiss your mother with that mouth?" I say with a grin, but also with an element of directness that seems to catch him off guard.

"So you're one of those. Then I'll leave you be with your martini," he says as he turns and tends to the end of the bar. His shirt is untucked from the back of his black trousers that wrap around his thick athletic body with a white waiter's sash and scuffed dress shoes.

And leave me alone he does, chatting with other male servers without lending even an eye in my direction. He's even more interesting to me like this, not ruining the brief chemistry with an awkward comment or an out-of-place word. He returns only momentary placing a small white bill in a metal clip in front of my empty drink without asking if I'd like another or even reinitiating eye contact. I pay without hesitation and make my way out of the bar.

Then the countdown to seeing David begins. I meander back to the hotel and freshen up before calling a car to take me to Belgravia for our 9:00 p.m. dinner. I want summer chic, so I wear a vintage pink Balenciaga puff dress that ties at the waist with a white knit sweater that I throw over my shoulder as I glide through the lobby to grab the awaiting cab. It's a little chilly for such a short dress. I sit in the back of the cab that buzzes through the pedestrian streets and congested thoroughfares of the city. London makes the mundane and ordinary seem privileged and civilized with its oversize advertisements and manicured urban parks wrapped in perfectly painted black iron.

"I'll be ten minutes late, have a drink in the bar, and I'll see you shortly. Work nightmares," David texts as the car approaches The Arts Club, a London member's club he's chosen to have dinner. Its imposing townhouse facade of red brick and perfect white windows rise several stories. A cluster of attendants opens a succession of sedan doors and mine, the lone taxi. I exit as gracefully as possible trying not to pull or snag my incredibly poufy dress. I think of how ridiculous I will look standing alone in the bar, me and this dress, waiting yet again on David who is not here when he really should be, whether out of love or sense of respect for this single woman in a foreign city all by herself.

The Arts Club is David embodied in every way, from the distinguished first impression of the entrance foyer. Its classic black and white marble floors and swooped iron baluster stands almost to attention while tracing the strong, tempered spine of the building. It tangents out into various floors that I explore from the basement dj lounge to the mannered dining room and studied library that has hosted patrons dating back to its original founders including Charles Dickens. I don't feel as out of place as I expected among the contrasting white Greek revival columns of the otherwise formal English space where I bide time at a bar once more.

"Let It Be" plays on a house track to the handful of guests in the lounge as my nerves alas relent, and the words sit down with me lingering in my mind to just continue this path to its ultimate outcome. The bartender pours my martini over ice in front of me without uttering more than the obliged word. My eyes struggle to take in all that is around me; an otherworldly place of the elite that's usually off limits even to me. I would rather be nowhere else than right here waiting for him.

"So embarrassed, I'm there already in heart. Fifteen-minutes max. In the car," David texts. My heart drops, and I sell myself on just a few minutes more of waiting. My thoughts turn to what life would really be like with David: long workdays that turn into weeks of him being gone, that insatiable appetite for sex, and always that wandering eye beyond the grasp of my watch or control. How scary life would be at this point in my life, giving up a sure thing for a maybe with someone so unpredictable. As I begin to drop in spirit and expectations, someone taps my shoulder. A turn of my head queues that rush of passion and adrenaline as his grinning eyes meet mine. I lean in for a kiss that begins this entire cycle again. My arms wrap around his silky-soft blazer, and my face finds that exposed skin just above his sweater where I'm able to grab his scent that is unlike any other I have smelled.

"Look at you. You're going to make the chaps here seethe with jealousy. You look sensational, Catherine."

My name even sounds better when he says it. I stand in stillness, unable to look away from him, the way his forehead wrinkles when he laughs and his eyes squint at the light above. I feel more beautiful with him here next to me, by my side, and it feels as if I am something altogether more, better, and complete. My life was supposed to be like this; this was the person meant for me, to be with and evolve as a person by his side.

"I apologize for leaving you here waiting. I hope it wasn't terribly uncomfortable," he says, nose to nose as the bartender hovers next to us waiting to tend to David's order.

When David is near, it's like everything else that was before or that is to come, is a blur, as if it doesn't matter or exist at this moment.

"I love this place. It's so pretty, and I had no idea what a literary haunt it was."

"I didn't really think about it, but it's really perfect for you as a writer."

"Although Charles Dickens wasn't really the struggling artist; he was one of the few writers of his time to have tremendous financial success during his lifetime."

"Are you saying he was an elitist bastard?"

"No, just that not all writers were able to afford such an extravagant lifestyle," I say.

"Would you prefer to go somewhere else?"

"No, no, not at all. That's not what I meant. Forget it, I love it, and I love it even more now that you are here."

"Shall we go into the dining room," he says with a mere look at the bartender who lingers on him without initiating verbal dialogue.

"Sure, yes, let's. Can I close my tab?" I say to the bartender.

"It's already taken care of, Miss Klein," he replies.

Klein is my last name, but I had never given it personally.

"Darby, we are going to go have dinner, but good seeing you, mate."

"As you, Mr. Summers," he replies as David leads me away from the bar with a gliding push of my lower back.

David seems tired or distracted as we walk silent between the rooms of the club and into the dining room that's brighter than I imagined. Its white cornice ceiling and veiny marble floors take some gentle steps to walk on. He chats to the maître d' as if he's there on a daily basis, but without introducing me. I stand attentive to the conversation, but the two men completely exclude me. Then the regal man with silvery-gray hair leads us past a group of packed tables to a large silvery-blue banquette that could easily seat six, but with just two place settings cozily arranged next to each other. I thought that even if the mood isn't perfectly romantic so far this evening, the backdrop couldn't be lovelier.

"So, I'm still a little cross that you wouldn't stay at my flat."

"Excuse me?"

"I said, I'm just a little disappointed you didn't choose to stay with me," he says with a whispered restraint.

"You know I would love to; it's just I am here for work, and they tend to call and fax directly to my hotel. It would appear as though I was goofing off to not actually be staying in the room."

"There's also another version of the story that goes, 'this incredibly lovely guy who never invites women to his flat finally found someone who he actually wanted to stay the night, and she shot him down.'"

"David, I didn't shoot you down. We have the whole weekend in front of us. You could just as easily stay with me at the hotel."

"Except for the one pesky word … job," he says in reply. "I have a seven o'clock meeting tomorrow morning, and the office is a good hour commute from your hotel in Covent Garden."

"Well, then, you understand my situation exactly," I say, taking his hand and holding it in my lap.

"It's just this is my hometown and that's my home, but I get it."

My heart stops at the thought of staying in David's home, but I also realize Matt would be calling me in the room. If I didn't answer and there was an emergency with Billy, I would never be able to forgive myself.

"So tell me about your assignment again. Are you interviewing someone here?"

"Yes, a US TV celebrity who's in a West End show." I make up a story on the quick, not wanting to tell him about the low-level travel assignment I've sought out just to be here with him again.

"What show?" he asks.

"Oh, just a US TV comedy actress on the rise."

"No, I mean, what West End show?"

"It's a new version of *West Side Story*," I blurt out, hoping it will satiate his inquisitiveness, which it does.

"So, what were you so busy working on the last few days?" I ask before sipping the iced water poured out of a hefty-looking glass bottle.

"It's one of the most intense jobs I've ever worked on, and without boring you too terribly much, it's a regional British bank acquiring a small German lender, but it's marred in all these subsidiary businesses that we are trying to risk access."

Three waiters bring a series of appetizers in three consecutive unveilings that reveal a full caviar spread and a fish carpaccio of some sort. They place the dishes in front of David. I hesitate to tell him I'm mostly vegetarian, especially if he doesn't remember by now, until I look closer and see the caviar is actually some sort of milled vegetable. I smear some on the endive leaf and attempt to eat it without displacing my lip liner.

David continues with the nuances of the deal; his intensity keeps me intrigued as he gestures with his thick hands, catching my eye in between delicate forks of the carpaccio and precise wipes of his mouth with the heavily starched white linen napkin in his lap. His manners are impeccable. He holds the fork in one hand while gently using the knife to smear the remaining pieces in one small heaping that enters his mouth without fail.

At moments, listening to David reminds me of Matt, from the way he gets frustrated at people of unlike mind, to the way he tries to appease me by passing the water before I ask or inquiring if my food is just right. I try to block the comparison from my head, as if it's some sort of Freudian undertone that we simply repeat all things from our past. It's neither comforting nor annoying but an awkward similarity of two men who have so little else in common.

"But let's forget about work and think about something more convivial. Tomorrow, you'll come over to my house, and we can leave together for Somerset?" he asks as he subtly makes obvious that we will not be spending the night together.

"Yes, of course," I say as I grab the stem of my orbed red wine glass. I bring it to my lips in a slow sip of the wine that I try to drink without having it touch my teeth.

"I'm going to drive, so we should probably leave by afternoon in order to avoid traffic," he says, "assuming you're done with your work by that time. Otherwise, we can always grab the train, but that's a bit grim, I'd say."

Dinner passes in a faster pace than I expect. David declines dessert or espresso, and I do the same. I glance at his thin gold dial Patek Philippe and its shiny black leather strap that alludes we completed dinner in little more than sixty minutes, which seems rather rushed for two people so desperate to be with each other. I think of ordering another drink, but resign myself to the evening ending. I hope to find better footing with David with a little sleep.

"So, my flat is very near here. Why don't we take a walk, and then I'll call my driver to give you a lift back to the West End later?" David says, grabbing my right hand and spreading my fingers to rub our palms together before getting up from the table. He helps me up from the booth as I contemplate a long walk in my now-ridiculous-feeling dress and heels. But it doesn't matter when with David as he leads me out of the restaurant and up the street, past galleries, closed cafés, and designer shops that line this part of Mayfair. It's no more than a few blocks where the narrow brick buildings open to the dramatic archways dotted in bold point lights that look like an old theater marquee along the entrance of the Ritz.

The streets are still crowded, and I try not to fall behind David's speedier pace. London beats with a racing heart even in the late evening. Taxis zoom past and busier commercial streets with posh brasseries and packed bars succumb to pockets of cozy residential buildings trimmed in glossy black frontages with wrought iron gates and women ready for bed in the windows cut out of the red and white brick on the upper floors.

"When I first moved to London after university, I didn't know how to get anywhere. I spent every moment in the back of a car to the point where I really didn't get to know the nuances of the city," David says.

"How old were you?"

"Maybe twenty-five or twenty-six. I'd come here all my life. But since then, I try to walk home every night from dinner as long as it's not terribly far or the weather isn't too bad. Seeing the people in the windows and on the street are my version of having dinner with the family every night."

I realize this is my time to tell him, to tell him the truth, in this moment of vulnerability when the night is still young and we have the weekend before us to work through the anger and deceit and come out the other side.

"You know, there is so much we really don't know about each other, things we might have missed in the process of this new relationship given the distance between us," I ease into the conversation.

"But I've had distance between the people I love all my life, from my parents sending me away to school and then with work that separates me from almost everyone I know."

"Do you want your life always to be on the road and away from the ones you love?" I ask softly, not wanting to come off as a woman who says she insists her husband not travel for work or otherwise.

"I love what I do, always meeting new people and seeing places that keep my mind and interests expanding. And that's what I love about you. You're not bogged down with conventional expectations and have found fulfillment as a person, a complete person, one who doesn't need a man or a child to have a full life."

"But I don't know if that's the exact case for me," I say.

"Of course it is. Normally, I'd be having fights at this point in the relationship about my lack of availability and endless travels, but with you, it works. It's the best relationship I've had with a woman, and I think that's because you know who you are and you know what you want."

The adulation stalls my advances as he holds my hand tighter, and the neighborhood around us becomes even more storybook-like. The perfectly green square lined in parked Mercedes sedans, encircled by rows of pure white Victorian houses and their proud Doric columns, varying striped window coverings and national flags of the respective Spanish and Finnish embassies, pass by us.

"This is my road," he says as I take a second look at the name Eaton Street. I savor this moment tracing the steps that he takes night after night. The sidewalk widens and the diplomatic houses yield to facades that are more residential and then his; it comes with a four-story white and brick face with an ebonized single door entry that opens to a narrow hallway. An iron staircase rises extravagantly above our heads. He opens his mailbox with a key from his pocket in a sort of coming-home routine that I couldn't find more captivating.

A small elevator opens and we both step inside. He presses the third-floor button and the door shuts. He leans in for a kiss without looking up from his fingering of envelopes and letters in large envelopes likely too important to be folded. I can't believe I'm here. The elevator stops and opens to a simple long corridor with doors spaced unevenly. His is the last one on the left, which he approaches with a key in hand and opens.

Two steps later, I stand inside the lair of the man I have been fixated on since our first meeting. I expected a dark boudoir of masculinity, and instead, a creamy white space surprises with its stylishness and purity.

"It's so lovely, David, and totally not what I was expecting," I say.

Two long powder-gray sofas are staggered on opposite walls with a Hermés throw laid over the arm, and an edgy photograph of a blonde woman smoking a cigarette on a bus stop sits on a white wall with plaster wainscoting and a crown of carved moldings. A marble fireplace looks inoperable, either out of lifestyle or in actuality, with its perfectly clean innards and wicker basket with birch branches in front of it. Two elaborately tall columns stride either side of a wall that leads to the dining room; its white lacquer table looks unused with its six cubist chairs that sit in a corner overlooking a storybook street scene. Two mirrored doors push open to the kitchen with its bare countertops and single coffeemaker that looks as if it had been left on from earlier in the day.

David doesn't do a tour or even mention much of anything about the apartment that feels like just another hotel room, albeit a bit larger with its decor that anyone would feel comfortable to live in and lack of personal touches that makes it feel like absolutely no one lives here.

"Do you mind if I use the bathroom, quickly?" I ask.

"No, not at all," he says, still consumed with his mail. "Just go through the living room, and you'll see it in the hall on the way to the bedroom."

Despite the continued lull in our conversations, the inside of his home captivates me. I make my way back through the living room with its few photographs of David and friends on vacation and a family photo at a formal wedding somewhere long ago. On a higher shelf, I notice another of him and a woman, which I cannot properly see on my turn down the short hall. I glimpse into his bedroom and see a perfectly made bed with a herringbone quilt and two oblong pillows in the same pattern.

Hoping the bathroom would be the lone one in the apartment stocked full of his personal items, I'm disappointed to find a simple sink protruding artistically from the wall with a Damien Hirst photo of a pill in place of a mirror and a toilet next to it. There's an arrangement of perfumes and hand soaps from Asprey that I test one by one, but none of which are the woodsy mandarin scent of him. His towel racks are lined in three pressed linen hand cloths, not towels like virtually every other person I know has in their bathroom.

"Catherine, come in here," David says as I exit the bathroom and see he's removed his suit and stands in his dress shirt and boxers in a corner of his bedroom. The fabric walls are the subtlest of gray colors, and I notice a television is on.

David flops on the bed. "Come sit with me."

I sit on the edge of the bed as he pulls the covers over him, now lying there in just his white boxers.

"This is my favorite place in the world, just lying right here in this bed and flicking on the TV set and letting my mind simply go blank."

My dress doesn't compress well when lying down, and I try to pull it under me as not to give the illusion of a fat ballerina.

"What do you watch?" I ask.

"It really doesn't matter. Sometimes, one of those singing quiz shows and other times whatever movie happens to be on."

"I didn't take you as the movie type," I say.

"I really don't watch it. I just let it wash over me and take away all that I was thinking about in the day."

My hand reaches over and caresses his warm body under the sheets; his smooth chest, with its spare few hairs and down his torso, he feels like a Greek athlete cut from marble and leaves me just a little self-conscious about my own body, even if it gets better and thinner with each day. My hand dips down to feel his dick, soft and lying to the side with its fleshy tip as a door buzz interrupts us.

"So I think that's your car. I was hoping we could cuddle a bit, but I know you have to work tomorrow," David says, somewhat to my dismay that we won't be having sex tonight after all. Perhaps he's upset that I chose not to stay with him, but that didn't mean I couldn't stay most of the night. I jump to my feet as David rises from the bed lingering with the covers in lieu of seeing me to the door.

"So, text me tomorrow when you are done with your interview," he says with a kiss on the mouth without a hint of second thoughts on his part.

"Yes, I will," I say, quietly making my way out the bedroom door. I can see the car through the window below, its lights beaming in the night sky.

"I'll send a car for you, and we will leave from here."

"Okay, see you tomorrow."

I retrace my steps through the living room and into the hallways, shutting the heavy wood door behind me. I take the staircase because it's prettier, rounding my way back through the lobby and outside where a shiny black Mercedes, like the one I saw on the walk, waits with a driver waving from the front seat. Even with my disappointment from what the night was to be, I find solace in plopping into the rear of the sedan with its new fragrant leather and dark windows. The London night flashes in the window like a movie of my own life: the marquees near Piccadilly, the store windows on Oxford Circus, toward Soho to Shaftsbury Avenue, and on to Convent Garden that feels so very far from him this night.

The following day, I busy myself with work through the morning and until the late checkout of two o'clock before texting David that I'm finished with my interview. I lunch quickly at a small bistro called da Polpo near the hotel that makes the best quinoa salad I've ever had, with crew of dining actors on break from their theater practices. It's overcast and intermittently rainy at times; a struggle for my mostly summer wardrobe that doesn't include a proper trench this season.

"Meet me in 30 at Paddington. Got delayed obvi, let's train it, more fun." Alas, at 4:00 p.m., a text finally arrives from David as I sit stranded in the hotel lobby with my plot of luggage. There's no car sent or excuse as to the delay, just a beckon to Paddington Station with which I gladly comply. The hotel clerk takes longer than usual to summon a cab, but it finally arrives. The driver hesitates to get out of the taxi as the bellman struggles with my hard-sided luggage into the rear of the cab. The rain is thicker than it was earlier; falling as if an angry man is sitting above in the heavens with endless buckets thrown on our windshield, and making me wonder how I will ever make it inside the train station without being drenched.

There, in the doorway of Paddington Station in a smart slicker and a cute hat, is the man I adore. The rain is falling on him as he rushes to grab my bag that he kiddingly struggles to lift before rushing it inside and me along with him. He could have easily remained inside, which I expected, but his presence on the street side, waiting for me in the rain, washes away all disappointment from the day before.

"I can't believe I made you come here in the rain, on your own, and in the worst of traffic!" he yells above the train announcements that lend a romantic soundtrack. He holds me tightly around the shoulder before rearranging our bags and making our way through the terminal that glows anew when on the arm of someone like David. We make our way to our rail track where the yellow and green locomotive purrs and uniformed agents whistle in the background as other trains ready for Chichester and Redding and Manchester.

"So, where is it we are going, exactly?" I ask.

"Well, technically the wedding is in Somerset, but we are going to Bath. That's closer to the hotel where we're staying," he says as we board the front of the train and make our way through the glass door and into a dark interior space with tables and booth-style seats; we take the third vacant one. David heaves our luggage onto the shelves above our seats, his bare stomach and small patch of hair below his naval exposed under his plaid shirt.

"You're not exactly a light packer, are you my love?" he says as he comes to a seat across from me. "That's good to know."

"It's actually the bag that's the heavy part; it really doesn't fit a lot."

"I see. And you advise people how to travel?" he asks with a sarcastic grin.

"Yes. I advise people how to travel fashionably and that bag is a hit," I reply as his grin widens.

We are seated in the first-class cabin. On the train, that simply means assigned seating, and I believe a free beverage of choice at the snack bar in the forward carriage. I can already smell its sizzling grill and too-fragrant meat pies. The train staggers to a forward motion before hitting a steady speed, and the rail station begins to retell the story of my previous day's journey to London in reverse. David's eyes home in on the weekend edition of the *Evening Standard*, his eyes speeding horizontally behind chunky black reading glasses that sit precariously low on his Roman nose.

The horizon turns from urban to rural in a matter of three pages of the *International Herald Tribune* with its condensed take on major news stories of the day and American trends that feel a little stale, likely by writers with stories that weren't immediately picked up by top-tier newspapers. The rolling grasslands of almost fluorescent foliage are suddenly interrupted by a horse-shaped figure carved out of the hillside.

"David, what is that on the hillside there?" I ask interrupting him from his paper folded over in fourths to an article that has enveloped him since boarding.

"You mean that … there?" he says, peering up from above his glasses. "That's one of the white horses. You'll see a lot of them along the way. They're really old. I think before Jesus Christ."

"What do they mean? Are they like crop circles?"

"Not sure, really. They're made of rock, I think. They usually represent some sort of historic figure or notorious battle, if I remember correctly," he says and returns to reading his paper.

I put down my own newspaper and pull out my iPad to do a quick research of hill figures and discover there are actually a variety of newer figures made for various advertising and cultural celebrations. But this particular figure is the Uffington White Horse that's almost five-hundred-feet long and made of hand-dug trenches filled with crushed white chalk dating back to three thousand BC. While questionable that the figure is even a horse, the carving was meant to symbolize the dominance of the nearby castle under the same jurisdiction.

I quickly check my e-mail to discover a picture that Matt sent me of Billy playing at daycare, which auto-expands on my screen. I attempt to conceal the reflection created on the window and glass behind me.

David looks up briefly, only to look down again at his newspaper that now resembles something that should be tossed in the trash. I fantasize about showing him the picture, falling into a conversation that absolutely must happen, and yet, I can never push myself to the point of uttering the words.

"So tell me about the wedding we are going to ... what's her name again?" I ask.

"Her name is Alexandra, we were very good friends in university. She's marrying Ben, who I also knew, but not as well, at the time."

"Did you date Alexandra?"

"Well, I wouldn't necessarily say date. But we were good mates for almost the entire time at university."

"Does she live in London now?"

"Yes, they live in East London. Ben is in advertising; his father started a very large PR firm in the fifties that he now assists in managing."

"And Alexandra, does she work? I assume not."

"She does work. She works at an art publication called *POP*. Have you heard of it?"

"No, not really. Although it sounds very familiar."

I truly wish he had told me a fellow journalist was getting married, as I probably would not have put myself in a position of meeting someone so connected to my New York life. While *POP* is really just a UK art publication, it also has a fashion component and likely overlapping contacts that could reach into my New York world. Given my own magazine is nowhere near as prestigious or hip as *POP*, I hope I have nothing to worry about.

"Well, it's a very big deal in London, and it's owned by Roman Abramovich, the Russian owner of Millhouse, and his girlfriend Dasha Zhukova runs the whole operation. You do know them, right?"

"Yes, of course, but just from what I've read."

"Well, they're lovely and know how to throw quite the party if you've ever been in Saint Barth or Miami for Art Basel."

There's an exclusionist tone to David when he speaks of people in his own world and me as an American, or maybe just as a normal not-wealthy woman. I'm sure he means nothing by it, but it rings

197

condescending, especially when he makes virtually no eye contact during the explanation.

There's little more conversation before the announcement calls out our stop in Bath, which is far more of a city than I was expecting, complete with its own large shopping street and jam-packed downtown.

Life moves at warp speed with David. The minute we step off the train, a driver greets him and takes everything, including my bulky purse, on him physically, so much so that he resembles a human mule in a full suit as he walks the terminal. Beads of sweat roll down his temple; he's a husky man with too much hair gel and a scent that's three spritzes too much of a fragrance from the early nineties. We make our way down the stairs and to his awaiting car that starts with a remote, and we seclude ourselves in a perfectly cool backseat.

"I'm so happy you were able to come with me." David leans in to kiss me on the cheek. "I told Alexandra you were the type of woman I'm proud to have on my arm."

I want to tell David exactly how I feel about him, how he makes every moment just a little better by being near. I want to tell him that I am as attracted to him with my eyes closed as with them wide open, and his hand is as comforting to hold, as his mouth is to kiss. However, I fear being the one who makes him feel too confined, too needed, and so in love with that he runs off for feeling suffocated or fearing intimacy. So instead, I sit silent and simply hold his hand tighter.

The evening sky turns to its last shade of purple before withdrawing into night as a horizon of manicured crops borders the hills. Elegant horses intersect rural roads as the car stops abruptly to let the four-hoofed traffic pass, an elegant rider on top. Ridiculously beautiful cows in all colors of brown sit within feet of white wooden fences along a narrow road barely wide enough for two cars to pass side by side. At the fork in the road is a small sign no bigger than a real estate marker with the words Babington House at one side of a tree-covered lane with a two-story cottage, long abandoned of its inhabitants.

"Is this where the wedding is tomorrow?" I ask. "It's amazingly beautiful."

"Oh no, this is where us poor folk stay without a countryseat in these parts. The wedding is at Alexandra's family estate nearby."

While easily impressed by such magnificence that appears through the windows, I mimic David and show no emotion. I concentrate on the series of footmen in my eye line who arrive to fetch our luggage, assist me out of the car, and welcome me with a glass of champagne. My eyes look away, taking in the edifice of Babington House and the manor's sixteenth-century exterior of grayish stone gripped in greenish-aged moss and flanked in a roofline of chimney stacks that connect to the sky in a line of smoke. Sculpted but somewhat spare landscaping of hedges and potted topiary surround the motor court traced in iron lanterns lit in candlelight.

David rounds the car as I exit, grabs my hand, and takes me under the threshold into the main reception hall that smells of another century. My eyes sneak a gaze inside the series of formal rooms with creaky wooden floors and cavernous ceilings that echo in the careful steps of my knee-high boots. David proceeds to a Biedermeier desk that doubles as the reception. I peer into a cozy library with walls of glossy photography books and intricate walnut paneling that surround heavily filled down sofas where a woman sits with an e-reader under a chandelier made of antlers. We smile at each other, and she returns to her book. I move back into the hall and farther along into a cozy bar trimmed in emerald fabric walls. The furnishings are a bit busier, and inside are a collection of gents in skinny suits seated in tufted wingchairs in mint-colored mohair.

Part member's club and part open-to-the-public hotel, there's an element of elitism in the air mixed with sounds of The Strokes and the ever-present thump of traversing footsteps through the main hall. Outside, the grounds come to life once more, as spotlights illuminate an endless lawn and outlying buildings, including a small chapel with a steeple immediately next to the main house. It feels like a house party where you don't know any other guests, but you really would like to meet them all. Everyone is fashionable and tucked deep into their own tête-à-têtes, looking up a second as I pass in my boots and jeans and flared black blazer, but then directly back into the depths of their conversations.

David returns, grabbing me from behind with a bite on my upper ear.

"Room key in hand. What do you say we head inside," he whispers in my ear and then follows with another bite.

"You lead the way."

The grand hall of the main house becomes quieter on this side. A cluster of heavy, old wooden doors leads to our own with a cumbersome deadbolt that David masters in a single attempt to unlock. He leads me inside and through a narrow hallway with a bathroom and into the bedroom with an alcove of three elaborately tall picture windows. At the center of the room, an ash-white four-poster bed is covered in a satin canopy next to a roaring fireplace. My eyes scan for our luggage tucked nicely on a stand side by side beside a white marble console with a sink.

My mind drifts to the idea of a bath or a change of clothes, but David's hands grip both sides of my waist and force me onto the bed. The bed is so fluffy that I actually bounce as he drops to the floor and begins to pull off my boots, first with one zipper and then another. He doesn't remove his coat or even his shoes as he strips away my jeans and then heaves me forward with a deep kiss while pulling my jacket off from behind.

"I want to taste you," he whispers in my ear. He removes my blouse, unbuttoning with his hands underneath me, grabbing my breasts, and wrestling with my bra that he unclips on the first try. I lie there unwillingly, leaping to my feet and onto the bed while grabbing the upper slats that support the canopy of the bed. Swinging a bit, I feel almost liberated with the warmth of the fireplace taking away any coldness on my breasts. David intersects my body with his face, and from above; I see only the top of his head and clothed body.

He enters me from behind with his tongue, abruptly and intensely, a tingling and almost euphoric feeling as he pries deeper while fingering me with his thumbs and spreading me apart as if trying to reach the deepest parts of my being. I yearn to see and touch his body, but alas, I let him simply devour me in this moment where I feel neither unfit nor average, but as the most wanted of women desired by a man who is nothing short of anatomical perfection. I cry out without control; he goes deeper and deeper inside me as the longing to have him inside me almost becomes overwhelming.

Finally, David rises and rips off his blazer and shirt. He stands there in his unzipped trousers and shoes fingering me as I hover above him still on the bed. Finally, his shoes come off and then his pants. He is standing there wearing nothing but his tall socks that he removes and then wraps each one around my hands on the bedposts. The socks are tight around my wrists, the bed is creaking, and I flail like a captured woman about to be ravaged by her conqueror. David vanishes from the room for just a moment and returns with a bottle of lotion that he holds in his masculine hands as I fall back onto the bed.

Slowly, from the foot up, he massages my body while manipulating his fingers inside and then outside, slowly sending me into frenzy while watching him bounce up and down as I alas yearn to have him enter me. He works his way up my body, finally making his way to my nipples, tense with anticipation, and then my mouth as he looks eye to eye with me. He then gets just close enough that I feel his hot breath on my face. He hesitates to kiss me, instead, he licks my neck and face before devouring my mouth with his own. He pulls on my hair, more aggressively than before. I feel his hard body pressing on mine before rounding around my back and then thrusting himself inside with a tip of my body and then in and out with all his might again and again and again.

His face has a focused stare while inside me, under a contorted brow and a vein that pops out of his left temple as if his mind and body are fully engaged. He never closes his eyes, studying my movements and reactions to him that fill the room in a soundtrack of desire and ecstasy. I climax in an arduous cry as I feel the warm sensation of him exploding inside me.

The following morning, I awoke to an empty bed still so fragrant with the smell of him on his pillow next to mine that I hold it against my face and inhale as much as my lungs will fill. The room is dark but for narrow slices of light that filter through the closed curtains. I pull off the sheet and make my way to open and see what the day holds before me. With a forceful heave, I push the blush-colored drapes open, and just beyond is a panorama of an almost neon-green lawn and bright blue sky with but a faint rejected cloud lost in the distance. A series of sun loungers line the perimeter of the garden, well spaced from one another as if each guest desired to be completely alone.

The scent of coffee lingers from a silver carafe on a large tray that sits on the coffee table. I plop onto the sofa and pour some coffee into a dainty white porcelain cup next to a small plate of pastries that I push to the side and cover in salt as not to be too tempted. A note sits on the tray, as well.

Been gone riding with the boys, back before midday, signed *David*.

In the meantime, I linger over the Soho House magazines that include more articles by more artists and actors than actual aristocrats do, as well as various edgy magazines that have probably sat in the room for years without actually being read. I wander over to David's bag and lean in to pull out his worn shirt, already picked up from the floor from last night and tossed in his bag, still with that incredible scent. He wears size thirty-two boxers, Dior Homme makes his pants, and his scarf is Hermés. His simple duffel bag is Tumi, his socks are made of cashmere, and he keeps his shoes in trees, even when he's traveling.

On the washbasin, there's a cloth overlaid with his toiletries, including a straight razor, aftershave by Eau d'Italie, and condoms tucked in the side of his dopp kit marked extra-large with an off branding. He uses cinnamon toothpaste that's not obvious, a hair balm by Santa Maria Novell, and keeps a prescription for Ambien. His computer sits on the nightstand; I open to see if it's passcode-protected, which it is, and alas, I am at the end of all things that occupy my interest in the room, and it's not even 10:00 a.m.

So, in my sexiest and most preppy tights and fluffy vest, I pull on my running shoes and make my way outside to join the daylight and incredible countryside. I make my way quietly through the main hall and out the front door to the main circle before hitting a jogging pace along the main drive that leads to the outside road. From there, I sprint to the road; a chilly breeze hits my face from under the leaning trees that smell of morning dew. At the road, I take a swift right, away from the direction in which we arrived and into the vast horizon of farm fields where in the distance I see three horses off the main road. I run faster and faster toward them. The road narrows as a taxi zips past, and the figures become larger on the horizon, one of which resembles the tall and lean man I so adore.

A rolling horizon erupts with yellow wildflowers as electric cables meander above in the only instance I've ever thought overhead wire looks almost pretty. And there, as I approach, a large black horse takes a step backward, and the rider turns. He's wearing a crisp white shirt juxtaposed by his wavy black locks under a sturdy cap with navy breaches that hug his thick thighs down to his high boots that are covered in mud.

"Is that who I think it is?" David says, his face chapped and rosy by the morning chill that makes his eyes penetrate even deeper inside me.

"Indeed, just out for a morning run."

"What a beautiful morning. So good you're taking advantage of it," says a slight woman in a red blazer who emerges from behind him. She has a porcelain complexion and perfect hair.

"You must be Catherine. Catherine the Great, from what I've heard," she says as I approach the bushes that separate them from the road and me.

"I am, and I hope it's all been kind things said," I reply.

"Is there anything else to say of you?" David interjects. "Catherine, this is Sophie Dale-Evans. She is the sister of today's bride and a dear friend."

I lean in to shake her hand. I find her beauty discomforting as well as the intimacy of them riding together on such a special morning. A smile is all I can muster as I tiptoe around the mud in the only pair of athletic shoes I own.

"Congratulations. You must be so happy for your sister," I say.

"Let's see. Sister marries rich and semi-successful city boy leaving but one sibling unwed in the Dale-Evans family. Happy wouldn't be the first emotion, but likely the third or fourth, and I do wish my sister the very best," she says with a smile directed to David, who responds with a smile to me.

David dismounts from the shiny black horse, jumps over the small brush to stand next to me, and plants a kiss on my lips. I bask in the attention; especially in front of this woman, knowing he would never kiss me in front of her if there was something between them.

"And this, now. You have to flaunt your romance. Am I not tortured enough today?" she says.

"My younger sister married before me, so I know your pain," I reply. Even though my younger sister is unwed and forty pounds overweight, Sophie could use some comforting words.

"Would you like a ride on my pony, young lady?" David says, patting his horse on the snout that lingers above the fence while grabbing my fingers.

"Oh, David. You and your zingers," Sophie laughs.

"But I'm not wearing the right clothes."

"That's okay, as long as you don't fall off or try to flee, my young one," he says.

"Really, I don't know. Are you sure?" The idea of horses has never really been my thing.

"Oh, come on. You can't wait for the one on the white horse," says Sophie, "from what my sister tells me anyway."

"Ouch. Now is that nice?" David rebuts.

"Okay, okay. Just don't go too fast or let me fall off," I say while making my way over the fence.

"I promise, as long as you do what I say."

"Today and forever more, I'm sure," Sophie laughs.

David rises atop the horse with a single lift of his leg; his pants perfectly tailored to his body as he leans over and tells me where to grab and where to step in order to join him. He flings me in front with a singular pull, and together the three of us leave the road and gallop through the hillside.

"Try to stand when we gallop, so you don't bounce as much, although I do like the way that feels, I must admit," he says, straddling me from behind.

"It's not the most comfortable position," I say, still a bit sore from last night, although I don't dare admit it.

"Well, practice makes perfect, my love."

We pass a series of undisturbed lakes surrounded by nothing more than grass and onto a dramatic gated entrance with a drive longer than that of the hotel and even more punctuated by large oak trees staggered perfectly along the curved cobblestone drive. In the distance, a sprawling manor stands out against a bare horizon with wide lawn and stables busied with riders and workers. Next to the house is a large white tent I assume is the site of today's wedding.

"See that marquee? That's where my sister will marry today and leave me the spinster sister!" Sophie screams to us in the back.

"I'm going to double back to the road and take Catherine back; I don't want her to get too dirty," David says in return.

"Oh, I'll be fine," I say.

"Accept the chivalry, Catherine, it's a bloody mess from the rains, and you'll be knee-deep," she insists.

Without further discussion, David turns away from the stables and gravel road and into the hills at a full gallop. I hold onto the thick leather reigns, and he firmly holds onto me as we cross the landscape. It's more familiar on the second time around the lake with the scowling goose and along the yellow-flower-dotted hillside to the gate where we crossed paths.

"This would be your stop, my lady," he says, squeezing me with his inner thighs.

"That was much better than a run on foot."

"I forgot how much I miss the country," he says. "But there's more of that later. You better hurry back; we are due at the house at one o'clock, prompt."

He hoists me off the horse and on to the ground with a pat on the head before galloping up the hill and away without even a wave good-bye, leaving me to my run that reverses back to the hotel.

David doesn't return to our hotel room for almost an hour, leaving me plenty of time to stare in every reflective surface, looking at myself sideways while changing my hair no less than three times in a dressing ritual best kept private in a new relationship. I chose a Sarah Burton creamy-pink chiffon dress for the wedding; a simple A-cut with a small bow detail at the neck that connects to a more dramatic lace cape of equal length. It's dressy without being formal.

"That was a wicked ride. Look at you ... you look ... ravishing."

The door opens and David walks in completely muddy and dropping little bits of grassy dried dirt in his wake. I immediately think of what the hotel management will say, but David is oblivious as he scatters his mud-covered clothes in a corner of the bathroom and in moments, stands there completely naked with the exception of his black equestrian helmet.

"Are you going to shower in that?" I say in jest, reminding myself that this is his world, and I should allow him to do as he wishes in the hotel room for which he is paying.

"Oh, right," he says as he pulls off the helmet and drops it with a thump, his hair falling in his eyes and his hands covered in dried mud.

"We got stuck, and I had to pull Sophie's horse out of a ditch. It was a bloody nightmare."

In a matter of no more than ten minutes, David is able to shower off the mud and simply throw on a three-piece Prince of Wales plaid suit with a bold blue shirt and tie that looks flawless even without a double take in the mirror. He proceeds to take his razor and freshen up his sideburns and facial hair before dabbing his index and middle finger into a tub of grayish clay that he slicks into his hair while leaning closer to the mirror and doing a roll of his neck. He spritzes more than a little fragrance in a similar motion from the back of his neck to his chest and arms before turning and looking at me with a wide smile.

"What is it?" he asks, stopping in the doorway.

"That was just so fast, and yet you look flawless."

"We need to hurry; the car is waiting for us. Oh, and grab some towels."

David leads the way curiously with a pile of white, fluffy towels that he carries through the main hall of the hotel. I follow alongside, struggling in my higher-than-normal heel as we round the front door. Outside, we find a steel-gray vintage car of some type and a fully outfitted driver waiting next to the passenger seat. A crowd of hotel guests has gathered to look at the car that I can't really recognize more than just being old and quite exquisite.

"So let me lay these down in the front seat; I'm afraid I made a mess of old Danny's car," David says to the driver as he lays the towels on the passenger floor.

"Mr. Summers, it will clean without trouble. No need to worry," the driver says.

I look in the front seat and notice it's covered in mud as well as the window that's rolled all the way down and crusted on top. David navigates the mud without much fuss, pushing the seat forward of what I see is a Ferrari of some type, and we both struggle to position ourselves in the snug seat.

"I love this car. What is it?" I allow myself to ask. The interior roof details and the burly driver's panel are nothing less than superb.

"It's a Ferrari 330 GT; their father has a fairly significant private car collection. This isn't really even one of the good ones."

We make the familiar drive out the long driveway of Babington House that now feels familiar and unintimidating to me. We retrace my morning path and make around a five-minute drive before approaching a gravel road barely noticeable from the main road. My eyes cannot wait to see more, and I'm hoping not to be so impressed that I feel intimidated or self-conscious of my dress, my job, or my social stature.

David's hand reaches over and holds my knee in the palm of his hand while he steadily watches the horizon. A home straight out of some Jane Austen novel appears different from what I saw earlier in the morning. Its stone is the color of pewter and its Jacobean architecture raises only two stories with a pointed roofline like a king's crown captured in a cloak of emerald lawn with few trees or shrubbery to impede its grandeur. I can't imagine anyone human in this day and age was born, lives, or exists in such a house.

"This is their main residence?" I whisper, not wanting to appear rapt or easily impressed.

"Yes, this is Dale Hall. I believe it's been part of their family since the fifteenth century," he says without batting an eye or noticing my eyes so engrossed in the spectacle.

A line of men stands alongside the main drive as our cars round to the front of the house. A cluster of men in morning coats hover within the interior foyer as our car comes to a halt. A man with a beard and Santa-like spectacles emerges.

"David, I hope Danny didn't drive like a bandit."

I struggle to step over the folded passenger seat that's front and center to the old man who watches as I attempt not to get dirty or misstep on the gravel in a five-inch heel.

"Not at all, but I'm afraid I made quite a mess of your car."

"No worries, chap, it won't be the first time. And this must be Miss Klein?"

"Yes, I am Catherine," I say as I extend my hand.

"Lovely for you to make it all the way here for my daughter's wedding; it means a great deal to Tess and myself."

"And myself as well," David says as he rejoins my side and holds my hand. Another car approaches to our rear.

"Well, I will let you head out to the north garden while I tend to the cars with the rest of the staff."

"So nice to meet you, Mr. Dale," I say.

"Griffin, call me Griffin. Or Dad, like the rest of the girl's friends calls me. Your choice."

David and I make our way into the house that feels less intimidating after having met the owner, who could just as easily be anyone's father if not for the eloquent speech pattern. Inside, a narrower-than-expected foyer is wrapped by a staircase tracing all four sides of the room with a black baluster and an ornate iron railing that rises above to a look down landing. A small crystal chandelier hangs above the middle of a room surrounded in bookcases on one side with a row of three marble busts of various Anglican figures. The room leads to a large parlor with doors that open to a stone terrace and 180-degree views of the sprawling gardens where guests holding champagne glasses are dressed in bursts of floral, opinionated hats, and smart day coats.

"David Summers; look at you," an older woman says approaching us before we've even stepped onto the lawn with its four rows of chairs and center aisle that leads to the main residence.

"Catherine, this is Victoria Evans," David chimes in.

The salutations and greetings linger no more than my explaining I am from New York and a writer, while David usually gets as far as explaining that he's mostly in London and traveling pretty much nonstop. The faces all look vaguely related; the younger women all slight with porcelain skin and exemplary fashion while the older women are much more matronly and struggle to go deeper in conversation.

Suddenly a bell rings and we are summoned to our seats. I realize that I am a married woman at a wedding with another man. My heart drops and my palm begins to sweat in David's hand before I pull it away and to my side. We sit in the second row directly behind the groom's family. Photographers are snapping photos in the distance, and I churn with anxiety remembering my own wedding in the Hamptons. I felt happy and fulfilled. Now, here I am, or at least a version of me.

David looks over at me with a deep-seated contentment that emanates from his steel-blue eyes. The orchestra begins a pastoral arrangement, the crowd hushes as the doors to the manor open behind us, and no less than twenty children emerge with flower pedals they throw along the glassy aisle. I had but only one flower girl at my own wedding, terrified at the expense that I helped my own parents cover. And then the bridesmaids, most likely an unwanted cousin or in this case five that the mother forced on the daughter, followed by her far more fashionable friends and best friend. They're tall and young and slender and the type of women David should really be with, and I'm likely not the only one thinking it.

Then the bridal processional plays pizzicato on the strings as a gust of wind blows across the crowd and sends a chill up my body. The bride in her simple strapless gown of pure white chiffon emerges under a simple veil and a bouquet of summer orange roses in an almost too-slow walk as she takes in the horizon and her awaiting groom standing at the end of her path as if no one else is present. In her, I see where I once walked and how somehow I ended up on this unlikely journey.

David reaches over and grabs my hand from my lap, holding it almost too tight and squeezing it each time the bride or groom says something he responds to. I want to excuse myself to the bathroom. I don't want to sit here. I don't want to be here right now. Yet, I continue to sit; I continue to hold his hand and continue to be unwilling to walk away or begin to tell him the truth. As the nuptials are almost complete, the landscape behind the couple becomes dotted with a herd of black and white horses that gather immediately at the fence behind them, and no less than twenty large hounds are let into the yards howling as the new couple embraces in a single kiss. We leap to our feet at the jubilant orchestral anthem; I try to endure and not collapse in emotion as David seals it with a perfect, slow, sympathetic kiss.

The mood transitions as soon as the bridal pair make their way back up the aisle; the music changing from aristocratic hymns to more upbeat guitar music by a band that we could hear inside the grand white tent. David leads the way as my eyes and spirit trail behind, taking in the larger-than-life setting and trying to imagine if I could ever truly fit into this world. A long corridor made from branches of white-painted birch and more amnesia roses than I've ever seen, lead into the pitched white tent with a large stage filled by a dapper rock group serenading raspy indie anthems that were likely lost on the older guests. Large round tables are dotted with exploding floral arrangements of French tulips and the largest white peonies I've ever seen. Twelve gold-rimmed plates with antique wine glasses and silver service made of actual sterling completed the table setting.

"It's absolutely stunning," I whisper to David.

"When they do things they really go all out."

David passes familiar faces with a courteous grab of the back of the arm for men who look similarly dressed as he does who give a nod of the head in return. Some faces appear perplexed in my direction followed by a whisper to their neighbor, mostly women, who seem shocked to see a new face among this very Old World crowd. David circles the tables immediately around the dance floor, and I eye up the few guests already seated and look for our names.

"You must be Catherine, we've heard much about you." An attractive woman around my age rises from across the table, her sparkling earrings the size of ice cubes with white gold encasing.

"And your name?" I ask. I extend my hand that she demurely takes with a limp wrist the way I imagine women are taught to do in these loftier circles.

"Ann Baxter, I'm a cousin of the bride. My parents are Lady and Count Baxter. I'm not sure if David has mentioned us to you."

She nods to David as if looking for reassurance or perhaps just stealing one more glance at his addictive face.

"Actually, even better Ann, we passed over your land this morning on our ride," David says with a cheeky charm.

"Oh, how lovely. Catherine, are you an avid equestrian?"

"Only when riding on David's horse, I mean, that came out wrong. I'm not, but David gave me a ride on his horse, which was fantastic."

"Yes, David has always been one to share his horse," she says with a condescending giggle that has me surveying the rest of the table for potential conversation partners.

"Catherine, that's Oli who I've known since we used to play blitzkrieg near the quarry on my parent's property, or their former property, I should say."

As David attempts to include me in the pleasantries of his inner circle that would most likely prefer to have him alone, my eyes gaze at the wedding program elaborately etched in gold leaf and lay with a sprig of lavender on each plate. Next to me, a tall, slender woman takes a seat, and my eyes take in her brightly colored dress that's a flamboyant juxtaposition to everyone around her.

"I'm Sam," she says with a direct stare and a handshake that's a welcome dose of real compared to everyone else at the table who seems to hover ever so slightly off the ground in their aristocratic air.

"This is obviously the wedding breakfast, I assume?" I ask in a somewhat embarrassed whisper looking at the day's program.

"Oh yes, this is the wedding breakfast."

"Why do they call it that when it's closer to lunchtime and dinner?"

"That's funny," she replies. "In the good old days of the eighteenth century, when women couldn't vote or hold land, people were not allowed to marry before noon. So ever since, especially in these posh circles, it's been called the wedding breakfast. I think you Americans call it a reception if I'm correct."

"Yes, exactly," I say. I notice the breakfast is just the first of an entire day of events that end in something called a Midnight Pig Roast, despite half the crowd already being drunk from the cocktails outside.

My eyes take in all the opulence around me; it's almost too much; the crystal chandeliers and the brocade silk detailing on the drapes made just for this day surrounding the elevated stage that must have cost a fortune. How could I ever expect David to go from this world to my everyday life that's so predictable and normal? He'd be bored so easily and lost in the mundane. How would I ever be good enough to compete with all this?

Men too old to be called waiters circle the room. Their worn faces look like the family has employed them for generations. They are passing champagne in squatty antique coupes. I take one and sip it as quickly as I can to get to a more relaxed place. Then on cue, a clink of another glass sends David up out of his chair and the few steps to the main stage.

"Is this thing working?" David lifts the microphone higher and to the level of his mouth as his manner is relaxed and natural in front of this large and intimidating crowd. His shoulders tower above his tall frame and his face silences the room without even having to ask.

"I am David Summers, or as the Dale-Evans family knows me, I'm 'that kid who moved into the game room and stayed for weeks at a time.'"

The crowd laughs, although the joke must be part of a larger story that I am unaware.

"I've never not known this family, these incredible people who have allowed me to become part of their lives and made me feel like their own son. This day looks as I always thought it would; Alexandra telling me repeatedly as a child how her wedding would be the most beautiful anyone had ever seen. She knew what color roses she wanted, where the marquee would be built on the property, and that the good man who would lead her down the aisle would be the kindest and most decent soul she'd ever encountered. When my father died, this family stepped in to tend to me like one of their own, and I hope that I've been able to take enough of them with me to one day be half the husband and father Griffin Dale-Evans is to his family."

David speaks without a script or notes, but simply and fluidly from his heart. My own heart drops just a bit; I am so taken by his innocent sincerity. What I thought was a terminal bachelor is a man who wants so much more. Suddenly, he seems a man ready for more than just a relationship of days or months. His words jolt my heart. David, being so much more than just the flirty bachelor I met on that Rio rooftop, confounds me. His words are flawless as I free fall in love all over again in this vulnerable moment where what I see and feel is nothing short of the perfect man. If only I had two lives, one to give to him right here and now.

"You've taught me that it's not about how many people you love, but how many people love you, and you are true to in return that really counts. They are the kind of people who not only know how to find love, but also hold onto it and make it deeper, richer, and better with time. I wish the new couple not only all the happiness in the world, but the resolve to face each day with passion and wonder and excitement. I can't thank you enough for being in my life, and I look forward to all the years and memories to come."

CHAPTER 8

PANAREA

*I*T'S BEEN SIX full weeks since I've seen Catherine. Missing a day of talking to her feels like weeks, one day becomes two and then four, as the progress and potential of our relationship laggards to the demands of everyday life at home. Whether it was some event at the wedding or a change of heart once at home, the irregularity of our communication makes me wonder if she's as into this relationship as I am. The lack of conversations or an attempt to keep a steady plan to see each other again isn't as it was before. She's evasive about solidifying plans, and more than being unavailable, sometimes she's almost entirely unreachable and inflexible.

I've ended up spending the waning months of summer in Taormina, eight days so far with about half of the work left to do. Sicily is not what most people imagine. The decayed buildings with porches where round grandmothers gather feels more like the South of France before writers were chased away to places like Capri, Positano, and Ravello, and then onto these dramatic hills and precarious mountains that cradle this incredible town where poets churned, actors agonized, and the Greeks left their magnificent ruins.

It's about as good a gig as you get in my line of work. An international luxury hotel group based in London purchased two iconic properties and embarked on a massive overhaul plagued with permitting hurdles and terminally over budget. After they had purchased two of the town's most iconic hotels, their British sensibility made them think the Italians would be less Italian and not put up as many obstacles and schemes as they've encountered given they would essentially be saving two iconic dilapidated landmarks. However, greed and corruption prevails in these parts.

Like a hilltop enclave of style and culture, Taormina is an irreverent antonym to bigger and brasher Palermo, and somewhere you actually imagine spending a lifetime in lieu of just a semester of school like in larger, more-urban Catania. Taormina lures you in even before you arrive, hilltop drama of structures you can't imagine could ever be built along terrifying roads that rise from the sea to twist along hairpin turns where century-old houses hug the land. Having come here as a teenager, I remember two things about the town, namely those colorful pots of various pottery heads where ferns and orchids grow. Then I remember the coliseum and some techno-style dance party that seemed so cool at 4:00 a.m. on an August night.

I'm given the dutiful job of assessing in-house budget forecasting and conversion options at their two hotel properties, made all the more difficult by late-summer weather in Sicily that means sweltering afternoons where men, women, children, and even pigeons vanish to the beach. Grand Hotel Timeo sits at the very top of the town next to the old Greek amphitheater. Its now-sibling property, Villa Sant'Andrea, lies on the seashore, and a stunning, somewhat stagnant rocky beach where hairy eighty-year-old men wear their underwear into the water and voluptuous nineteen-year-olds look for sex on the beach while sipping Malvasia wine, a super-sweet and bubbly local wine.

I've developed a routine I quite like in a relatively short time, which isn't very unusual except that I haven't tired of Taormina. To the contrary, I could linger doing pretty much nothing in this place for an undetermined amount of time. I began my first few days at the Villa Sant'Andrea with its seaside location that's truly incredible. The interiors reminded me of a rich Sicilian grandmother's house with a side of Versace at the beach. The crowd, however, wasn't one you'd want to see on the beach and the location so removed from town that getting back after dinner or drinks with friends was daunting, especially if the tram wasn't running.

I decided to move to the Gran Hotel Timeo, which is nestled within a compound at the very top of the town. After a honking and hollering journey up to the mountaintop, you'll see wrought iron gates open to indiscriminate glass doors that lead down a narrow hallway with herringbone floors that groan as you pass over them next to ornate vanities topped with marble busts of Zeus and Puccini.

The endless hallways dump out into unexpected gardens and terraces that face the Bay of Naxos in the identical visual once absorbed by the eyes of Goethe, Tennessee Williams, and D. H. Lawrence that I know would truly speak to Catherine. You want to be in love in this kind of place. There's femininity to the hotel's interiors despite its thoroughly dominant facade, mostly blue and pale pink decor in muted powdery finishes in the rooms. It's all a bit lost on me, especially the starched linen sheets that feel more like cardboard for the first half of the night until they conform to perfection around your body.

In Italy, your workday begins no earlier than 10:00 a.m., and in Sicily, it starts at 11:00 a.m. I kick it off with a 9:00 a.m. wake-up call with three double espressos and then an immediate early morning run. I don't try to adhere to the hotel's ridiculous dress code of long pants and shirts in the lobby that's out of sync with summer and especially its crotchety air-conditioning system. In nothing but a pair of shorts and running shoes, I run from the hotel and down into town as fast as I can through the old market that's a mix of mothers and grandmothers shopping, and tourists looking for a Starbucks equivalent. You can easily lose your bearings on a downhill run, but it's also impossible to avoid in a town built on a hilltop. At the entrance of town, I head through the main gate and down the side street that leads toward the beach. I gauge whether I want to take the tram down and run a longer distance on the beach or run the whole way down and then immediately head back.

Today, my arrival at the tram comes at the same time as a girl I've been watching for the entire week. She's not my usual type; she's on the short side with curves that makes her feel far taller. She wears the shortest shorts I've ever seen in public, and her thighs look like they were molded to fit just below. Her soft skin is crimson, and a deeper, richer bronze toward the knees and down to her filthy bare feet that look as if she's walked barefoot for a lifetime despite her young age.

We stand as the tram approaches, like a gondola in a snowless ski resort that links the town to the road at the bottom of the mountain next to the beach. There are four people waiting for the tram, two fully clothed, including a grandmother with plastic bag full of fruit that looks like it won't make it through the five-minute trip, and a city worker who looks to be heading toward the train station or bus terminal. Then of course, there's me, standing somewhat sweaty already in shorts that are probably too short for this crowd and bare chest, at which I notice the young woman concealing her stare between glances at the bus timetable and community bulletin board freckled with household items for sale and missing-dog notices.

I have not had sex since being in Somerset with Catherine, which is actually a record for me, amounting to almost six weeks. This results in constant erections and an easily stoked temper. I'm also almost constantly thinking about sex in some way. These are the tough moments, in the breeze that brings in the scent of game as the senses heighten and distractions come to quiet. She notices my constant gaze at her thighs. I imagine myself between them and touching every curve of her in a way that she's never felt. I imagine us alone in this tram that we now both enter at arm's length; she feeling the heat come off my readied body as we make our first eye contact of the day that forces me to hunch over to avoid the most inappropriate of silhouettes.

We face each other standing on opposite sides, not noticing the sun bouncing off the Ionian Sea below, or the handful of riders who just miss the closing door. We notice only each other, passing glances, and then easing into a long meeting of the eyes that breaks with her looking down at my chest, along my stomach, and me standing up just a bit to show her a tad more. Her breasts hang naturally under her sleeveless white shirt with a beach club name emblazoned across the front. She has that Italian sex appeal that lingers in its women from her age until

217

the day they die, that silent stalk of the eyes that lures you in and has you doing anything they desire to earn their attention. She looks away yet again and then back at me.

She's the type who orders you around during sex, telling you exactly what she wants, and how she wants you in a delirium of fantasies that come to an eruptive halt as the tram ends its short trip, and she leaves without another look. She marches down the sidewalk and toward a row of beach clubs lining the shore next to Villa Sant'Andrea, not turning around once, or lingering in step hoping I was to follow. My path leads farther up the beach and along the main highway where I could be the first person ever to run, or at least it feels as buses honk, cars swerve, and trucks inevitably boom their horns along my morning ritual.

The heat is blistering as I make my way up the narrow road past Lido la Pigna, and il Gabbiano with the best involtini I've had on the trip. It's essentially a piece of rolled-up swordfish grilled on the fire. I've completely sweat through my shorts as I forsake my run for a bypass onto the rocky beach that faces a series of offshore islands, including the much-talked-about and little-understood Isola Bella. The beach is essentially a shoreline of palm-size gray rocks that surround a swimming cove lined in thousands of loungers in royal blue and orangey-yellow stripes next to the water that seems thicker and soupier than you're used to with a slow-motion wake as my shoe touches the surface and sinks to the dark pebble bottom.

Even though it is the first day of fall, this midday feels like summer. The beach is essentially empty except for workers tending to nearby juice bars and cafés. Sun-withered venders are waiting for people like me to rent one of their chaise lounges. High season doesn't really end in these parts of Italy; it simply gets slower and slower to the point that workers no longer find the patience to show up anymore.

It's simply too glorious a day not to swim; the water is as if drawn for my own bath at its warmest temperature of the year that almost feels too hot to be refreshing. I take a seat on one of the larger rocks camouflaged among the equally colored stones around it. I pull off my running shoes and essentially sprint the distance between the shore and the deeper water that protects these sensitive feet that hate a pebble beach.

Few places are as visually stimulating as this, I think as I backstroke toward the small little island offshore. The Italian seaside is alit in colors with its murky green-blue waters that contrast against a beach of gray-blue rocks and a shoreline arranged in white and aged terra-cotta buildings awash in orange, yellow, and blue-striped awnings. Even the locals are a unique color, a sun-kissed bronze so dark the whites of their eyes allow you to see the subtleties between their dark brown and almost black pupils. The Taormina hilltop looks like an architectural Eden with its majestic ruins punctuated by teetering villas and timeless towers.

Despite all the passion and longing that I feel for Catherine, I still find myself fighting those inner demons of self-discipline. I'm constantly distracted, even from passersby along the beach, imagining what it might be like to take one of them back to my hotel or even to one of the private cabanas along the beach. This is why I insisted on Catherine visiting me for a few days despite bemoaning the endless flying and inability to settle back in New York. She resisted rather methodically, saying she's never going be much of a writer if she was constantly a hedonist tagalong. I insisted I had one of the best hotels of her career coming if she committed. She countered that the expenses were slowly adding up, that she's "not a banker after all," which is why I offered to give her the miles for a nonstop flight and not insist she stay any longer than a few days over a weekend.

With a swelling sex drive, I can only do so much Skype sex and texting. I've even resorted to preventative masturbation on my morning swims, whenever I can get a moment of privacy in the deep water. Which is essentially how I reasoned with her, at least somewhat successfully, after a few abrupt conversations and unanswered texts on my part. She obviously still wants to be in this relationship, but she must make the choice to grow our bond; otherwise, she's going to be one of those women who only have a job and not much else.

Alas, no privacy today as a familiar old man joins for a free swim and simply vanishes into the horizon with goggles and skin cap. I try to drift away from him, but he swims strategically around the Isola Bella and then back in my direction. Isola Bella manages to distract me with its own beauty as I backstroke in the stillness of the morning water. The small offshore island looks like a smaller version of Sveti Stefan in Montenegro. Today, it's a wild and overgrown nature reserve with a decaying monument to someone by the name of Lady Florence Trevelyan, who lived in Taormina and apparently was a cousin of Queen Victoria.

If you ask around, everyone seems to have a different version of Isola Bella, but from the stories I pieced together from the kiosk owner and hotel manager, it's long been a center of controversy and scandal.

Lady Florence Trevelyan was a Brit who would spend childhood summers with her cousin and confidante Queen Victoria. Although twenty-five years separated them in age, the two women shared a knobby penchant for birds and botany. They also shared a common interest in Queen Victoria's son, the future King Edward. Lady Florence Trevelyan became involved in a torrid and well-publicized affair with the future King Edward VII, who was already married, in a scandal that ended in Queen Victoria giving Lady Trevelyan just forty-eight hours to leave England.

Lured by the bohemian lifestyle and countless authors of the day who wrote of the area's beauty, Trevelyan relocated to Taormina and built a glamorous life of her own in the freethinking utopia. She went on to create this sort of ode to Florence Nightingale known as Isola Bella, with a series of ornate Asian-theme structures intersected by elaborate English gardens and populated with rare bird species that live on the island to this day.

Perhaps the legacy of that bohemian exile lingers today. No fetish lifestyle or crime goes judged as long as you're able find an island or hilltop to build another lifetime. Ever since I met Catherine, the isolation of life on the road has begun to wear on me, and I crave the continuation of such inner thoughts with someone who finds what I find just as interesting. It's not the physical as much as the mental that I crave of Catherine, like an inner companion who takes a two-color life and turns it into a rainbow of exponential color. When she leaves, it's as if my world returns to black and white.

The rocks hurt my feet more on the way out of the water. I struggle to find that camouflaged stone that's high enough to sit on to put my shoes back on. The beach is a bit busier in the distance as an older set make their way off the buses from Catania for day trips with lunch stops at the more affordable restaurants outside of town. I weave my way back along the shore and up to the road as my pace slowly increases to a steady uphill run. My shorts have now thoroughly dried. The sun beats down on my exposed shoulders, and my forehead struggles in the exposure as I try to stay tucked under the few trees that provide a space of shade along the side of the road.

The time leading up to Catherine's arrival always seems to pass in slow motion, a mix of inability to concentrate and to solidify last-minute plans of our seventy-two-hour weekend in Panarea. I must admit, she's a good sport to travel all this way, but my endless threats of taking an autumn break from work and following her around New York had her horrified. In the hours before her evening arrival, I have the blonde Swiss girl upgrade my room to a suite and assure the hotel car picks Catherine up promptly in Catania.

The suite sprawls from room to room with shiny parquet floors and powdery white walls strewn with satin-striped curtains that barely budge in the gusty wind. The room is sexy in a noble way with its polished antiques and gilded mirrors. The terrace wraps around the room with a ballast railing and a linen-covered pergola where two chairs face what looks like a painting of the Bay of Naxos and neighboring Greek theater. The inhospitable afternoon yields to an unexpected twilight of a rose-hued horizon framed by dramatic clouds that usually give way to booming thunder, but tonight just make a beautiful sky a little more dramatic.

Just before 7:00 p.m., the front desk rings to let me know her car has arrived. In a matter of seconds, I can hear a rolling sound echoing through the cavernous lobby mixed with the heavy heel of a woman walking. With no knock on the door or ring of the bell, the room door opens. I linger a bit on the balcony. The heavy heels circle the main room a bit before I hear her rattle a few words to the bellman, who promptly shuts the door behind him. I expect her to come out immediately, but instead, she lingers in the room as I get up to peek in to see what's keeping her.

She's even more beautiful than I remember. She's also thinner than she was last time. She's in a hot black skirt that tapers from her ass to her ankles with a simple white T-shirt that looks as if she changed in the lobby. She busies with her phone for longer than I expect, as I cough from the balcony.

"Oh my god, you're here," she cries as she presses long enough on her phone to shut off the power. She runs up to me, hugs me first, and then takes my lips with her mouth that smells of fresh waxy lipstick.

"I know that was a long haul, and I'm so glad you're here." I look into her eyes, and she absorbs the horizon that couldn't be of lesser interest to me with her standing near.

"Look at this place, David. It's just incredible. Is that Mount Etna?"

"Yes, and down there are the famous ruins."

"Roman ruins?" she asks.

"Greek. And that's the Ionian Sea just beyond what here is the Bay of Naxos. There's a sister hotel down by the water that I'll take you to if you want in the morning, but we need to get a fairly early start in order to get to Panarea."

"I'm so excited. I've heard it's just incredible, but seeing this makes me barely want to leave this place."

"Maybe you should come for longer than three days then, my love."

"I know, too bad I'm not one of your rich friends who only works professionally in order to maintain an approachable social decorum."

"Maybe we don't start off on that note; our time is so limited," I say, trying to disregard her snide comment.

Catherine struggles to sit in the iron garden chair in her tight skirt. It makes me wonder at what point exactly she changed; the taxi ride and flight from Rome would have been far too impractical for such a getup.

"You look incredible, *la dolce vita*," I say in my best accent surveying her legs. My pent-up libido makes me think of nothing else but thrusting inside of her as fast as I possibly can.

"Shouldn't you be strutting around in your Speedo? It's Italy after all," she says, unable to break free of the negativity that I choose not to address.

"That was earlier in the day; I've transitioned to my casual evening look." I wave my hand toward my ultra-thin trousers and white V-neck T-shirt.

"Stand up, let's see," Catherine says like a demanding schoolteacher on the first day of class.

I comply, rising from my entirely uncomfortable chair and hover above her as she takes another sip of wine, leaving behind a slight lipstick residue on the rim of the glass.

"There you go." I rise in front of her, walking forward almost to the point of straddling her legs. "Like that?"

I hover above her as our inner and outer legs touch.

"Take off your shirt," she commands, almost void of emotion.

I comply, pulling the back of the neck over my head, and adjusting my belt a bit lower on my pants. The breeze sends a chill up my spine, my body eager for what is to come.

"Tell me what you want," she says.

"Tell you what I want? Tell me what you want?" I say with a cutting flirtation.

"Tell me what you're thinking about right now," she says with a heartfelt lingering.

"I'm thinking about sliding my hands up that skirt and sticking my hands inside you, and then pulling them out and putting them back in before taking you in my mouth."

"Take off your shoes."

I kick them off with ease despite the laces and stand barefoot in front of her.

"Now back up a little and take off your pants."

I take a step back.

"Farther," she says as I take another short step back, not wanting to be outside of her any longer.

I take off my pants and stand there in briefs, well aware that portions of the hotel can see inside our balcony but hoping the view distracts from what's in front of them.

"Everything."

She barks the order as I move closer to the covered trellis to obscure the erection that flops from my white underwear that I fling in front of her. I wait for her to fall to her knees or jump to her feet; instead, she leans back in her chair.

"Touch it," she says like an innocent girl playing dominatrix, calling my dick *it* instead of some harsher, sexy, sleazy word.

I grab my dick around the base, which sends a jolt through it as I pull back the skin and then slide my hands a few times back and forth before stopping.

"Why are you stopping? I didn't tell you to stop."

"I've been jerking off nonstop for the past six weeks; it's sort of the last thing I want to do right now."

"What do you want to do?" she asks.

"I want to take my hands around your neck and rub my head around yours, smelling your hair as I send my hands through it, and tasting your mouth with my tongue."

She takes off her blouse and then her bra.

"And then I want to take my mouth to your breasts, biting them ever so softly as I arch your back with my hands. I want to smell your skin, taste its salty flavor with my tongue as my nose works its way from your shoulder to your hands that I take to my mouth and suck each finger one by one."

I stand there motionless, confessing the confines of all my thoughts and desires of her during the time since we've last seen each other.

"And then I would push you on your back and try to convey to you physically the way I feel about you emotionally, inside and out, every day since we met."

Catherine unzips her skirt and removes her black lace underwear in front of me in almost a single motion. She falls to the ground in front of me and takes me inside her mouth. Her movements portray a woman fully succumbing to me, like love's warrior laying down her defense in front of me that results in such immediate pleasure. She goes at it with the rigor of a woman who wants nothing more than to please me, and I willingly accept. She works me back and forth in an increasing rhythm; I stare down and watch her movements that aim to satiate me and send me into a thundering crescendo. With most women, I'm unable to cum from oral sex alone, but thoughts of being so intimately inside her sends me to another place. Without pause or hesitation to take my time, I explode in Catherine's unyielding mouth. I gasp in pleasure and bend until the continued sensation is too much to bear, and I pull away from her mouth.

We emerge from the hotel showered and connected as a couple once more. There's a connectedness between couples after sex, especially when you know that special someone won't disappear at the end. Our hands meet effortlessly, conjoined with the occasional glance to the other that makes everything else in the world seem secondary. We are both dressed uncharacteristically casual. The wind is gone, and an oppressive humidity has set in under a cloudy sky that's thicker than earlier in the evening.

We make our way down to Duomo Square, its gray-and-black marble stones and still-unpretentious cafés buzz with a menagerie of tourists and young locals gathered near a wrought iron edge that looks over the sea, striped this evening in a wide swath of moonlight. Summer evenings are the most social time in the Italian culture; grandmothers gather around the more comfortable benches away from the main square as their graying gents play bocce or chess at small parks below the cobblestone promenade. Teenagers fondle each other in the darker corners of closed department store entrances, and singles flock into a handful of bars and restaurants in a scene that's like a microcosm of your life's past and future visually spelled out in front of you within the few short blocks.

The following morning arrives too soon for Catherine, who lingers in bed as I take my run, which today is free of the many distractions that have slowed my pace of previous days. I return to a still dark room and Catherine sleeping on her stomach on one side of the bed, not sprawled in the center as I had expected. I've allowed her to sleep as long as possible, but alas, the day must begin. I heave open the weighty drapery and allow the unfettered sunshine that's retreated from under the earlier cloud cover to enter our room. I kiss the back of her neck to wake her, tracing my way gently down her back. I tuck a cappuccino cup next to her as her naked body stretches to wake.

Catherine is a silent morning person, and I leave her in the chosen stillness while I get ready to shower and pack for the weekend. The luggage is tedious on the road, separating what I need from the larger Tumi bag that will stay behind and wait for me at the hotel. We cross paths just outside the shower, she concealed behind a thick white robe and slippers. She watches my body more than most girlfriends I've had do. At first, it was a turn-on, but now it makes me think something's wrong or she's analyzing me in her deep Freudian stare that looks away when I catch her.

She's been awake for thirty minutes, and slowly the words come from her mouth. She asks about the day and the journey before us as we make our way out of the room. I am dressed in black and white and she is in a sexy white dress with a scarf wrapped around her head, which reminds me of the day I met her in Rio. I had no idea this is where I would be and who I would be with all these months later.

She leaves a wake of turned heads as we make our way through the lobby; even the Swiss girl at the reception desk cannot help taking notice as Catherine rounds through the area and toward the street where a brick of an old Mercedes S-Class awaits us in a plume of diesel smoke.

The hotel car leaves much to be desired, but inside you'd never know it wasn't the newest of models; the driver likely washes it inside and out every day. Two water bottles sit in the folds behind the driver and passenger seat. Catherine grabs hold of one and takes it to her mouth as I think to myself that I would never do such a thing not knowing who might have touched the top. I dare not school her; instead, I grab her hand and take in the descending horizon of Taormina and onto the swifter highway that leads to the north.

I've told her very little of the journey in front of us. About an hour on the highway leads us to a small turnout and a road toward the sea where on the plateau a blue whale of a helicopter sits on the grassy heliport with the words Air Panarea in faded white print on its side and a lone pilot standing next to it.

"Wait, is that for us?" she asks in a mix of excitement and nervousness.

"It is. I figured it beats the dinghy that stops at every island." My own excitement is fully engaged.

"I've never been in one before. Oh no, now I'm slightly nervous," she says in her girlish honesty.

"You'll love it, plus, it's all over water so not much to be afraid," I say while looking at the rather aged flying aircraft. It looks to be a good twenty years old with window tinting now half-peeled away and a worn metal door covering the motor that looks as though it's been pulled off and screwed on far too many times. It's a seamless transition from car to helicopter, and Catherine enters without hesitation. I tip the driver and make sure our two bags fit in the rear hatch. The pilot takes Catherine's heavier bag and places it on the seat next to him.

"We'll put that up here to balance the helicopter. I am Amerigo; I will be your pilot for the short flight."

He continues in surprisingly fluid and articulate English explaining the headphones to Catherine as well as the basic physics of how a helicopter works. I had no idea it was harder to fly a helicopter than a plane, not something you exactly want to hear on your first flight, but Catherine's face seems nonetheless engaged. He secures his door hatch with a strong pull and then a stretchy rope to secure it as I try to direct Catherine's eyes to the Aeolian Islands in the distance. The propellers thump to a steady purr, the chopper surges forward and to the side, and then up into the air.

Catherine holds my hand tight and then tighter as the chopper glides through the air with an occasional air pocket picked up from the afternoon heat that bounces us closer together. There's simplicity to helicopter flying, far beyond da Vinci's primitive sketches of vertical flight and closer to what it might be like as a lonely bird soaring across the water. Catherine looks over with her bulky headset.

"I love you," she whispers unexpectedly as our eyes meet.

"You mean me?" the pilot says with a baritone chuckle.

"Yes, you too. But only as long as we're airborne," Catherine laughs.

I look back at Catherine and mouth, "I love you, too." Her words catch me by surprise, but the moment couldn't be more appropriate. It's the first time I've said that to a woman in a very long time. She leans in with her soft hair on my shoulder, and we stare off into the distance as two large landmasses come into sight. One more dramatic than the other, volcanic Stromboli is a singular silhouette that appears identical to the volcano you would draw as a child, complete with an omnipresent billow of smoke that hovers around its head.

"That is Stromboli ahead," the pilot says as we look on. "You watch close, and you see smoke every hour or so, like clock," he continues, as the sight alone is mesmerizing, intimidating even at this distance.

"Do people live on Stromboli?" she asks.

"Yes, it is very famous in Italy. Roberto Cavalli and Dolce Gabbana both have homes. But you need be careful, volcano very active. They all have yachts if they need to get away fast. Most people not so lucky."

"But you have a helicopter; that's even better," I add.

"Yes, I guess that true. On the right here, is Panarea. We will circle and then land against the wind."

Panarea is larger than I expected. It's like a mountain topped with a high peak and collapsed lush green edges that descend along a terrain dotted in houses and farms that touch the sea with its jagged islands and rock formations that humble even Faraglioni off Capri.

"It's incredible," Catherine says from her headset clogged in static. She leans above the window for a better view.

Her head is framed by an aura of sun beating over the crystal blue sea as the white water can almost be felt crashing on the rocky shore. The helicopter finds its target, circles above the heliport, and descends as if pulled by a rope to the ground as it touches ever so gently onto the grassy pad.

"That was incredible," Catherine says in a sort of thank-you tone. The swoop of the propellers turned off and glided to a stop. We unbuckled and looked at a small converted golf cart parked at the edge of the grass.

"Welcome to Panarea. I'm Giuseppe and will be taking you to Hotel Raya," he yells from his seat in front of the cart emblazoned with the hotel logo. The lone pilot carries our luggage to the rear seat without help from the hotel driver or me.

Catherine takes a seat in the second row, her scarf wrapped tightly around her head to shield from the unyielding sun that's sent a bead of sweat down from the top of my head, along my neck behind the ear, down my spine, and through the rear of my pants.

"So we go to the hotel now, is that good?" the driver says without much of a good-bye to the pilot.

He zips away and the view of distant Stromboli and the jagged formations disappear along a shaded residential street that becomes more commercial with a series of terra-cotta-colored inns and family restaurants arranged on vine-covered terraces. Scooters whiz past us with a mix of shirtless beach-bound teenagers who double and sometime triple up on the rear behind speeding grandmothers and impatient fathers with cigarettes dangling precariously from their tanned faces.

"How many people live in Panarea?" Catherine addresses the driver.

"Right now, only about three hundred, but there are many visitors, so I would say somewhere closer to one thousand," he replies.

"That's not very many; it must be terribly quiet in winter."

"Quiet and beautiful. The ferries let you get away to Lipari and the busier islands, but here it's like a phantom town."

"When was the island first settled?" Catherine inquires further as the alleyways of the central town get narrower past small grocery stores with windows of pasta boxes, dated perfumery, and the type of shops frequented by locals rather than tourists. The streets are car free, and so is the island, maintaining an otherworldly simplicity that comes across in the calm faces of passing locals.

"It is very old, but it was really the Romans who came, and then later, it was occupied by pirates who made life terrible for those living here."

"Pirates?"

"Yes, pirates and ships that would come and stay the winter in village houses, eat all their food, and take their women."

"I hope they weren't Londoners," I interject.

"No, mostly North Africans and from the East. Very bad people."

The view opens as we arrive on the harbor. There is a bit more life along a single row of more commercial shops along the main port adjacent to a short, deserted seafront and incline in the distance where Hotel Raya rises.

The hotel is a simple cubist house in pinkish stucco framed in an all-white architecture that spreads out from the roofline. There are no manicured trees or grassy landscaping at the entrance; instead, a simple staircase descends from the cobblestone street with a sleeping cat perched atop the tenth step painted gleaming white.

Catherine is enveloped in the moment, absorbing every detail with her eyes and scribbling it down on a small notepad she carries with her every time we check into a hotel. I enjoy watching her, the lines in her forehead tensing when she sees something that piques her interest, whether good or bad, and then relaxing as she focuses back on her notes.

"Hello there, you must be David Summers," says an older woman inside a small office just up the main corridor leading into the hotel. My eyes play tricks on me in the direct sunlight making the interior spaces look far darker as all I can do against the light is look straight through the lobby and at Stromboli in the distance.

"Yes, that would be me," I say attempting to remove my sunglasses.

"I am Martina, this is my hotel, and I wish you both welcome," she says, extending her hand that's cold and soft to the touch. I feel a slight prick of well-manicured nails that touch my inner wrist. She smells of an Italian woman, a scent that evolves over a lifetime from that almost musky, sexy fragrance of a young woman to a sort of matronly floral scent of this likely grandmother.

"And I am Catherine. I've read so much about you."

Martina's eyes widen, happy or curious that someone new recognizes her as more than just front-of-the-house help.

"Oh, is that so? What have you read exactly?" she says coyly.

"Well, that you came to this deserted island in the sixties and built this hotel that is now as iconic as the island itself," Catherine explains.

"That is very nice, but I am just a woman trying to run a business despite these Italians that make this place impossible to do business."

"But you seem to be doing very well … I mean, look at this place," I add.

"Yes, but no thanks to them. They should build me a monument, but they don't respect women, and they don't like people from the outside. Hold on, let me finish up here, and I will take you to your room."

Martina has the command skills of a more efficient Napoleon, ordering her staff around in briefly punctuated Italian that probably translates far harsher than it sounds. Catherine walks ahead as I poke my head inside the small dining room and into the open-air lobby lined in white tiles and framed by a beam ceiling and a 220-degree view of a rugged seascape capped by architectural rock formations that look like Giacometti molded them. On the terrace, steamer chairs and loungers are vacant except for one with a single man sitting lost between a book and a cocktail.

"So let's go … where is your woman?" Martina barks.

"Catherine, love. Are you ready?" I yell ahead and see her silhouette turn back in our direction.

"You need to watch a woman who leaves your side in search of the unknown," Martina whispers pointing a long finger with a glossy red nail at me.

"Do you speak from experience?" I reply.

"Oh, I was worst of the worse. But I was never with such a handsome man. Beautiful men are delicious in bed and difficult in life. I prefer a man who's sometimes difficult in bed and delicious in life." Then she adds, "But I just speak very honest with you."

Catherine rejoins us as we walk swiftly to the parked golf cart. We all get in and Martina speeds up the hills.

"There are three parts of the hotel. You will be staying in Raya Alto that is up on the hill. Most times you will walk, but I'll take you this one time."

"Thank you. So has the island changed much since you arrived?" Catherine asks politely from the passenger seat.

"Everything has changed. When I arrived, I was beautiful and desired; now I am an old woman in a place where you have to bribe people to get anything done. What used to work with just a wink and some dinner, now takes years, and even then you don't know what's in store for you."

"When did you arrive here?" I ask.

"It was a lifetime ago. I was considered a foreigner because I am not from the islands. I met a man and we would embark on a love affair that became the best and worst times of my life. He was much older than I was with a life all his own. But when we were here, it was our life. I must say it feels like yesterday, but at the same time, a lifetime ago."

The town yields to a more residential setting with open plots of land that smell of trailing rosemary and citrus leaves among omnipresent olive trees. Martina turns the cart up a gravel road with an incline that requires a heavier foot. My eyes gaze up the hillside and at the edge of a mountain where a series of terraced villas looks almost identical to the main hotel lobby. A rounded driveway leads past a swimming pool that Martina says took forty years to build, and to a small roundabout near the foot of the buildings.

"This is Raya Alto where you will be staying," she says.

Catherine's eyes gaze up at the property that looks like a mix of Positano and Santorini with its earthy colors and white stucco architecture. The smell of fresh baked bread fills the air as two women busy about in white baker's uniforms in a small outdoor kitchen behind an old walnut tree. Martina says nothing to the women, but takes the lead up the slick white staircase that ends at a small landing and up to the left to a large terrace with white floor and a thatched roof.

"If you were here a month earlier, you could have danced at the disco that's outside the main house, but now you must entertain yourselves at night or go to the port. But looking at you, I think you will find something," she says.

Martina shoves the glossy-blue door open with a brute force as the metal key chimes against the metal key slot. The door opens to a spare space lacking the edgy design or trendy all-white decor that I expected. Instead, it's a room of blue hand-painted tiles, a simple white side table, and a platform bed that hovers in a scent of linen washed by hand and dried in the Aeolian wind.

"It's quite lovely. Simple, chic while making the most of that incredible view," Catherine says politely gazing out the window.

"If you need anything, you know where to find me. But I'm sure the long walk will make you really think about whether it's worth it," she says with a laugh and pulls the door behind her without much of a good-bye.

"What an incredible place. It's so not what I was expecting."

In a good sort of way, I assume?" I ask.

"Absolutely, although I take you for more of the Hotel de Paris type," she replies.

"Meaning?" I say, grabbing her around the pleated waist of her fluffy white sundress that's still as fresh as it was back in Taormina.

"Just that you don't seem the romantic boutique hotel type, that's all."

"Well, there are a lot of things you don't know about me yet," I say, resting my nose next to hers.

"Are you making your move already? We have to stretch the day, Mr. Summers. There's no Internet or TV here."

"No television? How totally awful," I say in my strongest American accent.

"I'm just saying we have to pace ourselves."

"I'm a couple-times-a-day kind of guy sometimes; I hope that's okay with you."

"You're insufferable, David, really."

"Okay, so I am going to jump in the shower and wash off my four hours of sweat, and maybe you'll feel differently when I come out, or at least I can hope."

"Go shower. I'm going to unpack both of us."

"That's so wifely, but I won't object," I say with a shut of the bathroom door.

The small bathroom just off the room is even bolder than the room with its hand-painted tiles and colorful sink with a row of toiletries contained in pottery vases. In the mirror, I catch my reflection and see dark circles under my eyes, greasy hair, and a thinner torso, lean from too much time on the road.

A chrome hand shower hangs from a hook that I try to lift higher so I do not have to hunch over to wash my hair. I spill the small container of shampoo into my palm. It smells like a mix of rosemary, citrus, and lavender and is soothing to the touch as I rub it on my scalp and the scent drips down my body. I want Catherine to join me, so I call out for her; I wait, but hear no response. As the moment passes, I turn the noisy knobs off and grab one of the towels that line a shelf opposite the shower, pale white and somewhat rough to the touch. I hold it near my nose and inhale its air-dried scent—smells of days in the country.

A thick robe doesn't smell nearly as good, as I tuck it around me and make my way back in the room to find what could be keeping Catherine. With few places needed to look, my eyes find her seated on a long bench at the edge of the balcony with a notepad in hand, her dress heaved-up around her thighs, and holding a glass of chilled white wine. I linger away from her view just a second longer, not wanting to interrupt what she's doing and becoming equally aroused watching her lost in the moment against a blue sea panorama with its rocky cutouts.

"Is this your David-in-a-robe look?" she hollers from the terrace.

"What's that?" I laugh.

"I said, is this your David-in-a-robe look?"

"I'm sorry; I thought you might find it irresistible."

"You're already irresistible," she says, rising from the chair and joining me back in the room. My robe falls open and my naked, wet body lies next to her. She grabs hold of my back from the inside and rests her face on my chest.

There is only silence, and I can feel my heart beat against her face; we hold each other tight in the most perfectly removed paradise around us.

By evening, we have napped and showered and cuddled, and yet still no sex. I resign myself to dressing for dinner, a quick shower-free change in the bathroom into some navy trousers, a crisp white shirt, and some sporty loafers. Catherine follows, barely uttering a word since arising from her nap, disappearing into the bathroom, which she locks behind her and doesn't emerge from for a good thirty minutes. Lack of Internet means no e-mail or calls, just idling away the last moments of the sun that sets without any notice from Catherine, who alas comes out in an outfit similar to what she was wearing earlier.

"Are you ready, love?" I say without a hint of frustration.

"Just about. Let me just change shoes," she replies, kicking off one pair of heels in the middle of the room for another pair in black that she pulls from her suitcase, which now looks as though its intestines have spilled from its cavity.

Finally, we make our way down the staircase that she struggles to navigate before finding flat ground and then down the hill back to the main hotel. I'm learning that Catherine isn't especially chatty upon waking up, preferring her own space for a good thirty minutes to an hour at a time that I would normally be fully engaged. There's moodiness to her, an irritability I have to traipse around before she's ready to engage fully.

In lieu of conversation, the landscape is my companion as the set sun now allows Stromboli to come into its own amid a turquoise sky with a few boats that try to connect the small dots of islands in front of us. Along the way, we see maids pulling down linens from the line, folding them perfectly on the first try, and setting them into extravagantly large baskets. There's no wave or acknowledgment of us walking past from the staff as Catherine grabs my hand and slowly emerges from her fog.

"Are you waking up still?" I say, trying to break the silence.

"No, I'm fine really."

"You seem to take awhile to wake up fully, am I wrong?"

"No, I don't think so. I'm just a little jet lagged still. It's a long way to get here, you know."

"Yes, and have I told you how happy I am that you are here?"

"I'm so happy to be here with you as well."

Hotel Raya is encircled in a flicker of candlelight as our five-minute walk that took more like ten minutes ends at the doorstep overlooking the port. My hand leads Catherine in first. She walks up the staircase and into the main reception where a larger crowd than earlier in the day has gathered. Catherine gravitates to the bar, which is adorned in Indonesian tribal art.

"You must be the love couple," says a young bartender rather abruptly. Her glowing brown hair falls on a simple tank top with white jeans that fit her ass perfectly.

"You must be the couple staying on the hill, am I right? Martina said you are both very attractive, like movie stars." Her dark eyes connect with mine as she aggressively juices limes with a wooden spoon.

"That's very sweet. I'm Catherine and this is David."

"Hi there," I say. "What's that you're making?"

"Well, there are some Americans over there who want something called a skinny margarita that's just lime juice and tequila. Doesn't sound very nice to me, but she insists that's what she wants," she says with a foreign, halfhearted laugh.

"That sounds like a lot of work to me. I'll just have one of your better tequilas on the rocks when you get done," I say.

"And I'll have a glass of rosé, please."

The girl maintains eye contact with me even though Catherine interjects her own order.

"We'll be sitting over there." Catherine points to the terraces alit in even more candles and soft lounge music barely heard above the chirps of crickets outside. We make our way to the terrace where only a single table is open. Catherine takes the chair facing the bartenders, either out of politeness to let me have the view or out of concern that I would linger in eye contact with the waitress the entire night. I have to imagine it gets lonely for a woman like her on the island, so full of couples and other women who fight for one of the 150 or so full-time residents.

I recognize seriousness to Catherine that she hasn't emerged from today. Usually her playful and vivacious self comes out by now, but today she seems lost in thought and unable to break free from her mind.

"You know, my friends at the wedding tried to send photos of us to you, but I guess they had your wrong e-mail or something."

"Oh really? I'd love to see them," Catherine says as she busies herself in the menu.

"She said they were great. I have yet to see them myself. Everyone was e-mailing me for days saying how much they enjoyed meeting you."

Catherine lingers her stare over the menu, which is the usual Italian hotel menu of carpaccio, pasta, and fish dishes. Her mood today has me to the point of frustration.

"Is there something wrong? You're awfully quiet, especially for someone who has traveled so far to see someone; you're now choosing to sit in total silence."

"Not at all," she says, looking up from the menu. "It's just sometimes I get lost in these incredible moments and get so scared they will go away."

"They're special to me as well. That's why I go out of my way to make them happen more and more often."

"But how realistic is it really? I mean we both have entirely different lives that are nowhere near going in the same direction."

"How can you say that? This is going incredibly well."

"How can it not? We go from Rio to Paris to Italy … how can we not get lost in the magic?"

"You just came home with me, and they loved you."

"Realistically, someone like you doesn't end up with someone like me."

The shadow of a woman across the floor materializes into the bartender who arrives with our drinks. She hands Catherine her wine glass without saying a word, and then with a heated stare, places mine on the table.

"Is there anything else I can get you?" she asks with a deep gaze.

"No, I believe that is all for the moment." I smile and return my concentration on Catherine who looks near tears.

Around us, the night couldn't be more perfect. A light wind blows away any separation between the sea and us, and the faint silhouette of Stromboli can be seen amid the bright moonlight. I wonder if it is something I'm saying wrong or not doing to make her feel like this, she being the closest I've ever come to a lasting relationship with a woman of substance.

"You know I would do anything for you if you just asked," I say.

"You're so wonderful. This has nothing to do with you. It's just my life is very demanding, and when I'm with you, I want it all to go away. You make me not really care about any of it. All I can see and think about is you."

I can't imagine the answer to her frustration is as simplistic as she says. She's an avid writer who likely invests heavily in her words even if they aren't entirely accurate. Her heart is there, but she's far too intelligent to lead with her emotions with the recklessness of an unseemly adolescent.

"So let's order and then get an early night of sleep. Maybe you're still jet lagged or something."

In my mind, I'm thinking maybe I should have made more of an effort to see her in her world. Visiting New York is always on my mind, but my company is mainly Europe-based, and my traveling rarely ends up in New York simply because when businesses want a New York company they hire someone local and not us in London. I have to change that. If this relationship is to work, she needs to know I am there for her. I want to know all about her and her life.

Dinner passes in less than an hour with little conversation between us. We make our way back to the room under a canopy of moonlight that illuminates the hillside and provides a seductive glow to both of us as we stop midway and push into a series of kisses. Back at the room, the chemistry simply takes a backseat to her jet lag. Catherine retreats into her own mental world, and I plop on the bed with a six-month-old *Vogue Italia* and watch her fade into a deep sleep.

The night lingers and morning arrives with a series of ground floor rumblings and an unforgettable scent, an unfamiliar one, which rises up the hotel and through the open windows of our room. Catherine is cuddled at the far corner of the bed and lying on her side away from me. Her arm is slipped beneath her pillow and her lacy negligee pushed tightly between her legs. A series of freckles dot her back and her hair is in a neat puddle next to her pillow. I roll over closer to her and mimic her form with my knees directly behind hers. I wrap my arm around her and grab her closer.

"What's the smell? It's insane," she says with a yawn. Her arm pulls me tighter around her as I thrust her from behind.

"I think the ladies are baking breakfast downstairs."

"It's making me hungry, baby," she says, lying still with her eyes closed.

"Should we sneak down for a taste? Or should I go grab you something?"

"Oh yes, a coffee and a little nibble would be delicious," she says.

"Okay, I'll be right back."

I pick up the robe, throw it over my boxers, and open the door to an explosion of sunlight reflected over the panorama of an even deeper blue sea than the previous day. My eyes struggle to adjust from the dark room; its curtains tightly bound and air-conditioned haze makes it feel as if it could just as easily be 9:00 a.m. as 3:00 p.m. The scent isn't as intense just outside the door, a mix of warm dirt and faint scent of bread rising on the heated air from below. I peek down and see Martina bossing about just the same as she did the day before. Her head cocks up and hushes the kitchen staff with a pat of her hand in midair as I make my way downstairs.

"Good morning, Mr. Summers. I hope you both had a very good night."

"Yes, I think the jet lag caught up with Catherine, however." My eyes fix on the bartender from last night. She's working the counter of the breakfast bar dressed in a white smock. Two bakers circle behind her with all eyes in my direction.

"Are you going to have a little breakfast?"

At the mere mention of the word, the heavier of the two bakers readies a place setting at a small wooden table with blue-plaid linens and pale-blue plates under the circle of shade from a giant olive tree.

"Well, I told Catherine I would bring her a bite, but I was also thinking of maybe a run or a swim in the pool."

"You sit here; you look like you get enough sport." Martina forces my shoulder into a wicker chair that's not made for outdoors, but such things are overlooked in these parts of Italy.

"You are from London, no?" Martina takes a cup of coffee with a saucer from the previous evening's bartender. I wrap my robe tighter, unaware I was going to be stuck staying for more than a pass by.

"Yes, I am from London."

"And your woman; is she also from London?"

"No, Catherine is from New York."

"And you are not married yet?"

"Yes, that's correct."

"You know, there were times in Italy that a hotel would turn you away without a wedding ring, especially here in the south. I don't understand, why no married?"

"Well, we met earlier in the year, and we see each other every few months as we find the time," I explain, well aware of the full attention coming from the kitchen, the women stopped in their tracks.

"She is older than you? She not want more babies?"

"No, she does. She is not yet a mother. I'm sure she very much would like to have a proper family," I clarify.

"She has no child?"

"No, neither of us have children," I reiterate.

"She will move to London with you?"

"We haven't really gotten that far, but I believe one of us would move to be near the other at a certain point."

"She not in love with you?"

"Actually, I believe she does love me, even if it's all very new and fast for her."

"She is older than you, yes?"

"Yes. Wow, this is brutal."

"My son, I am just trying to help you like a mother. You English shake your parents' hand. In Italy, your mama would tell you girl no good for you, and then show you the right one. That is Italy."

"No, thank you, I think, or perhaps this is all a little weird for me."

I rise from my chair and make my way to the breakfast bar. I survey the elaborate presentation of fresh baked fruit breads and petite pastries that are a mix of chocolate, lemon, and lavender.

"I make you uncomfortable; I tell you no more," Martina says from behind me.

"No, I appreciate all the help I can get."

"It's just I know a woman, I am a woman, I have daughter and granddaughter. The body do things when you have baby, some up, and some down. Your woman have baby maybe long time ago or not so long ago, but she have baby, I promise you."

"I can assure you, she has no baby."

"Okay, okay, okay, I tell you no more."

"Tell me about you. How old were you when you first married?" I ask attempting to divert the conversation from this starved woman with whom Catherine obviously got off on the wrong foot.

"I'm too old for you. Isabella over there maybe … a little young?" Martina looks for my nod as I sit motionless. "Or maybe not. And the other two, they more for good meal and clean house than bed."

"Wow, you're a tough one," I say.

"No, no, no, I just am very honest. I see life for its truths, and I find it impossible not to share it with people when I see it."

"And you married then?"

"That is unimportant; I will only tell you I was too old. You marry young, and you can make mistake and then marry again. You marry old and it no work, as woman, you might as well set off with the pirates. Or open a hotel in Italy."

She laughs and we all join in. I bite into perhaps the best muffin I've ever eaten, a crunchy top sprinkled with sugar and a fluffy lemon filling still piping hot.

"This muffin business is simply divine," I say with a full mouth.

"If only you could marry two women, my father used to say, one to sex and one to cook."

"Martina, so I take it you don't think I'm with the right woman," I whisper, opening my robe enough to stop the sweat that's beading on my chest.

"It is none of my business. I don't want to get in trouble. I always get in trouble for opening my mouth too much."

"But just this one time, I would appreciate the family advice."

"As your mother?"

"You're not nearly old enough to be, but as jest, pretend as my mother."

"You are very, very beautiful man. Every woman who works here tell me, did you see the Englishman? You can have anybody, any woman." She pauses and then studies my face. "That assumes you do like woman only?"

"Yes, I am not gay," I say directly and earnestly.

"No, please, forgive me; beautiful man often likes other beautiful man. I am sure you know that already. But I will say one thing and one thing only."

"A man always thinks about sex, and with a woman older than you, you will always be looking around. You will always be thinking where can I get different sex with young woman."

"But I have already done that and have come through it wanting someone I can talk to, someone I can connect with and love."

"You want her because she makes it difficult for you; she is impossible to know and please. That is why you love her. All other girls just say yes to that face."

She pats my leg and continues in a far more serious tone. "A woman not married at her age has problems or secrets. I hope for you it's problems and not the other."

"I was only supposed to be down here a few minutes for coffee and a snack to take to Catherine." I place a few muffins and pastries in a napkin and take a cup for coffee.

"An Italian woman gets the breakfast for her man, not the other way around. I don't understand this woman."

241

Martina stands, shakes both of her hands, and heaves them over both shoulders in a sort of exasperation.

"I will be on my way then. I think we rented a boat to go around the island this afternoon. What do you think?"

"I think you have a lot of work in front of you, that's what I think, my love," she says, pinching my cheeks. "Look at those eyes, just look at them. Make sure they get someone to love before all this turns to this," as she motions to her own face.

I make my way back to the room where Catherine has risen and started her day. I feel a little guilty that Martina was so critical of Catherine without even knowing her. From ridiculing her body to saying she wasn't young enough for me. I disagree; I am fully attracted to Catherine's body just as it is, but it's her mind and the years it's had to mature to which I am most attracted.

She's glowing this morning and a long way from the sullen state she seemed to be in last night, whether it was time change or jet lag or adjusting to me again.

"Wow, that took a long time, but it sure looks delicious," she says giving me a peck on the mouth.

She's freshly showered and wearing a simple pair of white shorts, a cotton button-down shirt undone halfway, and a colorful blue Bombay-print scarf wrapped around her neck.

"The lighter one is lemon lavender, and the darker one is raspberry and chocolate," I say, feeding the lighter one into her mouth.

"That's ridiculous … oh my god, did they make them all from scratch?"

"From the juice to the jam and pastries, they wanted to enroll you in the wife cooking class."

"No they didn't."

"Well, sort of, but then I told them you had no interest in being my wife."

"What business is it of theirs? Plus, why can't you be the cook in the relationship?"

"She didn't say, but I take it roles are a bit more rigid in Italy. It did make me think, we really need to see each other more often."

"Where is *this* coming from? All this for a cup of coffee?" Catherine crosses her arms in a sort of agitated annoyance that makes me weigh whether the conversation is even worth it. "Things are going really well for us. Why do you have to jinx it with this bored-maid chatter that's obviously gotten to your head? Now I don't want to even eat those."

"She was convinced you were some sort of harlot. I thought it sounded kind of hot."

"Excuse me, she said *what*?"

"She just thought you seemed like maybe you could have had a child at some point … she sees auras or something."

Catherine retreats to the bathroom, dumps the plate of pastries in the trash, lingers in the mirror for a moment, and then returns to the room.

"Can't we just be here right now with no drama, no fighting, and no gossip from the bored islanders?"

"Of course," I say. "I thought it was humorous. In no way did I intend on making you uncomfortable. I'm sorry for not being more sensitive."

"All these people have expectations of women based on their age. I bet she didn't count your waning biological years."

"I'm sorry, I think you're the most beautiful and amazing woman I have ever met. My intention was not to agitate you. Let's not allow it to ruin our day." I grab Catherine's hand and hold it next to my heart.

"So what's planned for our day?" she asks hesitantly.

"Well, I thought we'd grab a boat and troll around the island."

"That sounds lovely. Can I go dressed like this?"

"Absolutely, as long as you have a swimsuit on underneath. And they'll pack us a lunch and some wine we can take with us," I add.

"I'm sure they'll poison mine so they can have you to themselves. Was that bartender girl there? I could feel her eyeing you last night."

"We've moved on; no more talk of that. There will always be distractions. It is up to us to look past them."

Catherine retreats to the bathroom as I do a quick clothes change into my Etro shorts and Speedo underneath that will likely get a reaction from Catherine and her American prudishness. I throw a chambray shirt over it all, unbuttoned and preferably off, but trying to keep up appearances with Catherine, who is a bit sensitive to too much skin.

We make our way downstairs where only two kitchen helpers remain clearing up the dishes as almost mythical-looking maids hang morning laundry on long wires with a backdrop of yachts moored off the port. They pass us our picnic basket and a metal holder of three bottles of wine, which seems excessive for just the two of us, and we make our way down the hill and toward the harbor.

It's Saturday and the island is noticeably busier. The soot from scooters fills the air as couples pass walking hand in hand. We try to navigate the intense heat under partial awnings clinging from pastel-color houses and logoed storefronts.

At the harbor, we find an older man with skin the color of rubber. The whites of his eyes are pierced with black dots as he stares at Catherine as if in the presence of something magical.

"You must be the harbormaster?" I ask, interrupting his gaze.

"*Si, si, parla italiano?*"

His words eat at me, as obviously, everybody speaks some English in these tourist parts. Yet, he chooses to play dumb and simply ogle Catherine further to my annoyance.

"No, English. You have boat for David Summers from Hotel Raya?" I ask, surveying his inflatable fleet and nowhere near the Riva I was expecting.

"*Una barca lusso?*" Catherine interjects.

"*Barca, si. No lusso, no,*" he replies to her. He waves to the somewhat professional-looking zodiac boats next to him with a rear motor and two rows of seats made from long strips of blue-painted wood having already endured a summer's beating.

"I was picturing something a bit more wooden and vintage, maybe with a mattress on the back; not some sort of official rescue raft," I say.

"Well, it seems that's all he has, and I don't really see another option."

"We could go back to the hotel and see if Martina has any suggestions," I say.

"I'd rather take the raft … don't be such a snob."

"Snob? Dear, I just don't want you getting dirty in there. It's filthy."

"I'm a big girl; we'll be fine."

I pay the old man directly and lend my hand to Catherine who eases into the front of the boat tied with a rope along the wooden pier. I load the picnic basket and wine bottles inside and remove my shirt before untying the raft and heaving myself to the rear next to the outboard motor. I expect the motor to be temperamental, but a single pull ignites the motor, and I lead us in a circle away from the grumpy old man and toward the deeper water. The motor zips through the almost flat water taking the occasional wave that bounces Catherine in the air with her scarf blowing behind her.

The landscape of Panarea changes from one side of the island to the other. It goes from a more lush terrain around the village to a far rockier beach and barren hillside of dried shrub brush.

"Do you see the fish?" Catherine yells, leaning her head over the side.

"No, I just see a shark," I yell back. She turns and I throw her a sarcastic smile.

We pass a series of jagged cliffs that fall off the mainland with hundred-foot drops into the cobalt-blue water so clear you can see the putty-colored river rocks laid smoothly at the water's bottom. I idle the motor to a stop.

"David, the water feels like silk. It's so thick with sediment and yet so crystal clear."

"It must be the minerals. It looks so shallow, but it really is quite deep. It's an optical illusion."

I jump on the side of the raft and dive into the water with no notice, which catches Catherine a bit off guard. The water is warm but still refreshing. It feels like a layer of satin against your skin, soft to touch from all the volcanic minerals and the surrounding islands. I dive deep, opening my eyes while floating on my body flat and looking back up at the raft. The little motor with its propeller looks so unintimidating underwater. Life moves in slow motion as my wobbly bubbles make their back to the surface and life above waits as I linger until I can't take it anymore and erupt above the water.

"Are you going to jump in?" I yell to Catherine.

"Yes, I'm just taking it all in; it's truly incredible."

I swim closer to the towering rocks that jet out from the mainland, wondering what it would be like to jump from the top and into the water in a dead sprint. Behind me, I hear a splash. I turn and see just her feet above the splash as her head quickly emerges with a beaming smile and a wipe of the eyes.

"Come to me, baby," I say.

"I can't imagine being any happier than I am right now," she says, grabbing my waist.

She kisses me and we sink under the water. My hands wrap around her back and down to her rear end as she straddles her legs around my back. I can imagine being inside her right now. She pulls me in closer, tighter as I thrust myself against her, arousing both of us in the middle of the open water.

"It reminds me of Rio," she says in my ear.

"It reminds me of you and how much I adore you," I reply, nibbling the tip of her ear and then with my tongue down its edge.

I pull off my shorts, toss them into the boat, and swim fully naked against her body. I untie the back of her bikini and pull the straps from around her arms as she paddles fully exposed with her breasts floating half above the water. Our feet touch, my toes blindly feeling their way around her ankles and up her calf, meeting toes to toes together like held hands.

My hands grip both of her thighs, pulling her apart in the sea. I imagine how warm she'd be inside, easing myself into her and the warmth that lies within. She kisses me more aggressively, biting my neck harder and harder and pulling my hair to position my face exactly where she wants it, exploring the inside of my mouth with her own fingers as I do so often with her. We struggle to stay above the water. I go under and kiss my way down her back and to her ass before coming up again for a burst of air. I'm fully hard and ready. She grabs the base of me with a forceful grip, and I push her away not wanting to lose a minute once inside her.

"I want to be inside you; I want it so bad," I say as she swims toward the boat.

I chase her with ease and grab her foot. She flails onto her back, and my hands move their way up and inside her. She tries to swim farther away, but I hold her back. She slowly takes us both stroke-by-strokes back to the boat. She makes it all the way back with me riding attached to her legs. She grabs the small ladder that dangles from one side of the raft and allows me to see her rounded ass in its full-on beauty.

I try to grab her foot and pull her back in, but she makes her way into the boat.

"You don't want to stay in the water?" I ask.

"No, I want you here, back in the boat."

"But I like it here in the water, plus, I'm kind of totally naked."

There's a boat at the edge of the harbor that she seems oblivious to as she stands there in her salmon-colored bikini with bare breasts that kilt just to the side of her womanly torso with two tan lines that rise to her shoulders.

"You shouldn't care who sees you naked, especially with that body of yours," she says.

"And you?"

"Right now, I only care about you. And I want you back in the boat."

"I like it here in the water."

"I want you to keep me warm, please," she says with a girlish beg.

"Beg harder."

"Baby, please come back in the boat. Please, please, please," she squeals.

"Talk to me dirty. Tell me I can fuck you if I come back on."

"Baby, come back on the boat, and I'll let you fuck me."

"Tell me you'll let me fuck you, and you'll beg for more while I'm doing it."

"And I'll beg for more while you're doing it. Now, come back on," she says in a most seductive voice.

I make my way to the boat and rise out of the water. I stand dripping wet in front of her, my erection lost, and my dick adjusting to the cold air. I have only a towel in front of me as she extends her arms and touches my stomach, caressingly it slowly as she reaches lower and takes my dick in her hand and with the other, pulls the foreskin back and forth over the head. My interest returns as she puts me inside her warm mouth, rolls her tongue along the inside of the skin, and pushes it back with her lips.

I push her on her back between the two seats of the raft, her body exposed to the dirty bottom and all who has stepped there before. I prop her legs up on the seats and perch myself above her. I scoot as far back as possible, lowering my head between her legs and devouring her with my mouth. She sighs softly in delight, barely audible among the waves splashing against the boat, and I go deeper.

"Louder," I say. "Tell me how it feels. I want to know you from the inside."

"It feels warm, almost slippery, and then you hit a point that sends a chill up my spine. I want to yell stop, and at the same time, beg for more," she says in a soft voice.

I continue licking the inside of her legs, which she tries desperately to hold together. I push them apart with my arms and reposition myself above her. I attempt to prop her backward onto the seat while I take her fully from behind, shallow at first and then deeper and then so deep the warmness of her deepest desires are not beyond my touch. I continue harder and harder and the boat rocks back and forth. She gasps between sighs and moans that blur with the sounds of the surf and sea.

"Tell me what it feels like," she says. "Tell me what you feel inside."

"It's sweet and sticky to the tongue and feels like perfection as I enter you and push harder and harder trying to get deeper and deeper inside. I can see you watching me when I open my eyes, and I pound harder and harder like this grabbing your mouth and sticking my thumb inside imagining it was my dick that I roll around your lips and make you beg for more."

"And then," I say in breathlessness, "I listen as your voice edges over climax as I bring myself almost to the point of erupting before slowing almost to a stop, only to start it all over again."

Time slips away from us as we collapse in exhaustion cocooned in a blue picnic blanket laid along the interior of the boat. Catherine lulls into a soft sleep, and I lay wide-awake staring at the afternoon sky and attempting to keep our boat from washing into the rocks. Although exhausted, I don't want to close my eyes for fear of missing a single second of this perfect moment in time. I lean my head back as far as I can, staring at distant Stromboli as the piercing sun dips slowly behind the island leaving my bare body in a slight chill. I cover Catherine gently with our one last dry towel, careful not to wake her and interrupt this idyllic moment where she is fully mine, and I can pretend she'll never leave my side. The boat sways ever so slightly with each wave, like the even motion of a mother's lullaby. I gaze at her perfect face and imagine a day where our other worlds fade away and there is only us.

CHAPTER 9

NEW YORK

*I*T IS THE season of my redemption, or atonement, depending on the time of day. I linger at a point of no return between two men. In one realm, there is a life I no longer desire, and the other, a life that couldn't possibly exist outside the confines of hotel suites. I am paralyzed in a perpetual state of inaction while compulsively looking for the next opportunity to run away to my other life. In the dark harrows of the months since Italy, I managed to distance myself fully from the man I so love without any explanation other than a busy life.

That's how I end up in a crosstown cab from my offices in Midtown to Gramercy Park, where I've booked a room for David during the weekend before Christmas. It's an almost unbearable time of year for the deviant heart. Even unhappy couples pass by the window of my cab radiating a certain holiday satisfaction as they maintain held hands amid the pushing crowd of Grand Central and down Lexington and Park Avenues, where every condo and tower seems adorned with a human-size wreath or bold-red bow. My treachery only seems to reach new lows; defying my husband and child this time in our own city when I should be shopping for toys and manly gifts with which to surprise Matt. Instead, I lie about a work trip to Miami that will supposedly save me from having to work between Christmas and New Year's, just to meet him one last time.

In the meantime, David still fills my every dream, occupies almost every thought, and has made daily life excruciating to endure when I know somewhere in the world my hand could touch his, our bodies could once more meet, and this other lifetime that blossoms whenever he is near can begin again. But then there is my real life, the ever-anemic existence that I endure day after day in order to live up to my promise as a mother, even if inadequately, as I fade away as a person and from my own marriage that I don't know how to quit.

I didn't want to repeat Italy, having slept with Matt immediately before the trip and then arriving to David raring to go. I had to face the wretched truth, having two men within such a short period and yet, only one truly possesses all of my heart. I tried to be unresponsive to David's texts; I didn't return e-mails sometimes for a week or even two at a time, and I allowed my voice-mail to go full in order to avoid listening to his repeated messages. Yet, David would still get through somehow, and to me, like a drug, I simply could not resist. During the weeks, my loneliness and despair would only worsen as his scent, the touch of his hand, and the taste of his lips would all but fade from my immediate memory.

This part of the city has always seemed a sanctuary for me with its elegant apartment blocks that have weathered the far worse of world wars and fickle temperament of time with a stoic confidence reflected in their proud stone-carved facades and well-tended doors. Pin oak trees line either side of Twenty-Second Street, the insignificant trunks not big enough for signs or decoration under sensitive branches that flail in light wind and wither in the snow. Street level of the Gramercy Park Hotel is deceptively inconsequential with its modern squares of iron windows trimmed in super-sculpted topiary and cantilevered marquee trimmed in hundreds of bulbs that look as if they should blink or flash in lieu of their constant yellow light.

I exit the cab as my eyes rise to the hotel's upper-brick facade wondering which one is his of the windows hugged in masonry detail and decorative balconies briefly silencing my regrets of passing through this revolving door of deceit yet again.

The lobby's black and white checkerboard floor contrasts against imperial red carpets and equally red drapes with gold embroidery that interrupt stacked-timber columns and a mythical beam ceiling that rises above me and into a heaven of Murano chandeliers. Spare, exquisite pieces of original furniture picked through by designer John Pawson are placed like sculpture about a grand fireplace roaring for the season with walls festooned in ethereal artwork that transitions from Julian Schnabel's biblically allegorical pieces to Damien Hirst's kaleidoscopic butterflies, and Cy Twombly's painted optimism. With the world outside consumed in its December stupor, the deserted lobby keeps my secret safe as I make my way to the front desk where a key should be waiting for me.

"Can I help you?" says the timid clerk with her black and white Narciso Rodriguez uniform that's too big in the waist.

"Yes, I'm checking in. Actually, I'm with someone who has already checked into the hotel this morning."

"Guest's name, please?"

"Catherine, oh, I mean David Summers would be the room name."

"Catherine Summers?"

"No, Catherine Klein," I reply.

"For security purposes, could I see a driver's license to add your name to the room."

"Yes, of course," I comply as she types with the frantic index fingers of a serial texter as she returns my ID by placing it back on the wooden reception counter.

Under other circumstances, I would have been far better dressed for seeing David, instead of leaving from work in my boots and jeans and chunky winter coat that justified my quick trip to the airport and onto sunny Miami instead of this room-bound weekend that I hope is before me. Luckily, Matt didn't question my hefty luggage loaded with winter clothes in lieu of a weekender bag I would usually take to South Beach. But Matt doesn't really do questions, his mind never wandering farther than what's right in front of him with a sunny spin he puts on anything that isn't rosy. I can't even imagine how he would handle jealousy or another man; he's the type who's always gotten what he wants with little deviation.

I worry how David will react to me, whether he'll want to see where I live or meet friends or coworkers during his weekend that seems awkwardly timed right before the holidays. However, any trepidation is immediately wiped away by the thought of seeing him if even for an instant as I'm but steps away from that breath of life that lays a press-of-a-button away up the wood-lined elevator with its industrial lightbulb ceiling. The doors open to a dark hallway lined in red carpeting with gothic numbers marking each door. I reach his room where just a thin piece of wooden door separates me from that perfect physical world that exists just beyond.

I stand in the doorway for more than a minute, turning off my phone and adjusting my jeans a little lower on my hips, ready for him to open the door. As I listen, I hear his voice on the other side, but not so loud that I can make out the words that become louder with my knock. A series of footsteps are like a drumroll for a swing of the door opens, and his elongated torso stands in front of me in a soft-striped, gray-flannel suit that frames his eyes hidden behind black reading glasses perched at the end of his nose, his hair slicked back a bit different than I have seen it before.

"One second." He says in a whisper as he leans in for a perfunctory kiss and then turns around in the small foyer and returns to the desk cluttered with a shiny computer and stacked folders that bring a real worldliness to this otherworldly place.

He's the modern juxtaposition to this space that feels rooted in memories long ago when Edmund Wilson lived here with novelist Mary McCarthy whose experiences around Gramercy Park resulted in *The Company She Keeps.* I picture myself working where she did, snuggled in the corner of the mohair sofa pulled carefully close to the long-working desk with leather-bound top that David leans into with two hands.

An English bar cabinet draws the eyes with its backlit top that makes all the heavy crystal barware and stemmed wine glasses sparkle against the mirrored shelf. David is in mid-conversation discussing some sort of German bank that I remember him being involved with months ago. His face is serious and tense, his eyes more narrow than when we engage in conversations. His thick fingers grip a weighted ballpoint pen that he taps unknowingly on the overhead lamp that hangs awkwardly over the desk from a long arm that reaches from the corner of the room.

Glass doors concealed behind thick red velvet curtains divide the living room and bedroom. I wheel my overstuffed carry-on bag on the thick floral rugs and past the bed to a walk-in closet where just two perfectly pressed white shirts hang next to a pair of jeans with a pair of track pants lying on the floor next to his running shoes.

Then two hands sneak up behind me as I hang my new Lanvin black cocktail dress between his pants and shirts.

"I can't believe you actually came through," he says.

"What do you mean? I told you I'd be here," I reply as I turn and freefall into his scent. His eyes engulf my own and make me lose track of what he's saying.

"I know, but there seemed to be so much going on in your life. Yet, so many conversations were mostly silent or me trying to coax something out of you that you weren't ready to talk about or interested in discussing."

"Let's just be here now for a moment. I want to enjoy this minute that I've thought about for so long."

"And yet you make yourself so off-limits to me."

He says this with a tighter grip around my waist as I lay my face on his shoulder. I wish I could capture this moment and carry it with me all my life, feeling the heat of his breath on the back of my neck and knowing he is only inches away. I look up and our lips meet again as I dreamed. The passion is too much for either of us to fight. His hands reach down the back of my pants and make their way to my most intimate parts as I fall deeper and deeper into him without our lips parting. Then he pushes me away.

"Wait, let's wait a second and settle in a bit before this all happens again," he says.

He can tell I need him inside me to start where we left off, but he hesitates and pulls me back in the living room where the skyline behind Gramercy Park shines with twinkling office towers and the illuminated crown of a nearby clock tower.

"So what are you working on here in New York?" I ask in a tone that's disconnected and off.

"Actually, nothing. I'm still working mostly in Berlin."

"Wait, so this isn't a work trip?"

"No, it's not. I needed to see you any way I could get you, and this is the only weekend that seemed to work."

"I can't believe you did this just for me," I say in somewhat disbelief that he cares so much for me and with an increased sense of obligation to make the most of this weekend in New York.

"But what about you?" he asks. "You leave for your parents' on Christmas Eve, right?"

"Yes, that's right, and through the New Year."

"So no talking you into Saint Barth or Courchevel, I take it?"

"No, my parents are older, so I try to make sure I spend those moments with them while I have them."

"I respect that. I would do the same if my own parents were still around."

"I wish I could have met them. So what will you be doing?"

"The Dale-Evanses invited me back to Somerset for the holiday, and then I'll be in Verbier for New Year's."

"That sounds fabulous. I'm so jealous."

"Yes, but you're not into me enough to dare giving this whole situation a proper go, are you? Or at least that's what you have me believe."

"David, it's not that at all. I adore you. It's just we have incredibly incompatible lives."

There's something different about David. He looks away from me and out the window, avoiding our usual eye contact and his fluid conversation for a more distracted and distant tone. He's seated farther away than he would usually be, his hands held tight in his lap.

"But there's something else, too, isn't there Catherine?" he says, looking me dead in the eyes, his glazed as if just about to be engulfed in emotion.

"Something else, what do you mean?" I ask attempting to mask the inner feeling of doom I feel.

"You tell me, Catherine. If that's even your real name."

"David, please don't. Don't make this harder for me than it is already."

"Harder for you? Harder for you? What about your husband? Your husband, who is a kind and decent man who sits at home right now watching your child while you go fuck your way around the world?"

David says this in a soft monotone ache of words that my ears barely recognize upon hearing. My face struggles not to collapse, my hands tingle, and my feet feel as though they've fallen out from under me. There's the awkward, silent noise of the accused as all of me searches in peril for some word, some explanation before attempting to rise from the sofa and leave the room.

"No, you don't." He grabs my arm and pushes my body back down on the sofa with an intensity I have never before felt from a man.

"You will not leave until you explain yourself to me," he says.

"David, please don't make this any worse than it has to be," I say as tears gush from my soul, and I lean back on the sofa.

The pause of judgment and fear of the conversation that is about to come leaves my mind scrambling for what to say, how to fix, or save this from the very worst.

"You are an abysmal human being. I'd call you a whore, but in fact you're something far worse," he says. "A whore is at least upfront and honest with the men they use."

"Stop, David. David, I don't even know what to say to you."

"Then say something, Catherine. Please, just say something!" he yells across the room, throwing his folders to the ground as papers fly in the air.

I want to run away, seeing the other side of his love and adoration, he feels like a stranger I don't know. I see the pain in his eyes, more than I ever imagined he felt for me or was capable of feeling for anyone. He looks at me with the bewildered stare of someone who does not know me and me him, keeping his distance while still hovering without letting me move from the situation.

"Speak already, please Catherine. I need to understand!" he yells.

I want him to understand, even if I haven't comprehended my own decisions. I want to know how he found out, what he said to Matt, and how this all happened. I feel at the expiration of life, and on this precipice, I was always aware I would come to the end of this road, but with a far steeper cliff than even I had feared as all that I know and love now lays in ruins. There is no point of lying anymore; this is the end as these boundless secrets weigh heavy on my mind and have become too difficult to keep.

"What do you want to know? Where do you want me to begin?"

"Start from the beginning and tell me everything; I want complete honesty or at least as close to it as you are morally capable," he says.

With those words, my mind revisits that flight to Rio when I first saw him three rows in front of me on the plane. I watched him look at everyone else around him as some movie rolled on the screen, but he had no interest in allowing his incredible eyes to follow. I lingered behind him in the customs line and followed him to the coffee stand without saying a word or offering the least bit of notice. When you're married, there are people you see all the time and your mind will follow sometimes for years. Certain ones linger in your cognizance, and you fantasize *what if* or being with them when under the touch of a scripted lover who no longer craves or connects with you or you to him. They are never more than a fantasy, they pass from your thoughts, and you're thankful it was never more than a fantasy.

"Then why were you such a cold bitch to me at first in Rio?" he says with no more courteous regard for cursing or kindness.

"I could tell you were a guy who always got any girl you wanted, and I didn't want to simply be one more, even if merely with my eyes."

"Were you even attracted to me?" he asks.

"How could I not be attracted to you? Look at you; you're quite possibly the most beautiful man I have ever seen."

"But that's all you felt?" he says with a hint of tenderness.

I think of our afternoon in Rio as the rain poured and the vibration of thunderstorms seemed to force us closer and closer together as if beckoned from God. The more I learned of him the more I waited for that distasteful comment or inappropriate sentence that would inevitably repel me. Yet, his words and intelligence only made him more endearing as the thoughts of my own life faded farther away, and the enticement of what could be lay before my hands and became too much to fight.

"And then you found a crack in my wall, which was your brilliant mind and charm and kindness that took me away from my average life and to that place you only get glimpses of when you first meet someone and then never again," I plead.

"But why didn't you tell me you were married? I would have probably still gone after you, but why allow yourself to become the most despicable kind of liar?"

His question is the very one I've asked myself for almost an entire year. I've agonized about what it was that didn't allow me to simply tell him when we first started to embrace in the water off Rio or in my hotel room in Paris. This whole situation could have just been an inappropriate but forgivable fling and nothing more.

"I would have said and done anything to have just one more second with you. I didn't want you to just be a passing thing; I wanted you to be forever," I say in total vulnerability.

With those words, all my emotion manifests itself into a long and overdue breakdown. I lie two feet from him engulfed in tears and in full hysterics as he sits motionless watching with hands still in his lap. There is no sympathy or pity; there is only contempt and pain in those incredible eyes that now look at me as his heart's assailant.

"What about the fact that you're a fucking mother? I mean, who in the hell does that except women who drown their babies in a bathtub."

"Heartless sluts do it, I guess. What do you want me to say? I love my son, but I'm still a woman. I still crave someone who desires and wants me, someone who lingers with his hands over dinner and does more than jerk off inside me for sex when I'm lucky. And then there's the endless sleepless nights followed by twelve-hour workdays that aren't the chummy PTA bake sale I was imagining."

"PTA … what's PTA?" he says in all his British-ness with a glimpse of his former playful self. Even just for a passing moment, all I want is to see the carefree and loving eyes of the man I so love emerge from this fog of contempt.

"It's a parents program in the schools here; it's awful."

David disregards my comment, and the moment passes as if it didn't even arrive, and with it the last time I might ever see the carefree spirit of his inner soul.

"And Paris, what about Paris?"

"What do you mean? What was I doing in Paris?" I ask.

"Yes, that felt far too coincidental seeing you in Paris. Did you know I used to date Kelly? Is that why you did the interview?"

"No, not at all," I say as if offended. "The interview was entirely coincidental. But I moved the interview to Paris in hope of seeing you."

"So you stalked me."

"That's a harsh word. I didn't want to actually talk; I just wanted to see you once, just one more time."

"So you could ruin my life?"

"So that I could see your face, breathe the same air, daydream about what could have been in another lifetime without realizing that I could trip and fall and lose myself in this fantasy. It was you who came to my room, after all."

"You have no idea what you have done to my life," he says with emotion that appears to run deep.

"David, I am so very sorry. I can only tell you that every moment and emotion and word was real and true."

"I introduced you to my closest friends. I shared thoughts and plans with you that I have never shared with anyone. I was faithful to you even though we never even had the conversation, all the while you were getting it in both ends from me and your husband."

"But you didn't expect we would be happily ever after when we only saw each other every two months now, did you?"

"When people have real jobs they can't spend every waking hour staring at each other in their musty one-bedroom apartment in Brooklyn."

With David's words, I realize the worst. He's not only been to my home, but also inside, and he knows the exact details. I imagine the hurt that awaits me at home, my son in the midst of Christmas having lost his family and Mom to this unknown who turns up out of nowhere. I am at a loss of words for my treacherous behavior that leaves a battlefield of lost lives even beyond my comprehension.

"Did you sleep with more guys than just me?" he asks.

"You are the only man I have ever cheated with in my marriage or even while dating. I am not a cheater," I say emphatically.

"Well, you certainly play the part well."

No response I can give will quell his relentless barrage. I simply stare in contrite silence and hope some glimpse of the person I was to him before all of this, emerges with my blunt truthfulness and full culpability.

"Why did you invite me to Africa? And why did you ask me to fly you to my home when you knew it meant so much to me? My friends are all I have, my parents are fucking dead, and you take advantage of my deepest vulnerabilities."

"David, I love you. I wanted nothing more than to be with you."

"And live the good life sucking it up with all my friends and playing the posh girlfriend while her own family lives in squalor."

"I can't take much more of this, David, I really can't." Hearing what he thinks of my home wounds my soul beyond repair.

"You most certainly will until I am done. You have made me suffer, and now it's your turn to face your actions," he pauses. "Was Matt that bad of a guy? Did he beat you or ever let you down as a man?"

Talking about Matt stings, as if a parallel universe I never wanted to admit existed or discuss is forced down my throat. There's no other way to escape this moment other than to allow a clear, unfiltered line from my heart through my words.

"Matt and I met at a time in my life when I was one of the last women I knew who was still single. I was worried and scared that the life I had imagined I would have was no longer going to be an option if I didn't settle down soon with someone, maybe anyone."

Men don't know the agony of a woman at thirty-seven and still without a child, a man, or hope of one explainable in a single sentence that justifies she is still dreaming of having a family like everyone else. I'd meet men who wanted to date women who weren't so old that the conversation of marriage or children came up on the second date. They wanted women they could have fun with and then breakup with without having to feel guilty they left her just short of the gate where the ring, the baby, and the life were almost, and yet may never be again. Then I met Matt, who loved and accepted me, and my age was never an issue. He was my last exit to have that life, and I no longer felt in a position to say, "Not this guy."

"Or the alternative version is that you were too weak to leave or make it work when you could gallivant and meet another fool to take care of you," he says.

"No one takes care of me, if I haven't already made that clear. I work very hard and provide for my family regardless of how you might choose to believe. Then you came along and were like this prince who would allow me to be the woman in the relationship. You phoned when you said you would, you'd plan dinners, and special moments. You were always a step ahead of what my wildest dreams could expect. Then there was this passion, this incredible sex that made everything else in my life feel second. There was only you, David."

"And this is what I get; this is what I get when I give the very best of myself," he says as if speaking to the universe and me.

"David, you bear no fault in this situation. If anything, you were too perfect and made me willing to risk everything at the mere idea of seeing you just one more time."

"I came to New York—" he begins and then stops.

"You came to New York, why?" I ask after a few moments. His eyes begin to glass over, but not so much that a tear emerges.

"Nothing," he says.

"No, please, tell me."

Suddenly he stands and removes his tie and jacket, which he throws across the desk. There's urgency to his movement, as my mind wonders if Matt is soon to appear or some other surprise that even my mind cannot fathom in all this hellish chaos.

"So Catherine, I need a second. I'm going to head out for a while and you can leave, stay, or really do whatever you want. I can't really think about you anymore; it's just all too much for me."

"David, sit, please," I say rising next to him. I grab his hand, but he rips it away from me.

He doesn't say a word as he picks up his files from the floor and stuffs them into a briefcase that he leaves on a chair next to the table before exiting the room with a slam of the door. I want to chase after him; I don't want to lose him, but I also realize his mood is unpredictable, and I'm unsure of what would unfold in the hallway or lobby. I stand for a moment and take in the room. Suddenly, it feels like a prison cell for a thief who's forced to sit with her stolen treasures. David's clothes and leather duffel bag sit on the floor in the next room with my own luggage that seems like the criminal's forfeited weapon that someone will eventually use as evidence.

My mind flees outside the hotel walls that foretell my new reality. The hope of David returning to me is better than anywhere I could run away to right now. In all the turmoil, I hadn't even grasped that these are possibly the last few moments I will ever have with him. I wonder if I should go, but I believe if he really wanted me to leave, he would have said it outright. He wanted the conversation, and his absence was because he needed to regroup for a moment and not because he was done with me.

An hour turns to two. My stomach churns, and I venture from the couch to wander the room that feels a bit more comfortable with the passing of time. He thinks me a thief and a liar, which makes me uncomfortable to touch his shirts in the closet or the toiletries he's laid on a washcloth in the bathroom with its black veiny marble and translucent bulb chandelier that dangles above the distraught face of a broken woman who looks back from the mirror. I can't help but pick up the fragrance bottle that reminds me of him condensed in a single whiff, which dries my eyes before sending me into tears all over again. I look in the mirror at the outfit I wore to see him, dreaming as I put it on that the next time it was removed he would be ripping it off—a moment that will never be or likely ever be again.

Two hours turn to three as I return to the couch somewhat calmer and the anxiety of being exposed a fraud now ingrained within. Everybody now knows everything, and I'm left with only the ashes and not the fear of the fire. I consider turning on my cell phone, but know the message that is to come from Matt and the second wave of this battle that I will be forced to inevitably fight, but right now feel too weak to face. The unmade bed and his used pillows beckon my face and touch. I crave nothing but to roll up into a ball in the bed where he once lay and allow all this to fade away.

The 1:00 a.m. rouge of the room indicts my inner thoughts like a guilty harlot as some of the lights in the outside skyline begin to turn off, and I wonder if David might not come back at all with almost four hours gone. Will he be mad I'm still here, or simply kick me out in the middle of the night to walk along Park Avenue, as I deserve, my bag in tow as Christmas lights taunt in aggressive flicker?

Then I hear loaded footsteps in the hall just outside. I reposition myself on the sofa to appear as if I hadn't moved despite the hours of time. The air in the room is stale with dim light that hovers around the low-wattage bulbs of the delicate Victorian fixtures next to the bed. David enters, his unbuttoned white shirt and shoes held in hand, as he turns the corner immediately upon entering and sees me still here in this last corner of our life.

"You're still here?" he says as he takes a seat in the awkward rocker. His more relaxed face is chapped from the frigid weather outside that has frosted the edges of our windows.

"I'll leave if you want me to; I just wasn't sure."

"Wasn't sure of what?" he says, sitting motionless.

"I wasn't sure if you had more questions."

"Oh, I have a lot more questions, but none of which really get answered with your explanations."

He leans over his legs, elbows resting on his knees. His smart striped socks with orange stitch detailing seem to smile up from the serious woven rug of the living room.

"I have been completely honest with you," I say.

"I thought you were annoying when I first saw you, uptight and stuck in a constant inward reflection that was like some sort of introverted narcissism. Then you became more relaxed; a person I felt completely at ease with and wanted to linger more and more with in conversation. The sex was average at first, but you seemed comfortable being led into what became an entirely fulfilling emotional and physical relationship."

David struggles and wipes his eyes before continuing.

"In Paris, I felt there was some sort of divine intervention, maybe even from my mother who had you cross in my path. I felt redeemed after being so disappointed that you didn't contact me after Rio."

"I never got the information you left for me at the hotel, truly David."

"But there was a way to if you had really wanted. So I figured you didn't feel the same connection or had other priorities that didn't leave room for me. Paris was perfection, from the way we talked all night to the way you fixed the buttons back on my shirt without me knowing it after being ripped off the day before. And then when we parted, it was as if the time between allowed the relationship to grow; me sharing all there was to know about myself, and you listening and sharing all about yourself—much of what I now know to be lies and half-truths."

"It wasn't all a lie, David."

"And in Los Angeles, I was in awe of you and caught myself in conversation with people saying that you were the type of person I would be proud to say I loved and was loved by in return. Ibiza made me see your more playful side, and Italy made me completely certain you were the right one for me. I pursued a job offer with a New York company so our relationship could have some sort of future, and we wouldn't waste years getting to that place where I was yours and you were alas mine."

David tears up and pauses. He tucks his feet back into his shoes before getting up and packing his computer with the remaining items from the desk and lifting it up and into his lap as he settles into a chair that's soothingly closer to me.

"I wanted to get to know life with you. I wanted to know what it was like to take care of you when you were sick or food shop before coming home and making supper that would have been better than any hotel experience we could ever have. You were the type of woman I liked waking up next to as much as going to bed with. I didn't want to have just one child with you; I wanted to have four or five that we would raise in the country. I would have found a local job to keep me close to you, and you would transition to writing books and being the great mom I know you would be. The great mom I think you still can be contrary to whatever I feel about you now."

I begin to cry. David's sensitivity seems even less bearable than his previous anger, the kind heart of the betrayed that seems too good to me.

"But Catherine, you need to go be that mother and find joy in the life that you have instead of chasing it in places where you're never going to find it, and simply make what you do have all the less fulfilling."

David stands again and reaches into his bag. He pulls out a small ring box. Its Asprey logo and demure presence emotionally collapses me, and I begin to sob without control.

"I was going to surprise you with this before we parted, not so much a marriage proposal, but a ring that would remind you of my intentions and the path I felt we had long since embarked upon."

He holds the box dwarfed in his thick hands and sets it on a table in front of me.

"I didn't really want to give you this, but the truth is I think you should have it regardless, as they don't give refunds, and I really don't want it lying around reminding me of this time in my life."

I sit staring at the box as David moves into the bedroom and shuffles in the closet as if packing and then taking his duffel bag into the bathroom where a single swoop of commotion brings him back into the living room before me. He zips the opening of his black leather briefcase and puts his wallet in the lining of his inside jacket before looking over at me.

"So—" he begins, and then stops. He hovers above me appearing more emotional than he's been throughout the entire conversation.

"So," I say, looking up at him unable to fathom the moment where he is actually gone from my life.

"So, it's been interesting, to say the least," he says.

"David, I'm so sorry. I cannot even begin to tell you how sorry I am for deceiving you."

His eyes are almost neon blue and his cheeks are rosy and offset by his jet-black head of hair. He turns away from me and makes a direct line for the door without a hesitation, a look back, a good-bye. I want to chase him or grab his hand, especially if it's the last time to touch his skin, but I remain hopeful he will turn back. In the silence of a midnight hallway, the door slams shut. I run to the door and look out the peephole to watch him turn the corner into silence. I feel lost as I open the door and run for the elevator, and with a turn of the corner, I see the doors squeeze shut.

He will come back as he did last time, I tell myself, as there is something unfinished in his tone. There was no good-bye or mention of good-bye, I repeat to myself, walking back to the room resigned to wait out his return. He will return. As I enter, the dark wood furniture and haunting fabrics of the space seem confining and toxic left arranged in a remnant of memories that haunt as I recall the words and depth of my betrayal. I search the room looking for pieces of him left behind. He left nothing in the living room except for the lone ring box on the table, which I can't bear to recognize. I run to the closet where all that was hanging is gone including the dress I unpacked, which he must have taken in haste. The bathroom is also empty, just the solitary washcloth where his toiletries once lay. I hold the washcloth to my face with its crusted toothpaste and fragrant scent.

He will return. I know he will. I listen for the sound of the metal latch opening and the comforting tap of his footsteps to interrupt the silence. I see only the small purple box on the table that sits with a solemn darker purple bow, unaware it will never be opened between lovers. I return to the sofa and take his seat, now cold in his absence. I run my finger across the table to feel for any dirt or lingering element of him. Perhaps I should leave, but I lack the will to walk away from the only place in the world where he might return and tell me that despite all my treachery he might still love me.

Outside, a light snow falls over the park. I look for him as far as my eyes can see, but there is no one on the street at this hour, even on a weekend night. My feet ache from the constraint of my shoes that are a size too small, but I don't dare take them off should he return, not wanting him to see me feeling in the least bit at ease amid his sorrow. He left almost two hours ago. I do another look around the room checking under the fallen blanket in the bedroom and in the bathroom where I pull his damp towel from earlier in the day and take it with me back to the living room. I look it over for a single strand of his hair, which I find and hold close to my heart. I linger on the scent of the hotel's shampoo that smells of a lemony ginger and not of him.

At 5:00 a.m., the night turns to a faint dawn, the snowfall briefly stops, and the sunrise reflects in the buildings across Gramercy Park. I have been sitting in this chair for hours. I jump up to pull shut the weighted red curtains, not wanting to concede to a new day. He must return. I make my way into the bedroom and lie next to the fabric shadow of him still left in the bed, submerging my pain in his pillow that offers a faint smell of him initially and then of its feather fill. I pass my arm along the bed with its silky sheets. I close my eyes and try to pretend he is by my side once more.

And for a moment in my mind, he is here again. My leg reaches over and imagines our bare ankles intertwined as I study his sleeping face. His body is in stillness, his athletic legs, and bare torso exposed and ready, even when withdrawn in sleep with its dark hair that stops so abruptly at his elbows and thighs before returning to the small knap below his belly button that I take with my lips. I imagine us on that raft in Panarea as he emerges completely nude from the sea glistening in streams of water rolling down his body. I take his cold foreskin that's still wet inside my mouth and gaze into his eyes that study my face each time he penetrates me on the floor of the boat as the infinite sky frames his bare silhouette above me.

Though I am not asleep, I awaken from my thoughts and fantasy to realize I will never feel his touch again. I will never know what it is like to see his smile or feel him inside me again as he wanders the world far away from me. All our memories and thoughts of those times that I will savor for the rest of my days will likely rot in his mind as something he'd prefer not to remember.

The loss of him is simply incomprehensible. Let it be, I tell myself in this hour of my darkness where life seems so unlivable in my broken-heartedness. Part of me wants to die on this bed with him still here in some partial form in memory or smell or otherwise, falling into a deep and never-ending sleep where perhaps we can be together instead of having to face one day, this first day without him. I don't want to know what it's going to be like to count the days since we last talked, last touched, or last laughed as week by month by year the vividness of him disappears.'

It's been almost twelve hours since he left. My thoughts forward to him being gone long enough to already be back in London or waking up in another hotel in this vast city that even despite him being geographically near, might as well be a world away. I fully awaken from my semiconscious escape. A wedge of daylight is making its way through the curtain that I pull tight and see the clouds have once more blocked the sky in a gray, gloomy haze. The couch no longer has the indentation in the cushion from where we sat last night with a now-dry towel with no remnant of anything other than the hotel laundry smell. I turn on my cell phone to see if there are any texts or messages, but there's little more than work e-mails that come through.

Then there is the sound I have waited hours to hear again. I question if I'm actually even hearing it as the quiet has been almost deafening. But alas, the metal deadbolt on the door unlocks, and a hesitant foot steps into the room.

"Housekeeping."

Noise echoes through the vapid room and through me as all hope feels lost, and a glowing housekeeper whose head barely reaches the center of the door tepidly enters.

"You want housekeeping?" she asks.

"No, but thank you."

The last thing I can imagine is having someone erase every trace of him from this space that time is already expunging on its own. I imagine her patting the chairs clean of the smudges that his fingers made, the sink that still has residue of his shaving, and a bed that is the one last place we share even if he has long since departed. I don't want to leave this room, as I know that upon leaving, he will never be again; it will forever more close this chapter of my life with him, as all hope is likely lost for his return.

"Just a second. Did someone check out of this room yet?" I ask the housekeeper, realizing that David would have settled the bill before leaving. My heart stops, hoping that he hadn't while affording me hope that he might still return.

"Yes, miss, last night," she says in an almost baritone Spanish voice. "But you can take your time as hotel is no full. Hour or so no problem."

With her words my heart sinks. I imagine David checking out of the hotel in the middle of the night with no intention of ever turning back. The housekeeper leaves me in my broken-heart sanctuary as I return to the bed to smell his pillow in vain if for one last time. I lay my body and my head down on top of his print carved from the sheets and mattress, saying good-bye the only way I can for the last time. Part of me ends here and now, knowing that I will never truly love like this again for the rest of my life.

I look at my watch and realize that 4:00 p.m. is nearing, a lenient checkout time even at the most friendly of hotels. I return to his chair and brush the velvet seat clean of any trace as well as the bathroom sink, which I clean with my bare hand before going into the bedroom and stuffing his pillow inside my bag and pulling it out of the bedroom that never became what I imagined it would be for the weekend.

Then there is the box, the one last remaining trace of David that I can't bring myself to open as I stare at it on the table. I can't imagine actually unwinding the bow or pulling it apart to see the sentiment of his loving heart. I try to pull the ribbon, but stop myself knowing this is truly the last piece of him that I have as I stuff the small box in my bag. The creaks of the hardwood floors and the living room with its drawn blinds quarantine the emotions of the last day as I weep as I have not wept this entire time. I take my few steps to the door, which I touch, open, and step out of with a single look behind me at the nothingness that remains of us.

Then the door closes behind me as I take the first few steps back into my life. The narrow hallways retreat to the dark elevator that conceals my tears and into the lobby that's buzzing with laughter, conversations, and music. The walls strewn with rich artwork appears monochromatic in my misery and seems to boo my soul as I retreat. My head turns in every direction hoping to catch a glimpse of him anywhere in the lobby, but alas, nothing. As I stand on the curb where it is I belong and queue for a taxi, I begin to contemplate what is yet to come. The second front of this campaign of betrayal awaits my contrition.

The taxi driver arrives with a full holiday garland strewn across the dashboard. He's wearing a Santa hat that he holds on tight during speedy turns, even in the ice. The buildings seem to weep as they rise around me, and I contemplate what is to come at home and how I'll probably have to find a place to at least temporarily stay until I sort out exactly what's happening and where I'm going. I close my eyes and wonder if perhaps this is all a dream. I imagine the hate I will see in Matt's eyes, the hurt as he screams in our Christmas-tree-filled apartment as Billy lingers in rare silence watching his young world fall to pieces. I imagine the hurt Matt must feel as he sat at home maintaining our life while I was with this David the entire time during all those weeks away.

The city is immersed in Christmas. Lines form outside shops, even in the Lower East Side. Gramercy Park feels farther and farther away crossing the East River.

As the driver takes my exit and rounds our street, I yell for him to stop. I notice a light snow begins to fall once again.

"This is fine," I say.

"Are you sure? It's pretty cold out there," he says, looking at me with his black Italian eyes through the rearview mirror.

"No, I'll be fine. I don't mind," I say with as much of a smile as I can muster.

"And messy with that bag of yours," he continues.

"No, I really don't care … plus, I feel like walking."

I open the cab door and stand on a deserted street corner where wiser people have long since retreated to their happy homes. I need the time to figure out what exactly I will say to Matt, if he's even there. Should I be honest and explain how I feel, or should I be sensitive and just let things be the way they are as we come to some sort of agreement to separate?

I begin walking into the snow that falls against me. I take each step carefully as the wheels of my bag struggle between the ice and softer snow. There's a magical stillness to the air upon snowfall; sound no longer travels freely, and we hear the mechanical sounds of our own morality from our heartbeats to our own inhale and exhale.

I approach the front of our building with its iron fence and a scattering of padlocked bicycles that surround a concrete garden, which is where David must have stood in the last days looking up to wonder which one of the lighted cutouts was mine. I pass up the outside steps like a ghost of my old self, my heels slide on each slippery step with my filthy wheeled bag in tow. He would have taken these same steps and stared at the nonfunctional security box before pushing his way through the scratched red door and into the metal elevator that always smells like some sort of curry on the way up to the fourth floor. He would have seen the stained industrial carpet that lines our hallways as well as the occasional tricycle and uncollected newspaper on the way to our humble door that lies at the end of the hall.

My heart pauses in anticipation of what is to come. I don't know whether it's better if Matt is here ready for our collision or long since left me and gone to his parents. I wonder if our neighbors heard when the conversation became more intense, what David or Matt called me, and who will remember. I approach the door that will open to unleash the final effects of my selfish ways as I close in on the steel-gray handle, close my eyes, and push it open.

There's a sense of life inside as bacon hangs in the air. Maybe Matt made one of his breakfast dinners thinking he'd be alone for at least another day. There's a laundry basket piled on the dining room table that looks as if it's been there for a few days in some sort of contempt, and chairs pulled in all directions. Blankets lie on the couch as if it's been a refuge for a night or two, and homemade snowflakes hang from the windows that now frame real snowflakes outside. I take the three steps that are our foyer and recognize the more stylish furniture pieces from my single life hidden among an IKEA canvas selected for functionality and storage.

As I step farther into the living room, there on the other side of the door are Matt and Billy on the floor playing with cars in front of the Christmas tree and the TV booming a PBS cartoon. They pay no notice to me at first, as I hover in the background unsure of what the immediate reaction means. More than a minute seems to pass before I interrupt.

"Hi, guys."

There is no reply.

"Matt?" I say again.

As their faces turn, I prepare for their eyes of judgment and pain that will begin the final cycle of my demise for which I am ready to face and hope to come out anew.

"Mommy is home!"

Matt says this and jumps to his feet and walks in my direction with ignited eyes. His eyes piercing through his month-long beard hold no anger, no disappointment as he walks across the room, and I wait for the moment when his anger will emerge. He comes closer as I question what it is I'm seeing. I fear his closeness while wondering if he might grab me or do something entirely out of character given the extremity of the situation. He grabs me abruptly, and I stutter backward. He shocks my cold face with a kiss that stuns my soul and confuses my wind-chapped lips ready to begin in a scream of apologies and the inevitable story of David from the beginning. I can feel the loving hands of my son along my knees and around my thighs as he shifts his weight into me in the purest of affection.

The affection does anything but soothe my indicted heart. The misery and mourning inside me wants nothing to be normal again. This is the moment where I come clean, that I tell Matt how I feel, and what it is I really want for my life. This is where I tell him there's no longer a connection between us, and I've felt so displaced for the past few years.

Matt holds my body as the manly scent of his flannel and sweats uniform grabs me like the foreign touch of an unwanted advance that I don't know how to fight. I imagine what David thought of him on first sight, imagining me with Matt, living in this place, and in this life that couldn't be farther from his own.

"You're not supposed to be back until tomorrow," Matt says in more of a statement than a question, but with no hint of anger or pain that part of me so craves.

Tears begin to flow. Billy holds on so tight that for a moment everything seems okay, painfully okay as if nothing had happened, and we are all simply returned to where we were a year ago, a week ago, a day ago. I pick Billy up and hold him close, his soft baby hair dries my eyes as he flails to get away, and I struggle to hold up his weight with my knee.

"No, I came back early," I reply tepidly, still unsure if this too is a trap. Matt takes a seat at the dining room table and hides the basket of laundry underneath the table.

"Did you get everything you needed for your story?"

There's no question as to why I returned early, what my days entailed, or how I made my way through a treacherous snowstorm, as David would have asked. He has no curiosity for what I am feeling or have experienced in the days since we've parted as with those homecomings that have come before. Matt gets lost in his own immediate thoughts of holiday plans and dinner with no inquisitiveness for what happens beyond these walls, whom I met, or what he might have experienced had he joined me on this trip that didn't exist. My reality sets in; there is no other life than this for me now. There is just this.

"Wait, you're crying. Are you crying? Are you all right?" Matt asks as I try to hide my face.

"No, I'm okay," I reply, wiping tears from my face that simply continue to fall.

"Show Mommy what you made, Billy."

Matt points to the snowflakes that line all of our windows, their sills caked over in a mix of dirt and generations of paint. Billy wobbles about like a little man, a mini-version of his dad with almost identical gray pants and a sweatshirt. He returns to his toy cars next to the Christmas tree trimmed in a popcorn garland and a homemade star on top.

"I'm just going to put this away," I say with a finger pointed at my bag covered in salt residue and dirt that looks nothing as it did sitting on the floor of the hotel. My bag alone shares the secret of my broken heart.

I retreat to our bedroom and see our unmade bed. Glasses of water cluster on the side table with its LCD alarm clock and photos of happier days. My heart tells me to leave, to walk out the door and to a hotel for a few days as I manage to sort out the unwinding of this life. However, after a year of selfishness, I also know I need to be a better mother starting right now before it's truly too late. I tuck the bag in the back of our closet as I mutate into my home uniform of running pants and a sweatshirt, which I wouldn't have even worn to work out in when with David.

My hair is a mess, and I haven't showered in days. I glance down and reach back into my bag to finger the little box open, my last reminder of him as I return to this life. I untie the ribbon in haste as my fingers reach through the velvet packaging to feel the shiny stones and coldness of metal before me. I dare not look as I touch it to my face and lips, and my eyes open to catch shiny emerald stones wrapped around a single band of warm yellow gold. My eyes look closer to an inscription written inside: "Never further than right here inside." I repeat the inscription to myself and then again, as tears stream down my face. I fall to my knees as if life has forsaken me.

After hiding the ring back inside my bag and temporarily away from my thoughts, I return to the living room where Billy and Matt are curled up on the couch watching *Finding Nemo*. I join them as the reluctant third on the edge as I stare out the window contemplating how to go forward. They watch in an almost hypnotic gaze even though they've seen the movie a thousand times. The previous day spins like a filmstrip in my mind, and I wonder if David even came to the house or met with Matt at all. I truly can't figure out how he knew all that he did, even details like how many bedrooms we have.

"So did I miss anything while I was gone?" I ask.

There's a silence as if Matt is trying to wait until there's a lull in this child's film before engaging in conversation.

"No, not really. Just did some Christmas shopping. Oh, and we had a playdate," he says with brief eye contact and a passing smile as he reaches for my hand that stays limp. Then he returns to silence as I wonder if maybe he is just acting as if nothing happened, and he's simply trying to hold on to whatever it is we have. My agitated heart wants a confrontation with him; I want to tell him that this is no longer working for me and that I can't stand another day of this life with him. I gently pull my hand away.

"So I didn't really miss anything?"

"No, not really," he says.

"It's amazing that you can have this long journey and then return as if you were never even gone," I say in resignation.

"Oh, but we have a new neighbor. If that counts."

Yet another conversation that ventures no farther than this building's gossip and this apartment that suddenly feels like a cell. I imagine Christmas immediately before us that will be free of work, shopping, and friends to distract my broken soul as I'm forced to wait out the endless hours of these days that will pass in a dawdling pace.

"Do they have kids, pregnant wife?" I ask.

"I don't know. I didn't ask," he says in typically Matt fashion. "But he's a real sharp guy, probably gay, or maybe it's just that he's English or Irish or something."

With those words and the naivety of his impression, my heart sinks as I realize that David was actually here. I want to know more, but I hesitate, before the sheer desire to know all is too much to bear.

"What apartment? Where's he from?"

"He didn't say; he just asked my name and said he was introducing himself to his new neighbors."

"Did you ask him in?"

"He came in for a minute as Billy was being a terror, but that was it. He was real dressed up, kind of a snobby kind of guy. Didn't mention his own kids."

My soul collapses as I imagine his steps on the floor just feet away from where I sit. His eyes gazed on these endless taupe walls and rental innards littered in family life like the unkempt closet of my soul ripped open. I try to imagine the conversation in an instant, his face upon realizing this great lie that I've been living. Did he touch the table? Did he lean against the wall? Despite the hurt and pain he must have felt, he sought no comfort in the tale that would yield my demise.

I repeat the story through my head, trying to imagine why he did not spill the pain that's been caused to him by a woman who seems to fail all the men in her life. Instead, he simply left as he left me, unwilling to stoop to the level of confrontation or more disruption to his life than has already been caused. There was no manly brawl or fight of words; not even something subconscious that lingered with Matt to warrant a mention. There was nothing, saving me shame and instead, leaving me to rot in this life of my own making.

As I see the good of David, I feel even more paralyzed in this life. How will I recover? What is to become of me in these next days? I gaze at this charade of a life that I sit rejoined in and wonder how I will possibly endure the next day, let alone years, in this prison of my own making with David now lost.

As the sight of Nemo is simply too much to bear, I look down the couch at Billy's little feet kicking in idle as he takes in the movie. The sight comforts my heart as I study his little body that gets larger and larger by the day. His little eyes glance away to the windows and the solid white sky that has taken away all neighbors, buildings, and life outside this room.

"Billy, come let Mommy tell you a story," I suggest.

In the midst of such despair, the only solace is my son who has had an absent mother for far too long and perhaps the only relationship in this house not beyond saving. Billy takes my hand as we make our way to the kitchen table, leaving Matt behind to paw at the remote control.

Billy climbs atop the kitchen chair and sits attentively as I struggle to find our drawing journals out of one of three junk drawers. I place before him a box of crayons.

"Will you help me write a story? We'll draw it together," I say as his small hands grip the paper, and I pull a few colors out of the box. His hair still smells of baby as I stroke his warm neck that's piercingly white.

"What kind of story?" he asks.

"You tell me. It can be whatever you want it to be."

"What about a fish? Let's make fish story," he says with a nod. He grabs my hand and traces a fish as best he can.

"Did I ever tell you about the fish I swam with in Rio, swimming in the water between my feet and around all the people in the water that hot summer day?"

"No."

"Well, it was my last day in Rio, and I didn't like the city very much."

"It was yucky?"

"Yes, or at least I thought it was. But then it became the most magical of cities."

"Magic?" he asks.

"All of a sudden, one afternoon I saw it completely differently. I swore it was the most beautiful place I had ever been while swimming in the water with the most beautiful fish I'd ever seen."

"What did he look like Mommy?"

"He was very large and so handsome with these incredible blue eyes that were the most beautiful color I had ever seen and almost glowed in the dark."

"Were you scared?" Billy asks, looking into my eyes.

"At first, and then I was scared to lose him, so I kept swimming and swimming in the water so when I finally came up for air, I didn't know where I was anymore."

"And where did he go?"

"He swam with me awhile, and then I lost him into the deep blue sea. He was gone, and there was no way I would ever find him again even if I kept swimming and looking in every ocean in the entire world forever and ever."

"Can I go with you next time, Mommy?"

"Absolutely. There's nothing I would love more."